◆**ALTERNATIVES** *is a series under the general editorship of Eric S. Rabkin, Martin H. Greenberg, and Joseph D. Olander which has been established to serve the growing critical audience of science fiction, fantastic fiction, and speculative fiction.*

Other titles in this series are:
Bridges to Science Fiction, edited by George E. Slusser, George R. Guffey, and Mark Rose, 1980
The Science Fiction of Mark Clifton, edited by Barry N. Malzberg and Martin H. Greenberg, 1980
Fantastic Lives: Autobiographical Essays by Notable Science Fiction Writers, edited by Martin H. Greenberg, 1981
Astounding Science Fiction: July 1939, edited by Martin H. Greenberg, 1981
The Magazine of Fantasy and Science Fiction: April 1965, edited by Edward L. Ferman, 1981
The Fantastic Stories of Cornell Woolrich, edited by Charles G. Waugh and Martin H. Greenberg, 1981
The Best Science Fiction of Arthur Conan Doyle, edited by Charles G. Waugh and Martin H. Greenberg, 1981
Bridges to Fantasy, edited by George E. Slusser, Eric S. Rabkin, and Robert Scholes, 1982
The End of the World, edited by Eric S. Rabkin, Martin H. Greenberg, and Joseph D. Olander, 1983
No Place Else: Explorations in Utopian and Dystopian Fiction, edited by Eric S. Rabkin, Martin H. Greenberg, and Joseph D. Olander, 1983
Coordinates: Placing Science Fiction and Fantasy, edited by George E. Slusser, Eric S. Rabkin, and Robert Scholes, 1983
Shadows of the Magic Lamp: Fantasy and Science Fiction in Film, edited by George E. Slusser and Eric S. Rabkin, 1985
Hard Science Fiction, edited by George E. Slusser and Eric S. Rabkin, 1986

STORM WARNINGS
SCIENCE FICTION
CONFRONTS THE FUTURE

Edited by
George E. Slusser
Colin Greenland
and
Eric S. Rabkin

Southern Illinois University Press
Carbondale and Edwardsville

Copyright © 1987 by the Board of Trustees,
Southern Illinois University
All rights reserved
Printed in the United States of America
Edited by Carol Pierman
Designed by Quentin Fiore
Production supervised by Natalia Nadraga

90 89 88 87   4 3 2 1

Library of Congress Cataloging-in-Publication Data

Storm warnings.

(Alternatives)
Includes index.
1. Science fiction, American—History and criticism—
Congresses. 2. Future in literature—Congresses.
3. Science fiction, English—History and criticism—
Congresses. 4. Orwell, George, 1903–1950. Nineteen
eighty-four—Congresses. I. Slusser, George Edgar.
II. Greenland, Colin, 1954–   . III. Rabkin,
Eric S. IV. Series.
PS374.F86S86 1987   813'.0876'09   86-26111
ISBN 0-8093-1376-6

The paper used in this publication meets the minimum requirements
of American National Standard for Information Sciences
– Permanence of Paper for Printed Library Materials, ANSI Z39.48-
1984.   ∞™

To Jean-Pierre Barricelli
without whom the Eaton Conference
would not exist

Contents

Part 2
Orwell: An Interim Report

Part 3
Alienation, Prognostication, and Apocalypse

Introduction: Science Fiction Confronts the Future

George E. Slusser, Colin Greenland, and Eric S. Rabkin

Too often in the scholarly world essays are written as if they were miniature books, self-contained structures that in turn generate a larger, equally self-contained structure. Originally, however, an essay was an attempt, a suggestive, exploratory form whose nature was open and speculative. This volume of seventeen true essays, individual but interresponsive attempts to explore the nature of our fictions of the future, constitutes a gestalt of collective scholarship.

These essays examine the origins, forms, and, finally, the uses of our fictions of the future. On closer examination, however, these forms and uses in many cases constitute strategies for closure—specific ideas of the future used to limit our sense of a genuinely open future. Some are attempts to ground our imagining of the future in present conditions: social pressures, mental alienation, or historically determined epistemologies such as scientific "optimism" or humanist "pessimism." In and among these are attempts to argue for open futures. Nevertheless, overall and increasingly, openness is restricted, the science fictional sense of wonder qualified by a pessimism which strives, it seems, to be the dominant ideology of adumbrating the future. But no conclusions are drawn. What this symposium offers is a spectrum of possibilities, a broad variety of responses to the question of the future and how we frame it. The power to respond is vital; perhaps SF itself is, first and last, a system of response. For the human makers of fictions, no matter how absolute the hold of past or present may seem, there must be a future as well.

The relation of a text to its present—the circumstances of its conception, composition, production, and reception—are complex enough already. The relation of a fictive text to the future—the future it invents and simultaneously declares to be unreal by the very act of fictionalizing it—enters wondrous realms of paradox, particularly when we consider, as Marie-Hélène Huet does here, that this imaginary future is routinely narrated as if it were already in the past. In this popular arena of elegantly contrived uncertainty, does SF still have its legendary Delphic power of warning, or is this mode of fiction, as skeptical commentators still confidently maintain, automatically disqualified from significance by its commitment to inscribing those areas not, or not yet, embraced by human history? Do we call up images of future societies in order to prepare for them, or to forestall their ever coming into existence?

There was surely never a better opportunity to focus all such shifting questions than the historical moment when a calendar year and a fictive text both bore the same name. George Orwell's *Nineteen Eighty-Four*, read and discussed in 1984, provided a ready and fertile source of images, signs, and structures of language, comparisons, and disparities. Did Orwell, as John Huntington contends, present the future as closed and inevitable, using naturalistic anticipation to deny the possibility of meaningful political change? Or did he, as Elizabeth Maslen contends, anticipate such objections and cultivate a rhetoric, however oblique, to control the way that we, his future readers, receive and judge his text? A special section of essays dealing with or departing from Orwell's novel is contained in *Storm Warnings*.

All the essays contained here arise from the 1984 J. Lloyd Eaton Conference on Science Fiction, held, in recognition of that year, in two parts: the first at the University of California, Riverside, in April, and the second in July at North East London Polytechnic, organized by the Science Fiction Foundation. Each meeting was attended by writers and scholars from the other side of the Atlantic, allowing both American and European perspectives on the questions of science fiction's futures and the nature of fictional speculation to be brought to bear. The geographical surroundings were of more than contextual importance. Is Los Angeles, as the British mass media so often find it convenient to claim, the future of London? And what value do the readers of the New World place upon the fictional futures invented by writers of the Old World?

In conception, then, the conference itself was not merely a cross-cultural but a cross-futural symposium. It was science fictional in form as well as theme, offering the critic real alternate worlds of discourse, multiple 1984s of the mind and body. The topography of these speculations on speculation, gathered together as one might overlay the decor of *Metropolis* on that of *Bladerunner*, could only be unique; in constellation, though not, of course, in limitation. The result is this volume. As anatomy of the future, it describes a distinctive and intriguing version of the shape of things to come.

The coordinators of the conference wish to thank all the people at the University of California, Riverside, and North East London Polytechnic who sponsored and hosted this event so generously: Dean David Warren and librarian Joan Chambers of UCR; Colin Mably of NELP, and Joyce Day and the Council of the SFF. They are the ones who ensured that this conference on the future had a future.

Part I
Originating the Future

Storm Warnings and Dead Zones: Imagination and the Future

George E. Slusser

> . . . more like a man Flying from something that he dreads, than one
> Who sought the thing he loved.
>
> —Wordsworth, "Tintern Abbey"

We might think of science fiction as a literature in love with the future. For it is alone in possessing this dimension, alone in seeking to imagine, as things to come, realms that, in a maximum way, seem to respond to our sense of wonder. And yet, if we heed some of SF's most famous texts, and increasing numbers of its commentators, the very opposite is true. Seen in this light, SF's future imaginations are dominated instead by terror. And this terror is tautology, closure: for if SF lets us see the future, it is to enable us to experience dread, thus to be warned away from an activity which, if pursued, leads us inexorably from bad to worse.

But why is this so? Wonder and terror, the two valences I mentioned for SF's futures, make conflicting claims for its use of speculation. The question of why one is chosen over the other is a cultural matter. Such a mechanism of selection, however, elevating certain works out of a vast body of texts to represent a generic whole, must be dealt with, if we are to see through to the subtler nature, actual and potential, of future imagination. If many SF futures terrify us, and in doing so warn us away from the act of imagination itself, this does not mean that SF cannot imagine futures of wonder. There is a tradition of future "storm warnings" running from Wells to Orwell, one very influential in shaping our collective sense of the SF future. But this is not the only current. The issue here is much larger than Wells's relation to the development of SF. It is no less than the birth of an open literature of future imagination out of what seems, at

3

the heart of Western humanism, a terror of the future. It is the emergence of a sense of wonder out of a culture of fear and dread. The shape of our imagined futures is determined by seldom-examined assumptions that impose cultural restraints on fictional speculation. Let us discuss three of these briefly. The first I call the organistic assumption. Pervasive here is the romantic metaphor of growth which locates the realm of wonder *behind* us, as the place we are coming from rather than that to which we are going. Wonder, then, is the response of the child. Directed at the future, it can be no more than the projection of our intimations, a wish image of lost origins thrown on the forward screen. Thus, in a film like *Close Encounters*, man stands in gaping awe of his future, only to discover that future has taken childlike form. The child may be father to the man. But as both prepare to go off to the stars, these child aliens reveal it is a father figure they need, and allow Richard Dreyfus to herd them paternally on board and to their destiny. Beyond wonder, mankind, because it is engaged organically in the future, must grow up. And in this necessary light of common day, wonder is simply seen as childish.

In SF the "naive" analogue to wonder is that literature's claim to predict the future. As prediction SF seems little more than a desire to project our wishes, primarily the wish to control the course of events in order to restore, as something amazing, the lost glory. As "speculative" fiction, however, SF offers an "adult" future, one where the laws of organic evolution hold. But what we actually have is something grimmer, where these "laws" are inflected by a romantic sense of growth as a fall, devolution. In this sense, future imagination is a vision where, of necessity, wonder becomes terror, where Spielberg's child aliens give way to Wells's Eloi and their terrifying Morlock doubles. And yet, there are more ages of man than these polar opposites of child and adult. SF is often chided for being an adolescent literature. Adolescence, however, may be its rightful analogue. For it is the age of transition, of the *search* for wonder. An adolescent future then would be one in transit, constantly blending fear and awe. And as these interact, might they not create an open field for SF's future imaginations?

The second assumption, complementary to the first, I call the lapsarian assumption. Future imagination, here, is meddling, intrusion (despite all claims that evolution is nonteleological) in a predetermined design. It follows that our attempts to see the future become themselves factors that affect the course of that future. And further, because the course of that future, linked to the romantic sense of growth as fall, is necessarily downward, the only changes our visionary efforts can bring about are negative, an acceleration of the downward course. Mercifully, the naive predictions of SF fail. Speculation, however, is a more serious, an adult, hubris. Here our future imaginations lure us like the scythe in Bradbury's tale, upon which is written: he who wields me rules the world.[1] This story is cautionary to all who would use their future visions to change the way of things. That way here is clearly devolutionary—the postlapsarian rhythm of "natural" growth, which is really life tyrannized by death, the mowing of the "ripe" wheat. At one point the protagonist, as wielder of the scythe, is given a premonition of the future, and with it, the hope that, having seen the future, he can intervene to change it. He sees his family is to die, but will not take the swing that will cut their stalks. But this does not alter events; it only suspends them, and in doing so, creates a maddening blank zone of irresolution that drives him back to the field to mow ripe and green wheat alike, bringing premature holocaust upon the world. In seeking to divert the end through future imagination, Bradbury's protagonist hastens the apocalypse.

This process seems unrelenting. But it is fortunate too, insofar as these future imaginations warn us to abstain from imagining. Projecting visions from our present, the terrors perceived can function to bring us back, but this time to a new sense of presentness—the present seen as "structure." Instead of a process where we, in the extended space-time we call the future, engage natural forces in our visions in hopes of interacting with them, structuralism offers us, as the constant inhabitant of a field of human "systems," an endless present. Warned away from the storms and blank spaces of the future, we find refuge in a structure which, as man neither controls it nor can encompass it in vision, promises an existence that does not depend on either a past or a future. The retreat here is from time to the status quo of myth. Regained is the balance, however postlapsarian, of Bradbury's wheat field.

Structuralism is not just a literary or linguistic model. It is, as Robert Scholes has seen, an ideology: "A structural politics implies in particular a move away from adversary relationships in political processes at all levels . . . away from combat between countries, between parties, between factions, and above all between man and nature."[2] This last adversity, however, is all important for our sense of the future. For only where exists the possibility of struggle with nature can there arise the idea of an open future, and the fears that follow. Indeed, this condition is already there in Marlowe's *Doctor Faustus*, where the protagonist gains a future—so many years of control over natural forces—only by selling his soul.[3] Modern man, the structuralist says, may still be buying future imaginations at the risk of damnation.

For Scholes, this nonadversarial structuralism is today's humanism, replacing the similar claim Sartre made for his existential Marxism. This latter is betrayed by its positivistic faith in history, by the belief that man can direct change to utopian ends. But if Scholes is correct, dystopia, as the product of this betrayed faith, may represent a structuralist reaction. To Sartre, men live in history but seek refuge from it in myth. To structuralist Lévi-Strauss the opposite is true: men live in myth but seek refuge in history, and going farther, in their future speculations themselves. This "myth," Scholes tells us, is a system man may have created but which is "not necessarily arranged for his benefit." Where the relationship between man and nature has become arbitrary then, man can conceivably find himself powerless in a world where the arbitrary holds tyrannical sway over his future visions. Edward Said detects an antihumanist nightside to structuralism.[4] Its literary nightside, the refutation of Sartre's historicism, is dystopia: fictions that could be called structuralist warnings against visionary engagement in the idea of a future.

Scholes's claim, therefore, that the "role of the properly structuralist imagination will be futuristic," is not true. Nor is his claim true that this is a modern imagination.[5] Modern science, in fact, which offers the ideological base for SF, favors neither history nor myth. It is, in its vision, neither utopian nor dystopian, for both are closed systems, defined not only by beginnings and ends but, in the case of the latter, by an absence of these. Dystopia is typified by a tendency for the future to become system—a nightmare present where the process of change has been internalized, hence circumscribed. As if sensing this dystopian analogue of structuralism, Said sees Scholes's new man living "in a circle without a center."[6] This is "humanity" without man—*vir*, scientific man with his power to speculate on things to come.

The relation of history to myth we have described, where utopia has been co-opted by monitory dystopia, reveals these structuralist and organicist/lapsarian models conflating to limit severely our sense of an open future. If there is hope for a future of wonder, it is small. For, as Scholes tells us, man, if he speculates, can only do so in a system "beyond his control but not beyond his power to rearrange."[7] Under the sign of the Fall, however, even rearrangement is subject to devolution—in this case entropy, history overridden by nature. To Scholes, finally, "man's ability to exert his power in self-destructive ways exceeds the ability of his feedback systems to correct his behavior." If this man is to have any relation to the future, it is necessarily self-destructive. Indeed, the only possible "feedback" from dystopian terror is return to a place of minimum entropy—a "present" of rearrangement, of maximum predictability, where we embrace existence as system.[8] This new humanism then is a safe house, a huddling place.

The cultural forces against future imagination, therefore, are formidable, and we find them moving inside SF along a path that runs from Wells to Orwell. But are these storm warnings the only model? Isaac Asimov, for instance, has a different view of SF's capacity to imagine: "It presents a thousand possible futures and there is no way of telling which of these will resemble the real future or even whether any of them will resemble the real future."[9] Asimov's statement offers, in theory at least, two other aspects of future imagination: (1) inventiveness, the power to continue, in our future, to invent a myriad of futures; and (2) mystery, the possibility that one or a number of these invented futures might come true. Implied here is an act of faith: the belief that the real future is one of continuous change, and that our future fictions (however changing themselves) are themselves a factor of change affecting that future.[10] But SF that blindly espouses this credo is indeed naive. For in our culture, so fearful of change, terror blocks wonder. Terror is not the more profound emotion; it is simply more real, a fact that shapes all SF futures. Given this fact, my question is: might there not, beyond the either-or of child and adult, of awe and fear, be another future zone—one of process, of true anticipation? Might there not be a place of future growth that is open by virtue of being blank, not determined by ideas like the Fall—a "dead zone" offering our future imaginations, in the blending of terror and wonder, a way out of a cultural impasse?

To answer that question, let us first look at two "mythic" books
of future terror. Wells's *Time Machine*, poised at the beginning of
our speculative century, is the classic monitory text. The Traveller is
hurled, not by increments but absolutely and finally, into two equally
terminal futures. His real task is this: offered the future through his
machine, he must now imagine it. Having found wonder, he sees it
turn to terror. A speculative scientist by profession, he comes to
realize, as he offers theory after theory (*theorein*—to look at, speculate) to explain his futures, that he cannot figure it, let alone affect it.
Delving the mysteries of the Eloi, he gradually discovers the Morlocks. They seem at first biological opposites. For if the Eloi appear
to have returned to racial childhood, the Morlocks—carnivores and
machine tenders—offer a vision of extreme adulthood; with "pale
chinless faces and great lidless pinkish-grey eyes," they figure the
seventh age of man, the terror of the skull.[11] But these opposites
prove to be doubles as well. For the Traveller, change proves illusion, and these alternate futures of mankind are revealed to be not

only interdependent but self-consuming—cannibalistic Morlocks
feeding on our Eloi dreams of wonder and innocence. Indeed, both
futures, held in this terminal polarity, resolve finally into the face of
the White Sphinx, its glabrous marble features leprous with age.
Sight looks into sightless eyes; the Traveller's imaginations come to
rest on an inscrutable future which, insofar as it holds human forms,
bodes terror.

In the dark Morlock cavern, his last match spent, the Traveller
can only flee. If Wells takes him again into the future, this time it is to
the ultimate finality—the end of nature itself. In the Sphinx all
speculation on social process ends. This final scene is the physical end
of the visionary enterprise: speculation encountering a flat motion-
less sea, cold silence, the blurring of sky and earth in darkness. The
horror of this blank vision—devouring time's effect on differentiated
life—sends the Traveller not only clambering back on his machine
but scurrying back to his present, to his comfortable Edwardian
parlor, a place suddenly inviolate to any hint of futurity. As he left on
his speculative journey he saw his housekeeper Mrs. Watchett lunge
forward at rocket speed into time. His return reverses this lunge
exactly. In a fiction of symbols Mrs. Watchett's reversal figures the
end product of fiction's future imaginings: the inscrutable terrors of
the future mirrored in their safe opposite, in domestic futility.

This is only one lesson Wells's book teaches. But it is a powerful one, surely learned by Orwell in *Nineteen Eighty-Four*. For in Orwell's book Wells's two final futures have been telescoped into one monolith: entropy institutionalized, the final monitory terror to all speculation on the future.

Orwell's novel offers an interesting interplay of our three assumptions. The seeing eye into *Nineteen Eighty-Four*'s imagined future is Winston. He is in revolt against that future, and the direction of his revolt is clearly romantic. Fleeing this light of common day into hidden groves and rented rooms, he seeks to write a diary. He attempts, therefore, to exercise the Wordsworthian power of autobiography—to create the self-written life that sets itself, through a kind of imaginative friction, against the irreversible current of time and growth. This vision, because it is backward, fails. But it is more than simply childish. In its attempt and failure, Winston's dream is itself a replay of the general visionary fall that created the future of Big Brother. Our visionary acts, it is implied, cannot be neutral; they bear a burden of responsibility because they have contributed in some way to the creation of the nightmare. In a world of spectacles and slogans, Winston hopes, by means of the personally shaped written word, to see into the life of things, to reassert *vir* at the center of the visionary process. As with Bradbury's scythe, however, when he takes hold of the writer's tools—"archaic" pen and paper—he does not establish control but only creates more chaos. What flows forth, before his helpless eyes, is a "stream of rubbish," a degraded English "shedding first its capital letters and finally even its full stops," a written structure no longer capable of marking the least moral or grammatical distinctions.

As the visionary medium devolves, moving toward the state where all dialectic oppositions cease, we encounter inscrutable phrases like "war is peace," "hate is love." As in Wells's final vision, where sea and sun remain but without movement or warmth, language in *Nineteen Eighty-Four* has become a lifeless set of "pure" forms. This is endpoint—the closed system whose only capacity for change is the gradual leveling of all variable elements until only a fixity of parts remains. The sin of sins, however—and here the Faustian madman O'Brien is mirrored, if in reverse, by Winston and his diary—is to call this Newspeak. For this equates the future with entropy. Indeed, the claim, in this context, to speak anew, is a claim to total power, and at the same time an admission that one has no power at all, no active role in the evolutionary process of the future. "But at present," O'Brien tells Winston, "power is only a word as far as you are concerned . . . .The first thing you must realize is that power is collective. The individual only has power in so far as he ceases to be an individual. You know the Party slogan 'Freedom is Slavery.' Has it ever occurred to you that it is reversible? Slavery is Freedom."[12] By this same doublethink, antagonists become doubles, Winston becomes O'Brien. The former would rewrite society, the latter gravity. Yet do not both, believing they can enclose world in mind, effectively efface themselves from whatever futures these revisions promise? And in this novel, as O'Brien absorbs Winston and his fallen dreams, wonder becomes terror. Through Winston's eyes future imagination comes to rest on the sphinx-like face of Big Brother: "Forty years it had taken him to learn what kind of smile was hidden behind the dark mustache." O'Brien offers the visionary nightside: "If you want a picture of the future, imagine a boot stamping on a human face—forever."

Orwell created a future with a Gorgon face. Gazing on its paralyzing equations, we ourselves are frozen. And his carefully dated vision, in the act of mesmerizing its viewer, has turned its year to stone as well. The most terrible oxymoron in the novel is not that all power is no power; it is that one year is all years. The book's title is a date; but that does not designate an entity engaged in time, the year preceded by 1983 and followed by 1985. Instead that title is another hollow form, a chronological mark emptied of its futurity, fixed for all eternity as the perpetuation of a single date—a statement that one is all and forever. This ultimate act of timestop, drawing the reader himself into the equation, says that what is most feared here is the passage of time itself.

The final terror then, lurking in the imagination of the future, is not Gorgon but Proteus. For under the sign of the shape-changer, 1984 and all such fixities must finally be invalidated by their futures. The coming and going of years, leaving erasures instead of iron dates, shows us that future visions must be fluid and tentative, not monolithic. For the mind engaged in the protean future, facing the truly unpredictable, games of logic are invalid, as are all beliefs in growth or system or fall. It must rely on seeing, not foreseeing.

If, as Asimov claims, SF is the literature of open vision, then *The*

Time Machine and *Nineteen Eighty-Four*, as works of totalitarian closure, read like monitory tracts against the SF future. What is more, as such they have had a significant effect on the imaginative enterprise which is SF. For beside the extreme terrors of Wells and Orwell, the less radical futures of much SF seem suspect, naive by contrast. And, surprisingly, this contrast may serve, on a deeper level of our cultural psyche, a protective purpose. For, if we think about it, is not a tentative future more unsettling, in an epistemological sense, than Orwell's absolute nightmare? However terrible, Orwell's future is still knowable, whereas Asimov's remains fundamentally random and uncertain. There can be comfort then in radical terror. Given our cultural fears of the future, it is more reassuring even to see it through Faust's eyes, as inevitable process of vision and fall, than through the unclear glass of SF. This situation has had a real impact, first on the shape and direction of SF's future imaginations, and second on our need to define the *capacity* of SF, outside all such cultural restraints and fears, to imagine the future. It is to this latter need that I now turn.

The nature of future imagination is the subject of the recent film based on the Stephen King novel *The Dead Zone* (David Cronenberg, 1985). The problem, posed in the opening frame, is what the dead zone is, what it really signifies. The title sequence offers intriguing possibilities. We have the fixed view of a landscape in which appear, gradually, a number of irregular opaque shapes. As these multiply, they carve up the landscape, render it increasingly chaotic, until finally they regroup to form a series of superimposed block letters—presenting the film's title, *The Dead Zone*. Though it masks half the visual field with its foreboding words, this title stamps on the scene a new assurance of order. And when we soon realize that the film is not only about seeing but foreseeing, seeing into the future, the sequence takes on deeper meaning yet. The hero will later experience a series of terrible, and apparently unalterable visions. And as these unfold, we are seized with a sense of the future as nightmare. The hero is called the devil's spawn. Seen in this light, his visions become, increasingly, acts of meddling in a forbidden zone, acts obeying some primal curse that causes already fallen man to fall further into new horrors. The dead zone seems to be the future itself: a place of dark and destructive visions to which the sole alternative is no vision at all, the blind complacency of the film's tranquil-looking small-town present. Inscribed over what is now recognized as a future landscape, the title acts as a no trespassing sign.

The allusion here is to the final images of *Citizen Kane*. The camera pans slowly up an open chain-link fence, behind which lies foreboding darkness. That fence, like the letters "dead zone," and like the date "1984," is but another totalitarian *garde fou*, a fixed barrier that, quite mercifully given the alternative, halts and blocks out speculation. But Kane's fence is the last image in the film. Here the "dead zone" titles open the film. By the very forward motion of things, this warning is one we must get around. Intruders in the dead zone, we can just as well find, in its visionary blankness, a place of surprise, of freedom to act. Indeed, at a second glance, we notice that the protagonist's visionary acts, rather than being a simple descent into hell, follow a different, and significant, order. His first vision moves into an elsewhere that remains nonetheless in his present. Emerging from a coma after his accident, the protagonist is in the care of a nurse. Looking at her he sees, in a vision, that her house at the very same moment is on fire. He warns her, and she is able to get there in time to save her child. Here, imagination is moving in realms of simultaneity, not in sequential time. His next visions, however, go into the past. They not only cannot change the course of past events, but bring about a terrible degradation of the apparently stable here and now. He sees, first, the mother of his doctor, thought dead, escaping from German soldiers. Telephoning her, the doctor hears her voice but (the opposite of the nurse who saves her child) refuses to make contact, claiming that such was not meant to be, that reunion would not build but destroy. Which is exactly the result of his second excursion into the past, for by revealing a brutal sex murderer to be a local policeman, he brings the murderer to commit an even more grisly act of suicide in the present. The moral is clear: visionary interaction with the past can only bring horrific disorder to the present.

We are thus prepared, with fear and trembling, for the direction of the next visionary projection—the future. It comes when the protagonist, talking to a young boy he is tutoring, sees the boy drowning. Learning the boy is to go ice skating the next day, he breaks his silence and warns him, which, in this case, is a positive, future-directed act, not an act of negative disengagement from the future. And because the accident occurs, but without the boy, this act literally pulls the face out of the vision, creating a different sort of dead zone. The areas in the future where we do not see are no longer a priori fearful; they are simply undetermined. And, something not predicted, they allow at least the possibility that our speculative visions may themselves be actions that affect the future, if in unpredictable ways. What we learn here is that seeing is not, necessarily, fixing. For what we see on the screen, the boy drowning, does not come true.

The protagonist's final act of future vision involves a demagogue politician. He sees him, having become president, pushing the nuclear button in an act of totalitarian madness, triggering apocalypse. Seeking to assassinate him, the protagonist fails. But this sacrifice erases the politician's future as well. For to shield himself from the protagonist's bullet, the latter holds up a young child, and by doing so reveals his true nature to his voting public. Dying, the protagonist has a horrific vision which, in a sense, reverses the polarity of an earlier horror—the suicide of the policeman whose murderous past was exposed. We see our politician, unmasked as a brutal coward, graphically blow his brains out. The visionary splatter of blood, it seems, creates another grisly dead zone. This one, however, has become the mark of an undetermined future, a place where our future imaginings engage the process of history, and can even alter it, if to unknown ends. The claim of the title then is belied. The dead zone no longer, by blocking all visions, forces us to sit paralyzed and watch the totalitarian end take shape, stamp itself on the field of our future imaginings. It has become just the opposite—the place of open vision.

This 1985 film is, in a sense, a science fictional answer to Orwell's 1984. It is interesting, however, that in the wake of 1984, this film must come at the question of future vision backwards, must in a sense reactivate as seeing zones what has been declared horror, must relocate visionary freedom within the interdictions of an overdetermined future. The film is proof that, beyond 1984, a struggle is going on for the shape of the future, a shape which governs, as it molds our visions, our relationship to time and change altogether.

SF, however, in film and book, continues to project future visions, and we continue to react to them. And the legacy of Wells and Orwell has taught us to question their legitimacy. There seem to be two common responses to SF futures today, which I call the literalist and the mythicalist responses. And both of these, if we look carefully, appear to be attempts to "horrifize" those visionary futures they scrutinize. Following the example of *The Dead Zone*, but in reverse, they strive to effect a generic shift. For if these responses are, in fact, strategies of disengagement from the future, their operations, converting apparently open vistas, one by one, into dark spaces, designate the SF vision a realm of horror.

The literalist seeks to hoist science fiction with its own petard by applying the concept of change literally. He challenges SF's ability to project genuinely extrapolated worlds beyond a very limited point in the close future, because such visions cannot imagine even a fraction of the possible changes that would have occurred. The literalist will read a few pages into Asimov's *Foundation*, set in the year 12,000 of the Galactic Era, and discover that there are still Ph.D.'s. He will read Samuel Delany's *Nova*, carefully dated "Draco, Earth, Paris, 3162," and find celebrity parties and jet-sets, mores and institutions that surely could not survive the passage of 1,100 years, any more than they existed in 900 A.D. The analogy with history, in this perspective, tells us we cannot possibly imagine what change and historical process will bring, even in the near future. Our fault lies, therefore, in attempting to depict the future at all. Film here is even more at fault, because it knows it is image-bound, and cannot hide behind the imprecision of words. David Lynch's film version of *Dune*, for example, is a vulnerable target. For even if we conceive that empires and feudal governments might recur in that far future, we cannot accept that their subjects, seen on the screen, would dress and act like figures we see today in our dictionaries and encyclopedias, the products of our limited (and probably false) sense of the past.

Clearly, this literalist challenge to our ability to imagine plausible futures has an undercurrent of warning—a suggestion that the point beyond which we cannot see is perhaps the point beyond which we were not *meant* to see. To the literalist that point can be located, reversing the time line, in the past as well as the future. In fact, his most telling argument against the imagination of the future is just such a reversal. For unlike the future, the past has happened, has left images. The task, therefore, of organizing these into coherent visionary wholes should be much easier. Upon reflection, however, past reconstructions, except for dates very near to us, prove not only difficult, but ultimately impossible. This impossibility must serve, in turn, as warning against our future visions, for in that direction there are no artifacts, no images to rely on. This is the point, for instance, that Federico Fellini seeks to prove, quite consciously, in his film *Satyricon*. And the manner in which he proves it, by revealing the too-distant past to be a place of inscrutability, finally of horror, casts a grim storm warning forward upon SF's futures.

Fellini and his associates are aware of the relationship of their enterprise to science fiction. Refusing to make a period film, he claims his efforts are, instead, science fiction: "It's a film about Martians, a science-fiction film."[13] By this comparison, however, Fellini shows us how he feels about the speculative capacity of SF. For neither the period film nor the SF film can pretend, beyond modest temporal limits, to give us a complete vision, let alone a "real" one: "Could you do a satire on Martians?" One of Fellini's associates calls the *Satyricon* "historical science fiction, a journey into time, a planetary world, away from our everyday logic and rhythm: counterimages, counterdialogue."[14] The film then is a visionary voyage down the time line to a point, Rome, which is beyond the limits of the recognizable: "It's a lost, vanished, defunct world, about which we really know hardly anything and with which we have no real relationship. . . . It's a completely alien world, in fact."[15] The problem with vision then is the past or the future themselves, "the leprosy of time" which renders all projected images finally "indecipherable, obscure."

Fellini's *Satyricon* is a vision of fragments and ruins, a dead zone to which we react with terror. Again, however, this is not horror as alienness, visions of things never before seen and therefore new. It is horror as alienation, the totalitarian vision of Orwell's slogans and Wells's sphinx, something both recognizable *and* unrecognizable. The faces and forms are there, shoring up what still appears a structure of intercourse. But they are ruins, emptied of significance, yet still organizing their timescape with a mocking semblance of human control. To call such a vision science fiction is to set rigid limits on SF's speculative power. To do so is to prescribe, as well, fearful consequences for overstepping those limits. Fellini typifies the literalist response; his film tells us two things. First, compared to the task of envisioning historical Rome, SF's projection of the Roman Empire into the future appears both a banal and a futile enterprise. For if our vision fails two thousand years in the past, where there are images extant, how can we possibly imagine anything two thousand years in the future? Second, if our visualization of the past, as in *Satyricon*, proves fearful, might not any attempt to create images in and of the future be doubly so? For against this total unknown we can only project images from past or present, turning its blank face into a mirror, and illusion into the terrible fixity of 1984 timestop.

The mythicalist approaches the future from an opposite angle of vision. His basic tenet is not alienation but familiarization. He does not say we cannot see the future. He says, on the contrary, that we easily see the future, and that we do because its images, ultimately, must obey the configurations of what we call myth. These are super-temporal situations that, as they deprivilege the time line, can be seen to shape all our visions, past and future. Myth allows us to see the alpha and omega, to look beyond the limits, at either end of the chronological scale, of history itself. But this mythic vision too may be a form of mirror vision. For looking into the past or the future, mythicalist man hopes to see, in his myths, his own face. Time, in this process, is converted into a vertical dimension, one that finds its center of gravity in the human form. By this logic Fellini was able to comb the streets of today's world and find faces that resemble those painted on the walls of Pompeii. And the recent film of *Dune* can be accused of taking this same synchronist assumption and turning it around, pointing it at the future. The costumes for this future world were derived from at least ten different past times and places. The reason is surely this: if we assume that army officers, 24,000 years in the future, will still exist, then a nineteenth century Russian officer's uniform, chosen at random from the past field of possibilities, is as likely to recur at that time as any other possible style. The mythicalist considers both past and future as forming a finite system of social and vestimentary permutations—a system whose symmetry is regulated by the human form that abides at its centerpoint.

The mythicalist vision is deep-rooted, because it is, in a sense, man's defense against his imagination. Indeed, because he considers our future imaginations generated by patterns that are both super-temporal *and* human, the mythicalist is not raising the problem of man's engagement in time so much as his desire to disengage from time. Even Asimov cannot escape the pull of this desire. For if, on one hand, he proclaims SF's need for visionary engagement in the future, on the other, he shades toward "humanist" nonengagement when he defines SF as the literature that measures the impact of technological change on human beings. The assumption is that there is some constant we call "human" that naturally resists or controls change. This same assumption informs his division of speculative scenarios into two sorts—the "chess game" and the "chess puzzle" models. The chess board in question is that of human society and history. In the "puzzle" story, for instance, the "rules," the set of patterns that govern human behavior in history, must hold; the pieces alone are out of place, and the "plot" is the process of restoring them to their rightful order. And yet, despite a belief that history repeats itself "with surprising regularity," Asimov in the same essay reaches a point where vision becomes dangerous, and the gameboard possibly invalid because mankind has ceased to be *Homo sapiens*. Asimov in the end cannot abandon his human norm. But this possibility reveals an ominous, and quite specific, dead zone—the sense that today "for the first time in history, the future is a complete puzzle even in its most general aspects."[16]

This particular prospect, where the human system undergoes such change that it becomes itself something undetermined and potentially chaotic, brings the mythicalist mind to establish new games. In these, myth has become a totalitarian structure, one that must subsume darkness and chaos itself in the workings of its closed system—a system that both determines and overdetermines our futures. An example is Delany's use of Tarot cards as mythic underpinning for his far-flung future visions in *Nova*. In this novel historical and even natural processes appear to be drifting into areas of uncontrollable change—of "heterotropic" or "psychomorphic" elements. To control the uncontrollable, however, Delany brings forth, at the heart of this future, Tarot cards which, coming from the night of time, organize in mythic, and predictive, configurations the most potentially disruptive struggles of human ambition. Held in the confines of these cards, and promising to fix human futures in the same confines, is the primal struggle of chaos and order itself. Much as in the slogans of *Nineteen Eighty-Four,* these cards link total opposites—Manichean forces of light and darkness—in fearful and tyrannical images: the Dioscuri, immortal Pollux and mortal Castor, who are both deadly rivals and twins; or the Sun, the trinary pattern of two rivals and their common goal, microcosm of hero Lorq's deathless battle with, and undying likeness to, his rival Prince. The Tarot enfolds all instability, even that of the darkest futures, in a balance that, if it still claims to be human, is grotesque and terrifying to the gaze. Indeed, the dark perversity of the struggle for the future in *Nova* opens, beyond these cards and their patterns of order, a black hole of potential chaos. At such an extreme juncture there can only be this choice: man or nonman, Wells's end of the world or (what we get by leaping back on the time machine and reversing vision) totalitarian myth. As in Blake's engraving *A Divine Image*, mythicalist man must stamp his own face on his sun and his future. But here, as in that drawing, the man is fraught with anxiety, his sun's face is angry. This mirror situation, man gazing on his terrible 1984 constructs so as not to see beyond to unknown futures, conceals that deep "humanist" nightmare where "terror" has become "the Human Form Divine . [and] . the Human Face, a Furnace seal'd, the Human Heart, its hungry Gorge."[17]

Jean Gattégno, in his book *La Science-fiction*, suggests that SF may be a literature of hate.[18] This is a profound observation, but it needs qualification. I would argue, in this context of future imaginations, that it is not SF per se but the Orwellian literature of terror that is founded on hatred—a hatred of the future. Indeed both the literalist and the mythicalist positions, as emissaries of 1984, create an adversary relationship between the future and the present. And this relationship is the product, on the polite level of critical discourse, of our deep cultural fear of the future. For rather than concede that the future is open, both the literalist and the mythicalist would rather see it as a place of vengeance. In their last-ditch warnings, there is more than tyranny; there is Orwell's boot, the Morlocks's cannibalism, the Hitler-like ravings of Cronenberg's "president." These are monstrous visions, meant finally to crush those who dare look beyond their own present. The hate reflected in these futures is our hate, a hate against the whole speculative enterprise, itself become the work of some mad scientist tampering with a divinely ordained order of things. Fellini shocks us, Orwell bludgeons us; there is no refuge in the past or the future. Humanity is helpless except in the confines of its own present, for as Bradbury says, everywhere else "there be tigers." Indeed, Bradbury's story "Zero Hour" is a perfect statement of the degree zero of our pastless, futureless existence. For in its future utopian world the conduit of hate, what brings the pitiless

Martian exterminators, is the children themselves, those seers into our innocent past.

The role of hate in SF, then, is more complex. For SF, in general, may not be so much a literature of hate as one which, in its search for wonder at least, draws hate, becomes the object of hate. Works like *Nineteen Eighty-Four* are attacks on wonder because, at the deepest level of their operation, they seek to annihilate the purveyor of wonder—the individual imagination of the future. Their absolutely collective worlds, a finality perpetrated by never-ending acts of hatred against the individual's claims to a future, seem to be created this way in order to show that all intermediate or tentative wonders, by terrible contrast, are banal and finally inconsequential.

Daydreams then, in the light of *Nineteen Eighty-Four*, must become nightmares. Perhaps another reason for this is that our fear of the future is a fear of science, or what science has become. As Gary Zukav tells us, today "there is no single 'experience' of physics."[19] This physics, like the multiple future visions of SF that take inspiration from it, "is a sparkling realm of continual creation, transformation, and annihilation." Against this, the Morlocks or Big Brother erect Newtonian totality. What they oppose to the dance of the Wu Li Masters is the myth-bound game of gods and dragons. Their sky god is Urizen, whose name means "limits," and whose form has cruelly aged, Northrop Frye's "white terror" become the enemy not only of life but of vision as well.[20] Their "science" not only created the word "future," that which is about to *be*, but made it the extreme adversary of man by re-casting change as the dragon that must be frozen and slain. For Zukav's science, however, the future is simply that which is to come. And SF's imaginations of the future should be free to engage this neutral dead zone, to explore the nondetermined "way" from now to then.

SF's imaginations of the future, therefore, if they are to respond to this new science, must be tentative. And, if they are to throw off all vestiges of Faustian hubris, they must be collective as well. They do not seek finality, but rather continuity of vision. There are examples of collective speculation in the body of SF, examples often obscured by the higher profile of its storm warnings. A striking recent example is the *Dune Encyclopedia*. This is a collective act of speculation on a speculation, the spontaneous extension, by our society in the fictional form of a future world, of what otherwise seems an individual obsession. The *Encyclopedia* moves in the opposite direction from that prescribed by Michel Butor in his famous attack on SF.[21] Telling us that SF's realm of operation is not the future but the present, Butor gives SF a zone of imagination only if this is carefully, and absolutely, circumscribed. For instead of allowing each individual writer to project his own future city, we (whoever "we" are) must dictate a single city, one that "would become a common possession to the same degree as an ancient city that has vanished." But SF writers, unlike Heraclitus, are dreamers who do not all want to wake in the same world. To Butor, however, these individual dreams must yield to the tyrannical whole, a "same world" by fiat, the future again as a 1984 enterprise. *Dune*, however, is a world, created by an individual, which now proves it has a future by freely attracting other individuals to speculate within its framework, and beyond it. Seen from the perspective of the *Dune Encyclopedia*, Herbert's future world has become more than just history. It is the subject of anatomy and analysis, by people in our later future, for the *use* of other generations who will need the knowledge in order to imagine more Dune futures to come. There is a Dune Tarot described here as well. But this is but one entry—nonprivileged—among others in a vast compendium. These cards then in no way can determine and close (as in *Nova*) Dune's future. They are an open structure, a speculative device in the true sense. Their description provides, better than I can do perhaps, the key to the speculative imagination of science fiction: "Meaning resides not in the cards but in the mind of the reader; the cards provide only a focus and a symbology for the channelling of energy, for the clearing of the vision, for the opening of the eyes of the seeker."[22]

Origins of Futuristic Fiction:
Felix Bodin's *Novel of the Future*

Paul Alkon

Attempts to explain the origins of futuristic fiction have concentrated on backgrounds: the industrial revolution; acceleration of technological change; the rise of capitalism; expansion of geological time-scales together with Darwinian theories of evolution; and political revolutions towards the end of the eighteenth century.[1] All these phenomena doubtless play some role in the emergence of a genre unknown to classical, medieval, and Renaissance literature. But until we have more completely described the works themselves, our explanations of why they came into being will perforce remain incomplete. Another problem is the temptation to scrutinize early futuristic fiction with an eye mainly on the accuracy of its predictions instead of asking what role such predictions play in the formal structure of particular works.[2] We should defer sociological explanations until we have a better picture of what it is we are trying to account for. We might remember too that questions about causation, however interesting, are, finally, less significant for criticism than questions about the manner in which a new form achieves its full power; only by looking more closely than we have at the first steps along the road to *Nineteen Eighty-Four* can we fully appreciate the nature of an achievement like Orwell's. It was no easy leap to such mastery of the future.

By "futuristic fiction" I mean prose narratives explicitly set in future time. Prior to 1659, when Jacques Guttin published his romance *Epigone: Histoire du siècle futur*, no writer of fiction chose the future as a narrative setting.[3] That part of time was left to prophets, astrologers, and practitioners of deliberative rhetoric. Fiction taking the future as its milieu is a significant new development of early post-Renaissance literature.[4] The French maintained their lead in this form, although the next such work after *Epigone*, and the first to be located with specific future dates, was Samuel Madden's anonymously published and quickly suppressed satire *Memoirs of the Twentieth Century* (London 1733). This was followed in 1763 by *The Reign of George VI, 1900–1925*: a fantasy of relentless conquest whose unknown author claims the ambiguous honor of initiating the genre of future warfare. It was a second French writer, Louis-Sébastien Mercier, who in 1771 took the far more crucial step of decisively moving utopia from no place to future time in his widely translated and often imitated *L'An 2440: Rêve s'il en fut jamais*.[5] In 1802, Restif de la Bretonne's *Les Posthumes* portrayed a very far future marked by planetary and biological evolution. In 1805, Jean-Baptiste Cousin de Grainville's *Le dernier homme* initiated the secularization of apocalypse—a watershed event for the history of science fiction, which is so widely described today as "the contemporary form of apocalyptic literature."[6]

In 1834, Felix Bodin's *Le Roman de l'avenir* provided the first literary criticism of works set in future time as well as the first—and arguably still the best—poetics of the genre. Bodin invented an apt term for the new form: "littérature futuriste." He also remarked, quite correctly, that no fully realized novelistic examples of it yet existed. I believe Bodin's discussion is the first instance of generic criticism written predictively *before* emergence of the genre in question for the purpose of encouraging its creation: an altogether fitting sequence for futuristic fiction. In this essay I want to suggest that Bodin's remarkable work, which deserves to be far better known, is the locus classicus for understanding both the origins and formal innovations of futuristic fiction.

Let us approach Felix Bodin's tour of the horizon in 1834 by glancing ahead to a text dealing with similar issues in our own period: Robert Scholes's *Structural Fabulation: An Essay on Fiction of the Future*. I single out Scholes's excellent discussion both for its aid and comfort to students of futuristic fiction and to underscore by comparison the astonishing prescience of Bodin's criticism in a book that is almost totally neglected, to their loss, by twentieth century critics who could still find its insights of more than merely historical interest. Scholes argues "that the most appropriate kind of fiction that can be written in the present and the immediate future is fiction that takes place in future time." He rightly notes that such fiction can achieve a power unequalled by other kinds, and supports his case on several grounds, of which two are especially relevant to the origins of futuristic fiction. There is first an ethical argument: "If we accept Jean-Paul Sartre's imperative for literature, that it be a force for improvement of the human situation, and if we nevertheless would not see fiction reduced to the level of propaganda, then the idea of fiction freely speculating on possible futures must appeal to us." Secondly, Scholes addresses what he calls a metaphysical issue: given widespread rejection of the idea that language can or should refer to anything outside its own system, a solipsistic notion that undercuts all relationship of literature to life, futuristic fiction offers a way out, because "all future projection is obviously model-making, poesis not mimesis." It follows, according to Scholes, that because such extrapolation is bounded only by "current notions of what is probable"—notions that science renders increasingly latitudinarian—the resulting literature is not only useful in the sense which Sartre urges as an imperative for improving the human condition, but it is also a literature in which "realism and fantasy must have a more intricate and elaborate relationship with one another."[7] There is, thus, a distinctive aesthetic advantage, along with the utilitarian possibilities of encouraging efforts to create a better world. This is our best defense of futuristic fiction: as a form uniquely appealing because it is potentially more able than any other kind to further human progress by serving a variety of cognitive purposes without sacrificing either the appeal of fantasy or the claim to probability that is a hallmark of realism.

Bodin too, although writing in a cultural context whose differences from our own I need hardly labor, saw futuristic fiction as an instructive mode that could better than any other enlist writing in the service of progress by combining the pleasures of fantasy with the reassurance of verisimilitude. He identified the main philosophical dispute of his day as an opposition between those who located mankind's golden age in the past, regarding the world as going downhill to an iron age that would mark its deathbed, and those who believed in the possibility of progress, for whom the golden age lies in a future which presents itself to the imagination, "resplendent with light." In ages dominated by the conviction that things are getting worse, Bodin notes, our dreams are of endings for the world and of the last man.[8] When belief in progress prevails, other dreams are possible. But, as yet, futuristic literature, Bodin laments, has offered nothing but utopias or apocalypses: he does not know of any *novelistic* action transported to the setting of a future social or political condition.[9]

The trouble with utopian literature, according to Bodin, is that its authors only try to find a basis for unfolding some religious, political, or moral system without attaching it to an action, without giving either depth or movement to *things or persons*, and without finally achieving the living creation of any kind of world to come (p. 17).[10] Apocalypses, in Bodin's view, may at best provide poetic visions of the sort exemplified in "the mysterious and gigantic scenes" found in the Book of Revelation and its derivatives focusing on the Last Judgment. But such images, although respectable, are not consoling. Nor do they encourage either hope or efforts to work for progress. They lead to despair and apathy. Bodin's critique of previous futuristic literature thus firmly links the aesthetic issue of imaginative appeal with the moral issue of how readers may best be roused from indifference to their own future.

When Bodin considers what, ideally, futuristic fiction ought to be, he specifies with even greater precision the most desirable relationships between verisimilitude, imaginative appeal, and the moral consequences for society of the new genre:

> If ever anyone succeeds in creating the novel, the epic of the future, he will have tapped a vast source of the marvelous, and of a marvelous entirely in accord with verisimilitude . . . which will dignify reason instead of shocking or deprecating it as all the marvelous epic machinery conventionally employed up to now has done. In suggesting perfectibility via a picturesque, narrative, and dramatic form, he will have found a method of seizing, of moving the imagination and of hastening the progress of humanity in a manner very much more effective than the best expositions of systems presented with even the highest eloquence. (P. 20)[11]

What Bodin envisions is a literature of rational wonders that can play a useful role in the real world *without surrendering the lure of the fantastic.* He also recognizes a problem peculiar to the issue of verisimilitude in novels attempting to enact plausible dreams of possible futures: it will be harder for such works to attain universal appeal, he says, because everyone shapes an ideal future according to their own fantasies; such fantasies are more likely to differ from those perceptions of the world which we make our yardstick for measuring verisimilitude in realistic fiction.[12]

Turning at the end of his discussion from the relationship between literature and society to what he describes as the "purely literary considerations" involved in the question of how people view the future—whether as leading to progress or decay—Bodin provides an aphorism of his own, which, he affirms, contains the entire poetics of the novel of the future: "Civilization tends to separate us from all that is poetic in the past; but civilization also has its poetry and its marvelous" (p. 29). Applying this thought to novels set in future time, Bodin winds up his essay with a remarkably accurate prediction of future novelistic possibilities as well as a perceptive location of such possibilities with respect to previous literary history. The two most striking statements from this section especially deserve wider familiarity not only for their historical interest, but for the help which I believe they can still provide to students of futuristic fiction.

To find subject matter, Bodin suggests leaving what he calls the sad past, which has been sufficiently exploited, and making a leap into the more seductive unknown future:

> There [in the future] can be found the revelations of those under hypnotic trance, races in the air, voyages to the bottom of the sea—just as one sees in the poetry of the past sibyls, hippogriffs, and nymphs' grottoes; but the marvelous of the future is entirely different from these other poetic marvels in that it is entirely believable, entirely natural, entirely possible, and on that account it can strike the imagination more vividly and seize it via realism. Thus we will have discovered a new world, an environment utterly fantastic and yet not lacking in verisimilitude. (P. 30)[13]

Here the imaginative role of plausibly extrapolated scientific wonders such as voyages under the sea and aerial races—very workable themes indeed, as we now know—is clearly affiliated to those purposes formerly served by the fantastic marvels of classical literature. Bodin affirms the desire for such marvels as an emotional and imaginative need: what Samuel Johnson in another context called the hunger of the imagination. Bodin also suggests a way of enlisting such marvels, changed to modern form, in the service of rational speculation. This insight is still a valid answer to those who question our need for fictions of the future. Such fictions—perhaps uniquely among literary kinds—may serve cognitive purposes both necessary and acceptable to reason in a scientific age of rapid change while *also* feeding our hunger for the marvelous.

The final paragraph of Bodin's essay is even more specific in spelling out the tradition to which novels of the future, when they are written, should be affiliated:

> For the moment the question is to know whether, after the grotesque and audacious fantasies of Rabelais, the amusing and satiric inventions of Cyrano and Swift, and the sparkling philosophical novels of Voltaire, it would be possible to find something new and at the same time analogous; something which would be neither a too licentious fantasy, nor of a purely critical intent, nor of that philosophical spirit which is an obstacle to interest and illusion by always substituting ideas for people, and by subordinating both action and characters to the thesis which it argues; something at once fantastic, novelistic, philosophic, and a little critical; a book where an imagination brilliant, rich and wandering can range at ease; and, finally, a book amusing without being futile. I believe such a book would be possible; but I am still perfectly convinced that it is not yet written. (Pp. 31–32)[14]

Bodin's own novel of the future, to which his discussion serves as preface, was published incomplete. Even this lengthy fragment is of considerable interest, both as a revealing historical document, and as an intriguing bit of fiction that stands up well if measured by the high standards articulated in its preface. Bodin, however, was not up to following his own counsel of perfection. That remained for H. G. Wells and his successors—whose best writing may certainly be seen as providing among other things just the kind of analogues to Rabelais, Cyrano, Swift, and Voltaire which Bodin here urges.

Bodin's statement of the tradition for which novels of the future could be the logical next development marks a noteworthy step toward that self-consciousness which has become one hallmark of futuristic fiction. But I must note too that despite Bodin's foresight, his essay was apparently neither itself instrumental in bringing about the development he recommended, nor even very widely known in its own day. There was no rush to adopt his useful term *littérature futuriste* by way of encouraging, as Bodin hoped to do, the realization of a new form designed to achieve what had previously been accomplished only separately by the fantastic voyage, the marvelous machinery of epics, the utopian projection, and the *conte philoso-phique*. The isolation from each other among early writers of futuris-tic fiction is one of the most striking features of their situation and of that genre's origins. I have found little evidence that futuristic writers before 1850 knew of their predecessors' efforts apart from Mercier's famous book. Nor are there textual signs that their readers were expected to recall earlier works *of the same kind* for comparison with the book in hand. It is not until very much later that one commonly finds mutual awareness manifested by writers of futuristic fiction along with inclusion of what had become obviously conventional elements such as time machines or future warfare in the didactic mode of G. T. Chesney's *Battle of Dorking*.

Early futuristic fiction is indeed, as Pierre Versins, I. F. Clarke, Darko Suvin, and others have suggested, a series of largely indepen-dent efforts that cut across the usual national, cultural, and formal boundaries. The degree to which previous forms were in fact tran-scended by the evolution of futuristic fiction has been obscured by its scattered origins. Despite the popularity of Mercier's *L'An 2440*, there was in the rise of futuristic fiction nothing exactly comparable to what Raymond Trousson describes as the monogenesis of forms like the utopia or the robinsonade for which a single text is clearly recognized as so distinctive that it sets the parameters for recognition of all subsequent examples while also retroactively casting some earlier works in the role of forerunners—as More's *Utopia* did for Plato's *Republic*.[15] Nor for most theories of genre has resort to future time as the setting for narrative action seemed a variation sufficiently distinctive to count as a form in its own right.[16] Usually that resort has simply been taken for granted as nothing more than one attribute of science fiction. But tales of the future are not necessarily science fiction. Although undeniably liberated by the possibilities of displac-ing action to the future, science fiction does not require such displace-ment, as Mary Shelley's *Frankenstein* may remind us, along with other early science fiction set in the present or close past—most notably, of course, all the major works of Jules Verne.[17]

Nor did new technology or social transformations in the wake of the American, French, and industrial revolutions provide a more evident stimulus to invention of the first futuristic fictions than the literary system itself. Bodin, after all, was able to point out gaps in that system which remained to be filled by futuristic fiction: most notably, as I have remarked, the need for some acceptable novelistic equivalent of the fantastic voyage, the marvelous machinery of epics, the utopian projection, and the *conte philosophique*. Bodin's very stress on the need for novelistic future fictions subordinating ideas and extrapolation to vivid portrayal of action and environment obliquely acknowledges the rise of the novel as a preeminent form during the eighteenth century. The aesthetic virtues of those other genres whose masters are Rabelais, More, Cyrano, Swift, and Voltaire are acknowledged by Bodin's insistence upon the need to achieve effects *analogous* to theirs within the framework of plausible tales of the future—that is to say, in a variation of the realistic novel. Underlying Bodin's argument, to be sure, is a profound transformation in standards of verisimilitude brought about by the rise of science and technology. That transformation, however, as Bodin was perhaps the first to recognize, primarily altered the basis of the marvelous in a way that allowed its inclusion within new forms of realistic literature. Developments such as hypnosis, aeronautics, and submarine travel (to mention only what attracted Bodin's attention) offered the prospect of marvelous phenomena especially suitable to futuristic fiction, but—as Jules Verne demonstrated—without necessarily requiring a leap to future time for effective use.

Evidence available in the relevant texts themselves suggests that resort to future time for the setting of fiction was stimulated more immediately by a climate of literary experimentation that persisted throughout the eighteenth century. The most innovative writers encouraged by their example an extraordinarily vigorous search for viable new kinds of writing whose novelty would be apparent by implicit or explicit contrast with traditional forms. Thus, Alexander Pope responded to the classical epic by creating mock-epics: *The Rape of the Lock* and *The Dunciad*. Extraordinary voyages like *Gulliver's Travels* were among many other things obvious parodic inversions of conventional travel literature. Swift turned the serious projection upside-down in *A Modest Proposal*. The forms of biblical exegesis are twisted to new modes of satire in *A Tale of a Tub*. Handel's operas and their style of grand opera, once established as a major form, immediately served as foils for *The Beggar's Opera*. This was also termed a Newgate Pastoral in allusion to another formal contrast, and in turn it became the ancestor of a viable new theatrical kind: the musical comedy. The realistic novel itself had scarcely been established in England when Sterne inverted most of its conventions to create a new variety of mock-novel in *Tristram Shandy*.

It was in that challenging context of authors trying to outvie each other in the game of providing anti-forms to match accepted forms, as I have argued elsewhere, that the first English book set in future time, Samuel Madden's *Memoirs of the Twentieth Century*, exploited yet another possibility of turning a familiar genre around by taking history, the form which deals with the past, and converting it for satiric purposes into its absurdist opposite: a history of the future.[18]

Succeeding novelistic fictions of the future are also less closely affiliated to the rise of science than to the eighteenth century endorsement of formal variation. In the remaining space available here I can perhaps best illustrate how this particular impetus to creation fostered tales of the future by turning briefly to the one novel published prior to Bodin's essay which comes closest to satisfying his ideal prescription for futuristic fiction, a novel alas unknown to him: Jane Webb's lively 1827 anticipation *The Mummy! A Tale of the Twenty-Second Century*.

Webb prefaces *The Mummy* with an introduction that begins: "I have long wished to write a novel, but I could not determine what it was to be about. I could not bear anything common-place, and I did not know what to do for a hero." The narrator then describes walking down "a shady lane, one fine evening in June," mulling over the problem: "I could think of nothing that had not been thought of before. . . . 'Surely,' thought I . . . 'there must be some new ideas left, if I could but find them.'" Coming to a hill with a superb prospect ("It was quite a Claude-Lorraine scene") the narrator sleeps. We are then reminded of how such sleep on a picturesque hillside is conventionally used by writers: "It would be of no use to go to sleep without dreaming; and, accordingly, I had scarcely closed my eyes when, me-thought, a spirit stood before me. His head was crowned with flowers; his azure wings fluttered in the breeze. . . . In his hand he held a scroll . . . 'take this,' said he, smiling . . . it is the Chronicle of a future age. Weave it into a story. It will so far gratify your wishes, as to give you a hero totally different from any hero that ever appeared before."[19] Such an introduction encourages readers to think less about the real future than about the literary past.

Webb arouses curiosity about her book itself. She classifies it as a tale, thus using a term that smacks more of unabashed make believe than representation, however fictionalized, of what might really happen in the future. Her introduction directs attention not so much to what the twenty-second century may possibly be like, but to the very different question of how her story will bring off the feat of achieving novelty when its twenty-second century events are compared, not with life in the reader's nineteenth century present, but with previous novels. Readers are not invited to take stock of what the nineteenth century is like before plunging into an imagined future, but rather to think of heroes they have previously encountered in other books. Only thus can a new kind of hero be appreciated. Of course this does not preclude comparisons between the present and her imagined future. Throughout *The Mummy* such comparisons are, in fact, often elicited for purposes of satirizing nineteenth century trends in education and technology. Nor does the self-reflexive announcement of its own fictionality, its status as a work of makebelieve entered in the contest of wit for the prize awarded to originality, necessarily prevent Webb's readers from surrendering to the charm of a coherent and plausibly worked out future.

The book's plot is nevertheless more compelling—and I believe most accurately accounted for—as a self-conscious variation on gothic conventions than as a response to shifting ideas about the future, or as a forecast of its possible technology in the form of dirigible travel and the like, or even as a response to aspects of Webb's nineteenth-century world such as schemes for universal education, which she amusingly satirizes in the form of garrulous servants who talk in the elaborate jargon of college professors and cook gourmet meals, while their masters speak simply and eat boiled potatoes. Such aspects of Webb's twenty-second century—like its England converted to Roman Catholicism again and ruled despotically, though harmlessly, by a lethargic queen while sinister scheming priests plot to alter the royal succession—are certainly intended to elicit from readers some thought about possible futures and the role of present choices in creating or forestalling them. A romantic love story distracts attention from such matters, however, converting Webb's comically dystopian future into a mere exotic background, although surely one sketched with sufficient depth, and sufficiently subordinated to novelistic action, to have won Bodin's approval, had he known of the book.

The mummy itself serves a more traditional literary purpose, not much related to futuristic fiction as such. The Egyptian Pharoah Cheops is brought back to life apparently (but, as it turns out, not really) by the galvanic experiments of a comical mad scientist named Entwurfen. Cheops then escapes to London via dirigible, and terrorizes the populace in scenes that invite comparison, not between the reader's world and a possible future, but between Webb's book and the works of Ann Radcliffe and her followers. Cheops resurrected as protagonist of a futuristic fiction is indeed an original hero. In this figure, the novel satisfies expectations aroused by its introduction. There are also some truly powerful scenes describing the moment of Cheops's revival, the impact of this event on witnesses, and his initial bewilderment after leaving his tomb in the pyramid when he tries to understand the steamboats which he sees on the Nile: a sight that does not correspond to his notions of the afterlife. Thereafter, however, Cheops operates at the level of magical fantasy rather than as an exemplification of the scientifically plausible marvelous.

We no longer learn what Cheops is thinking. Despite initial menacing appearances he always acts to thwart the tale's villains while aiding its virtuous young lovers. His principle of action is out of the arbitrary world of fairytale or supernatural gothic: if you sincerely appeal for his help in a good cause he will help you; if you try to enlist his aid for a vicous scheme, as the book's villains do, he will seem to help but in fact will prevent all evil plans from succeeding. We discover at the end that it was not galvanism at all, but (somehow) God's mysterious will that brought Cheops back to life. Here is another twist on the kind of gothic romance in which apparently supernatural events turn out to have a natural explanation: in *The Mummy* what seems like a scientific achievement—revival of a corpse via galvanism—is discovered to have been no such thing, but a genuine miracle. The moral is clear: do not meddle with nature.

By treating that theme in a gothic mode, without recourse to the supernatural, Mary Shelley's *Frankenstein* became a prototype for science fiction as well as an enduring myth of how science may destroy those who misuse it. Webb's novel, despite the extreme originality of a future setting which, as such, warrants very high praise, remains a comic fable without either tragic force, mythic power, or the sustained cognitive and emotional interest that may be achieved by scientifically plausible marvels. In reverting to the gothic marvelous of the supernatural after what at first seems like a scientifically marvelous feat of reviving the dead by natural means, Webb's book falls short of achieving the true novel of the future as Bodin was to define it only seven years later.

Jane Webb's achievement commands respect and deserves far more recognition than it has received. Nevertheless, her novel, precisely because it does come so remarkably close to meeting Bodin's standards, without quite doing so, best illustrates the incomplete evolution of futuristic fiction up to the 1830s. Only later, toward the middle of the nineteenth century—well after the first beginnings of futuristic fiction—are technology and social changes in the real world manifest in the futuristic texts themselves as decisive influences upon the form of that new genre. Before Bodin's 1834 manifesto, *Le Roman de l'avenir*, futuristic fiction is mostly a response to the demand for literary novelty within a framework of proliferating genres whose conventions, like those of the realistic novel, narrative history, and the gothic novel, were at once sufficiently fluid to encourage experiment, and sufficiently familiar to an expanding reading public so that variations on familiar types were in themselves desirable and increasingly sought after.

I do not propose this as an entire explanation for the origin of futuristic fiction, but as a corrective to what I believe has been undue neglect of the purely formal impetus to its invention. Mercier's displacement of utopian narratives to the future is not so clearly motivated by reaction to established conventions of the utopian voyage, nor by reaction to any other traditional form. But neither is *L'An 2440* the work of a writer evidently moved by the rising currents of technological change or the advent of capitalism. Mercier's resort to the future as a venue for advocating reform and the idea of progress, despite its air of inevitable rightness when looked at from our vantage point in Orwell's century, remains a puzzling step that challenges further enquiry. So does the related development of utopias taking the form of alternative past histories. This essay is only the sketch for a picture that remains to be drawn in much greater detail. That said, I hope to have illustrated here both the enduring significance of Bodin's *Novel of the Future* and the way in which it should alert us to the role of those formal variations encouraged by prevailing Enlightenment genres which played a role no less crucial than other cultural contexts in calling into existence the forerunners of *Nineteen Eighty-Four*.[20]

Anticipating the Past: The Time Riddle in Science Fiction

Marie-Hélène Huet

What is prophecy? We know of several different types, spanning many centuries. In biblical prophecy, the vision of future times takes the form of a privileged dialogue between God and his spokesman. The prophetic voice speaks of a future determined by God alone, and the prophet receives his apocalyptic knowledge with an incomparable immediacy, in the very presence of God.[1] Another type of prophecy developed in the Middle Ages and during the Renaissance. Far from being God's chosen interlocutor and witness, the Renaissance prophet was, in fact, often excommunicated by the church, since it was felt that knowledge of the future should be confined to the biblical prophecies. Any other form of insight was therefore suspect; thus, the prophet stood alone, and had access to a vision of the future through a text which was invisible to all but himself. In this type of prophecy, the prophet makes the invisible visible: he can read the stars and decipher the meaning of their movements; he can write the history of centuries to come. Nostradamus is perhaps the best known of these figures: half astronomer, half visionary, his writings are inextricably linked to the movements of the heavens. For example, the following quatrain allegedly speaks of the 1980s: "Lorsque Venus du Sol sera couverte / Sous l'esplendeur seront formes occultes/ Mercure au feu les aura découvertes / Par bruit bellique sera mis à l'insulte." (When Venus is eclipsed by the Sun / Occult shapes will hide under the splendor / And they will be uncovered and ignited by Mercury / Warlike tumult will follow provocation.)[2]

Thus the world reads like a book of future eras, but in such a mysterious and coded form that the prophecy itself remains unclear: the text is never explicit, but is loaded with symbols which often defy interpretation. Because of its inherent obscurity, the prophetic text requires an interpreter: at different times, Nostradamus's *Centuries* has been understood to convey dozens of different predictions. Thus the prophecy, although read by the prophet and given to the public in a visible form, remains extraordinarily difficult to understand. Either it is too obscure, or, on the contrary, it lends itself to an excessive number of conflicting interpretations. Ultimately, the images and symbols resist a definitive reading, and the prophetic word remains hermetically closed.

The prophetic text is mysterious in still another way. While it opens the doors of the future, it never assigns precise temporal limits to the prophecy. There are no specific dates in this vision, which is inspired by a future that could best be described as timeless. For this reason, the texts never cease to produce different meanings. A quatrain of Nostradamus's *Centuries* was interpeted in the sixteenth century as pertaining to Henry II, in the seventeenth century as relating to Louis XVI, and in the nineteenth century as bearing upon the French Revolution. At different times, the same line has been said to describe Bonaparte, the Second Empire, even General de Gaulle. Thus the paradox of prophecy becomes more evident: it always remains a text yet to be translated. It is a reading open to new events, never definitely rooted in a given period of time. Prophecy, it would seem, can never be exhausted by history. This peculiarity entails a double constraint: prophecy is only "recognized" as such at the moment when it seems to have been fulfilled. Here lies the profoundly useless character of the prophetic text, its inherent futility: it is only when it has lost its prophetic quality that it can be recognized as having been prophetic at all. Moreover, at that point, the formerly sacred meaning of biblical prophecy, of prophecy as *warning*, has been lost.

Science fiction has been perceived by a wide audience as a modern, postindustrial version of prophecy. Focusing on times to come, its scientific bias confers upon this recent literature the nearly sacred aura which formerly belonged to religious prophecy. But we, of course, know that prophecy can no longer work according to the same rules. In science fiction, the future is rooted. There is an extrordinarily specific calendar which our reading of the great classics has made familiar, years away, but years already filled with known events: 1984, 2001, 2002, 2026, 2075, and so on.[3] The chronology is implacable; the scientific terms are explicit, luminous, and they cast no shadows. In the disguise of fiction, it would seem that prophecy finally speaks our language.

Yet when we consider the beginnings of science fiction—and I will focus especially upon the works of Jules Verne—we can see that this image of a future, already made familiar by its specificity, conceals astonishing displacements of time, as well as remarkable manipulation of history. As we have all read, the first rocket to the moon was launched from the Florida coast on 30 November in the 1860s, shortly after the Civil War. In fact, the architects of such a feat were none other than ingenious soldiers eager to find a way out of the sudden, tiresome inactivity which peace had imposed upon them. On board their ship were two Americans, Barbicane and Nicholl; a Frenchman, Michel Ardan; and two dogs, Diane and Satellite. The spaceship traveled around the moon, returned to the earth's atmosphere and was recovered in the Pacific Ocean, northwest of San Francisco, on December 20. We all known that this voyage has been described in great detail by Jules Verne in two novels published in 1865 and 1870, respectively. They are entitled *From the Earth to the Moon* and *Around the Moon*.

Was this prophetic fiction? To a remarkable degree, if one considers the geographical location of the launch site(near what is now Cape Canaveral),the dimensions of the rocket, and the approximate spot where the first actual astronauts were recovered in the Pacific. In spite of their lack of verisimilitude, these texts can doubtless be seen as giving support to the idea that a new literary genre was being born, one which emphasized the fictional construct of a future that was a priori fantastic and unlikely, yet still not entirely impossible. As a fiction of the future, as a sketch of a scientific world which was yet to be born, and yet nearly perfectly conceivable, the works of Jules Verne in France, like those of H. G. Wells in England, thus became the standard by which early science fiction would be measured: the science of a fictional futurity in a fictional scientific mode.

However,—and this is the subject of my paper—I would like to emphasize that particular displacement of time which makes Verne's work curiously and insistently turn toward a certain past; and beyond Jules Verne, I would like to propose a reconsideration of the use of the future and anticipation in science fiction.

What is indeed most remarkable about *From the Earth to the Moon* is neither the cosmonauts' heroic journey, nor the stunning precision of various geographical locations, nor even the bold project of a moon rocket, but rather the fact that this nearly inconceivable exploit is presented by Jules Verne in 1866 as *having already taken place*, a few years before the narration and the book's publication. Such as it is, the orbit of Verne's astronauts, far from being the measure of times to come, that distant era of interplanetary travel, is instead inscribed in a specific, dated, recent past, a past which the first readers of the work *should have been able to remember*. It is quite clearly stated on the first page, indeed the first sentence of *Around the Moon*: "During the year 186_ the whole world was singularly moved by a scientific experiment without precedent in the annals of science."[4] Another well known novel, *20,000 Leagues beneath the Sea*, starts with a similar statement: "The year 1866 was marked by a strange event, an unexplained and inexplicable phenomenon which surely no one has forgotten."[5] These beginnings suggest a double perspective on the question of time. First, the dating is absolute; the past is written and closed. Throughout the novel, everything is meant to remind us of a historically dated voyage: the Second Empire style of the Nautilus's dining room, the comfortable interior of the moon rocket, even Barbicane's top hat and coat are already slightly outmoded. Only the machine would appear to transcend history, but even the machine's decoration, if not its concept, comes from a recent past. On board, a perfectly dated lifestyle is maintained.

These opening sentences also suggest a more complex manipulation of time and history, one, I would argue, that might provide us with a key to the critical organization of Jules Verne's narrative and of science fiction in general. In the lines quoted above, Jules Verne appeals to the reader's memory: "An unexplained and inexplicable phenomenon which surely no one has forgotten." It is clearly not a matter of imagination, but of memory. Moreover, these memories have nothing personal about them; they are collective: "The whole world was singularly moved." Indeed the event in question has stunned everybody. Obviously, the strategy is not without deviousness. At the very moment when he appeals to his readers' memory, Jules Verne anticipates that their memory is faulty; the fantastic tale then becomes just the thing needed to fill in the gaps, to save history from sudden oblivion. Thus the narrative does not fit into the past, but rather it slips into an abrupt and collective memory lapse.

This curious appeal to both memory and oblivion is repeated in all of the Jules Verne novels which can be described as belonging to the genre of scientific anticipation. It is significant that the first example of such a literature should have as its privileged slice of time the interstices of a defective group memory. Except for two short stories, "L'Eternel Adam" and "La Journée d'un journaliste américan en l'an 2889",[6] all the novels take place in a recent but forgotten past. This repeated rupture in historical continuity deserves further consideration, not just as a curious exception to the genre, but more specifically, as the very element that allowed the genre to emerge as a new literary form towards the end of the nineteenth century. To describe this genre, one would say that with Jules Verne a style of writing emerges which fuses, in a single datable rhetoric, the invention of future technologies and the narration of a bygone era. This process could be called: anticipating the past.

Needless to say, the anticipation is thus, twice and forever, out of reach; it not only falls short of the lost memory of the events in question, it also misses out on their expected realization. As we have repeatedly been told, these events have already taken place. While we have slowly grown accustomed to appreciating in science fiction a sense of prophetic accuracy—which the media have certainly emphasized in their treatment of *Nineteen Eighty-Four*—from the outset, Jules Verne deprives us of this type of suspended expectation. Instead of authorizing the sentence, "It happened as he said it would," he only allows for the possibility of acknowledging, "It happened as he said it had." So that the moon landing of 1969, far from being the fulfillment of a prophecy, turned out to be only the repetition of an event which had always already taken place, even when the prophetic text which described it first appeared. Nothing could emphasize more dramatically the unreachable character of the past. We always are (and always will be) too late to witness the first moon voyage, the first submarine, the first flying machine. Furthermore, the memory which we should have retained of these unforgettable events has mysteriously vanished, so that we are reduced to a retrospective reading of an unattainable past. Such is the extraordinary constraint which is imposed upon the reader and his memory by the temporal structure in Verne's works: those events which confirm that Verne's amazing scientific fiction will always appear as simple repetitions. The prophecy can never be fulfilled, because every single anticipation is presented as having already happened. Jules Verne writes at the beginning of *Le Chateau des Carpathes*: "Nous sommes d'un temps où tout arrive—on a presque le droit de dire où tout est arrivé." (We live in a time when anything can happen—we may almost say, when everything has happened.)[7] The reader will never recover from the prodigious memory lapse which first kept him from witnessing the departure of Nicholl, Barbicane, and Michel Ardan, or from following the Nautilus under the sea. His only memories will come from books. The text, and science fiction in general, will serve as a supplement to the reader's defective memory, to that collective memory lapse which is vaguely echoed by a sketch of things to come.

It could be argued that this is a strategy specific to Jules Verne, whose goal was to endow scientific exploration with a greater degree of certainty, by positing the narrator as an observer rather than a prophet. At best, this strategy would serve to reduce the unavoidable skepticism with which such unlikely exploits would likely be met. However, the structure posited by Verne as the premise of his novels, the memory lapse presiding over all scientific inventions, which is the very condition of narrative, is in fact one of the most important conceptual figures of the nineteenth century episteme. In other words, what links Verne to the great technological developments of the nineteenth century is not the ingenuity of his scientific constructs, but this very emphasis upon a past which has become lost to memory, a past which has left no trace behind, and which becomes the beginning of history.

In the wake of eighteenth century empiricism, the notion of the *chain* became the double metaphor for the organization of reality and the possibility of knowledge. Locke, Condillac, and especially Diderot viewed the universe "as a multitude of different systems which blend with each other, so as to form a single order of things."[8] In this system, memory is a key element, the function that allows for the constitution of the subject's own sense of identity.[9] The metaphor of the chain, the image of universe where all the systems are linked together, and more specifically, the conceptualization of time as a chain became prevalent in nineteenth century thought. In their examination of various systems, many of the great disciplines of that period consistently turned toward the past—history, philosophy of history, natural sciences, philology—and from the past they gained a privileged insight into the future. At the end of *The Origin of Species*, Darwin writes: "*Judging from the past* we may safely infer that not one living species will transmit its unaltered likeness to a *distant futurity*." Yet as we well know from the model of the natural sciences, this past is not continuous; it has missing links. Darwin calls them "very wide intervals," or "blank intervals."[10] Ernst Haeckel describes them as "appreciable gaps."[11] Many efforts were made to fill in these gaps. One of the most interesting was the theory that embryonic life reproduces the various stages of the evolution of man. Yet even that constant reproduction of history, a replay of the past within the life of an individual, falls short of completing the chain. As Haeckel writes in *The Evolution of Man*: "But such a repetition of the ancestral history by the individual in its embryonic life is rarely complete. *We do not find our full alphabet*" (emphasis mine).[12] Freud will suggest a similar model, a vertiginous *mise en abîme*, comparing the early stages of life in society, and the repressed murder of the father, with the early stages of child psychology—I am thinking of course of *Totem and Taboo*.[13] Yet, no matter how many fossils may happen to be found, or how many lost memories surface, the gaps, the blanks, the missing letters remain, by principle and definition, unattainable, impossible to fill in.

Speaking of the comparatively "small" intervals between the respective mental powers of man and ape, Darwin writes: "Yet this interval is filled by *numberless* gradations" (emphasis mine).[14] As it happens, the missing link is both constitutive of, and inseparable from, the concept of universal life as a chain. For this reason the missing link will always be approximated but never actually found. At any rate, the gaps, the blank intervals of the past are really at the center of nineteenth century scientific discourse. For biologists, this took the form of a search for vanished species; for historians, the quest for lost archives; for Freud, the conjuring up of repressed memories.

The memory lapse, the blank which presides over scientific anticipation in Jules Verne, has the same structure and application—conceptually and teleologically—as the blank intervals in Cuvier, Lamarck, Darwin, or Freud. It is the very space of speculation. In its search for a lost past which alone holds the key to times to come, the science fiction text thus choses and explores the privileged space of a memory blank, a sudden absence, as that which both emphasizes and undermines the scientific and historical chain, and points to its inherent fragility.

From this point of view, science fiction is not the simple and nearly always predictable illustration of an inspiring scientific development; it is rather the manifestation of an episteme which seeks to master the universe in a vast and coherent system, which nonetheless implies an insistent, if sometimes half-forgotten, discontinuity. Far from being the expression of a simple-minded positivism, science fiction is the very form of modern scientific anxiety.

The uncanny use of a missing past in science fiction (and while I have chosen Jules Verne as a rather striking example, similar cases could be made with Rosny aîné, René Barjavel, Pierre Boulle, A. E. Van Vogt, or Philip K. Dick,)[15] parallels the very specific temporal structure of the mystery novel which also emerged in the nineteenth century. The classical structural frame of the detective novel—Poe's *Murders in the Rue Morgue* is the first and perfect example of this— consists in the reconstruction of an event, murder, which has already taken place, but to which there have been no visible witnesses. The novel ends when the missing scene has been perfectly reconstructed, the gaps filled, the murder symbolically reenacted, told, made present by the detective: an exemplary archeology of crime. It has been thought that the search for the murderer's identity reproduced many elements of the Oedipus myth: enigma and death, blindness and truth. It is, thus, interesting to note that one of the early and most famous science fiction texts also used the Oedipus story in a very explicit way. In H. G. Wells's *Time Machine* a Sphinx greets the Time Traveller and hides the way to the terrifying underworld of the Morlocks. A modern Oedipus, the Time Traveller is *lame* when he comes back to the present to tell us his story. Both genres, mystery and scientific anticipation, appealed to several writers, among them Edgar Allan Poe and Arthur Conan Doyle.

The black hole of history, the missing alphabet, the chosen lost time of science fiction, thus becomes the very space of fiction. Whether or not we choose to take a Freudian approach, we can emphasize that early speculative fiction supplements the discontinuities of the past in the form of an anticipation which insistently replays a myth of the origin, a conceptualization of origin and foundation and departure. Jules Verne's books speak of nothing else: the extraordinary machines, the scientific exploits (which all suggest starting over), and the attempt to recover lost beginnings. As we know, such beginnings are not innocent; they carry violence, murder, and the foundations of new laws.

Although the very specific temporality of Jules Verne's novels may have disappeared from most science fiction texts, a considerable number of novels continue to propose—in a future which may or may not be dated—the history of a beginning, an origin which we would finally be allowed to witness: Clarke's *2001: A Space Odyssey* Stewart's *Earth Abides*, Heinlein's *Past through Tomorrow*, Hogan's *Genesis Machine*, Pohl's *Way the Future Was*, or Dick's *Now Wait for Last Year*, all tangle with the genealogy of a time which is discontinuous, a broken chain of events which often ends up in murder, even if the intended victim is only a machine. (The "murder" of Hal, the computer in *2001: A Space Odyssey* is in a truly Vernian tradition: all of Jules Verne's machines are systematically destroyed at the end of the voyage.) Another recurrent obsession is the theme of the power and weakness of memory and dreams (Le Guin's *Lathe of Heaven* or Barjavel's *Le Voyageur imprudent*) and the presence of past oriented fantasy in future oriented science fiction.

In this conflictual anticipation of the past, it could be said that the narrative strategy of science fiction parallels what Eric S. Rabkin describes as the most fundamental mechanism of the fantastic: "The fantastic does more than extend experience; the fantastic contradicts perspectives."[16] If science fiction is prophecy, then we may imagine that, since its inception, this modern prophetic genre has been repeatedly telling us: "The future is near and clear, but the past is unforeseeable."

The Thing of Shapes to Come:
Science Fiction as Anatomy of the Future

Howard V. Hendrix

When H. G. Wells entitled one of his myriad works *The Shape of Things to Come*, he played directly upon the science fiction reader's desire to know what the future looks like. Certainly this desire for an authoritative perspective on the future and what it holds is an ancient human need—astrology, fortune-telling, and scores of divination methods have been with us a very long time. Only relatively recently, however, has a significant genre of literature developed which takes as its special concern the shape of things to come, the anatomy of the future.

The most obvious difference between science fiction and other human activities anatomizing the future is that science fiction relates its futures in past or sometimes present tense, while other forms of future anatomy simply use the future tense. The astrologer and the trend-predictor say this *will* or this *might* happen; the science fiction narrator says this *has* happened—in *my* vision of the future.[1] The diviner takes signs, granted by the external world, as the ultimate basis of his or her authority; the science fiction writer takes not the external world but rather, like the epic poet, his or her own personal vision of the future as the ultimate basis of his or her authority. In doing so, the science fiction writer engages in a form of visionary poetics, a long-standing tradition with its ancient roots in pre-Christian epic and religious writings; in John the Apostle's delineation of Apocalypse in the Book of Revelations, in medieval dream-vision (particularly *Piers Plowman*); in Dante's *Divina Commedia*; and in Milton's *Paradise Lost* (especially books 11 and 12).

Engaging in visionary poetics in the secular and materialistic world of the twentieth century is rather difficult business, however. John the Apostle could claim that his vision came directly from God.

Piers Plowman's author, William Langland, could claim his story came to him in a dream. Milton could claim the stance of vatic poet inspired by a heavenly muse. But such stances, such claims of divine dreams advocated seriously by any twentieth century writer, would seriously tax the reader's willing suspension of disbelief. The rise of the secular and materialistic scientific world view has meant the death of the traditional visionary stance, and with it the death of the traditional epic. In the end, the science fiction writer, like all other twentieth century writers, can only fall back on the authority of the storyteller—no mean authority, but one which presents special difficulties for the science fiction writer.

The storyteller says, "Once upon a time, there was—"; the diviner says, "In the future, there will be—"; but the science fiction writer must say, "Once upon a time in the future, there was—." Storytelling gains its authority from the past: the storyteller says this *has* happened; therefore, it *is* real or valid. This orientation toward the past (or at least the past tense) as signifier of authority is a distinguishing characteristic of fiction and of the literary culture as a whole. Science fiction, however, concerns itself primarily with the ramifications of a future oriented scientific culture. The science fiction writer is deprived of much of the authority of pastness and history simply because he or she most often writes about the future, about a world and time that is not yet and may never be—a world markedly different from the more historically fixed worlds of the traditional literary artist. The science fiction writer, in presuming to write about the future in the past tense, attempts to transmogrify the storyteller's role into a role for which it does not possess the authority—namely, that of visionary.

In the past, a storyteller could claim divine inspiration as a powerful authority for the story—and once he or she claimed such authority, the story was no longer just story, but also vision, and the storyteller a visionary. Today, however, claiming divine inspiration doesn't get one as far as it once did, and the storyteller seeking the status of visionary must look elsewhere for the authority that will inform his or her vision. For the science fiction writer, science itself, its accomplishments, its practice, and its possible future, provides the authority that informs the writer's personal vision of that future. Science provides the twentieth century version of "divine inspiration" that makes the science fiction writer's visionary stance plausible and, indeed, possible. But, where the epic poet supported vision by appealing to the audience's shared sense of a transcendant order beyond understanding, a god or gods ultimately above and beyond the material world, the science fiction writer appeals to the audience's faith in the accomplishments of science, a human ordering and understanding of the material world.

The paradigm, or model, in science is analogous to the vision in visionary poetics. Over time, the scientific model gets remodeled and the poetic vision gets revised. Of all the genres, science fiction is the one in which both these processes can most clearly be seen proceeding simultaneously. If by *anatomy* we mean a detailed examination or analysis, then every work of science fiction produced that deals with future time is, in a sense, an anatomy of a future, and future-oriented science fiction as a generic category is concerned with the anatomy of *the* future. Science fiction presents us with a host of competing paradigms, competing models of the future, competing shapes of things to come. Science fiction as a genre is much like the shape-changing Thing of Campbell's novella *Who Goes There?*: it modifies its shape in response to a remodeling of scientific models, the revision of visions. As a genre, it is the Thing of Shapes to Come.

I will deal now with what I believe are the three major models of the future with which science fiction currently presents to us. These models are literal shapes of things to come, shapes I've cribbed from undoubtedly outdated physics textbook discussions of the shape of the universe.[2] According to these texts, the most plausible shapes of the universe are: (1) spherical; (2) flat; (3) saddle shaped (or "hyperspherical," "hyperflat," and "hypersaddle," as all are more-than-three-dimensional shapes).

A universe of hyperspheric shape results when we propose that the momentum imparted to the universe system at the time of the Big Bang is significantly less than the mutual attraction of the system's elements for each other. In other words, the universe does not achieve escape velocity but rather expands only to a certain size before the gravitational forces inherent in the system cause it to collapse in upon itself again, faster and faster, until the universe has contracted into a point called the Big Stop. At that point perhaps the universe will explode outward again in a new Big Bang, expanding and contracting, Big Banging and Big Stopping until the end of time. The analogous visionary model in science fiction is the catastrophic or cyclic catastrophic model, in which the benefits of scientific and technological progress are significantly less than the dangers inherent in that progress. In this model, scientific and technological expansion ultimately create more problems than they solve, and human society, as a result, suffers a devastating collapse in the form of nuclear war, overpopulation, and ecological breakdown, or other similar self-induced catastrophies.

Though there are many stories in this vein, *A Canticle for Leibowitz* seems to be a premier example of this model. The novel begins half a millenium after a nuclear holocaust has plunged humankind into a new dark age, proceeds through the progressive reawakening of human culture, and culminates in yet another and even more devastating nuclear apocalypse. Cyclic catastrophism and the related notion that human progress ultimately results in more problems than its solves (and thus is finally not progress at all) are two of the key themes of the book:

> Listen, are we helpless? Are we doomed to do it again and again and again? Have we no choice but to play the Phoenix in an unending sequence of rise and fall? Assyria, Babylon, Egypt, Greece, Carthage, Rome, the Empires of Charlemagne and the Turk. Ground to dust and plowed with salt. Spain, France, Britain, America—burned into the oblivion of the centuries. And again and again and again.
> *Are we doomed to it, Lord, chained to the pendulum of our own mad clockwork, helpless to halt its swing?* (P. 217)[3]

> The closer men came to perfecting for themselves a paradise, the more impatient they seemed to become with it, and with themselves as well. They made a garden of pleasure, and became progressively more miserable with it as it grew in richness and power and beauty; for then, perhaps, it was easier for them to see that something was missing in the garden, some tree or shrub that would not grow. When the world was in darkness and wretchedness, it could believe in perfection and yearn for it. But when the world became bright with reason and riches, it began to sense the narrowness of the needle's eye, and that rankled for a world no longer willing to believe or yearn. Well, they were going to destroy it again, were they—this garden Earth, civilized and knowing, to be torn apart again that Man might hope again in wretched darkness. (Pp. 235–36)

The first of the above quoted passages emphasizes the cyclic catastrophic view of human history and human possibility presented in *Canticle*. Particularly interesting are the image of the Phoenix and the image of the clock. The Phoenix is trapped in time, a bird that, according to Egyptian mythology, consumed itself in fire every five hundred years, undying, to rise renewed from its own ashes. Like *Canticle*'s other noteworthy prisoner of time, the Wandering Jew who appears throughout the book, the Phoenix is doomed to a sort of immortality and denied what peace death might bring. That both Phoenix and Jew are meant to serve as types for humanity in history is clear from the image of mankind "chained to the pendulum of our own mad clockwork, helpless to halt its swing." In this image, human existence and entrapment in time—a product of the Fall, before which human existence was timeless—is specifically linked to the fallen state of human technology and human history, which, no matter what greatness they encompass, can be finally only a "mad clockwork."

Dom Zerchi, whose thought that first passage expresses, also thinks "this time, [the pendulum] will swing us clean into oblivion" (p. 218). But this is only true in a limited sense. True, in *Canticle*, we are led to believe that all human life will be blasted from the Earth, but this does not mean that the seed of man shall die from the universe. There are human colonists on a few distant planets; hope exists that the catastrophic cycling will continue even after Earth is done:

> [Brother Joshua] peered up again at the dusty stars of morning. Well, there would be no Edens found out there, they said. Yet there were men out there now, men who looked up to strange suns in stranger skies, gasped strange air, tilled strange earth . . . enough like Earth so that Man might live somehow by the same sweat of his brow. They were but a handful, . . . there in their new non-Edens even less like Paradise than the Earth had been. Fortunately for them, perhaps. (p. 235)

The reason Brother Joshua, a monk of the Order of Leibowitz who will lead his order's contingent to the stars, feels that the less Edenic a world is the more fortunate that world will be for its human settlers is made clear by that second passage quoted above. The closer human beings come, through the aid of their fallen technology, to an Edenic state, the more impatient and frustrated they become with their pseudo-Eden, until in the global equivalent of a tantrum, they kick themselves and their world apart. Because man and all his works are fallen, he can only approximate Eden—never really achieve it—and he is doomed to the constant cycle of hope, near attainment, realization of ultimate unattainability, frustration, and self-destruction (so that the cycle may begin again). The longer the fall, the more fortunate the fallen, in the Leibowitzian scheme of things.

What exactly the "something" is that is "missing in the garden" created by man, what exactly the "tree or shrub that would not grow" is never made clear, but knowing the Eden myth, we can postulate that it might be the tree of eternal life or the shrub of human happiness in a perfect world. But even if man through his technology succeeds in creating his own Edenic order, will the result necessarily be good?

In Damon Knight's brilliant but sorely neglected novella *Dio*, we find just such an Edenic state. Like many another utopian/dystopian vision, the future in *Dio* follows the hyperflat model. In physical speculations, the hyperflat or Euclidean universe results when we propose that the momentum imparted to the universe system at the time of the Big Bang equals or just barely exceeds the forces of attraction inherent in the system. The universe achieves escape velocity, but just barely, so it expands forever at an ever-decreasing rate of expansion. The science fiction analogue is the utopian/dystopian model, in which human sciences and technology solve problems faster than they generate them, but just barely, so that the civilizations of this model fight a long battle with entropy as they slowly crumble back into deserts of vast eternity. Barring radical change, these pseudo-Edens created by technology become increasingly sterile and possessed of a false animation that is part of the process of their long death.

Such a world we find in *Dio*. Technology has ended death and want and supplied in their place immortality and the happiness of dominion over the Earth and all its elements. The virtues of Eden are created, or recreated, in this future landscape populated by two cultures: the Students, or producers, and the Players, or consumers. The story's three main characters are Dio, a student who holds the rank of Sector Planner; Claire, a beautiful and eternally young player who loves Dio; and Benarra, an eternally young student with interest in the biological sciences who becomes interested professionally and personally in Dio when it is discovered that Dio will grow old and die, unlike everyone else in his world. Tangentially, Benarra also becomes interested in Claire and her response to Dio's mortal condition. Much of the story's exposition takes place in conversations in which Benarra explains Dio's condition and the history of human mortality and immortality to Claire, as in the following passage which occurs after Claire sees Dio as clearly mortal and suffering uniquely from a once common viral infection:

> *"What's wrong with him?"* she says.
>
> [Benarra] sighs, looking down at her modish robe with its delicate clasps of gold. "How can I tell you? Does the verb 'to die' mean anything to you?"
>
> She is puzzled and apprehensive. "I don't know . . . isn't it something that happens to the lower animals?"
>
> He gives her a quick mock bow. "Very good." (P. 118)⁴

Benarra then shows her a visual recording of a white lab rat's death, to help explain to Claire just what it means "to die."

> Watching, Claire tries to control her nausea. Students' cabinets are full of nastinesses like this; they expect you not to show any distaste. "Something's the matter with it," is all she can find to say.
>
> "Yes. It's dying. That means to cease living: to stop. Not to be any more. Understand?"
>
> "No," she breathes. In the box, the small body has stopped moving. The mouth is stiffly open, the lip drawn back from the yellow teeth. The eye does not move, but glares up sightless.
>
> "That's all," says her companion. "No more rat. Finished. After a while it begins to decompose and make a bad smell, and a while after that, there's nothing left but bones. And that has happened to every rat that was ever born."
>
> "I don't *believe* you," she says. "It isn't like that; I never heard of such a thing." (P. 119)

The reason no one knows death any more, the reason death doesn't happen to people in Dio's world is simple: disease, debility, and death have been expunged from Dio's Edenic future Earth. His world is a world of eternal youth:

> "Now this," says Benarra, "this long shallow curve represents man as he was. You notice it starts far to the left of the animal curve. The planners had this much to work with: man was already unique, in that he had this very long juvenile period before sexual maturity. Here: see what they did." With a gesture he imposes another chart on the first.
>
> "It looks almost the same," says Claire.

"Yes. Almost. What they did was quite a simple thing, in principle. They lengthened the juvenile period still further, they made the
curve rise still more slowly . . . and never quite reach the top. The curve
now becomes asymptotic, that is, it approaches sexual maturity by
smaller and smaller amounts, and never gets there, no matter how long
it goes on." Gravely, he returns her stare.

"Are you saying," she asks, "that we're *not* sexually mature? Not
anybody?"

"Correct," he says. "Maturity in every other complex organism is
the first stage of death. We never mature, Claire, and that's why we
don't die. We're the eternal adolescents of the universe. That's the price
we paid." (P. 128)

In this conversation between the student Benarra and the player
Claire we learn the crucial information of the story. Dio, through a
fluke, is doomed to grow up, to become the mortal adult in a world of
immortal superhuman adolescents. In a world where normally "people endure, things pass away," Dio builds for permanence. He becomes the Great Artist, who sculpts by hand with hammer and chisel
rather than by machine. We are led to see him as a tragic and heroic
figure in a world peopled by frivolous immortals. The technologically
created Eden where Dio lives is a sad farce with a dark secret; though
its inhabitants can't die of old age, they *can* commit suicide:

Leaving the circle toward midnight, [Claire] roams the apartment
alone, eased by comradeship, content to hear the singing blur and fade
behind her. In the playroom, she stands idly looking down into the deep
darkness of the diving well. How luxurious, she thinks, to fall and fall,
and never reach the bottom. . . .

But the bottom is always there, of course, or it would not be a
diving well. A paradox: the well must be a shaft closed at the bottom;
it's the sense of danger, the imagined smashing impact, that gives it its
thrill. And yet there is no danger of injury: levitation and survival
instinct will always prevent it.

"*We have such a tidy world.*" (P. 141)

Dio's pseudo-Eden is a place where, after thousands of years of life,
everything seems frivolous whether it is or not, a place where frivolity
becomes boring, where boredom leads to a desire for death, where
the desire for death ultimately becomes more powerful than the
survival instinct. Every diving well is potentially a suicide chamber.
Science, in *Dio*, has solved human problems more quickly than it has

engendered new ones, but just barely. Though the people of Dio's world are like gods, they can't ultimately manipulate, levitate, or fornicate their way out of boredom's grasp. They are fallen human forms who, though they can claim with Satan in book 6 of *Paradise Lost* and with Benarra (p. 127) that "We did it, we created ourselves," they also must hold the flip side of that coin: we also destroy ourselves, in the distant end.

And Dio's deathless, so nearly perfect world is, in fact, dying slowly because it is killing itself. There is no escape from entropy or original sin. Dio's world, though bright with reason and riches, feels the narrowness of the needle's eye; the secular and material immortality that science provides is not enough to save it. No one transcends the deserts of vast eternity into which Dio's civilization is slowly crumbling.

In *Dio* the message is that science and technology, though powerful manifestations of the mind, cannot bring about transcendance; in Arthur C. Clarke's *2010: Odyssey Two*, the message is quite the opposite: mind, particularly in its scientific and technological manifestations, is the only means available for ultimately transcending the secular and material world. This is a crucial paradox of much of Clarke's work. A secular and material worldview provides the very means by which the secular and material are transcended.

Such a paradox is in some ways a logical outgrowth of the shape of the future in *2010*. The universe of the novel is hypersaddle in shape. The hypersaddle model in physics results when the momentum imparted to the universe system at the time of the Big Bang vastly exceeds the mutually attractive forces inherent in the system itself. The universe achieves escape velocity strongly and expands steadily and undecreasingly forever. The analogous visionary model in science fiction is the final but unending frontier model, in which the benefits of scientific and technological progress far outweigh the dangers inherent in that progress. Scientific and technological expansion are ultimately forms of mind expansion and solve far more problems than they create.

This is perhaps the most optimistic of the models cited here. In contrast to the burstable balloon of *Canticle*'s spherical model and the lone and level sands of *Dio*'s flat model, *2010* presents a model to boldly go and split infinity by, sapience back in the saddle again, riding the range on the final frontier. Chapter 51, "The Great

Game," gives perhaps the clearest statement in all of Clarke's fiction of his open ended universe, and of mind to match that universe:

> And now, out among the stars, evolution was driving toward new goals. The first explorers of Earth had long since come to the limits of flesh and blood; as soon as their machines were better than their bodies, it was time to move. First their brains, and then their thoughts alone, they transferred into shining new homes of metal and plastic.
>
> In these they roamed among the stars. They no longer built spaceships. They *were* spaceships.
>
> But the age of the Machine-entities swiftly passed. In their ceaseless experimenting, they had learned to store knowledge in the structure of space itself, and to preserve their thoughts for eternity in frozen lattices of light. They could become creatures of radiation, free at last from the tyranny of matter.
>
> Into pure energy, therefore, they presently transformed themselves. . . .
>
> They were lords of the Galaxy, and beyond the reach of time. (Pp. 307–8)[5]

The "lords of the Galaxy" here are grand experimenters, scientists writ cosmically large. Through their science, which began as the study of matter, time and space, they have become "free at last from the tyranny of matter," pure energy "beyond the reach of time" that can "rove at will among the stars and sink like a subtle mist through the very interstices of space." Immortality and eternity are theirs. Just as, given time enough and chance, inanimate matter can, in theory, produce life, so too, in the Clarkean scheme, can science, given time enough and chance, transcend its roots in matter and time. In classic Miltonic fashion, Clarke's self-transcending mind from body up to spirit works.

Like *Paradise Lost*, *Canticle*, *Dio*, and many another visionary works, *2010* concerns itself with Edens and apocalypses, beginnings and ends. *2010* has obvious parallels to both the Genesis and apocalypse stories. The grand experimenters create a Jovian star system by inducing Jupiter, via their monoliths, to condense to fusion point and become a star. In this apocalyptic destruction of Jupiter, the grand experimenters simultaneously let there be light and improve the conditions for life on the Jovian moons. Apocalypse becomes genesis, and even brings with it a new Edenic prohibition:

ALL THESE WORLDS ARE YOURS—EXCEPT EUROPA
ATTEMPT NO LANDINGS THERE.
(P. 320)

Europa is in a very real sense a new Eden, waiting for a new (and perhaps unfallen) sentient species to inhabit it. I would not go so far as to push Tanya as an Eve figure or Heywood Floyd as an Adam, but I do find a striking parallel with God's prohibition to Adam and Eve in the Garden (Genesis 2:16–17): "And the Lord God commanded the man, saying, 'From any tree of the garden you may eat freely; but from the tree of the knowledge of good and evil you shall not eat, for in that day you eat of it you shall surely die.'" Both prohibitions originate with superhuman entities and are tests of human obedience which humanity fails. Just as Adam and Eve eat of the fruit of the tree of the knowledge of good and evil and, thus, become mortal, so too do later humans attempt landings on Europa to try to discover what's going on there and, thus, get shot down again and again by the monolith the experimenters have left behind. This monolith, stationed by the experimenters, is designed to protect their new experiment from human intrusion, much the same way God stationed a cherubim with a flaming sword in Eden to guard the way to the tree of life from human intrusion after the Fall.

In a sense, I suppose, the apocalyptic genesis of a new Jovian Eden in *2010* is something of a spherical, cyclic catastrophic, Big Stop—new Big Bang model. It is, however, always contained within the larger purview of the saddle shaped model of the future that pervades the book. The models I have proposed here are obviously not absolutes, and I hope they will not be approached that way. They are heuristics, paradigms, models about models, all of which are concerned with whether knowledge, in particular *scientific* knowledge, brings about more good or more evil. In the spherical model we saw how, in *Canticle*, partaking of the fruit of the knowledge of good and evil results more in evil than in good, culminating ultimately in nuclear apocalypse. In the flat model of *Dio*, we saw how the pursuit of knowledge results in more good, relatively speaking, than evil, but the evil in knowledge persists so strongly that the victory of the good in knowledge is meaningless. In the saddle shaped model of *2010*, we saw how the good in the pursuit of knowledge, in eating the forbidden fruit, far outweighs the evil involved in that pursuit, and results, at last, in mind without end. Each model, and each story, is an interpretation of what the beginning will mean in the end, how genesis affects apocalypse.

That visionary works should be very much concerned with beginnings and ends, Edens and apocalypses, is not surprising when we consider that all art, all science, all religion—all knowledge—is perhaps in its final reduction and elaboration, concerned with just three questions: How did it begin? How is it going? How will it end?

"But why only three?" asks Tanya. I don't know; perhaps because we exist in time. Clarke's Ramans do everything in threes, and I'm not greedy for reasons more.

Knowing the Unknown:
Heinlein, Lem, and the Future

Bradford Lyau

In spite of experiencing some periods of uncertainty in the recent past, Americans, unlike Europeans, remain, for the most part, optimistic about their prospects for the 1980s and beyond. The causes of this difference surely lie in the respective historical circumstances of Europe and America. These circumstances, in turn, have produced two very different modes of thought. And because these modes are not merely attitudes, but ways of dealing with the material world (and of knowing and potentially controlling that world), they may be called epistemologies. Such a divergence of epistemologies may help explain the different reactions in Europe and America to future possibilities in general.

The epistemologically derived attitudes in question here are the pessimism from theoretical skepticism in Europe and the optimism from empirical pragmatism in the United States. Isolating these stances in their most extreme forms will readily reveal how they operate. Two works of fiction will be chosen as exemplars for analysis, since they both, despite widely varying first appearances, have as their central concern the examination of epistemological approaches to the unknown as the basis for arriving at the best decision for action. *Solaris*, by Stanislaw Lem, and *Time Enough For Love*, by Robert A. Heinlein, are two such works.[1] Furthermore, not only do their opposite views of knowledge also become the basis for their conclusions about human nature and its future, these novels also serve to define and identify two distinct modes of science fiction—European and American.

This selection of two works from the field of science fiction was made by design and was not a result of serendipity. Science fiction is the literary form that most purports to deal with alien encounters in

55

the future, making it a prominent branch of epistemological literature. More importantly, however, it provides a much needed meeting point at which to examine differing cultural attitudes toward a
common problem—in this case, that of knowledge.

Leonard Krieger, in his article "The Autonomy of Intellectual
History,"[2] refers to a spectrum that exists for this form of history. At
one end of the spectrum lies the study of the ideas and systems of the
great thinkers, the intellectual elite who were, more often than not,
isolated from society in general; at the other end resides the study of
mass attitudes, the thoughts of the people themselves. Science fiction
is perhaps the only literary form today that can mediate between
these "high" and "low" cultures, that can translate the ideas of one
into the language of the other—and visa versa. This branch of literature is at once both a "popular" medium (i.e., widely read and
discussed mostly by people not necessarily of the intellectual elite)
and a vehicle for "high ideas" (i.e., issues and problems usually
viewed as being the province of the great thinkers of a society).
Because of science fiction's claim of association with the methods of
science, its field of inquiry can encompass the empirical and practical,
as well as the abstract and systematic approaches to knowledge.

The systematic and theoretical characterize the ideas about
knowledge at the elite end of the intellectual spectrum. This is
representative of European thought, as this continent has been settled long enough to produce enduring traditions of ideas. Lem's
epistemological concerns fall there. Heinlein's, meanwhile, belong
at the other end, that of the masses, where action, experience, and
practicality characterize the approach to knowledge. This also is
representative of American epistemology in general. Daniel J. Boorstin identifies the American colonial and frontier experiences as
being responsible for this attitude.[3] Whereas Europe was well settled,
America became the place in which to start anew. Both the desire to
escape the more constricting societies of Europe, and the having to
face the harsh conditions of an unknown wilderness, led Americans
to abandon Europe's intellectual heritage. Preconceived notions
became useless in unexplored terrain. Expecting the unexpected
turned out to be the rule of thumb for action; so serendipity and
versatility, and not abstraction and specialization, emerged as the
required attributes for survival and success. Whatever worked became the basis of knowledge.

Lem's *Solaris* satirizes the European approach to knowledge by making fun of that familiar symbol of long-lasting studies, the compendium. By piling up speculation after speculation, theory after theory, and result after result, Lem shows the inadequacies and follies of human endeavors to explain the unknown—in this case, it is an alien planet. The novel centers around a team of scientists' attempts to understand a mysterious alien presence, in the form of an ocean, on a planet named Solaris. Heinlein's *Time Enough for Love* is also a compendium of sorts, full of casual, sometimes long discourses on politics, religion, science, and many other fields of human knowledge. Unlike Lem's story, Heinlein's novel is not satirical but rather something that could be called exploratory; the novel focuses on the life and ideas of one single person, Lazarus Long—Heinlein's version of a Methuselah of the future. This long-lived character's search to know turns out to be a personal quest for new experiences that would add to an already full and knowledgeable life.

Both of these novels center on humanity's attempts to comprehend the unknown, and, as a result, serve as perfect counterpoints to each other. While Lem deals with the shortcomings of theories, Heinlein focuses on the opportunities that emerge from experiences. And while Lem's criticizing of ideas result in pessimistic visions, Heinlein's examination of the empirical way leads to optimistic views.

So opposite in their epistemological directions, these two works do share a common structure. Both novels move back and forth between reviews of past knowledge and the present actions of their protagonists. Besides focusing on the advancement of knowledge, both also center on encounters which appear to limit knowledge. When addressing the problems of these limits, the protagonists in the present are drawn to reexamine the past—in *Solaris*, the large body of writings on the ocean; in *Time Enough for Love*, the experiences of Lazarus Long himself—in hopes of finding an epistemological breakthrough. The following analysis will be organized accordingly: first, an examination of the reviews of past knowledge, and then a consideration of the protagonists' attempts to transcend the seemingly impenetrable limits to knowledge.

Solaris's past is progressively unveiled as the protagonist, Kelvin, explores the historical and theoretical works that make up the library of Solaristics. The historical knowledge which Kelvin seeks becomes a metaphor for the history of thought in general as he studies the changing hypotheses and scientific attitudes toward the planet. Arriving on Station Solaris and planning to join scientists Gibarian, Sartorius, and Snow, he encounters Snow who is raving like a madman. Snow tells him to rejoin him in an hour. During this interval Kelvin examines two books about Solaris.

Here, Lem sets the satirical tone which will characterize Kelvin's subsequent investigations. The first book that Kelvin leafs through is *Historia Solaris*. It recounts the early history of the exploration of Solaris. Explorations of the planet reveal its ocean to be an organic formation, thus igniting the debate as to whether this body of water was living or nonliving. Many theoretical systems are used to support both sides of the argument. Kelvin ponders after leafing through the book: "Revered and universally accepted theories foundered; the specialist literature was swamped by outrageous and heretical treatises" (p. 26). Kelvin then peruses another volume which contains a review of the countless attempts to make contact with the ocean, and he notes, "Compared with the proliferation of speculative ideas which were triggered off by this problem, medieval scholasticism seemed a model of scientific enlightenment" (pp. 26–27). After reviewing how mathematical models failed to establish contact with the ocean, Kelvin notices:

> Yet others . . . but would-be experts were legion and each had his own theory. A comparison of the "contact" school of thought with other branches of Solarist studies, in which specialization had rapidly developed, made it clear that a Solarist-cybernetician had difficulty in making himself understood to a Solarist-symmetriadologist. Veukebe, director of the Institute when I was studying there, had asked jokingly one day: "How do you expect to communicate with the ocean, when you can't even understand each other?" The jest contained more than a grain of truth. (P. 28)

This Solaris Affair made many give up, but it also inspired others, for quite another reason, to persist. As Kelvin reflects: "Many people in the world of science, however especially among the young, had unconsciously come to regard the 'affair' as a touchstone of individual values. All things considered, it was not simply a question penetrating Solarist civilization, it was essentially a test of ourselves, of the limitations of human knowledge" (pp. 29–30). This passage introduces a central epistemological theme to the novel: the limits of humanity's ability to obtain new knowledge.

The idea of the testing of one's self soon becomes an all-pervasive influence on Kelvin's present actions. This becomes especially so when he encounters strange apparitions, the most important being a simulacrum of Rheya, his wife who had killed herself after a quarrel with him ten years earlier. Kelvin attempts to extricate himself from this situation (which is increasingly complicated by the fact they they are falling in love with each other all over again) by trying to get rid of her actual presence. Continual failure results, even after he ships her into orbit in a space shuttle, as Rheya reappears after each attempt. Eventually he realizes that Solaris is drawing the image of Rheya from some deeper level of his own mind—far deeper than his rational scientific mind. Thus the limits of knowledge to be tested reside in the inquiring mind of Kelvin himself.

Meanwhile, the apparition Rheya becomes like a mirror image of Kelvin's self. And while Rheya is temporarily away in the shuttle, Kelvin has another discussion with Snow. Snow expounds on the limitations of human knowledge. According to him, "We don't want to conquer the cosmos, we simply want to extend the boundaries of Earth to the frontiers of the cosmos" (p. 81). Humanity is not really seeking contact with alien races, but "we are only seeking Man. We have no need of other worlds. We need mirrors. . . . We are searching for an ideal image of our own world." (p. 81). Snow concludes: "We arrive here as we are in reality, and when the page is turned and that reality is revealed to us—that part of our reality which we could prefer to pass over in silence—then we don't like it any more" (p. 81). Here, theories and abstract systems fail because they try to construct humanity's preferred reality, no matter how incongruous it is with the actual one of Solaris.

Later, Snow gives Kelvin an antique volume of Gibarian's, called *The Little Apocrypha*. The part of the book that Kelvin reads is an inquiry into the actions of a pilot involved in a search for a missing explorer. The pilot, Breton, describes the unbelievable formations of Solaris's ocean, but then refuses to go further unless the commission believes his testimony. The commission claims it cannot make such a decision on his findings, and later (with one dissenting member, a Dr. Messenger) rejects Breton's report as a product of hallucinations caused by the planet's atmosphere. Breton disagrees and describes the rest of his observations to Dr. Messenger, who claims: "If the Council disregarded Breton's testimony, it was basically because Breton has no scientific training, although any scientist would envy the presence of mind and the gift of observation shown by this pilot" (p. 96). Earlier, Messenger had described the members of the commission as "obtuse minds, a pyramid of stupidity" (p. 96). Again Lem stresses his skepticism of theoretical approaches by showing how their use as a basis of judgment can even override someone's own evidence.

Twice more in the novel Kelvin reads historical accounts of past events. First he studies *Solaris—Ten Years of Exploration*, by Giese. The work contains countless examples of systems and categories which attempt to organize the activities of the ocean into some semblance of order. Kelvin's musings again suggest Lem's skepticism of theoretical approaches. On encountering Giese's classifications, Kelvin notices "that in spite of his cautious nature the scrupulous Giese more than once jumped to premature conclusions. Even when on their guard, human beings inevitably theorize" (p. 120). And further on, he declares that "there was no escaping the impressions that grew out of man's experience on Earth" (p. 132). As if to combine the point of man's futility with a sense of finality, Kelvin recalls how an expedition with Giese perished when an oceanic formation erupted and swallowed all up.

Later Kelvin comes across Gravinsky's twenty-year old *Compendium*. As the title indicates, the book contains a summary of the almost innumerable ideas and theories about Solaris. Gravinsky divides the first sixty years of Solaris studies into several periods. The first period lasted nine years, in which "nobody had produced theories in the strict sense. 'Common sense' suggested that the ocean was a lifeless chemical conglomerate" (pp. 172–73). The second period witnessed many theoretical accounts of an ocean now thought of as living and extremely complex. During the third period, however, "scientific opinion, hitherto practically unanimous, became divided. What followed was internecine warfare between scores of new schools of thought" (p. 173). The book also related the story of the great scientist Sevada and his mysterious death that occured while flying over the ocean. There were various speculations on his demise, but Kelvin had "always believed that his was in fact the first suicide, brought on by the first crisis of despair" (p. 174). These events seem to reemphasize Lem's skepticism towards theoretical explanations. For this approach appears, with the death of a scholar once again occurring, to lead towards despair and suicide. Once more Kelvin continues reading the *Compendium*'s summaries: "Still the hypotheses rained down—old, 'resurrected' hypotheses, superficially modified, simplified, or complicated to the extreme—and Solaristics, a relatively well-defined discipline in spite of its scope, became an increasingly tangled maze where every apparent exit led to a dead end. In the despondency, the ocean of Solaris was submerging under an ocean of printed paper" (pp. 176–77).

Kelvin replaces Gravinsky's tome on a bookshelf and accidentally discovers another work, a short pamphlet by Grastrom. It turns out to be an abstract reflection on the limits of human speculative theories. According to Kelvin:

> Grastrom set out to demonstrate that the most abstract achievements of science, the most advanced theories and victories of mathematics represented nothing more than a stumbling one or two-step progression form our rude, prehistoric, anthropomorphic understanding of the universe around us. . . . Grastrom's conclusion was that there neither was, nor could be, any question of "contact" between mankind and any nonhuman civilization. (P. 178)

This could very well serve as Lem's final statement for this part of the novel as well.

Time Enough for Love starts off with a short introduction that identifies the main character, Lazarus Long, and sets the forty-third century background of the novel. Long, an unexplainable mutant over twenty-three and a half centuries years old, is a member of the Howard Families, a family group which seeks ways to lengthen the human life span. By the forty-third century, science has developed life-prolongation procedures to the point that they can be repeated indefinitely in readily available rejuvenation centers.

The introduction sets the empirical tone of the novel. In describing the Howard Families, it explains their methods, "The Foundation started its work as a prescientific breeding experiment, as nothing was then known of genetics: adults of long-lived stock were encouraged to mate with others like them . . . unsurprisingly this experiment worked, as it was an empirical method used by stock breeders for centuries before the science of genetics came into being." When recounting how the rest of humanity developed these techniques, the notion of serendipidity in learning appears for the first time: "The short-lived humans back on Terra, still convinced that the families possessed a 'secret,' set about trying to find it by wide and systematic research, and, as always, research paid off serendipitously, not with the nonexistent 'secret,' but with something almost as good: a therapy, and eventually a sheaf of therapies for postponing old age, and extending vigor, virility, and fertility (p. 18). Throughout the novel the ideas of action and serendipity emerge. The focus on these two notions reflects *how* things are or happen. The question of *why* observations or events are so does not enter into picture.

Most of the first part of the novel deals with Long reviewing his past life, with the bulk of his memories contained in three major reminiscences. There are two sections of aphorisms surrounding the last major reminiscence. The story opens on the planet Secundus where Long finds himself confined in a strange room against his will. He comes to Secundus expecting a peaceful death, choosing not to rejuvenate himself. Ira Weatheral, acting head of the Howard Families Trustees, enters and explains that Long has been rescued and placed in a rejuvenation center because the human race needs his wisdom. Incensed, Long agrees to cooperate only if someone can think of something new for him to do; for the reason why he wanted to die was that he was tired and bored with life, having done all that a person could do.

It does not take much time for Long to start giving opinions. In his first discussion with Weatheral, when informed that a planet is being settled in order to test whether or not a democratic government works, Long gives a negative response. Weatheral claims that the project may work since all involved believe in the democratic theory. Long responds; "I was about to shove my own experience with such governments down your throat. But you're right, this is a brand-new situation—and we *don't* know. Oh, I have strong opinions, but a thousand reasoned opinions are never equal to one case of diving in and finding out. Galileo proved that and it may be the only certainty we have" (p. 31). He then goes on giving his reasons why democracies do not work and later asks Weatheral for his opinion. Weatheral refrains, claiming he lacks sufficient experience for an opinion. But long interjects, "To get anywhere, or even to live a long time, a man has to guess, and guess right, over and over again, without enough data for a logical answer" (p. 31). These two statements are to be taken as complementary and not as contradictory. The first utters the constant theme of action and experience as the primary components of knowledge. The second warns against letting a lack of total knowledge of a situation prevent one from trying on his or her own.

Later, Long warns about the human race needing his wisdom:

> "If you think I have gazed upon the Naked Face of God, think again. I haven't even begun to find out how the Universe works, much less what it is for. To figure out the basic questions about this World it would be necessary to stand *outside* and look at it. Not inside. No, not in two thousand years, not in twenty thousand. When a man dies, he may shake loose his local perspective and see the thing as a whole."
>
> "Then you believe in an afterlife?" [Weatheral asks]
>
> "Slow up! I don't '*believe*' in anything. I *know* certain things— little things . . . from experience. But I have *no* beliefs. Belief gets in the way of learning." (P. 41)

Here is Long's first statement concerning nonempirical knowledge. Speculations that do not involve experience have no place in knowledge. This means that such questions about the existence of an afterlife become superfluous, not because of their unimportance, but due to their unreachable nature. As Long later states in one of his aphorisms, "There is no conclusive evidence of life after death. But there is no evidence of any sort against it. Soon enough you will *know*. So why fret about it?" (p. 257).

In a later scene the personal computers of Long and Weatheral, named Dora and Minerva respectively, become the topic of discussion. Their capacity for learning is significantly compared with that of their human makers. Indeed they are so advanced that they can duplicate almost all human thinking functions, including conversation with humans. In this scene, Long discusses with the computers a basic human emotion, love. It is interesting to see that he approaches this in the same way he does other human endeavors. According to him:

> The trouble with defining in words anything as basic as love is that the definition can't be understood by anyone who has not experienced it. It's like the ancient dilemma of explaining a rainbow to a person blind from birth . . . one could teach such an unfortunate all the physical theory of the electromagnetic spectrum, tell him precisely what fre-

quencies the eye can pick up . . . until he knew *all* about rainbows in a
scientific sense . . . but you still can't make him feel the breathless
wonder that the sight of a rainbow inspires in a man. (P. 143)

This subject of love turns out to be the central topic of the novel and
the key to Long's finding the new experience he has been searching
for.

Long now embarks on a long reminiscence. He tells of the days
when he was an interplanetary trader and guardian of twins, a boy,
Joe, and a girl, Llita, whom he bought as slaves. He tries to bring
them up as free people, but encounters difficulty, as their slave
background and its resulting mentality prove quite resistant to
change. However, a long stretch of time aboard a ship in interstellar
flight provides an opportunity for pedagogical experiments. He applies the same empirical learning-by-doing method to them as he
does to himself:

> I did not hesitate to use fiction in teaching them. Fiction is a faster way
> to get a feeling for alien patterns of human behavior than is nonfiction; it
> is one stage short of actual experience . . . I could have offered them
> psychology and sociology and comparative anthropology . . . but Joe
> and Llita could not have put them together into a Gestalt . . . and I
> recall another teacher who used parables in putting over ideas. (P. 193)

Experience remains the basic criterion. As far as teaching them how
to think and act as free individuals, there is no substitute for action.
Instead of reading them ideas on freedom, Long forces Joe and Llita
to think for themselves as often as possible. And in order to show
them "that aggressive self-reliance necessary to a free human,"
(p. 193) he teaches them how to fight.

During this reminiscence Long makes his most extended statement of his ideas on marriage. And in it, his epistemological
approach to this important act is clearly revealed:

> Every so often some idiot tries to abolish marriage. Such attempts work
> as well as repealing the law of gravity. . . . Marriage is not something
> thought up by priests . . . marriage is as much part of mankind's
> evolutionary equipment as his eyes, and as useful to the race as eyes are
> to the individual. . . .
>   Why do bees split up into queens, drones, and workers, then live
> as one big family? Because, for them, it *works*. . . . Why is it that
> "marriage"—by whatever name—is a universal institution among hu-

man beings everywhere? . . . It *works*, that's all; for all its faults it works far better by the only universal test—survival—than any of the endless inventions that shallow-pates over the millenia have tried to substitute for it.

I am not speaking monogamy; I mean *all* forms of marriage. (Pp. 210–11)

Again, what has worked in the past becomes knowledge and the basis for human behavior in the future.

At the heart of the novel, and surrounded by two sections of aphorisms by Long, is another reminiscence, his third and most extensive, where he recounts what he calls the happiest of his lives. The aphorisms were composed over an extended period by Long as crystallizations of his thought at particular times under particular conditions; hence, they often seem contradictory in the sense of being unsystematic. In their very refusal of systematic deductive logic, however, they demonstrate Long's pragmatic approach to future events. One aphorism discusses this very idea: "What are the facts? Again and again and again—what are the *facts*? Shun wishful thinking, ignore divine revelation, forget what 'the stars foretell,' avoid opinion, care not what neighbors think, never mind the un-guessable 'verdict of history'—what are the facts, and to how many decimal places? You pilot always into an unknown future; facts are your single clue. Get the facts!" (p. 264). Human futures are not guided by theories, but by the ability to change and adapt to circumstances, to master the unknown by experiencing and doing. Another aphorism points this out: "A human being should be able to change a diaper, plan an invasion, butcher a hog, conn a ship, design a building, write a sonnet, balance accounts, build a wall, set a bone, comfort the dying, take orders, give orders, cooperate, act alone, solve equations, analyze a new problem, pitch manure, program a computer, cook a tasty meal, fight efficiently, die gallantly. Specialization is for insects" (p. 265).

The setting for this major reminiscence is the planet New Beginnings, a newly settled planet with a similar setting to that of the nineteenth century American frontier. Long tells of his life with Dora, whom Long raised from childhood and eventually married. Most of the story details their life together as struggling settlers. The opening passages set an optimistic tone by encouraging learning by action: "Learn to grow it, learn to eat it. You can't buy it; learn to *make* it! How do you know until you've tried it? Try again and keep on trying" (p. 271). The following passage, describing Long's search for suitable building materials for his home, shows the preference for practicality over speculation.

> I walked past the answer hundreds of times before I recognized it. When wind and weather and rot and lopers and insects have done their worst on a dead dragon, what is left is almost indestructible. I discovered this when I tried to burn what was left of a big brute that was unpleasantly close to our compound. I never did find out why this was so. Perhaps the biochemistry of these dragons has been investigated since then, but I had neither the equipment nor time nor interest; I was too busy scratching a living for my family and was simply delighted to learn that it was true. (P. 346)

The notion of serendipity is also present in this situation. In the first part of Heinlein's novel, the notions of action, practicality, and serendipity are indeed the dominant epistemological characteristics.

The second part of Lem's and Heinlein's, as mentioned earlier, present the actions of the respective protagonists and their individual attempts to solve a similar problem—that of understanding the alien or new situation that challenges their capacities to know. In *Solaris*, Kelvin, Snow, and Sartorius attempt to destroy the apparitions. In *Time Enough for Love*, Long experiments with different forms of human relationships as he searches for that long-sought new experience in life.

Solaris's second part begins with Kelvin's examining a blood sample from Rheya. From his results Kelvin speculates that the apparitions are probably composed of neutrinos. More theoretical discussion follows. For Sartorius ponders: "I have the impression— only an impression, mark you—that Dr. Kelvin's hypothesis is not without validity. . . . Our knowledge in this field is purely theoretical. We did not know if there was any possibility of stabilizing such structures. Now a clearly defined solution offers itself to us" (p. 114). Later, Snow informs Kelvin of Sartorius's attempts to produce a negative neutrino field that will disintegrate the apparitions and leave normal matter unharmed. Kelvin fears this action, but Snow responds by questioning Kelvin's doubts. Kelvin then retorts with a skepticism towards Sartorius's theories: "Sartorius follows the Frazer-Cajolla school . . . [he] has faith in his tutors. I don't say we

can't respect that, but there are other tutors, and other theories. . . .
It seems to me that we can't afford to back Sartorius against the ocean
as well as the other theories" (p. 138). Then he criticizes Sartorius
himself:

> You realize that these theories have never been tested experimentally:
> neutrino structures have been abstractions until now. Sartorius is re-
> lying on Frazer, and I've followed Sion's theory. He'll say I'm no
> physicist, or Sion either, not from his point of view, at least. He will
> dispute my figures, and I'm not going to get into the kind of argument
> where he tries to browbeat me for his own satisfaction. (P. 138)

Rheya's discovery of the nature of her existence further compli-
cates Kelvin's attitude toward this experiment. She has previously
tried to kill herself by swallowing liquid oxygen, but she instantly
regenerated, a power seemingly possessed by all of the apparitions.
Her second attempt at suicide provides the novel's climax.

Sartorius actually succeeds in disintegrating Rheya, who had
voluntarily submitted to the experiment. Knowing Kelvin's reluctance to see her go, she has to drug him into a deep sleep the night
before the experiment. At last a theory works. The scientists finally
succeed in one of their attempts at mastering the ocean's actions.
However, this success is only an illusory one, as very little, if anything
at all, is gained in understanding the nature of the ocean.

In the concluding chapter, Kelvin and Snow spin off yet another
theory about the ocean. It turns out to be the most speculative in the
novel. They talk of the ocean as being a god struggling out of the
childhood stage of development; this idea is reminiscent of Olaf
Stapledon's divine creator in his *Star Maker*.[4] Snow concludes,
however, with a disclaimer: "I renounce paternity of the theory"
(p. 206). The novel ends with Kelvin remaining on the station. He
remains, to the end, skeptical about the future of speculation on
Solaris and about his own future. Knowing nothing, he can hope for
nothing: "I was not absolutely certain, but leaving would mean giving
up a chance, perhaps an infinitesimal one, perhaps only imaginary.
. . . I hoped for nothing. And yet I live in expectation. . . . I did not
know what achievements, what mockery, even what tortures still
awaited me. I knew nothing, and I persisted in the faith that the time
of cruel miracles was not past" (p. 212).

The second part of *Time Enough for Love* presents Long's *new* experiences in love. He has already told of his past; now he searches for—and seeks to justify—his future. New characters are introduced. The first two are females, Lapis Lazuli and Lorelei, twins who were cloned from Long himself. The third is Minerva, Weatheral's personal computer, cloned into human female form. Long, now completely rejuvenate, is offered something new to do: the possibility of time travel. He decides to travel back to the period of his early childhood.

Before going back in time, however, he becomes romantically involved with the twins and with Minerva. The reason for these affairs is the exploration of the nature of love, a topic Long has discussed earlier with Minerva (when she was still in the form of a computer). This inquiry leads to a contest between two types of reasoning. Agreeing with Long and others that the highest purpose and expression of love is the reproduction and raising of offspring, the twins are upset that Long has never shown his love to them in this fashion. Long explains that he does indeed love them, but two reasons prevent him from fulfilling their requests. One is scientific; the other emotional. The former reflects Long's concern over genetics. Since the twins are clones of him, negative reenforcement of genes emerges as a legitimate worry. The latter is a product of his childhood upbringing. Even though the taboos of early twentieth century Bible Belt America have been proven nonsensical, they are still hard for Long to abandon. Long's personal computer informs him that there exists no threat of genetic mishap between himself and the twins. So he eventually gives in to both of them.

Long's trip back to the place and time of his childhood, Kansas City, Missouri, in the early twentieth century, finishes the novel. Using the name of Ted Bronson to conceal his identity, he eventually meets his family, and encounters his six-year-old self. The most unlikely of events occurs when Long falls in love with his mother. This is further complicated by his mother, unaware of Long's relationship to her, who wants to reciprocate his affections. The threat of changing the future—i.e., Long's past—becomes quite possible. And to finish the mix-up of events, Long joins the army in order to remain in good favor with his patriotic family, especially his mother, for the United States has just entered World War I. Long, knowing about the futility of the war, as well as its dangers, lets his emotions and sentiments overrule his reasoning. After a series of botched attempts, he and his mother finally consummate their desires during Long's last night before he is shipped out.

Throughout the events leading up to and including that night, there are discussions about the morality of the relationship. His mother reveals that she is one month pregnant, thus eliminating the worry of unwanted offspring. Relieved of worry, Long can now consider this affair as another experiment in his ongoing search to learn more about the emotion of love. Long takes the same approach toward exploring this emotion as he would any other endeavor, via increased varieties of experience. As he states in one of his aphorisms, "The more you love, the more you *can* love—and the more intensely you love. Nor is there any limit on how *many* you can love . . ." (p. 266).

Long is sent over to France to fight. He is fatally wounded in a battle, and, while calmly waiting for death, experiences a mysterious encounter:

> "You still don't understand," the Gray Voice droned on. "There is no time, there is no space. What was, is, and ever shall be. You are you, playing chess with yourself, and again you have checkmated yourself. You are the referee. Morals are your agreement with yourself to abide by our own rules. To thine own self be true or you spoil the game."
>
> "Crazy." [Long responds.]
>
> "Then vary the rules and play a different game. You cannot exhaust her infinite variety."
>
> "If you would just let me look at your face," Lazarus muttered pettishly.
>
> "Try a mirror." (P. 602)

If the novel ended with this passage, one could say that the conclusion parallels that of Lem's novel in which the individual is left alone facing the hopeless situation of solipsism: a person ultimately trapped in his own perpetual system, unable to break out into the future and new experiences. One last section follows, however, in which Long's friends arrive from the future and rescue him in the nick of time from certain death. Unlike Kelvin, Long will go on to other things. The above passage reflects one last time Heinlein's view of what humanity's approach toward new encounters should be. If one can choose which way to act, and to change course if success is not forthcoming, failure eventually becomes only a delay—not a finality.

What remains to be asked is whether or not there exists any intersection between the two novel's epistemological stances. Do Lem's theoretical skepticism and Heinlein's pragmatic optimism have any meeting point in this particular analysis? If there is, it would show that the two epistemological approaches chosen by the writers are not categorically exclusive—i.e., closed to any different and opposing ways of thinking—and that they selected these modes either to reveal their inherent weaknesses or to emphasize their possible strengths.

Such an intersection exists when analyzing two characters: Rheya, from *Solaris*, and Minerva, from *Time Enough for Love*. For despite all the differences in their respective intellectual contexts, Rheya and Minerva have very similar human situations, those which act upon and inflect the epistemological views of the male protagonists, Kelvin and Long. Two other common aspects help sharpen the focus in this particular examination. First of all, both women are recreations of other characters that have existed in the male protagonists' pasts. Rheya is a duplicate of Kelvin's dead wife, while Minerva is the computer-made human who has taken the form of the former slave Llita whom Long raised. Second, and more important, both women take active roles in the searching for solutions to the main problems facing each of the protagonists. This latter point provides for the epistemological intersection, because both Rheya and Minerva, at crucial points in the action, cause their respective protagonists to act counter to their usual methods.

In *Solaris*, Rheya causes Kelvin to experience a conflict of duty, and at one point Kelvin decides to resist. In a key passage he examines the nature of his action:

> They can't force me to cooperate. But I can't tell them the truth, I'll have to dissemble and lie, and keep on doing it. . . . Because there may be thoughts, intentions and cruel hopes in my mind of which I know nothing, because I am a murderer unawares. Man has gone out to explore other worlds and other civilizations without having explored his own labyrinth of dark passages and secret chambers, and without finding out what lies behind doorways that he himself has sealed. (P. 165)

Kelvin, still skeptical of pragmatic action, now sees—under the pressure of his relationship with Rheya—the human mind itself as being unexplored. However, he cannot open those "doorways that he himself has sealed." Rheya, meanwhile, shows him a way through her love and ultimate sacrifice of self. She teaches Kelvin that if one makes theories, one must also act upon them (as she does in submiting herself to the neutrino theory, thus allowing herself to be disintegrated)—even if the consequences, as in this case, are irreversible and emotionally painful.

In an analogous scene from *Time Enough for Love*, Minerva is upset at Long because he will not consummate their relationship. As a computer, Minerva has discussed with Long human experiences which a machine (Minerva) could only think about but not feel. One of them is what she calls Eros:

> I found it fascinating, Lazarus, I now know all about sex . . . in the sense that a man who has always been blind can be taught the physics of a rainbow. I am even a gene surgeon now, in theory, and would not hesitate to be one in practice since I had time to construct the ultramicrominiature waldoes needed for such fine work. I am equally expert as obstetrician and gynecologist and rejuvenator. . . .
>
> "Eros" alone I cannot know . . . and [I] know at last that I am blind. (P. 174)

Minerva makes Long promise to give her that experience. In the novel's second part, when she takes human form, she confronts him on why he has reneged on his promise. She deduces that Long's reluctance comes from the fact that her human form is that of Llita's and that emotionally he can not come to grips with this. Long's refusal to act, to give and take experience, is to act counter to his pragmatic method and to the notion that, no matter how many times it has been repeated, an action need not have the same result. Recalling his earlier remarks (especially those about democracy), his reluctance to act here reminds us more of the scientists in *Solaris* than of his own past methods. Minerva must, like Rheya, take the active role. By convincing Long to fulfill his promise, she leads him back to experience and to the discovery of new things in what seem (for the theoretical mind) to be dead ends.

Two novels do not make a generalization, but rather an indication. This analysis does illustrate, finally, how a society's particular epistemology, which is usually thought of as being discussed in academies and ivory towers, is seriously discussed at the popular level. The fact that both writers are widely read means that their methods of reasoning as well as their ideas are disseminated among the general populations. Thus, people of Lem's persuasion may tend to doubt new ideas because they may appear to be contrary to long-held theories, while people of Heinlein's may support those ideas for their past successes in application. The former may try to speculate about the future in comprehensive and total terms while the latter may do so in respect to certain proven issues. Therefore, since comprehensive theoretical structures could be easily upset by any new discovery, those on Lem's side would view, from this mode of thinking, the future prospects of knowledge with pessimism. And, since any new idea could be readily acted upon for its possible success (whether foreseen or not) and not for its facility for supporting systematic explanations on the nature of things, those on Heinlein's side would view, with this way of doing things, their future possibilities of action with optimism. If these generalizations hold, then such writers as Robert A. Heinlein and Stanislaw Lem become important indicators of how people at large feel towards new and future situations.

Reactionary Utopias

Gregory Benford

One of the striking facets of fictional utopias is that nobody really
wants to live there. Perhaps the author, or a few friends, will profess
some eagerness. But seldom do utopian fictions awaken a real longing to take part.

I suspect this is because most visions of supposedly better
societies have features which violate our innate sense of human
progress—they don't look like the future; they resemble a warped,
malignant form of the past.

Time and again, utopists envision worlds where one aspect of
human character is enhanced, and much else is suppressed. Plato's
Republic was the first and most easily understandable of these; he
thought that artists and similar unreliable sorts should be expelled.
Too disruptive, you know.

Should we be uncomfortable with this fact? If we value Western
European ideals, yes.

Five Regressive Ideas

How can we codify this notion? Utopian fictions stress ideas, so
we need a way to advance the background assumptions, while suppressing the foreground of plot and character.

Nearly all utopias have one or more characteristics which I shall
term *reactionary*, in the sense that they recall the past, often in its
worst aspects. Here, "reactionary" means an aesthetic analogy, no
more. It may apply to works which are to the left in the usual political
spectrum, though I feel this one-dimensional spectrum is so misleading that the customary use of reactionary means little. *Regressive*
might be an alternate term, meaning that a utopia seeks to turn back

the tide of Western thought. Looking at the range of utopian literature, I sense five dominant reactionary characteristics:

1. Lack of diversity. Culture is everywhere the same, with few
ethnic or other divergences.

2. Static in time. Like diversity, change in time would imply that
either the past or the present of the utopia was less than perfect (i.e.,
not utopian).

3. Nostalgic and technophobic. Usually this takes the form of
isolation in a rural environment, organization harkening back to the
village or even the farm, and only the simplest technology. Many
writers here reveal their fondness for medieval society. The few
pieces of technology superior to today's usually exist only to speed
the plot or provide metaphorical substance; they seldom spring from
the society itself. (Only those utopias which include some notion of
scientific advancement qualify as SF. Otherwise they are usually
simple rural fantasies. Also, this point calls into question classifying
any utopia as SF if it is drastically technophobic. Simply setting it in
the future isn't enough.)

4. Presence of an authority figure. In real utopian communities,
frequently patriarchal, this is a present person. Historically, nearly
all utopian experiments in the West have quickly molded themselves
around patriarchal figures. In literary utopias, the authority is the
prophet who set up the utopia. Often the prophet is invoked in
conversations as a guide to proper, right-thinking behavior.

5. Social regulation through guilt. Social responsibility is ex-
alted as *the* standard of behavior. Frequently the authority figure is
the focus of guilt-inducing rules. Once the authority figure dies, he or
she becomes a virtual saint-like figure. Guilt is used to the extreme of
controlling people's actions *in detail*, serving as the constant standard
and overseer of the citizen's actions.

These five points outline a constellation of values which utopists
often unconsciously assume.

Before backing up these points with specific arguments, consider some utopias which *don't* share all or most of them. Samuel
Delany's *Triton* seems to have none of these features; indeed, it
proclaims itself a "heterotopia," stressing its disagreement with the
first point. Often Delany depicts societies which express his delight in
the freakish. Franz Werfel's *Star of the Unborn* (1946) depicts a
heavily technological future with many desirable aspects, while

accepting the inevitability of war, rebellion, and unsavory aspects. Advanced technology is carefully weighed for its moral implications in Norman Spinrad's *Songs from the Stars*.

Nonreactionary, or genuinely progressive utopias, often reject regulation through guilt. This divides utopias roughly along the axis of Europian versus American, with the Europeans typically favoring social conscience, that is, guilt. Consider Edward Bellamy's *Looking Backward* (the most prominent American utopia of the nineteenth century) and William Morris's reply to it, *News from Nowhere*. Both stabilize society more through gratification of individual needs than through guilt. Indeed, one of the keys to American politics is just this idea. Huxley's *Island* (written after his move to California) sides more with gratification, though his *Brave New World* (written in England) depicts the horrific side of a state devoted to gratification without our "sentimental" humanist principles.

LeGuin as Reactionary

I want to argue that utopists often thought to be forward-looking and left-wing may be in fact reactionary. Consider, for example, Ursula Le Guin. Arguably, *The Dispossessed* is the finest American utopian novel of our time, and much of her work touches on these issues.

A first clue comes from the strangely nineteenth-century middle-European "feel" of her background society in *The Dispossessed*. This gives a curious static flavor, and, of course, recalls her reverence for the European tradition of utopian thought.

Her utopian experiment on the world Annares is strikingly technophobic. Except for minor intrusions of a faster-than-light communicator and interplanetary travel (old SF staples), there is little which suggests the future at all. The vague middle-European feel to the architecture, organization of work, and so on, is clearly nostalgic; rural Europe itself isn't even like that any more. Plainly, the author disapproves of the techno-flash and dazzle of the opposite world, Urras.

There, Shevek can't connect with the womanly embodiment of Urras's temptation, and he symbolically spills his seed on the ground before her. Indeed, in later works, Le Guin sees space travel as "a bunch of crap flying around the world, just garbage in the sky."[1]

NASA's planetary missions, or Shevek's science, can be clean, serene. Technology, though, is practical, dirty and liable to fall into the wrong hands.

We learn that the Hainish, who began the colony worlds, are burdened and driven by some strange guilt. Considering their superiority in so many fields, it is difficult not to conclude that Le Guin feels we should regard their guilt as admirable, too. This book is the culmination of her utopian thinking, a path which leads through the short story, "Those Who Walk Away from Omelas." (This parable might be titled "Those Who Walk Away from Omelettes," because we know what it takes to make one—you must break some eggs.)

The Dispossessed reeks with Old Testament themes and images, using guilt as the principal social control. The founder, Odo, is the central saint of a communal society. Her pain and suffering during nine years' imprisonment *make possible* the virtue of the later Anarres society. Citizens remind each other of the events and connect her suffering with their dedication. The implied lesson is that utopia will not arrive until man comes to grip with his own inner nature, which means in turn that a citizen is *born guilty*, must repay Odo's pain with his submission to the general will and society's precepts. Living on Anarres has an uncanny resemblance to being nagged by your mother.

The marriage vows in Castro's Cuba explicitly require a couple to raise all children according to socialist morality. On Anarres a child is not a true citizen, psychically, until he has undergone a guilt-inducing experience—an unconscious, implicit rite. Both processes seek to induce early control. The crucial scene in the protagonist Shevek's childhood is the boy's imprisonment game, described in careful detail. (This incident is clearly central, an act of juvenile deliquency taking up more space than Shevek's entire courtship of his wife!)

Odo is clearly the guilt-inducing authority figure which appears so often in reactionary utopias, though she is not the customary type: that is, male, dynamic, assertive. Odo dies just before her utopia begins (see the short story, "The Day before the Revolution") and has some resemblance to Le Guin herself. It is interesting, then, that Odo avoids the problems of building a real utopia, for Le Guin does this too.

Reading the Silences

I propose a further method of investigating utopian writings, after first applying the litmus test of the above characteristics: reading the author's silences.

Plausibly, the yearning which motivates a writer to contruct a utopia, devoting narrative energy to it, will in turn lead the author to neglect certain disturbing problems. The novel reflects the author's avoidance of crucial questions that arise naturally from the imagined world. Conscious avoidance (or, more importantly, unconscious neglect) of these tells us what the writer fears and feels uncomfortable with. Also then we might expect the inhabitants of a utopia never to think of the blind areas in their own society.

The principal ignored problem of Anarres is the problem of evil and thus violence; to Le Guin they are often synonomous. Guilt (social conscience) simply overcomes such discordant elements. In the middle of a drought in which people starve, no matter how evenly food is shared, somehow no one thinks of taking up arms with some friends and seizing, say, the grain reserves. Similarly, there is no on-stage evidence in *The Dispossessed* of hardened criminals, insane people, or naturally violent types (indeed, violence is "unnatural," and an impulse toward it is the principal offense which calls up guilt). There *is* a prison camp for undesirables, evidence for the ambiguity of this utopia. But people seem to go there for offenses such as writing unpopular plays or, perhaps, voting Republican.

Le Guin's silence is conspicuous. This arouses the suspicion that shying away from violence of any sort is part and parcel of an emotional posture of which *The Dispossessed* is only one reflection.

Tolstoy is the obvious father of many of Le Guin's ideas, techniques, and even literary mannerisms. As Samuel R. Delany has remarked in "To Read *The Dispossessed*,"[2] whenever Le Guin begins to discuss politics (a common occasion) or show it (quite rare), she uses a language which "sentence by sentence is pompous, ponderous, and leaden." He surmises that her style owes much to the Victorian translations of the great European novels, and that when she attempts depth she unconciously lapses into this voice. These are "signs of a 'European' or 'Russian' profundity that the [translated] texts do not have." (This brilliant essay stresses the microtext and ignores the book's principal strength, its beautiful structuring. As Delany deftly shows, hidden assumptions or avoided problems often show up best at the sentence or even phrase level. He also misses some of the lovely passages which her style achieves.)

Why Tolstoy? He, as well as the Russian anarchist Prince Kropotkin, took an absolutist position—no cooperation with any state control which used force. It is worth noting that the home of much idealist anarchist thinking, Russia, is now the largest prison state in history. One suspects that this comes in part from the inability of the nineteenth century socialist thinkers there to confront the problem of violence in any moderate way.

One would then expect Le Guin's Anarres to evolve, if it ever slipped free of the authorial hand, in the direction of nineteenth century Russia—without, of course, the apparatus of the Czar, and so on. Failing to confront the problem of evil and violence gives these forces more power, not less. A quite plausible outcome, then, would see the reduction of Annares to warring camps, each promising to restore order and ideological purity, perhaps even concluding with a Bolshevik-style victory. Le Guin attempts to finesse this entire problem. Her ignoring of a remarkable historical parallel (the demise of Russian socialist idealism at the hands of Lenin) marks *The Dispossessed* as a deeply reactionary work, concerned more with repealing history, than with understanding it in order to make a better future.

This came up recently when I was discussing Soviet SF with one of the principal SF critics there, M. Gakov. Appropriately enough, it was a cold day in 1984 and we were crossing Red Square. He remarked that *The Dispossessed* was not translated into Russian, in part because it referred to ideas the regime didn't like. Then he said rather wistfully, "For us, you know, it is terribly nostalgic. And irrelevant."

Le Guin seems to have tentatively approached the problem of real-world violence in the cartoon version of real politics depicted in *The Eye of the Heron*. There, descendants of the mafia confront nonviolent anarchists in highly implausible fashion, leading to a retreat of the anarchists into the wilderness—a note oddly reminiscent of many American escape-adventures. One must conclude that Le Guin can hardly bear to confront this crucial issue, and, when she does, sees no solution.

But there seems to be a deeper reason for Le Guin's silence

about the realities of the world: fundamentally, the real world does not matter.

As the British critic Roz Kaveny has remarked in a review of *Malafrena*, "Throughout there is the sense that fills all of Le Guin's work: that politics is important less for what it can do for other people than as a way of achieving personal moral self-realisation. Altruism is seen as good for its own sake and not because it may be useful to the under-privileged, although the altruist is supposed to be too busy to ever think in precisely those terms."

A utopia of hard-scrabbling scarcity solves so many problems quite cheaply. No worries of distribution of wealth, no leverage for power relationships. And it casts all in a superior light: poor people can have few sins. Throughout, no one questions a system which produces poverty, because, after all, it provides lovely opportunities for sacrifice.

A genuine revolutionary in such a place would be he who puts productivity over political theory. No such figure appears—another author's silence. But reality, after all, is not the principal concern of such narratives.

So the crucial scene in *The Eye of the Heron*, in which anarchist confronts mafia thug and the protagonist dies, is *skipped*. We learn of it obliquely, via dialogue, in flashback. Partly, this comes no doubt from her aversion for violence, but I suspect we are meant to see the moral grandeur of the survivors as the central fact. Even death is another way to strike a moral posture—or rather, to *be seen* doing so.

The street controntations on Urras in *The Dispossessed* rang false to many reviewers, and for good reason: they are the only examples of real-world political confrontation in the book, and Le Guin knows very little of such things.

So her anarchists, confronting theory rather than facts, come over as nice, reasonable, and fairly boring. They behave like middle-class middle-brows, except that they are scrupulously horrified at the idea of property. (One of the book's assets lies in reassuring the middle-brow reader that revolutions will let him feel moral and yet comfortable. Everyone, after all, believes himself capable of over-coming his own greed and being a nice guy.) The conspicuous villians of the book are a physicist who steals Shevek's work, and, of course, lots of pseudo-American capitalists on Urras.

But not quite. As Delany points out in his essay, she treats the homosexual Bedap with an unconscious condescension. It is clear that Bedap should reform himself—stop being gay—because it does not fit in with the utopia she is constructing in her head. Which in turn intersects with the reactionary utopist's dislike of cultural diversity. Homosexuals cannot be eliminated from human society (without genetic engineering at least); they are a fact impossible to ignore, but clearly their presence troubles Le Guin's blueprints.

In her world, a quiet talk over herbal tea will surely fix matters up. A romantic, she ignores the problem of evil. In Le Guin's land, crowds watching a potential suicide on a window ledge never shout "Jump!" Averting her gaze from the twentieth century, she sees evil people as those unfortunates who have not been given sufficient chance to be good.

The real question here is not the use of violence—which is, in Le Guin's work, an invariable sign of wrongness—but rather, is moral order compatible with human diversity? Her answer is clear: her societies should opt for the age-old solution, known to the pharoahs—moral authoritarianism. Even in the dystopian future America of her novella *The New Atlantis*, dissidents retreat to classical music and romantic humanism as a counter to the oppressive state. Old world values can, perhaps, redeem us.

Active thwarting of violence is not allowed, though. Le Guin labels her utopia as ambiguous, clearly knows something is wrong, but does not confront the deep problems. Rather than think through the hidden assumptions of Anarres, Shevek returns to pursue his own moral self-realization. Perhaps he, too, will become a martyr, like Odo—and thus engender more guilt, more attendant control.

Looking Backward

As perhaps the best modern utopian novelist, Le Guin is worth studying to illumiate *why* utopists are so pervasively reactionary. I suggest that some underlying aspects of her thought come from the failures of European utopian theory. But there's more to it than that.

While there is much in reactionary utopias we should scorn, I think we should properly look at *The Dispossessed* and some more obviously feminist utopias as responses to earlier, more mechanistic and masculine utopias. (As examples of novels which clearly are such reactions, see Suzy McKee Charnas's *Motherlines*, Marge Piercy's *Woman on the Edge of Time*, and Joanna Russ's *Female Man*.) They depict communal societies with pleasant characteristics: relative lack of government, ecological virtue, diffusion of parenting, freedom of movement, sexual freedom, and no crime.

Feminist utopias often use the family as a model for social structure, but "the unowned, non-patriarchal family, headed by nobody."[3] This, with their classlessness, makes them seem like fantasies about how families ought to be (and seldom are). If masculine utopias fret over the means of production, feminist ones are bothered by the means of reproduction. They uncouple sex from power. But this is not enough to provide social ordering.

Perhaps it is natural for women to extend the family as a model, since they have not, up to now, experienced society as a whole from a more masculine viewpoint—as a focus of conflicting forces. It isn't surprising that the problem of control doesn't rear its vexing head in such utopias, and the principal problem seems to be work assignments (who's going to do the dishes?). No trace remains of general competitiveness and the desire to be better than others; somehow, they have been laundered from the human psyche. (Interestingly, feminist utopists support this by asserting that women are inherently better, that is, non-competitive. The idea seems to be that men have merely taken a wrong turn lately.)

There is no doubt which authority figure is to set the house rules, as Joanna Russ's choice of words signifies: "Careful inspection of the manless societies usually reveals the intention (or wish) to allow men in . . . if only they can be trusted to behave."[3] If you don't, presumably you are sent to your room, i.e., exiled—unless it's James Tiptree, Jr.'s utopia in "Houston, Houston, Do you Read?" where you'll be killed with minimal regrets. In no case should divisive ideas or surging hormones be allowed to thwart the communal good. Unsurprisingly, the authority figure is the only fallback enforcer in such worlds. The problem of control is simply neglected.

These feminist utopias are primarily reactive, responding to perceived masculine evils. The qualities they long for—stronger communal feeling, harmony with the natural world, violence only if it expresses anger in limited ways or in self-defense, country versus city (where the streets are unsafe)—reflect current needs. But by concentrating on these concerns they run the risk of forsaking the gains of the present, and becoming reactionary because they cannot imagine new ways to organize community.

Freedom to do as we please, so long as we all agree with each other and remain in a state of harmony with the cosmos, is no freedom at all. It is little better than a religion in which faith in a deity has been replaced by faith in some supposed truths of the human spirit. It is a single-party system that is as superficially benign, yet as subtly authoritarian as Disneyland.

Why does much utopian thought tend in this direction? The central difficulty confronting social planners is just that contained in the name—they must *plan*, and so must fear the wild card, the diverse, the self-regulating. History provides methods for governing errant wild spirits, so a planner looks longingly backward for models. Few peer ahead to landscapes where men and women have more freedom, can interact swiftly and chaotically, yet with good results.

Some SF authors have seen this. Norman Spinrad's depictions of electronic democracy, from *Bug Jack Barron* onward, are deliberately saturated with lust for power and sharp contradictions. Frederik Pohl has meditated throughout a long career on these problems, notably in the recent *The Years of the City*, which abounds in utopian visions threaded with practical lore. It would be interesting to apply the criteria for a reactionary utopia and for reading silences to such works, as well as older (more apparently right-wing) utopian novels such as Heinlein's *Beyond This Horizon* and Niven and Pournelle's *Oath of Fealty*.

I conclude that reactionary facets spring in part from lack of imagination. And feminists, searching for ways to revise our society, fall upon analogies with the family, even if these do not provide solutions to the genuine problems of a diverse, urban, cantankerous world. Fundamentally, what we sense as most reactionary about these fanciful worlds is their fixation on a final, glorious endpoint: utopia as stasis.

We intuitively understand now, in a world ever in flux, that no society will stay put. The modern spirit is less concerned with ends than with means. We wrinkle our noses at frozen goals, sensing that our longing for a better world must fasten on making the process of change better, rather than nailing down eternal, theory-bound specifics. We need utopias which satisfy many human needs while all about them is changing, being made new by the insights of science and art.

It is no longer enough to depict flawed utopias, ambiguous ones, or the like. What literature needs, and plainly isn't getting, are utopias of *process*, which tell us something about how to reach goals and be happy during the journey. Such visions people could respond to creatively.

Instead, present utopists long for sweeping simplicities. The supremacy of communal values, the need to suppress the individual, the fear of diversity or of science, the longing for a respite from change—these find many echoes in socialist thinking, in third world societies, in all those who look hopefully forward to a restful era when we could, thank god, sleep off the binge known as modern times.[4]

Media, Messages, and Myths: Three Fictionists for the Near Future

José Manuel Mota

> In broadcasting your audience is conjectural, but it is an audience of one. Millions may be listening, but each is listening alone, or as a member of a small group, and each has (or ought to have) the feeling that you are speaking to him individually. More than this it is reasonable to assume that your audience is sympathetic or at least interested, for anyone who is bored can promptly switch you off by turning a knob. But though presumably sympathetic, the audience has no power over you.
> —Orwell, "Poetry and the Microphone" (1943)[1]

In a text from the late twenties the German poet and dramatist Bertolt Brecht, speaking of radio broadcasting and what it is (was) being used for, comments acidly, "I look forward to yet another invention by this bourgeoisie who have invented radio: one that will establish forever the contents of radio broadcasting. Forthcoming races could then see with astonishment how a caste which made possible for themselves to tell the whole world what they had to say, at the same time made it possible for the whole world to see that they had nothing to say."[2] If you have nothing to say through the media, the media will be an end in themselves: the McLuhanish maxim is here anticipated and disenchantedly demystified. From this ascertainment Brecht proceeds with the proposal of transforming broadcasting from a means of distribution into a means of communication. Instead of minority-owned, ruling-class-controlled radio stations acting as suppliers of dominant ideology, there should be truly democratic broadcasting, where useful information would be brought to audiences, allowing them not only to listen to the radio, but to speak and be listened to through the medium.[3]

The text where this specific proposal is made is dated 1932, early in the history of broadcasting and quite accurate in describing a situation which has not changed that much in the forty years that followed. Another German, also a leftwing poet, Hans Magnus Enzensberger, is no less pessimistic and radical in analyzing the contemporary situation of "ethereal" mass media. It was in his essay of 1969 that I first found elements that struck me as relevant to my purpose:

> Electronic technology knows no contradiction in principle between transmitter and receiver. Every transistor wireless set is, as far as its manufacture is concerned, also a potential transmitter: it can interfere with other sets through feedback. To develop a means of communication out of a medium of mere distribution involves no technical problem. It is prevented on political grounds, good as well as bad. The technical differentiation between transmitter and receiver mirrors the social division of labor between producers and consumers, which in the mind industry displays itself with peculiar political acuity.

Enzensberger seems to argue that all would be well if a listener has the right to strike back whenever he feels irritated by the radio station he is tuned to. Later on, in his diatribe (which is mainly directed against the ideological weakness of the left in their confrontation with the problem of the media) he mentions *Nineteen Eighty-Four's* mythic patron: George Orwell's understanding of the media is, he argues, both "undialectic and obsolete." It is easy to prove that, in order to control the whole social system (by means of the telescreen), you would need a still more complex system of surveyors;[5] technically, this means that the monitoring system would have to be one order of magnitude wider and more complex than the telescreen system itself. Things being as they are, the only surveillance possible is through probing at random—and then extrapolating (the safety of the universe) on a statistical basis. Of course Enzensberger deliberately misses the literary point, bypassing the allegorical, perhaps even mythical intentions of Orwell concerning totalitarianism. But he is entirely right, and Brecht with him, in establishing the dichotomy between distribution and communication in broadcasting, and in insisting on the democratization of the media through the freest access for audiences to broadcasting facilities. And here enters the great technological flaw of George Orwell's *Nineteen Eighty-Four*. "The telescreen received and transmitted simultaneously." Winston "could be seen as well as heard. There was of course no way of knowing whether you were being watched at any given moment. How often the Thought Police plugged in on any individual wire was guesswork. It was even conceivable that they watched everybody all the time." Anticipating Enzensberger's critique, the text follows: "But *at any rate* they could plug in your wire whenever they wanted" (p. 1, chap. 1; my italics).

Here we find, at best, a lay undertanding of the media: a cable television (wire!) network, having, as such, very restricted functions: musical entertainment: wake-up slimnastics; (war-) news and other announcements read to listeners rather than viewers. There seems to be no understanding of the visual capacity of television: you come across Big Brother's face everywhere—but not so often on the telescreen; apart from the Two Minutes Hate, people do not seem to watch the screen, rather to listen to it. The social function of the telescreen,[6] as far as an audience is concerned, is pure radioish. People are not educated through it (extensively) by visual means: there aren't even live transmissions of the hangings that the Parsons kids are so anxious about. And the BBC had already (before the publication of *Nineteen Eighty-Four*) transmitted the V-Day Parade, Princess Elizabeth's marriage, and the 1948 Olympic Games!

You think, speak, or write of mass media—and you eventually get paranoid. If you use the word "paranoid" at face value—or, at any rate, its current value—of obsession with the idea of being persecuted, then you can endorse this fearful definition by the late Philip K. Dick: "The ultimate in paranoia is not when everybody is against you, but when everything is against you. Instead of 'my boss is plotting against me' it would be 'My boss's phone is plotting against me.'"[7] In this sense, Orwell's "paranoid" obsession with totalitarianism does not encompass the media problem, which is dealt with clumsily and without foresight. What the two German theorists claim—rightly, it seems to me—is that, as far as communications are concerned, a two-way flow is desirable, nay, a necessary condition for a democratic functioning of mass media, an interactive structure as proposed by Raymond Williams.[8] This purported bi-directionality works here as "my boss's phone": in a way, the thoroughness and internal logic typical of paranoid thought, which we find in the writings of Emmanuel Goldstein and, later, in the teachings of O'Brien, does not cover the other facet of depicted reality which is my concern here. And Orwell himself was a media man, he knew what it meant to have an audience, what it was like to make propaganda—even subtle, but nonetheless unashamedly colonialist propaganda: simply read *all* of his "Poetry and the Microphone," from where I took my epigraph. The impossibility of switching off the telescreen is explained in that quote. But what about "having no power over you," if you can answer back?

Let *Nineteen Eighty-Four* remain, then, as a tale of the near future with the professed intention of a political warning. Near future fictions need not be warnings or prophecies: they project the worries of the present in a less metaphoric way, perhaps, than a tale of a galactic empire (or a historical novel for that matter). Nonetheless, in spite of that greater transparency, the fictional veil acts in the same manner; the fantastic element, being mixed with more real-life features from our own time makes it easier, on the one hand, for the reader to sense the strangeness in a broadly familiar world, referred to in his own terms of social cognition, and, on the other hand, to draw the line between the acceptable and the nonacceptable in terms of empirical realism.[9]

If an author chooses the near future as scenery for his plot, and if he does it as a reaction to so many distant future fictions, then the near future may act as a merely formal device. If he does it as a warning, he will most probably become a pedantic bore, who, against his will, invokes the status of prophet—and in doing so, makes his extrapolations all the more subject to extrinsic criticism. Orwell does this—even if he were not a science-fiction author, he still bores.[10] Ballard does not: his near future is no mere formal device (we would call that a "generic" near future). It is indeed a reaction, but as a modality of inner space it both allows for metaphorized poetic readings of the acknowledged polysemy of the discourse and a textual reading of the described universe that makes up for the sense of wonder conventionally expected of science fiction.

J. G. Ballard in British science fiction and Philip K. Dick in American can be said to be responsible for the foremost examples of this subgenre in our time, if not the modern classics of near future fiction.[11] Do these authors have a more reasonable understanding of mass media than Orwell? Are mass media crucial to their fictions, as the telescreen is to *Nineteen Eighty-Four*? Do their ways of dealing with mass media reflect persona, or rather cultural trends or features, British versus American? Any conclusion would be a distorted argument, but so are they all.

Philip K. Dick's work is obviously pervaded with references to mass media. And, in his more paranoid stories, both means and two ends may be after you: boss, phone/medium, message. And all of these—medium and message and boss—will massage you as well. Most of all in *Ubik* (1969) there is the boss, Runciter; there is the medium, TV, radio and tele(vid)phone; and all the messages from Ubik (a bossing medium, a message password) and others. Advertising erects itself as a mass medium:[12] through advertising you can see the nature of our consumerism (*Ubik* as "the theological super-ad . . . confirming the strange identification of religion and capitalist consumerism"[13].

In a communicative process the emitter is the first instance. In Dick's conventional media situations, this is mostly an entertainer or disc jockey. He may also be a robot, or an actor, as are, respectively, the ever-on-the-air Buster Friendly and his counterpart in religion, the prophet Mercer, in *Do Androids Dream of Electric Sheep?* (1968), turning the communicative scheme into something prearranged by You-know-not-who (or perhaps you do!). Jason Taverner, the leading character in *Flow My Tears, the Policeman Said* (1974) is nonetheless revealed in his intrinsic emptiness, his sterile egoism and neutral role in the main drama of the novel, which is the drama of Alys and Felix Buckman. The only positive entertainer I can find in Dick is an entertainer malgré lui, trapped forever in his capsule: the astronaut Dangerfield, in *Dr. Bloodmoney* (1965). Alone, he is the subversion of the network of disc jockeys around the colonized planets mentioned in *The Three Stigmata of Palmer Eldritch* (1964). In this mood, Alan Faine, the one who comes to meet Barney, acts as a secret agent of Bullero and even spies on Barney's and Anne's lovemaking. "The feeling that (the announcer/entertainer is) speaking to you individually" turns into the feeling that you are being scanned by him, that he will expose you to others, or abandon you. Once more, this ill treatment of the listener by the entertainer has its counterpart in *Dr. Bloodmoney*'s Dangerfield, who, after being himself bullied around by Hoppy, willingly undergoes psychotherapy. The unique, two-way, telephonic relationship between him and Dr.

Stockstill becomes predominantly and ironically one way when people listen mainly to his free-association talk. And while the request program has been demystified, the phone-in is really made to help people on both ends of the line, becoming the prototype of the intercommunicative situation.

Dick's worlds show us the totalitarian capitalist state at work. Here the Big Brother, pervasive, sadistic, destructive, is the capitalist.[14] Instead of blaring out an intoxicating ideology, Dick's Big Brothers *sell* an ideological toxin: any sort of drug that distorts reality and/or the perception of reality. Life being drab, it is illusion that makes it bearable. But while in Airstrip One you had to fabricate ideological propaganda everyday just to keep things going, even with the excuse of there being a war on,[15] drugs and other commodities, being addictive,[16] go on by themselves. Propaganda in Dick's world is directed against competing capitalists. The totalitarianism and hierarchization of the Three Power Earth in *Nineteen Eighty-Four* appears now in the shape of the feudal relationship between the capitalist and his employees, to whom he gives protection in exchange for fealty. "This process towards the instauration of a neo-feudal post-bourgeois system," to use the words of Gérard Klein,[17] seems to be assumed by Dick from the very beginning: it is the concept of *Solar Lottery* (1955), of *The Three Stigmata of Palmer Eldritch* (1964), and, when Dick enters his "mystical phase," of *A Scanner Darkly* (1977).[18]

The fundamental dishonesty and mischievousness of the capitalist reveals itself in still another of his products: the android.[19] In *The Simulacra* (1964) government and a private corporation join to defraud the nation: the President of the United States is a simulacrum, the glamorous matriarchal First Lady is an actress.[20] Through androids or show-biz people, with drugs and advertising, Big Brother becomes the Big Boss. And the natural opponents (as far as the fictional structure is concerned) are people who are not capitalists, who fight downright consumerism and industrialism: those who go in for craftmanship; repairmen, pet-lovers; small rebellious executives—like Winston Smith, who adopts the craftsmanship of writing a diary when nobody writes even letters any more, who repairs the Parsons' waterpipes, who becomes fond, if not of an animal, at least of a glass paperweight. Robert Plank argues beautifully that the paperweights of both Winston Smith and Charles Foster Kane are symbols of lost childhood:[21] I believe there is a similar nostalgia in Dick's heroes and their "precious artifacts."

In all these fictions the communications situation and the mass media system at large are explored to the point of becoming metaphors for the world. Since the material function of the communications situation is the production of signs, and signs are mere substitutes for the real thing, androids, simulacra and drugs can be understood as parts of the communication system set up in capitalist society. In a world where everything is sold, signs become commodities, and commodities are emitted as signs are sold. The capitalist sells images: commercial advertisements; entertainment programs where there are no entertainers, just simulacra; drugs that addict from the first dose; androids that can be taken for real people. Those who in some way are conscious of the fraud are sure to become paranoid. And once more, "my boss's phone is plotting against me": the medium/message will chase you to the end of any time or any place,[22] and you feel the Big Boss (yours or someone else's), the Big Brother, God, the Authority and Father Figure lurking behind everything. All messages are false: so, there is no message. This lack of truth, which is the lack of a valid content, gives the "message," reified in the sign, an index function (indicial character): it stands not for its alleged meaning, but for its emitter. This, however, is not signifying, but manifesting: the drug, the android, the commercial advertisement, all manifest their dispenser, their maker, they are their god's ubiquity. And if God is (nearly) everywhere, there is no point in sinning out of his sight. The telescreen can be done without. The shift to gnosticism in Dick's later work accompanies these views, as drugs are seen as a mystical experience and God is still a delusion. This seems to allow us to generalize, from the identification of religion and consumerism in *Ubik*, to Dick's other novels.[23]

If we turn now to Ballard's "inner space," which did not appear in the beginning so notoriously illustrated with metaphorical or real communicative devices, we must start by taking into account his initial reaction against "the literature of technological optimism, born in America in the twenties."[24] This reaction is radical: he was the first to subvert the British tradition of the disaster novel by giving his heroes a defeatism that made him very unpopular with his American editors. Estrangement operates here by will of the hero and/or narrator, and becomes his way of knowing and of projecting his self by means of a cognition which transmogrifies the landscape and determines the action. The plot acquires, then, in most novels and longer stories, its typical spiraling structure, as though slowly funneling towards a whirlpool where the water is least clear.

Centered in these vortices of the mind, Ballard's stories make no great fuss about communication as a technological device. In a world where people isolate themselves, where you cannot run away "for there is never anywhere to go but in" (Doris Lessing), a universe of derelictions, the technical inventions used by the industries of mass communications cannot have their original role. That explains why Ballard selects as motif the communications satellite Echo, which he puts to several mythical uses, none of which is the open denunciation of the evils of manipulated information or of the alienating character of its "content." As conveyors of information, the Echo orbiters are, first of all, misread because they are directly inscribed in the observed landscape: their meaning turned inside out, they are exposed as objects for which there is no justification per se.[25] The Echo satellite in "A Question of Re-entry" (1963) is totally outside its natural setting: for the Nambiquara Indians it is a messiah, a god announced to them by Ryker the Baptist. A messianic religion is not the same as cannibalistic god-eating; the purity of the Indians had been soiled by Ryker; "By using the Echo satellite [he] had brought the twentieth century and its projects into the heart of the Amazonian deep, transforming the Indians into a community of superstitious and materialistic sightseers, their whole culture oriented around the mythical god of the puppet star." For Ryker, who has fled from the civilization into the Mato Grosso, is another failed "Mistah Kurz" figure, whose "futile attempts to identify himself with the forest" reveal him as a narcissus (see his many-mirrored dresser!)—as unnecessary as his mythic counterpart Echo.[26]

Ballard does not deny that "the surrealist influence applies especially to [his] work before *The Atrocity Exhibition*,"[27] and has said elsewhere that it was then that he "began to make direct references to the Pop Artists."[28] Those condensed novels of the mid- and late-sixties have brought about a new emphasis on urban and technical civilization and its myths; if this concern accounts for the new influence of Pop Art, the fact is that only since then does Ballard write as Dali had painted, "split[ting] the elements of reality and assembl[ing] them to constitute a kind of Freudian landscape."[29] This new style derives from the literary prophet of Surrealism, Lautréamont; *The Atrocity Exhibition* (1970) and *Crash* (1973) teem with *rencontres fortuites* of the sewing machines and umbrellas of our uneasy late twentieth century, copulations of "the new sexuality borne from a perverse technology" (*Crash*, chap. 1).

His Vermilion Sands vision of the near future as a global village of vacationists, or "country-club paradise,"[30] can be best understood through the following words of Enzensberger: "Other, more recent branches of the [mind] industry still remain largely unexplored: fashion and industrial design, the propagation of established religions and of esoteric cults, opinion polls, simulation and, last but not least, *tourism*, which can be considered as a mass medium in its own right" (my italics).[31] A couple of lines below, the editor of *Kursbuch* mentions the industrialization of education: "the language laboratory and closed circuit TV" (he forgets the computer but says nevertheless that "in the process, education will become a mass medium, the most powerful of all, and a million dollar business"). Enzensberger may be, for the sake of argument, giving mass media and the "mind industry" too similar and too general a meaning, but his model noticeably shares the discontent of Ivan Illich with "non-convivial" trends in the civilization of continual growth: mass media (current sense), education, transportation. Ryker's question about the "real reasons" for the moon trips,[32] is echoed in Ivan Illich's following words: "If a moon vehicle can be designed so can the demand of going to the moon. Not to go where one can go would be subversive. . . . The state of mind of the modern city-dweller appears in the mythical tradition only under the image of Hell: Sisyphus . . . Tantalus."[33] Tourism, transportation, broadcasting at large, computers and the like: all are facets of the "mind industry" of Enzensberger, to Illich all are distorted in their potential conviviality, and, in Ballard's fiction, they become mythically ambiguous topoi, such as tourism in derelict resorts, fool's errands, and all sorts of funfair techniques from fireworks to holograms and ICBMs in the hands of wilful showmen.[34]

In *Hello America* (1981), for example, the robots of the Presidents and the singers, or the holograms of John Wayne and Charles Manson, have much the same semiotic function as Dick's simulacra, indeed, for that matter, as the stunts in *Crash*. The vicariousness of the media for the real persons and things is obviously destructive (e.g., in "The Sound Sweep" [1960] or "Studio 5, the Stars" [1960]). But the emphasis here is not on the institutional fake, as in Dick, but on the mythical relevance of the images transmitted and/or built by the media. And the growing obsession with violence, which has turned his heroes from passive, death-seeking victims into quasi-maniac theoreticians or practitioners of sadistic fantasies, expresses itself not only in the slow motion and closeup techniques,[35] but also in the growing number of characters and the abundance of short chapters, even in the replacement of an imagined Vermilion Sands by the "real" Shepperton of "the enormous novel we live in," a reality whose invention is said to be "the writer's task."[36]

The threat to the established world, which in the beginning came from wind or drought, the external revenge of a Jungian nature, now comes solely from that established world itself: from the highways, the president, the movie-star killers, the apartment blocks. The disaster novel has been turned inside out, and divested of those nostalgic potentialities of bourgeois robinsonade still found in a classic like *The Day of the Triffids*, so as to reveal the autonomous dynamics of a diseased, yet fascinating, modern world.[37] In a way, one can speak of a shift of perspective from the Marlowes to the Kurtzes, to use once more the Conradian frame of reference. Where else is the heart of darkness, but within?

Ballard appears, then, as the conspicuous myth maker of contemporary science fiction. He does consciously what Orwell did involuntarily, when he made the wrong choice about the title of his novel, and, by that choice, allowed a date to become a myth. Philip K. Dick, on the other hand, found an inner space version for the Orwellian nightmare: long before Ingsoc, Big Brother will be among us, as a corollary of free competition and technological sophistication. And all these fictions bear testimony to this same world. A world where the telescreen, the not-so-hidden camera spies on shoplifters in supermarkets, or on speed limit breakers on highways, or on sneak attacks on military satellites; and where, instead of novel-writing machines, we have the feverish activities of cable-TV industrialists; a world which, after all, vindicates the sombre vision of the "tory anarchist" who first mythified the near future.

Part 2
Orwell: An Interim Report

Coming Up on 1984

Frederik Pohl

The year 1984 suffered greatly from some really bad advance publicity. The source of the publicity, of course, is George Orwell's novel of
the same name.

What Orwell did in the way of making that year a household-
term, the book did for Orwell. To be sure, he was already well
known. It was the novel just before *Nineteen Eighty-Four, Animal
Farm*, that transformed Orwell from a fairly well known local writer
to a world figure. But *Nineteen Eighty-Four* greatly magnified his
renown, and surely has had a more lasting effect both on Orwell's
fame and on the world itself. It was also the last book he wrote. And,
I think, it was very close to being his worst.

I know that this view is not widely shared. *Nineteen Eighty-Four*
is legendary. It is possible that it is the most famous novel published
in the twentieth century. There are sensible people who believe that
the reasons we have been spared the emergence of a real-life
"1984"—i.e., a soul-deadening and unchallengeable dictatorship—is
that we had the example of the novel, *Nineteen Eighty-Four*, to warn
us off. There may be some truth to that, at least to the extent that
terms like Newspeak and Big Brother have kept such dangers alive in
the public consciousness by becoming standard epithets of political
invective. If this is so, then *Nineteen Eighty-Four* can only be judged
by its effectiveness, and literary merit matters no more than it did for,
say, *Uncle Tom's Cabin*.

Yet . . . what a very bad book it is! You can measure it by any
literary standards—grace in the use of language, originality, fulfillment of the author's intentions, internal consistency, or, if you view it
as science fiction, by accuracy of prophecy, reflection of technology
on the human condition, understanding of the impact of science on
society. It fails every test.

What is most queer about this failure is that Orwell's literary gifts were immense. How ironic that fame and vast financial rewards should have come to him, at the very end of his life, from a book that he himself called "a balls-up."

If you do not share my views on this (or Orwell's own), that's all right, but I would like to persuade you to them if I can. Failing that, at least to show you why I think as I do.

"George Orwell" was a man named Eric Blair, poor but well connected, a writer by profession (though seldom a well paid one), a lefty in politics, and a moody, often dour and unhappy man.

He was also a man who guarded his privacy to such an extent that he forbade any biography of him during his lifetime and, by testament, after it (though several have appeared). He had, as any psychological counselor would tell him now, a rather poor self-image. Writing of his own perception of himself as a schoolboy, he said, "I had no money, I was weak, I was ugly, I was unpopular, I had a chronic cough, I was cowardly, I smelt. . . . The conviction that it was not *possible* for me to be a success went deep enough to influence my actions far into my adult life."

Not all of that was fantasy. He did cough; he was poor; he was not popular; it may even have been so that he smelt, then and later. He continued to think that he gave off an offensive odor until his death, and that may have been true—at least toward the end of his life, when, says William Empson, "The truth is [Orwell] stank, and evidently knew it—well, his wife talked to mine about it quite frankly. . . . It was the rotten lungs that you could smell, not at once but increasingly as the evening wore on, in a confined room; a sweetish smell of decay."

And, of course, his prophetic vision was for once clear. A success he was not, at least in terms of money or fame, until almost his last years. His average earnings as a writer in the 1930s came to about three pounds a week, most of it in tiny checks for writing reviews and occasional pieces for left-wing periodicals. His early books—which were among his best—received tiny advances, and he never earned them back until *Animal Farm* and *Nineteen Eighty-Four* made anything with his name on it sell. At the age of forty, during World War II, he had to work at a job he hated—as Burma Editor (which he translated as "paid propagandist") for the BBC.

School was an ordeal for him. Adult life was not much better. At the age of nineteen he signed for a tour in the Indian Imperial Police in Burma, enforcing the sahibs' law. "It did not suit me" (he wrote twenty-five years later, in 1947) "and made me hate imperialism." It also made him, after resigning the service and returning to London, write *Burmese Days*.

There is a scene in *Burmese Days* in which the hero, Ellis, is walking along a road carrying a cane. Five Burmese students, "jeering like a row of yellow images," try to provoke him. There is an exchange of words, and then, "There was about a second during which Ellis did not know what he was doing. In that second he hit out with all his strength, and the cane landed, crack! right across the boy's eyes."

It is a moving scene. It is taken from life, and "Ellis" was Orwell himself. Maung Htin Aung, who was a student on the actual scene, says a boy accidentally bumped Orwell on the steps of the train station in Rangoon; Orwell fell, got up in a rage "and raised the heavy cane which he was carrying, to hit the boy on the head, but checked himself, and struck him on the back instead."

There is no doubt that Orwell felt guilt for enforcing imperial law on the Burmese, and it is a reasonable speculation that he did not think writing a novel was expiation enough. For when he left Burma he did not at once settle down. Instead he went to Paris and lived on almost nothing while he tried some unsuccessful writing. (All of it he later destroyed.) Then he plunged himself into the life of the poorest people. Out of that came what I think to be his greatest book, *Down and Out in Paris and London*, and it was at that time that he decided, never to change during his life, that he was a socialist.

Both *Burmese Days* and *Down and Out in Paris and London* were published. They did not sell well, but they were actual books, in print, reviewed by critics, available in libraries, read by strangers; Orwell's literary career was launched. It did not, however, prosper.

All told, Orwell published nine unitary books, and that's all. There were five early novels (assuming you consider *Down and Out* a novel rather than loosely fictionalized reportage): *Down and Out in Paris and London*; *Burmese Days*; *A Clergyman's Daughter*; *Keep the Aspidistra Flying*; and *Coming Up for Air*. Then two nonfiction books, both reportage, but not (any more than any other reportage) fictionalized: *The Road to Wigan Pier* and *Homage to Catalonia*. And the final two immense commercial and media successes: *Animal Farm* and *Nineteen Eighty-Four*.

What Orwell's first seven books have in common is that they are about things he had seen with his own eyes, in places where he had been, viewed through characters who feel what he felt. He saw a lot, and he felt strongly. In fact, every one of his books, and many of his shorter pieces, is a cry of pain. The pain in the first five novels is the agony of poverty and oppression by the rich; the same theme is in *The Road to Wigan Pier*. It is only in his last books that his theme becomes wholly political.

I wish I thought I could impose on your patience long enough to speak about each of the books in detail—especially the earlier ones, because I think among them is Orwell's strongest claim to greatness. There is no more searing account—not even in Dostoevsky, or in Upton Sinclair's *Jungle*, which Orwell read without much admiring— of the dehumanization of the poor than *Down and Out in Paris and London*. And each one of the other books has its special merits, either on its own or as a rite of passage in the development of George Orwell as a writer.

But what we are talking about when we talk about Orwell is really *Nineteen Eighty-Four*, and, with Herculean effort, I will turn from his early novels, and even *The Road to Wigan Pier*, to the first of his really political books, the one that came out of his brief service with the anarchist loyalist forces in the Spanish Civil War, *Homage to Catalonia*. It is not even that book that I feel free to discuss here— fascinating though it is—but only the part that that book played in his development, for it was the one in which rage against the Bolshevik communists of Joseph Stalin became equally incandescent with the constant and continuing rage against the capitalist oppressors . . . and also the one which led to his break with his publisher, Victor Gollancz.

Gollancz was my own primary English publisher for the last few years of his life. I knew him only slightly, though I have had the help of longtime associates to help piece together what went wrong between him and Orwell. There was more, I think, than a political difference.

It is my opinion that part of Orwell's difficulty in getting along with Victor Gollancz lay in the fact that Gollancz was a Jew. I don't mean that Orwell was a thoroughgoing anti-Semite. He certainly did not think of himself as one, but there is every indication that at bottom he thought Jews, blacks, and Catholics were—how can you say it?—less fully human, at least, than his own kind. When he refers casually to a Catholic in a letter, it is as "D. B. Wyndham Lewis, a stinking RC." In "Hop-Picking," he says there was no hope of forming a union "for about half the pickers are women and gypsies and are too stupid to see the advantages of it." In the same essay, almost all the persons he runs into are given names, except for "a little Liverpool Jew of eighteen, a thorough gutter-snipe," who is referred to only as "the Jew."

Publicly, however, he deplored anti-Semitism in England, particularly among the working classes. There was gossip that Jews took all the places in the best air-raid shelters during the war, and pushed to the head of ration lines. He spoke out against the rumor and then, to make sure, went around to the shelters and the lines himself to study the features of offenders and see how many he could identify as Jewish. (His conclusion: Slightly more than the proportion of Jews in England would justify, but not by much.) When he came to write *Nineteen Eighty-Four* and had his Trotsky-figure Emmanuel Goldstein list the evil practices of the period just after 1930, anti-Semitism was not among them, although one of the regimes he was discussing was Nazi Germany. When Orwell reviewed *Mein Kampf* in *New English Weekly* in 1940, he was able to say, "I should like to put it on the record that I have never been able to dislike Hitler. . . . The fact is that there is something deeply appealing about him. One feels it again when one sees his photographs. . . . It is a pathetic, dog-like face, the face of a man suffering under intolerable wrongs. In a rather more manly way it reproduces the expression of innumerable pictures of Christ crucified."

In any case, once Orwell came back from Spain the irritations between him and Victor Gollancz became terminal. By contract, Orwell was obligated to show *Homage to Catalonia* to Gollancz. He did.

Orwell must have known that Victor Gollancz would not publish a work that described the Communists as criminals and murderers, but he went through the motions of offering it. Ultimately it was published elsewhere. It was the last real book (as distinct from a collection of essays) that Orwell wrote for five years, until *Animal Farm*.

Animal Farm was easy enough to write, and quick: less than three months. Finding a publisher for it was harder and longer. The book was owed to Victor Gollancz by contract, but Gollancz could not possibly, by conviction, publish so inimical an attack on the Soviet Union, as Orwell knew. Gollancz turned it down; then Jonathan Cape turned it down; then Faber & Faber turned it down. Orwell submitted it to Secker and Warburg as a last hope in July 1944, but at the same time he wrote a friend that if Warburg didn't take it, "I am not going to tout it round further publishers, which wastes time & may lead to nothing, but shall publish it myself as a pamphlet at 2/–. I have already arranged to do so & have got the necessary financial backing." Warburg's acceptance saved him that trouble.

Animal Farm was published in England on 17 August 1945, and fame and fortune began to pour down on George Orwell.

Animal Farm is a savage political fable. Its target is the Soviet Union of Joseph Stalin. It is not aimed at socialism—certainly not at small *d*, big *S* democratic Socialism—and Orwell meant that to be perfectly clear. Farmer Jones and all the other human beings in the story (that is, the capitalists) are entirely as evil as Napoleon and Squealer and all the other Stalin-pigs. In fact, the end of the story shows that they are no longer distinguishable. The pigs have learned to drink, smoke, talk, and walk on their hind legs, and the humans have come to look like pigs. There is only one hero in *Animal Farm*, and that is the great horse Boxer, whose response to every wickedness or tragedy is "I will work harder."

There is a curiosity there, and irony. Surely Orwell meant Boxer to stand for the honest proletarian (even democratic socialist) who always attempts to be noble and is always betrayed. But did Orwell also mean him to echo that other hero of socialist agitprop literature who always responded to the same stimuli with the precise same words? The character is Jurgis Rudkus; the novel is Upton Sinclair's *Jungle*.

That is the curiosity. The irony is more complicated. Sinclair meant *The Jungle* as a tract for socialism. When it was taken only as an exposé of meat-packing in Chicago he was astonished and annoyed. It was even taken so by Orwell, it seems, for when Orwell reviewed the Sinclair book he could only say that it was "good if you like facts."

Orwell never doubted democratic socialism. Even while he was writing *Animal Farm*, he was also writing, in his regular column for the *Tribune*, "Socialists don't claim to be able to make the world perfect; they claim to be able to make it better. . . . It is all summed up in Marx's saying that after Socialism has arrived, human history can begin." But his publisher's own report on *Animal Farm* said, "This I take to be a deliberate and sadistic attack on socialism and socialist parties generally." Reviewers saw it the same way, particularly in America. Orwell's intention was understood no better than he had understood Sinclair's, and he fumed.

The American edition was slow in coming; twelve publishers turned it down before it found a home. (One because "animal stories don't sell well in America.") But the success, if slow, was vast. Secker and Warburg had printed 4,500 copies of the first English edition; they sold out at once, and as soon as possible (not very soon because of postwar economic problems) they printed another 10,000, which went almost as fast. In America, the Book-of-the-Month Club alone sold half a million copies. Orwell's words might be misunderstood, but they were being read, and the money rolled in.

Yet the success, if vast, was slow. It relieved Orwell for the first time in his life of frantic money worries, but it was too late to make up for years of poverty. His health had been irreparably harmed. His wife, the former Eileen O'Shaughnessy, an attractive and loyal psychotherapist whom he had married young and who stuck to him through the trying times, did not live to see the rewards. She needed a hysterectomy. Orwell opposed it on shadowy grounds, perhaps because he had a hope for children, perhaps because he did not think her condition really serious; Eileen delayed the operation, apparently, because she did not wish to spend the money. Or didn't think Orwell did. When Orwell was briefly out of the country, between the acceptance of *Animal Farm* and its first publication, she went in for the operation, on the cheap. She died under the anesthesia.

For the first time in his life Orwell was solvent and famous. But his life had only a few years left to go.

Angry, unsettled, sick, alone—those are the words that seem best to fit Orwell for the period just after *Animal Farm* and Eileen's death. He spent his time trying to set the record straight on what he really meant by his book . . . on writing furious polemics . . . on trying to find another wife. He and Eileen had adopted a four-week-old boy, Richard, and it was perhaps to find a mother for the child as well as a wife for himself that he began to propose to other women quite soon. Sometimes his courtship was arrogant and even brutal—one of the women he approached while drunk thought he came close to rape—sometimes humble, even wry. "What I am really asking you," he wrote one, "is whether you would like to be the widow of a literary man." And amid all that he began to write his last, and most famous, book, *Nineteen Eighty-Four*.

One of the things wrong with literary criticism is that familiarity actually does breed contempt. The more you know about a writer, so that you see behind the mystic veil which hides the sometimes grubby process of creation, the less you are inclined to regard him as semi-divine. The best part of any writer is in his work. As well, reading any writer's lesser works—the ones that are generally forgotten—dilutes the impact of the greater ones that attracted you to the writer in the first place. And even the greatest of works show flaws on the second and nth readings that weren't apparent on the first. For these reasons, scholarship can often diminish its subject. I don't doubt that these processes have been operating on my opinion of Orwell.

What saves us all, though, is that if we are very lucky the same processes of research, or even simple rereading, can often find new values missed the first time around, or not detectable without some knowledge of background and sources. Good books tend to get better as you know them better. Bad books get worse; and the most damaging thing I know about George Orwell's *Nineteen Eighty-Four* is that if you look at it closely it simply falls apart in you hands. For it is a very badly written book.

I'm not talking about style—Orwell is not a person one reads for literary style in any case. What destroys *Nineteen Eighty-Four* is that it is riddled with self-contradictions and failures of logic; it does not fulfill Orwell's purpose, as he discribes his purpose himself; it betrays a failure to understand what was really going on in the world, devastating in what is meant to be a revelatory and pointed cautionary satire; and (although this is less important) it is a thoroughly unoriginal work, in that almost everything it says has been said before—often by Orwell himself.

Masterpieces don't have to follow rules. Masterpieces are sui generis. They create the rules for others to follow. If you think of *Nineteen Eighty-Four* as a masterpiece you can say, as Harold Berger does, "It stands so central in the history of the genre that previous dystopias are seemingly but anticipations and later ones variations of Orwell's definitive hell." Or you can exempt *Nineteen Eighty-Four* from conventional standards on other grounds. You can assign it to that special class of literature called "socialist agitprop"—short for agitation/propaganda—which has its own rules. Agitprop does not attempt to comply with conventional literary standards. What is important in agitprop is the degree to which it moves its audience in the direction the author intends.

Orwell's primary intention in writing *Nineteen Eighty-Four* was clearly to whip up public (and vent his own) anger and loathing against the Bolshevik regime of Joseph Stalin in the USSR. The objective was the same as in *Animal Farm* before it, and in *Nineteen Eighty-Four* Orwell discarded the talking animals for realism. *Animal Farm* can be read as a children's story; *Nineteen Eighty-Four* cannot. At the same time, Orwell wholly supported the cause of small *d*, big *S* democratic Socialisms, and not only expected, but devoutly desired, a socialist revolution. So he had a tightrope to walk, and knew it was chancy. Long before he began either novel he wrote, "It is an unfortunate fact that any hostile criticism of the present Russian regime is liable to be taken as propaganda *against Socialism*." When the books were in print he discovered that exactly that had happened, and so spent a lot of time trying to correct the misreadings: "My recent novel in NOT intended as an attack on Socialism or on the British Labour Party (of which I am a supporter) but as a show-up of the perversions to which a centralised economy is liable." It didn't help. Overwhelmingly *Nineteen Eighty-Four* and *Animal Farm* before it were taken as propaganda *against socialism*, to repeat Orwell's own emphasis; and so the propaganda splattered beyond its target to smear what Orwell cherished. However effective it was, the effect was not what he intended. As to whether *Nineteen Eighty-Four* is a "definitive" masterpiece . . . well, let's look at the book itself.

The central character is Winston Smith. He works for the Ministry of Truth, and his function is to rewrite history to make it conform to the party line of the moment. The world is divided into three great superpowers, incessantly engaged in a sort of desultory war among themselves. Alliances change; and, if yesterday's ally becomes today's enemy, Smith has to search out old newpaper files and alter them to show that that was the enemy all along. If a high official becomes a "non-person" his task is to remove all references to him, especially favorable ones.

It is this "gimmick" in *Nineteen Eighty-Four*, I think, that struck most readers as fresh and exciting. It wasn't original with Orwell. It comes verbatim from Arthur Koestler's *Darkness at Noon* in which the old Bolshevik Rubashov, about to be sacrificed in a purge, remarks jokingly to his assistant, Arlova, "that the only thing left to be done was to publish a new and revised edition of the back numbers of all newspapers." (There was no doubt that Orwell knew both the book and its author—in fact, Koestler became perhaps Orwell's closest friend.) In *Darkness at Noon* the remark was meant to be jocular, but Orwell didn't see it as a joke. He didn't see jokes very well, except as weapons, and in this particular joke he found the weapon that became *Nineteen Eighty-Four*.

The world in which Winston Smith lives is a soul-destroying tyranny:

> It is a stifling, stultifying world in which to live. It is a world in which every word and every thought is censored. . . . [E]ven friendship can hardly exist when every . . . man is a cog in the wheels of despotism. Free speech is unthinkable. All other kinds of freedom are permitted. You are free to be a drunkard, an idler, a coward, a backbiter . . . ; but you are not free to think for yourself. Your opinion on every subject of any conceivable importance is dictated for you.

It has features that appall us, like the Two Minutes Hate in which a Party agitator pumps everyone up to fury: "It was a voice that sounded as if it could go on for a fortnight without stopping. It's a ghastly thing, really, to have a sort of human barrel-organ shooting propaganda at you by the hour. The same thing over and over again. Hate, hate, hate. Let's all get together and have a good hate. Over and over. It gives you the feeling that something has got inside your skull and is hammering down on your brain."

Yet what makes Winston Smith dissatisfied is cloudy. It is not the work he does that troubles him. In fact, he rather enjoys it, though he can't help wondering if revising old newspaper stories so that "history" will conform to what the Party wants it to show is really a good thing. It is not, particularly, the depressing physical environment: the elevators don't work, food is miserable, the only drink is vile synthetic gin, and razor blades are unobtainable, but Smith is so used to these things that they are hardly noticed. He is disturbed little more by the fact that sex is forbidden him, and privacy does not exist, not to speak of the always-present expectation that a slip may cause him to be dragged off to the basements of the Ministry of Love to be beaten, tortured, and probably shot. He sleepwalks through a life of vague discontent until a woman, Julia, seduces him. He seduces her, in turn—this time politically; they both become rebels. They seek out O'Brien, a member of the Inner Party, and tell him they are revolutionaries—they choose O'Brien to confide in for no better reason than that a passing flash of expression makes them think he, too, is discontented. Of course, O'Brien is a highranking member of the Thought Police. Smith and Julia are captured and tortured to the point where they betray each other.

Attempting to analyze a fable like *Nineteen Eighty-Four* is not much more useful than trying to parse a poem. Listing contradictions won't change anyone's opinion. The only flaws that matter are the ones that spoil the fable, and contradictions that one doesn't notice can't spoil it.

But how many of these there are in *Nineteen Eighty-Four*! When Winston Smith begins his diary he writes the date "April 6th, 1984," and then muses that he isn't really sure it *is* 1984: "It was never possible nowadays to pin down any date within a year or two." Really? But a few pages later we find that the *Times* is still being published every day, dated with month, day, and year. How can he not know what year it is? Again: We are told "Oceania has no capital." But a capital is only the place where the bureaus of government are built, and we already know that all four Ministries—Truth, Love, Plenty, and Peace—are in London; so how can it have no capital? Again: We are told "the Party [is] not a hereditary body" and admission to it "is by examination, taken at the age of sixteen." But we are told on the same page, "Proletarians, in practice, are not allowed to graduate into the Party," and there is no sign, there or anywhere else, of children of Party members who have failed the sixteen-plus among the proles. (In fact, elsewhere we are shown a clear progression from youngest childhood on, beginning with the tiny "spies.") Again: Smith wistfully regrets that he allowed a slip of paper that proved history had been falsified to pass into the destructor; if only he had saved it—but every document he handles, every working day, is exactly such proof; putting these proofs into the destructor is what he does for a living. So why need he lack proof?

Of course, writers often make slips, and copyeditors sometimes fail to flag them—but rarely has any author so often contradicted himself in the fundamental arguments of his work as Orwell did in *Nineteen Eighty-Four*.

As to originality, I believe that every element in *Nineteen Eighty-Four* that cannot be shown to come from someone else's work came from Orwell himself. In that connection, I must confess to having played a small trick. The paragraph a page or so earlier which so well describes the "stifling, stultifying world" of *Nineteen Eighty-Four* does not come from *Nineteen Eighty-Four*; it is taken from *Burmese Days*, and the world it describes is the pukka-sahib society of which Orwell was a part. The quoted paragraph after it, so apt to *Nineteen Eighty-Four*'s Two Minutes Hate is again not from *Nineteen Eighty-Four*. It is from *Coming Up for Air*, and the hate-purveyor is actually an anti-Hitler lecturer for the Left Book Club. I have already mentioned Orwell's debt to Koestler for the notion of rewriting old newspapers. The three superpowers dividing up the world Orwell owes to James Burnham. (In February 1945 he wrote in his column, *I Write As I Please*, "Already . . . the world is splitting up into the two or three huge super-states forecast in James Burnham's *Managerial Revolution*.") The rats of Room 101: "If there is one thing I hate worse than another it is a rat running over me in the darkness," Orwell wrote in 1936.

It is tempting to go on listing repetitions, contradictions, and failures of memory, but maybe unnecessary—the author's own views might suffice. Orwell's letter to Roger Senhouse, December 1947, while he was in the process of writing the first draft: "it's a most dreadful mess." To Anthony Powell, November 1948, when the book was just finished: "it's a ghastly mess now, a good idea ruined." To his publisher, F. J. Warburg, after the book had been accepted, December 1948: "it isn't a book I would gamble on for a big sale." To Julian Symons, February 1949: "I ballsed it up rather, partly owing to being so ill while I was writing it." Authors are not always good judges of their own work, but I think here George Orwell was dead on target, and for the right reason. He was sick. In fact, his life was nearly over, and it is rather likely that *Nineteen Eighty-Four* helped to kill him. He stayed doggedly and foolishly with the novel on the remote and primitive island of Jura until he collapsed into bed. Overwork, bad weather, and his never very strong body combined to make the illness terminal. When it was published he had only a year left to live.

So in reading *Nineteen Eighty-Four* one must always remember that what Orwell said was said by a sick man, racing against what he knew to be the end of his health, and must have suspected would be the end of his life. If Orwell had had better health and more time, *Nineteen Eighty-Four* might have been more logical and more lucid— qualities he always strove for. He didn't, and it isn't. It was very widely misunderstood even in its central polemical theme, which even his own publisher took to be a high-temperature blast at socialism of all kinds. When Orwell, still sicker and even closer to death, tried to untangle that particular misreading with a press statement, he achieved only a muddle—had even to send out an amendment to the clarification (and the amendment itself was not very clear). There can be no question about Orwell's political faith. He was a committed socialist from his return from Burma until his death. He never wavered. He longed for the revolution. At least until the actual time of writing *Nineteen Eighty-Four* he even expected it; and sometimes expected it almost any day. *Nineteen Eighty-Four* is not a statement of changed beliefs, only of blighted hope. "If there is hope it lies in the proles," he says. But, "until they become conscious they will never rebel, and until after they have rebelled they cannot become conscious." What Orwell intended is certain, from his own collateral writings and from the text of the book itself; unfortunately, he did not make his intentions clear. There is almost no other writing of Orwell's that can be misread. But in 1947, 1948 and 1949 he was too sick, too exhausted, and too rushed to achieve his customary clarity.

There is no doubt Orwell's main target in *Nineteen Eighty-Four* was Stalin's Russia. He said so explicitly. But it was not his only target. The shabby misery of Airstrip One reflects a lot of postwar Moscow, but even more of postwar England, when the bills for the victorious war all came in and most Britons found themselves rather worse off than they had been during hostilities. And it is not an accident that the currency of Oceania is neither the ruble nor the pound. It is the dollar. T. R. Fyvel, in his valuable memoir, says of Orwell, "He was profoundly afraid of what he saw as a larger, inevitable social change which was simultaneously in progress: the growth of a dehumanized, technological collective life lying ahead, particularly within the big Soviet State in the East, but for that matter also within the State of depersonalized Big Business in the West."

It is likely that the reading of *Nineteen Eighty-Four* as a tract against *all* socialism contributed greatly to its success. The book came out at the precisely perfect moment; the Cold War had just been launched, ex-socialists denouncing the Reds were in a sellers' market. Such powerful advocates of the book as the New York *Daily News* were no more in favor of small *d*, Big *S* democratic Socialism than of any other kind; if they misread Orwell's purpose, it was surely good for Orwell's success that they did. The misreading did not stop in 1948; in 1983, Norman Podhoretz was able to say with a straight face, "I am convinced that if Orwell were alive today, he would be taking his stand with the new-conservatives and against the Left." Well, to be sure, if Orwell were alive today he would be in his eighties and who knows what stands he might be taking? But he isn't alive today. When he was alive, through all of his life to the very end, the Left is where he stood.

Orwell is, in fact, almost archetypical of lefty writers. Left writers, by and large, are absolutely superb at seeing and describing what is wrong with the world. Think of Upton Sinclair's *Jungle*; think of Jack London (a great early influence on Orwell), of H. G. Wells (whose last works are as despairing as Orwell's); think of all the American proletarian writers of the 1920s and 1930s and all the British Fabians of a generation earlier. In this respect, Orwell stands high in a distinguished company.

Left writers, on the other hand, are singularly wrong-headed in their predictions of the future, and here too Orwell stands out. He was wronger than most.

As forecast, *Nineteen Eighty-Four* has failed seriously. But as warning, it has succeeded perhaps far beyond any of Orwell's hopes, and very likely even beyond his desires. He wrote it as agitprop to get us to hate the wickedness of Stalin's Russia; it had exactly that effect on an immense scale. But he did not mean to make us hate socialism, and yet as a contribution to the anticommunist hysteria of the 1950s, to the Cold War, to that state of mind which has led us to define socialist governments as evil, and nonsocialist governments as good (no matter what good things the former do or what murders, tortures, tyrannies, and exploitations occur in the latter) . . . in that way it succeeded tremendously, too, and Orwell would surely not have been pleased.

George Orwell was a conscientious, perceptive, and talented writer. Sometimes, as in *Down and Out in Paris and London* and in many of his essays, he has claim to having been a great one. His mood was tragic, and so was his life. He suffered from the greatest of all tragedies: he got nearly everything he desired, but, always, only when it was too late to mean anything to him. He wanted love, and found it with his first wife, Eileen; but much of their life was marred by separations caused by work or health, and all of it was blighted by poverty. He wanted a child to complete his family, and adopted one—just before Eileen died and the family was destroyed anyway. He wanted to be widely read and widely praised—and was, with *Animal Farm* and *Nineteen Eighty-Four*, but only when his life was almost over. He wanted a wife to replace Eileen—and got one, in his second wife, Sonia, but it was a deathbed marriage. One hundred days later, on 21 January 1950, he hemorrhaged and died.

Orwell was not gifted at expressing love. In his courtship of women, he sometimes amused them with his clumsiness and sometimes frightened them with his violence. He seems to have considered violence one way to express love. In 1944, he wrote to John Middleton Murry, "You may not understand this, but I . . . think that there are times when you can only show your feelings of brotherhood for somebody else by killing him, or trying to." The recollections of those who knew him speak of terrible, slow-motion, drunken fights with fists, sticks, and furniture, and of the slow, methodical destruction of an adder he trapped under his heel on Jura. But he surely felt love, and wanted love. When his closest friend, Arthur Koestler, wrote his obituary for the *Observer*, Koestler said: "The greater the distance from intimacy and the wider the radius of the circle, the more warming became the radiation of this lonely man's great power of love." Lucky for those on the fringes. Unlucky for those at the core.

Unluckiest of all, of course, for Orwell himself. "It is sad and paradoxical," wrote Burnham Beckwith, "that this earnest socialist writer should have achieved recognition as an author, near the end of his life, primarily because two of his satires proved useful as anti-Socialist propaganda."

Perhaps it is only because I so completely agree with Beckwith that I believe that Orwell himself, in those last declining, hopeless weeks before his death, must have thought the same.

So Orwell's year of 1984 has come and gone, and what can we learn from Orwell?

The first lesson is of course to become cynics. That's an easy lesson. Orwell learned it himself, over and over. He learned that, if you put your trust in a party, or a cause, or a state, that trust can be betrayed. Sooner or later, more often that not, it will be.

We can learn that words, even the most beautiful and inspirational of words, can be lies.

This whole subject of lies, and in particular the social and political lies we organize our lives by, is one that has absorbed me for some time; I spoke about it a length in Santa Barbara and elsewhere, and Orwell's vision was always a part of what I had to say. For that much has come true. His Ministry of Peace, which was devoted to its opposite, war, is mirrored in our own Department of Defense. We have no defense. No technological defense, least of all the Star Wars particle-beam satellites, can guarantee that no Russian missile could destroy any one of our cities or all of them, on minutes' warning. This is almost certainly true forever, and is certainly true now; wherefore the proper name for our DOD should be only the Department of Revenge. So the word "defense" is a lie, just as the word "peace" was a lie for Orwell and for ourselves, as long as it means building weapons and deploying troops; and democracy" is a lie when it is applied to many of the countries we call our allies. When Orwell warns us to disbelieve these lies we should listen.

Despairing on his deathbed, Orwell had perhaps little belief left at all. But there is something that can be trusted, and Orwell knew it, at least until he became too sick and angry and defeated to remember it. That is the essential love, decency, and brotherhood that is somewhere in all of us.

Orwell didn't believe in God, but he did believe in that core of goodness. In 1940, in one of his columns, he wrote: "Brotherhood implies a common father. Therefore it is often argued that men can never develop the sense of a community unless they believe in God. The answer is that in a half-conscious way most of them have developed it anyway. Man is not an individual, he is only a cell in an everlasting body, and he is dimly aware of it."

The marvelous part of that is that it's true. However the origin of man took place, whether out of Adam or *A. afarensis*, there was a common parent. So we are all blood relatives, members of the same family, you and I and the Eskimos and the Hottentots; it is from that fact that brotherhood and altruism and an nontheistic Golden Rule can be derived.

That is what I would learn from George Orwell.

O'Brien's Interim Report

George Hay

Nineteen eighty-four is also the year of timestop. In that sense, all years are the year of timestop, 31 December of that year being followed by 1 January 1984, like Fabre's caterpillars. (There was, of course, no such person as Fabre, though caterpillars, for reasons pertaining to the Ministry of Agriculture and Fish, still remain, pending further investigation.) Still remain, similarly, Goldstein and his loathesome followers, whom we have simultaneously to persecute and preserve. Thus, our security forces have to occupy themselves with the regulation of those years outside of 1984 which still exist for us in the Party, though not for those we govern. An intricate system of timetravel policing allows us to vet each of those years. To avoid the temptation of our police by overlarge amounts of dangerous knowledge, only I, O'Brien, am allowed the total overview of all these years: each police unit reports back on one complete year, no more—thus extending into time our normal cell-system.

Limiting police units to policing of one year only of Oldspeak time has, of course, its drawbacks. Notably, it is difficult for these officers, when preparing their reports, to write with an integrated understanding of the errors and confusions they confront. For this reason, I have ensured that, as each officer enters a given year, he is issued a briefing prepared by me. The paper I now read to you constitutes the briefing for 1984 itself—that is, not the real, immutable, and eternal 1984, but the illusory and dangerous 1984 of the Oldspeak calendar. As a further limitation, this particular briefing refers only to science fiction, that being your own area of operation.

Let me start by referring you to page 214 of the Penguin edition of my Handbook for Timestop Police Officers, more popularly entitled *Nineteen Eighty-Four*. This work, in the guise of a work of fiction by George Orwell—an old penname of mine—was issued in Old-speak year 1984, as a disinformation ploy. Were one of my officers to mislay my handbook, as such, where one of Goldstein's mob were to come across it, the results could have been calamitous. By using the Purloined Letter ploy, calling it fiction and flooding the market with it, Goldstein is disarmed in advance. As the mythical Hitler explained before us, the one thing people never will believe is the truth under their own eyes.

But to return to page 214. I quote: "Only the disciplined mind can see reality," and again, "you can become sane." Further, my remarks to Winston Smith as listed on pages 228–29.

> "The earth is as old as we are, no older. How could it be older? Nothing exists except through human consciousness. . . . For certain purposes, of course, that is not true. When we navigate the ocean, or when we predict an eclipse, we often find it convenient to assume that the earth goes round the sun and that the stars are millions upon millions of kilometres away. But what of it? Do you suppose it is beyond us to produce a dual system of astronomy? The stars can be near or distant, according as we need them. Do you suppose our mathematicians are unequal to that? Have you forgotten doublethink? . . . metaphysics is not your strong point. The word that you are trying to think of is solipsism. But you are mistaken. This is not solipsism. Collective solipsism, if you like. But that is a different thing; in fact, the opposite thing."

The successful takeup of the principles I expressed to Winston Smith cannot be better shown than by a quote from the editorial of *Interzone* magazine no. 8, summer 1984 issue. An appeal is being made for a new type of story. "What we're looking for is a fiction that is as radical and hard as the implications of the new technology itself. It will be *radical* SF because it will be critical and investigative, facing up to the science and technology of the present and future as we see them now, rather than as John W. Campbell saw them. At the same time it will be *hard* SF, using the hard-edged language and imagery of technology for imaginative interpretations rather than departures into fantasy. Radical, hard SF; not necessarily future realism, or applied sociology, or breezy tales of technological fixes in an all too familiar vein."

Really, I could hardly have created more obfuscation in less time myself! The beauty of the thing! A story that will be hard-edged without realism and without technology . . . and thrown in for *bonne bouche* the implication that Campbell was neither critical nor radical, had a very fixed view of the future, and understood science as being something "hard." This, about the man whose novel *Uncertainty*, in 1936, described the effect of the Heisenberg uncertainty equations on classical science, and whose fiction under the penname of Don A. Stuart opened onto science fiction the doors of poetry and feeling. *Unerhört!* My own success in supressing the editorials of Campbell over recent decades fades to nothing in comparison with such misdirection. I recently learned with regret that, despite our best efforts, Campbell's correspondence may shortly become available. I can only ask you to exert what pressures you can on the editorial board of *Interzone* so that they may bend their efforts in this direction.

Enough on that. Now for a general briefing on SF. Looking back through Oldspeak years from the time of, say, Jules Verne, you will see that up to the 1930s no real threat exists to our way of life. The science in SF of those days refers practically 100 percent to the so-called Newtonian view of life and the universe. I say, "so-called": the self-suppression of Newton's real views during his lifetime, and the blindness of his followers thereafter, allowed what was laughingly called "the known world" to be governed from his days almost to ours by an entirely mechanistic view. This consists, if I may allow myself the pun, of the idea that this universe is all balls—little, hard billiard balls of molecules, building up into huge balls called suns and planets. That older and most sinister notion that these objects themselves symbolized something else was allowed to quietly lapse, the entire culture having become symbologically illiterate.

Probably the first real threat emerging in the 1930s was from the works of Olaf Stapledon, particularly *Star-Maker*. This threat was not that there could actually be a meaningful god—Stapledon was far too "enlightened" and liberal to be so blunt—but in the incitement to other writers. Fortunately, our American office had by this time taken advantage of Campbell's accession to the editorship of *Astounding Science Fiction*, flooding the world with copies of this and similar magazines to ensure that any burgeoning attempts at all-round thought and philosophical investigation were knocked on the head. Establishment education we could by then discount, it being dominated by the twin reinforcing floods of Marxism and logical positivism, a deluge that could be counted upon to drown out most dissenting voices until well after World War II. Now, you may be surprised that I cite Campbell as being on the side of the ang—er— that is to say, on our side, in view of earlier remarks on his dangerously radical views. Well, you must bear in mind that the man is on record as saying that what he was after was really the encouragement of rigorous thought, and that it was simply an accident that, in these days, such thought was most found in the area of science. Since "science" meant, in the minds of Campbell's public and writers alike, that Newtonian billiard ball world, it was relatively easy for us, judo-fashion, to create the impression that science fiction represented that very world. Indeed, to a large degree, it did. Our problem was to deal with those parts that did not.

There was, for example, general semantics, and then dianetics, with its Big Brother, scientology. Both of these presented very real threats, inasmuch as any serious involvement with them tends to provoke in the student a serious look at the fundamentals of his existence. Fortunately, stateside office proved more than equal to the threat. In each case it sufficed once again to turn the strongest points of these disciplines against themselves. In the case of scientology, all that was called for was an increased belief among its practitioners of the "holiness" of their "cause"; the dissensions that followed tore the whole organization part. It is true that there now remains the danger that those cast into the outer darkness may be free to tell the public what the whole thing is actually about—still, you may count upon me when I say that the matter is in hand. As to general semantics, as originally popularized by A. E. Van Vogt— well, there again, a double bind could be invoked. A study of the subject tends to create in the student an increased tolerance and objectivity. Bravo! All that was needed was to increase this effect— and, lo and behold, the practitioners became so tolerant as to practically fade away. Of late there has been some attempt at a revival. Do not alarm yourselves: Korzybski's "Bible," *Science and Sanity*, is large, thick, and dense; only those who are both well-motivated and intelligent will study it—and how many are there of those? There do exist popularized versions by such as S. I. Hayakawa—but we have ensured that they are not widely available. I see, though, that Van Vogt is preparing a third novel in the *Null-A* series—ah, well, we'll get to that when it comes.

All this while our main offensive in SF has been going ahead, all guns firing. While Jerry Pournelle, Larry Niven, and their supporters have been achieving success in enlisting the support of President Reagan in their Star Wars campaign, Frank Herbert has been mixing science and mysticism to a point where, with any reasonable luck, the general public will have the one totally confused with the other. Such confusion, I need hardly say, is an essential preliminary to the total elimination of any opposition still remaining to us in the field of SF. That it can be done, there is no doubt—witness the supreme irony of Robert Heinlein's *Stranger in a Strange Land* becoming the bible of an entire hippy generation. Heinlein, mark you, the man who wrote *Starship Troopers*!

Bear in mind that we still face danger as long as it is possible to reach the general public with any clear and accurate exposition of either real science or real religion. Once someone has acquired from science the habit of rigorous thought, the risk is there that he may extend his investigations into the field of the mind. Should he get to grasp the difference between religion and superstition, he becomes equally dangerous. Yet we cannot overtly suppress reference to science or religion in SF. What, then, Comrades, is our solution? It is to head off those authors who have any real grasp of these areas, and to encourage those who do not, but think that they have.

We can safely claim to have made real headway on this latter task. Any SF bookshop today is packed with novels out of Tolkien via Ursula Le Guin, novels which duplicate the length of the former's work without its style, and the trappings of the latter's work without its understanding. The fact that this mishmash of ancient magics, eldritch wizards, towering heroes, and liberated heroines is passed off as science fiction is already a triumph for us; the inculcation in the young that religion is something on a par with Royal Queen jelly is an added bonus. As an example of our equal success in suppressing the real thing let me give an example reinforcing my earlier remarks about John W. Campbell. I refer to his novella *The Elder Gods*, which appeared under his Don A. Stuart persona in the fantasy magazine *Unknown*, which he also edited. This tale is an exact opposite of the kind to which I have just referred, inasmuch as, while it appeared to belong to the genre of what would nowadays be called "sword-and-sorcery," it actually dealt in a very hard-edged manner with the nexus between ethics and science. Any detailed account would, I fear, greatly offend your own sense of ethics: I shall restrict myself to saying that it deals with the—from the author's point of view—harmful effects on society of a religious regime whose priesthood could actually, through the use of science, predict the future, hence undermine any attempt on the part of the public of the use of free will. I see from your expressions that, as I expected, you find the revelation of such views revolting. You will appreciate, then, my pleasure in being able to point out our success in ensuring that this work has never been reprinted since it first appeared. With continued good staffwork, it never will be. I quote it simply as an example of how menacing it can be for us when someone with some real grasp of these issues is allowed to publish a fictionalized presentation of them. Ethics, let me remind you, must always be presented to the public in such a way as to ensure that it is confused with sentiment. Theodore Sturgeon is a master at this, which is why I have always supported the presentation of his work, even in the face of criticism from some of my best officers. I know that on several occasions he has produced works capable of awakening the sleeping conscience, but I am convinced that, on balance, the overall effect of his writings has been to convince his readers that science and ethics are really at odds. No doubt his own belief is the opposite—but what do we care about that? It is the broad view, gentlemen, that we must take. Remember, the power to dream is not our opponent, but our ally—it is the power to *decide* that is the threat. And the simplest way to suppress such decisions is to ensure that rationality is removed in the power of choice.

At this point, I should advert to the works of Ayn Rand, and particularly to her near-future novel, *Atlas Shrugged*. You will, of course, be aware of her philosophy of Objectivism, and its immense emphasis on rationality and the objective testing of events in the physical world. Frankly, the damage done here has been immense: anyone exposed to this kind of thing will find his capacity for doublethink almost crippled. There is a way round this, but the remedy is almost as bad as the disease. Our Philosophy Office points out that Rand's atheism leaves her exposed to a charge of suppressing the spiritual side of existence, while her Aristotelian either/or stand risks leading her into self-destructive conflicts. After all, as Blake said, contraries are not negations. I notice that some of you are now looking pained at these references to matters spiritual, but, gentlemen, please! After all, you are members of our Inner Party, and I trust you have not forgotten that our entire campaign against the spirit would have no motivating power, and indeed, no point, did we not recognize its existence in the first place. Indeed, our motto might well be, "Since it exists, it must be destroyed." There are two main pathways to the spirit: reason and art. Which path is the more dangerous is not something I want to get into here: at all events, sustained rationality, such as Rand's, must be a main priority in our attack. Fortunately, Rand herself tended to overreact toward the end of her career, producing a healthy counterreaction. Still, her books have sold in the millions, and we are now reduced in this matter to the rather old fashioned, but still effective policy of pretending as hard as we can that they do not exist. Successful we may be, but the cost of that success is ceaseless vigilance. SF writers tend to be ever on the alert for new sources of inspiration, which means we must equally be on the lookout for these. Let me take two areas, both in the context of the growing field of computer operations. Great Britain is often in the lead here, particularly in interactive networks. *Micronet 800*, for example, has for some time had an electronic SF news magazine, *Starlight*, possibly a world-first, and an extremely interesting game, *Starnet*, with multiple access. Our Censorship Bureau, I regret to say, has not been able to obtain much leverage in these areas. My recommendation, therefore, to officers dealing with these activities is that they should seek to insist that any games, news services, and so on, should be both exciting and trivial. In that way, where we lose out on suppressing dangerous individuals, we may at least be able to drown them out as more and more thousands of people obtain access to these networks. It may well be that newsprint will lose out entirely to this medium. You will recall how we defeated a reactionary, but still dangerous, Catholic church by our backing of Martin Luther and his call for a free bible, freely interpreted, thus ensuring distracting conflicts of faith which, happily, persist to this day. In the same way, the transfer of data from the newspaper to the television/computer terminal, with its far narrower range and short persistence, may yet work to our gain.

There are real intellectual dangers, also. Let me give here a direct quote from Arnold Arnold, cyberneticist and mathematician:

> Science fiction has often predicted what science turns into reality. Unfortunately the opposite is also sometimes true. For example, it has long been a theme in science fiction that one day machines might

achieve equality with man's intellect or even surpass it. In the 18th century, clever mechanics like Vaucanson managed to fool royal and public audiences with little machines that appeared to behave like their organic counterparts. Vaucanson's famous silver duck waddled about, pecked, swallowed grain and defecated to the amazement of the populace and crowned heads of Europe.

The human race seems slow to learn, despite the lessons provided by science fiction writers like Swift, Samuel Butler, Wells, Orwell or Pohl. The computer scientists of today have adopted their phantasies and promise us that these will be the realities of the future. Thousands of millions are now allocated by governments in the industrialized portions of the world to permit today's computer scientists to develop "thinking" and "decision-making" machines that will equal or better their masters.

The machine myth is deeply rooted in our unfortunate history. It has been used by the priesthoods in the past to fool the people. In ancient Egypt priests pretended to foretell the rise and fall of the Nile because they were in direct communication with the Gods. But the mechanisms of their secret underground reservoirs provided them with that knowledge. Today's science does it the other way round. It builds machines hardly anyone understands and then predicts that it can imbue those machines with God-like attributes. It is hard in our day to tell science from fiction.

In good science fiction the impossible is either satirized or exaggerated and the consequences of irrationality are dramatized. But in today's science the irrational is rationalized and the consequences are ignored or glossed over. The difference is profound and it would seem that science fiction comes out ahead of science as far as integrity is concerned.

You can see for yourselves that there is no way of getting around these statements: no way of watering them down. Our general rule is to attack science by accusing it of lacking spirituality, and religion by accusing it of ignoring science. Here, we are stymied on both counts. All that remains to us is direct suppression, and you may count upon it that no effort is being spared in that context. Mr. Arnold, of course, is no SF writer—but SF writers might read or hear him, and then. . . .

Let me conclude my references to our opponents by citing John Crowley, a recent writer, but possibly the most dangerous since the appearance of Ursula Le Guin. The particular danger with Crowley is that he is equally at home in myth, religion, and the nastier aspects of modern life. All our own success depends on our insistence that the world of Winston Smith is the *real* world, the *only* world. Imagine, then, the effect produced on our dupes when they read a passage like this:

> The difference between the Ancient concept of the nature of the world and the New concept is, in the ancient concept the world has a framework of Time, and, in the new concept, a framework of Space.
>
> To look at the Ancient concept through the spectacles of the New concept is to see absurdity: seas that never were, worlds claimed to have fallen to pieces and been created newly, a congeries of unlocatable Trees, Islands, Mountains and Maelstroms. But the Ancients were not fools with a poor sense of direction; it was only not Urbis Terrae that they were looking at. When they spoke of the four corners of the earth, they meant of course no four physical places; they meant four repeated situations of the world, equidistant in time from one another: they meant the solstices and the equinoxes. When they spoke of seven spheres, they did not mean (until Ptolemy foolishly tried to take their portrait) seven spheres in space: they meant those circles described in Time by the motions of the stars: Time, that roomy seven-storied mountain where Dante's sinners wait for eternity. When Plato tells of a river girdling the earth, which is somewhere (as the New concept would have it) up in the air, and also somewhere in the middle of the earth, he means by that river the same river Heraclitus could never step in twice. Just as a lamp waved in darkness creates a figure of light in the air, which remains for so long as the lamp repeats its motion exactly, so the universe retains its shape by repetition: the Universe is Time's body. And how will we perceive this body, and how operate on it? Not by the means we perceive extension, relation, colour, form—the qualities of Space. Not by measurement and exploration. No, but by the means we perceive duration and repetition and change: by Memory.

Well, enough of such sickening material. I dislike exposing you to it, but how can you learn to insist on the promotion of the misleading and the fifth-rate without at least some contact with the real thing? Our task as realists is a hard one, and I will not pretend otherwise. Every day and every hour we must inculcate the image of the boot descending forever on the face. The alternative—I must be brutal here—is that the knowledge be allowed to escape, that the Gates of Paradise remain forever open. Yes, you may flinch, but it is fact. Of my own record in combating happiness I am confident: it is your own careers that concern me, and if I conclude on such a frightening note, it is done for your own good. To succeed, you need only to ensure that science fiction remains dominated by the effete, the misleading, and the ineffectual. With the aid of the writings available from our Literary Office, this is hardly difficult. Should you fail, the offices of our Correction Unit remain—but come; why should I threaten you? Let evil for evil's sake remain your blazon, and you shall not find your efforts unrewarded. If, on the other hand, any of you should slacken—well, just remember this: our Court of No Appeal sits in judgment night and day, and never rises.

Gentlemen, my maledictions to you all.

Images of *Nineteen Eighty-Four*: Fiction and Prediction

Colin Greenland

To live in London during the first months of 1984 was a surreal experience. Coming through a dingy alley into Wardour Street, I passed torn posters of Big Brother, his image taken from Michael Anderson's film of George Orwell's *Nineteen Eighty-Four*. There I was in 1984, looking at a real picture of an imaginary picture from 1955 of an imaginary person of 1984, an imaginary year in a real book written in 1948. I began to feel like Winston Smith, who wasn't sure what year it was.

In fact, in Britain in 1984 nobody could possibly have escaped knowing what year it was. Since months earlier, politicians, publishers, journalists, booksellers, television personalities and advertising copywriters had been falling over each other to remind us that this was the year of George Orwell, adapted from his book of the same name. In Orwell's book, people walked through dingy alleys past posters of Big Brother. The prediction had come true!

How people appropriate Orwell's creation, and how it offers itself for appropriation, make an interesting study. After all, George Orwell was not the first author to invent 1984. G. K. Chesterton had already done so, in 1904. No one appropriates Chesterton's invention, because he published it under the title of *The Napoleon of Notting Hill*, referring it to the past rather than the future. Orwell, in an act of conceptual piracy, stole the year and copyrighted it, so that when it eventually appeared, it would carry his face as trademark: our very own Big Brother watching us with consumptive concern from his Hebridean retreat thirty-six years before.

January was his peak. By April he was looking decidedly unfashionable. This Big Brother could be taken down from the wall, his image changed for that of Harrison Ford or a packet of Quaker Oats.

We could even change the channel on the telly screen. Orwell, ultimately, was just one more bit of information. The inhabitants of Airstrip One have no information. They have propaganda, meaningless statistics, pornography, sentimental music, and lotteries. Winston Smith has more information than most. He has seen the photograph of Jones, Aaronson, and Rutherford in New York on a midsummer day, when history says they were in Siberia. Winston Smith is in possession of the facts, for just a moment, before they are whisked away into the "memory hole" and incinerated. Information can be destroyed. Winston's job is to destroy information:

> The written which Winston received, and which he invariably got rid of as soon as he had dealt with them, never stated or implied that an act of forgery was to be committed: always the reference was to slips, errors, misprints, or misquotations which is was necessary to put right in the interests of accuracy.
>
> But actually, he thought as he re-adjusted the Ministry of Plenty's figures, it was not even forgery. It was merely the substitution of one piece of nonsense for another. Most of the material that you were dealing with had no connection with anything in the real world, not even the kind of connection that is contained in a direct lie.[1]

The difference between Airstrip One and Britain is that our state does not entirely monopolize the media. We have many Ministries of Truth. They sell us detergent and video recorders, George Orwell and Margaret Thatcher. In America, in 1981, the Boise Cascade Corporation went to an advertising agency and bought a package with the motto: "Wood and paper for today, trees for tomorrow." Their advertising copy began: "We're betting $2.3 billion Orwell was wrong. We see a sunnier future today than George Orwell did in 1948, which is one reason we've launched our most ambitious capital investment program ever. If all goes according to plan, we'll have invested $2.3 billion in our operations by the time 1984 arrives, and we'll have doubled our company's size." The illustration showed a blond, blue-eyed couple with backpacks. He wears clean faded jeans and a lumberjack shirt; she wears cowboy boots and a quilted jacket, and embraces her man with glee. He is five inches taller than she. Together with infant son and panting dog they stride through a spectral calendar for 1984 into a sunlit glade, complete with deer, bluejay, rabbits, and of course trees for tomorrow.

Boise Cascade had tidied the place up since Winston Smith was
there:

> Suddenly he was standing on short springy turf, on a summer evening
> when the slanting rays of the sun gilded the ground. The landscape that
> he was looking at recurred so often in his dreams that he was never fully
> certain whether or not he had seen it in the real world. In his waking
> thoughts he called it the Golden Country. It was an old, rabbit-bitten
> pasture, with a foot-track wandering across it and a molehill here and
> there. In the ragged hedge on the opposite side of the field the boughs of
> the elm trees were swaying very faintly in the breeze, their leaves just
> stirring in dense masses like women's hair.[2]

Ninety pages later Winston finds the Golden Country, this
scruffy English Eden, and consummates his sexuality with Julia. This
naked couple in the field wake from the innocence of sexual symbolism to the experience of sexual politics. "You could not have pure
love or pure lust nowadays. No emotion was pure, because everything was mixed up with fear and hatred. Their embrace had been a
battle, the climax a victory. It was a blow struck against the Party. It
was a political act."[3] Mr. and Mrs. Boise Cascade, on the other hand,
have rediscovered purity. Transplanted west to the pastoral New
World, they defy the knowledge of good and evil. They defy economic recession. They have *investments*. They defy the dystopian
image of 1984. Just as long as all goes according to plan.

"We're betting $2.3 billion Orwell was wrong," Boise Cascade
announced. On the last day of 1983, Neil Kinnock, Leader of the
British Labour Party, contributed an article to the *Times* under the
title "Shadow of the Thought Police."[4] Bleary, perhaps, from the
festive season, an editor added the subtitle "Are we helping to fulfill
George Orwell's prophecies?" without even looking at Kinnock's
first sentence: "*Nineteen Eighty-Four* was satire, not prophecy."
"The question for us now in 1984 is not 'have we reached *Nineteen
Eighty-Four?*' We plainly have not and never will, any more than
anyone has ever lived in Lilliput or Brobdignag. The question must
be 'what elements in our current condition give substance to the
satire of Orwell?' The answer cannot be comforting." Kinnock cited
"starving nations and deadlocked empires," militaristic international
policies fuelled by hate, a mass media full of "prolefeed" and an
intelligentsia who "know better, but stick to their positions rather

than their convictions." The state, he observed, "is being reduced as a source of care and opportunity while being extended as a means of control." The rhetoric strikes, and the echo answers, *Nineteen Eighty-Four*.

The analysis Kinnock proposed was necessary, and not difficult. It is the proper response to the literary form in question. In the same way we might have asked, "What elements in our current condition give substance to the satire of Jonathan Swift or for that matter G. K. Chesterton?" Their rhetoric continues to resonate too. We might have asked that, but we didn't; at least not in 1984. In 1984 we felt a duty to ask about the satire of George Orwell, because, so to speak, it had our number on it.

Satirists and writers of utopian and dystopian fantasy often give their fictions titles that show them to be rhetorical rather than oracular: satire, not prophecy. Thomas More wrote *Utopia*; Samuel Butler, *Erewhon*; William Morris, more frankly, called his book *News from Nowhere*. Orwell could not afford such a disclaimer. "I do not believe," he wrote, "that the kind of society I describe will arrive, but I believe that something resembling it could arrive."[5] So he called his work after something that did not exist, but one day almost certainly would, in the lifetimes of many of his readers. *Nineteen Eighty-Four* explicitly deals with the possibility of the irresistible totalitarian state being founded by postwar thought and technology. It is a memo to the future, addressed to "1984." In 1984 we received the memo, and we read it. We read it in classrooms and seminars, in program planning meetings and science fiction discussion groups. Early in 1984 I asked a University of London extension class what would happen to *Nineteen Eighty-Four* now that the year itself was upon us? With one voice they answered me: "It will sell a lot." And it did. In September 1984, even before the release of Michael Radford's new film and attendant publicity, Penguin Books were already reporting three times their usual annual sales of a quarter of a million in paperback.

Reading *Nineteen Eighty-Four* against a background of science fiction, the first thing we notice is the inadequacy of its technology. Every time Winston Smith rewrites a *Times* article, somebody must have to go out and locate and destroy every copy of the prior version. The telescreen apparently requires active surveillance by the broadcaster of every single transceiver. ("'Smith!' screamed the shrewish

voice from the telescreen. '6079 Smith W.! Yes, *you*!' "⁶) The military
technology of Oceania is astonishingly primitive by comparison with
what one writer has called the "baroque arsenal" of the modern
state. But science fiction readers, of course, ought to be the last to
complain that Orwell's machines wouldn't work. Science fiction is
full of machines that wouldn't work, from the Time Machine to the
faster-than-light drive, from the spindizzy to the ansible. They are
all, in a quite literal sense, plot devices: contrivances that enable the
imagination to reach into inaccessible distances of space and time, to
resolve paradoxes, to bring aliens together, to extend and amplify
human control. The machines don't work, but they make the plot
work. The same is true of Orwell's machines, which reach into the
midst of privacy, overhaul history, and achieve the will of the Party,
extensively and intensively, globally and personally. The world is
locked in perpetual war. Winston's Smith's nervous system is
annexed. Nothing is too much trouble for the party. In fact, *Nineteen
Eighty-Four* is the story of the perfect machine, the solid state,
omnipotent, and infallible machine. It regenerates itself. It regenerates Winston Smith. The fact that it does so with a minimum of
equipment that now seems hopelessly outdated was originally part of
the satirical distortion. Orwell's technological extrapolations were
provocative rather than predictive. He was writing a novel in which
the writing of novels had been automated.

Examining *Nineteen Eighty-Four* from the height of our technology, it is obvious that its machines are science fictional devices,
symbolic not literal. They function in just the same way as the coral
paperweight, the engraving of the church of St. Clement Danes, and
the fat prole hanging out the washing: that is, they furnish Winston's
moral understanding as it is first enlarged and enlightened, then
reduced and simplified. The telescreen; Newspeak; the Thought
Police; Room 101: they are not only sufficient, they are definitive, as
the technology of tyranny. As the blurb on the Penguin edition has it,
"The language of 1984 has passed into the English language as a
symbol of the horrors of totalitarianism."⁷ Neil Kinnock had no need
to explain the terms of his article "Shadow of the Thought Police,"
not only, not even primarily, because he was addressing the literate
audience of the *Times*. Everyone knows, or thinks they know, *Nineteen Eighty-Four* by George Orwell,even if they have not read it. In
addition to *Nineteen Eighty-Four* the book, and 1984 the year, there

is "1984" the myth, common property, public domain, appearing in forms whose content is not usually derived from English Literature: American advertising, for instance, or rock music. Hugh Hopper, Rick Wakeman, and Herbie Hancock have all released albums called *1984*; David Bowie's *Diamond Dogs* features three tracks called "We Are the Dead," "1984," and "Big Brother." The imagery of *Diamond Dogs* is a bizarre blend of elements from *Nineteen Eighty-Four*, Clifford Simak's *City*, and Harlan Ellison's "A Boy and his Dog": "Beware the savage jaw / Of 1984."[8]

"1984" the myth is exploited by left and right alike, each eager to dissociate itself as far as possible from Big Brother, while casting the other firmly in that role. On the opposite page to Neil Kinnock's article in the *Times* appeared its New Year editorial, "1984speak," which maintains that "the principal message" of *Nineteen Eighty-Four* is "Orwell's prediction of the debasement of language."[9] The argument is worth recapitulating in some detail. Alexander Solzhenitsyn is cited as witness to "the twin motors of degeneration; the abuse by design in the totalitarian world from which he was exiled, and by default in the liberal world whose light shone on him from afar, only to dim when on closer inspection he discovered its canker of doubt and self destruction within." Note the opposition: the deliberate attack on language comes from elsewhere; at home there is only weakness, a failure to be deliberate enough. The choice of Solzhenitsyn as authority reinforces a familiar polarity of East and West, which Orwell himself saw through and displaced with his rotating system of two virtually identical power blocs eternally ganging up on a third. The *Times* editorial goes on to describe Marxist-Leninist crimes against language—the lies, the contradictions, the silencing of opponents—all much as Orwell himself did. "What is harder to recognise," says the *Times*, "and harder still to cope with is the widespread indigenous debasement of our language which cannot be attributed to some clearly defined external conspiracy and ideological assault."

The conspiracy is external; it is foreign; it is hostile. We must stand firm against it. But intellectuals are allowing their desire for political change to threaten the stability of the language which is in their custody. "This condition," says the writer, "is at its most pervasive in the social sciences, and any discipline relating to the study of economics." Thus, definition of the socio-political functions of sexuality is said to depersonalize sex by bringing politics into it. New critical language which articulates what colloquial language excludes is said to be, therefore, unrealistic and unreasonable. Dissent is interpreted as a failure of faith; radicalism as vandalism. This whole inversion of values is conducted under the banner of "pluralism," championing individual freedom against the inhuman uniformity of the foe; and yet, it is a formidable orthodoxy which is being preached.

"In the subsoil of a pluralist society lie the roots of individual freedom and morality. They are nourished by the gentle rain of a million words and ideas. No rain; no roots. No words; no freedom." The imagery associated with pluralism is organic—"subsoil," "roots," "nourished"—as opposed to communism which, we learn elsewhere, "doctors" and "gelds" truth. The implication is that pluralism is somehow natural, a primal state rather than a laborious and difficult balancing act. The "gentle rain," we remember, was Portia's simile for the quality of mercy, which, according to her, was similarly "not strained," but the effortless gift of divine grace. British democracy seeks to disguise itself as a romanticized, benevolent nature, invisibly mediated by the poetry of Renaissance humanism, Albion as Arcadia, and Shakespeare is summoned to endorse the metaphor.

Thus the *Times* repossesses Orwell's Golden Country, where the pastoral encompasses delight and desire, identified as the first principles of freedom and opposed to urban oppression, "the May sunshine" opposed to "the sooty dust of London." We recall that after his dream of the Golden Country, "Winston woke up with the word 'Shakespeare' on his lips."[10]

Remarkably, the *Times* editorial nowhere acknowledges that in Orwell's novel the principal organ of officially degraded language was the *Times* itself. Indeed, Orwell tells of Winston's work, "on occasion he had even been entrusted with the rectification of the *Times* leading articles, which were written entirely in Newspeak."[11] An embarrassing thing for a *Times* leading article to mention, perhaps, but a curious omission nonetheless—unless the writer actually wished to conceal the fact that in our world too the *Times* is an ideological construct, an organ rather than an oracle. Not once does he admit (and it certainly is "he") that the English language is also under attack by totalitarian forces within, which are not at all foreign, but claim their power from nationalism and tradition: the authoritarian forces of the political right. Other commentators have noticed the absolutism of Margaret Thatcher's rhetoric, her habitual denial of even the *possibility* of dissent. A couple of examples will suffice here. "There is no hard and fast line between economic and other forms of responsibility to self, family, firm, community, nation, God." Monetarism becomes a spiritual virtue; capitalism is natural and inevitable. "We Conservatives," Thatcher declares, "did not invent these ideas, nor did we find them in books. This is the sense of the people, which we simply accept and try to clothe in laws and policies. There are difficulties. But we are strengthened by the knowledge that there is no other way."[12]

Thatcher attacks pluralism every time she opens her mouth. She attacks it by appropriating the terminology of moral and religious rightness to that of her chosen position on the political right. It is as much an abuse of language as any practice of the Marxist-Leninist left. Yet the *Times* article does not even mention it, does not even acknowledge that it is being done, and done more powerfully than anything the left can do, because done by the party in power. And the *Times* hopes that we will not notice that in the novel under discussion, a British newspaper called the *Times* is the organ of the party in power, the only party. Could it be that this heaven-blessed pluralism of ours is really only conservatism in disguise? Perhaps not, or not altogether, while Neil Kinnock is allowed his say on the opposite page.

The *Times* of 31 December 1983 exemplifies how *Nineteen Eighty-Four* can still be brandished as a weapon by right as well as left, just as when Orwell's publisher, F. J. Warburg, described the book in a company memorandum as "worth a cool million votes to the Conservative Party." *Nineteen Eighty-Four* has been swallowed up by "1984," the myth, which is available for anyone to exploit, Neil Kinnock or Margaret Thatcher, David Bowie or Boise Cascade. Ironically, despite six current editions of the book, 1984 was primarily the year of the myth, the dissolution of the book into an all-purpose rhetorical figure, a catchphrase, a slogan. But now the year is past, George Orwell's *Nineteen Eighty-Four* is finally detached from its spurious claim to describe a piece of reality twelve months long; not in the facile sense of being "disproved," but in the sense of at least becoming visible in its true identity.

In 1984 the media of Britain and America tended to address *Nineteen Eighty-Four* as a set of predictions, which, of course, it could not possibly be. Orwell himself wrote, "I do not believe that the kind of society I describe will arrive." Fiction is more useful than prediction. Prediction is either right or wrong. Fiction cannot be either, because it consists of statements about things that do not exist. Orwell cunningly labeled his fiction as prediction, calling it by the name of a future year, thus ensuring our continuing attention. As a Danish journalist observed, if Orwell had finished writing a year later, he would have called it *Nineteen Ninety-Four*. No doubt the same pundits would have found predictions in it for that year too, just as interpreters of Nostradamus blithely reallocate his pronouncements to whatever year seems to fit them best.

Internally, Orwell's text shows its ambiguity. The first things we look for are correspondences with our own time, but to its first readers in 1949 the most obvious elements were those transcribed directly from theirs. Anthony Burgess identifies many in the first part of his book *1985*.[13] Victory cigarettes were the brand dispensed on ration to British forces overseas; "Let Me Be Your Big Brother" was the slogan in advertisements for the Bennett Correspondence College; Room 101, in the basement of the British Broadcasting Corporation, was the studio from which Orwell broadcast propaganda to India. 1984 is 1948 turned around. Orwell satirized the present by pretending it was the future. We, the future, think it belongs to us; in 1949 they thought it belonged to them; as fiction, it belongs to both. Despite its title, *Nineteen Eighty-Four* is adrift in time. Winston Smith, whose job it is to rewrite history, knows this well. "He wondered again for whom he was writing the diary. For the future, for the past—for an age that might be imaginary."[14]

What became obvious in 1984 was that *Nineteen Eighty-Four* is a work of science fiction: an alternate history, a parallel world. In our world the nuclear war of 1950 did not happen. Since then our time-track and Winston Smith's have been steadily diverging. From his viewpoint, ours is the imaginary age: in the future, in the past, in both at once, and neither. Burgess comments, "We can talk to the past as we can talk to the future. . . . Both acts are absurd, but the absurdity is necessary to freedom."[15] We are not accustomed to thinking of science fiction as intrinsically absurd, but it is, as a special case of the absurdity of all fiction. Science fiction consists of statements about things that do not exist and demonstrably cannot exist in the same reality as the book. While mundane fiction, contemporary or historical, is sustained within a field of consensual mimetic tolerances, which it cannot transgress, science fiction must transgress the bounds of experiential reality before it can begin. Its mode of extrapolation may be logical, symbolic, comic, or didactic, but it is always existentially absurd.

As satire, *Nineteen Eighty-Four* is absurd in character as well as kind. Burgess points to the clock that strikes thirteen, the television that talks back, and the running gag about a razorblade shortage. In the second part of *1985* he emulates Orwell, focusing on the absurdity of an economic system in which "taking industrial action" does not mean working diligently (as, from the Latin, it should), but refusing to work at all. In Burgess's story the Islamic Oil Union finances a fascist private army of Free Britons to fight the trade unions, and all the derelicts have degrees in humanities.

A novel by the Hungarian poet György Dalos, also called *1985*, is published in an English translation as "a sequel to George Orwell's 1984."[16] It features all the characters of *Nineteen Eighty-Four*, including several unpersons, and begins with the death of Big Brother from "a temporary indisposition." O'Brien calls Winston Smith into his office and invites him to become the editor of a new journal, to be called the *Times Literary Supplement*, which will rally the disaffected intelligentsia and speak out for peace and reform. Winston's group, the Intellectuals' Reform Association (or IRA), meets in the Chestnut Tree Cafe and discusses ways of getting in touch with the proles. A new moderate Thought Police prepares for a visiting Eurasian delegation by re-equipping a department store for them to do their Christmas shopping.

Clearly, neither Burgess nor Dalos has much time for Orwell's politics, but each of them has seized upon his dark, frightening humor and developed a quite separate political farce. The institutions of dystopia are always absurd. It is the very establishment of unreason, in doublethink, that seals the power of the Party. Certainly O'Brien can demolish Winston's memory, and his emotions, but he wins by demolishing mathematics. The terror of the absurd is spelled out by the giant slogans on the wall of the Ministry of Truth: War is Peace; Freedom is Slavery; Ignorance is Strength.

There is more than an echo of this in contemporary American

dystopian SF. Thomas Disch's "The Man Who Had No Idea" is set in a bland dystopia where you need a license to have a conversation.[17] "Remember," cautions the accompanying document, "that direct, interactive personal communications are one of our most valuable heritages. Use your license wisely. Do not abuse the privilege of free speech." Disch's equivalent of the Ministry of Truth is the Federal Communications Agency. The giant slogan on its wall reads: "Planned Freedom Is the Road to Lasting Progress." The grim America of Ursula Le Guin's "New Atlantis" has "planned freedom" too, or at least "planned implementation of recreational leisure"—which does not include playing the viola, marrying someone and living with them, or inventing the perfect solar cell.[18] Le Guin's United States, perpetually at war while keeping its population cheerful with community hikes, imports *Nineteen Eighty-Four* to America with very little adjustment to Orwell's original design; while the alarming aspect of Disch's story is that "planned freedom" can be accommodated and enforced by a system which is essentially that of American society today.

Yet no one will ever speak of Disch's story or Le Guin's as predictions. They have been written and published within the generic bounds of science fiction—"The Man Who Had No Idea" in *The Magazine of Fantasy and Science Fiction* and "The New Atlantis" in Robert Silverberg's anthology of the same name. Here it is perfectly obvious that fictional times and places, even when given the names of historical ones, do not have a relationship of linear succession to history. They will not come to be; they are: satire, not prophecy; fiction, not prediction. Orwell's book was not published as a genre work, despite its conformity with the principles of the genre, and it is still regarded as an exception by readers both generic and general. Its ambiguous classification, fortunately, has also prevented it from being tidied away out of sight. *Nineteen Eighty-Four* was not erased by 1984; nor has its satire become any less urgent.

Orwell and the Uses of the Future

John Huntington

It is a commonplace that the union of technology and science and the modern modes of organizing production—in short, the Industrial Revolution—have changed the conditions of life in such a way as to change the ways human can think about and shape the future. *Nineteen Eighty-Four* is famous for the success with which it *closes off* that future. In part, this is a conscious aim of Orwell's. But it is also a quality which may go beyond his control and which derives from the implications of certain ways of looking at the future.

In a letter to F. J. Warburg, Orwell described how he conceived his generic options in *Nineteen Eighty-Four*, which he was then just beginning. It was not simply to be a prophecy: "I don't like talking about books before they are written, but I will tell you now that this is a novel about the future—that is, it is in a sense a fantasy, but in the form of a naturalistic novel. That is what makes it a difficult job—of course as a book of anticipations it would be comparatively simple to write."[1] "Anticipations" is, of course, H. G. Wells's word, and, in distinguishing *Nineteen Eighty-Four* in this way, Orwell separates himself from one part of the Wells tradition. In *The Road to Wigan Pier* and in numerous essays Orwell had expressed his dissatisfaction with Wells's future and his modes of imagining it. "I want a civilization in which 'progress' is not definable as making the world safe for little fat men" (*RWP*, p. 210).

The totalitarianism of *Nineteen Eighty-Four* is certainly a rejection of such "progress." The novel itself marks an attempt to imagine the end of history, the reduction of process to the simple, repeated, dominating images of the rat and of the boot stamping on a human face. At the middle of the novel, however, this process is challenged by a second book, a book within the book, Goldstein's *Theory and Practice of Oligarchic Collectivism*, which constitutes an attempt within the novel itself to reopen history by subjecting the totalitarian state to rational analysis. Certainly, the experience of Winston Smith and, I imagine, of many readers of the novel, is one of exhilaration at the prospects of understanding and, therefore, of control that Goldstein's book seems to offer.

There are, of course, questions about what Goldstein's book is *really* doing in the world of *Nineteen Eighty-Four*. In a world of complete totalitarian control, the rationality the book stands for may simply be bait to lure minds such as Winston Smith's into the open. But putting aside for now the issue of how Goldstein's book works in the novel itself, I want to view it, not in the frame of *Nineteen Eighty-Four*, but in the frame of 1948, when Orwell wrote it. Though in 1984 Goldstein's book is a piece of sociological analysis, in 1948 his book is an *anticipation*. Like Wells's *Anticipations* of 1900, it describes in nondramatic terms the rationale by which the future will be organized.[2] It gives up the "difficult" work of naturalist fiction and tells us in schematic and general terms what the world will be.

An important model for Goldstein's book is the work of James Burnham. William Steinhof has explicated how much Orwell is indebted to Burnham for elements of structure and detail in his depiction of the future world.[3] What is of interest for us, however, is not the explicit debt, but Orwell's own reaction to Burnham, which will tell much about the attractions and distortions of anticipations.

Burnham was much discussed in the forties, especially by the anti-Stalinist left involved with *The Partisan Review*. Orwell, who was then writing a regular letter from London for *The Partisan Review*, wrote two essays on Burnham. In *The Managerial Revolution* (1940), Burnham, picking up some slightly Wellsian ideas about technocratic competence, foresees the victory of "managerial" Germany over socialist USSR and capitalist Britain. What is important for us, and for Orwell, is that at this stage Burnham can envision a "new" era in history, managerial totalitarianism. In his next work, *The Machiavellians* (1944), Burnham performs a variation on the first and sees history as always being manipulated by an oligarchic elite even when the action is in the name of "The People." By the time this book came out, however, Burnham had published an essay in *Partisan Review* entitled "Lenin's Heir," which Orwell at least read as a panegyric on Stalin. And then, in 1947, he published *The Struggle for the World*, in which he urged a preemptive attack with atomic weapons by the USA on the USSR as the only way to preserve democratic capitalism against totalitarian socialism in a world of atomic arms.

The shifts in political allegiance emphasized by this summary of Burnham's intellectual journey (we might note that he began in the thirties as a Trotskyite) are of less interest to us than are Orwell's insights into the continuities that allow Burnham to perform such radical changes of direction and yet, at the same time, maintain the prophetic pose. Orwell points to Burnham's fascination with power and apocalypse. For Burnham, the present crisis is always the ultimate, final crisis, and it is one that will be resolved by the victory of powerful elites of one sort or another. Though he prophesizes about the indefinite future, at the moment of prophecy he admires those who right now *are* powerful—thus, Hitler in 1940, Stalin in 1945, the USA in 1947. Yet these very limitations to Burnham's vision contribute to what Orwell finds to be his great attraction. The analyses Burnham performs all carry the air of confident, dispassionate objectivity; there is no sentimental shying away from brutal realities, no finding silver linings in dismal situations.[4] Burnham represents a model of a kind of anticipation.

But there is a problem here: was Orwell misreading Burnham? In 1944 Burnham objected publicly to Orwell's reading of him. In his 1959 reissue of *The Managerial Revolution*, he disavows having given any support to Hitler. Orwell himself, in his second essay on Burnham, remarks on the difficulty one has knowing what political meaning is to be given to Burnham's analyses (*Essays*, 4: 325). Goldstein's book, while imitating the tone of confident authority and fearless objectivity essential to the anticipation, raises the same problem: how does such a text make its intended meaning clear? Just as Orwell can "misread" Burnham, so can we or Winston Smith "misread" Goldstein.

This ambiguity is essential to the successful anticipation and derives from the form's evasion of its own political implications. In claiming to be a dispassionate analysis of the future, an anticipation hides its true rhetorical purpose and, perhaps unintentionally, diminishes the importance of "history" itself. Though the novel itself provides us with some understanding of the problem, we will have to look outside of *Nineteen Eighty-Four* to other anticipators, their purposes and effects, in order to understand the full implications of such foresight.

In the ultimate totalitarianism based on Newspeak and Doublethink, all textuality is completely malleable. But consider an earlier stage, which Winston Smith represents in the first half of the novel, in which rational, empirical thought of some sort is still possible. Here Orwell raises the most interesting issues. In the later phase, one might say, there is no longer such a thing as an issue.

In this earlier stage of simply strong propaganda, we observe an event which raises some deep questions about the intrinsic significance of a text. Near the beginning of *Nineteen Eighty-Four*, in his first diary entry, Winston Smith describes a propaganda film designed to rouse him against the Eastasian enemy. Though already a critic of Oceanian totalitarianism, and even though conscious of the film's purpose, Winston Smith reacts in exactly the way the makers of the film intended. The film describes the massacre of Eastasian refugees by the fighter planes of Oceania and asks us and Winston Smith to side with the planes, to see the women and children as unworthy of compassion, to take sadistic pleasure in their helplessness, and to read violence aesthetically. It is a skillful piece of irony: Smith objectively describes the film, and for a long while it seems possible that he might be critical of the stance the film asks him to take. But his scornful reaction to the prole response at the end shows that he has been describing without irony, that when he said that the film was a "very good one," he meant it:

> then you saw a lifeboat full of children with a helicopter hovering over it. there was a middleaged woman might have been a jewess sitting up in the bow with a little boy about three years old in her arms. little boy screaming with fright and hiding his head between her breasts as if he was trying to burrow right into her and the woman putting her arms around him and comforting him although she was blue with fright herself. all the time covering him up as much as possible as if she thought her arms could keep the bullets off him. then the helicopter planted a 20 kilo bomb in among them terrific flash and the boat went all to matchwood. then there was a wonderful shot of a childs arm going up up up right up into the air a helicopter with a camera in its nose must have followed it up and there was a lot of applause from the party seats

but a woman down in the prole part of the house suddenly started
kicking up a fuss and shouting they didn't oughter of showed it not in
front of the kids they didn't it aint right not in front of kids it aint until
the police turned her out i dont suppose anything happened to her
nobody cares what the proles say typical prole reaction they never—
(P. 11)

I bring up this episode because, quite in addition to any kind of
measure it may give us of Smith's "consciousness," it raises a problem of how can a text insure its proper reading? Here, in the propaganda film, is a text which we read as a depiction of the suffering of
innocence but which even a man as aware as Winston Smith can read
as the triumph of righteous power.

We ourselves frequently experience such reversals of the value
of images. Soviet films of the twenties and thirties in praise of
electrification and industrialization show up now as cruelly naive.
Margaret Bourke-White photographs of rows of telephone oper-
ators, intended to praise national productivity, now speak of alienation and the oppression of women. Riefensthal's celebration of the
Nuremberg rallies of 1934, intended to glorify national vigor, unity,
and might, becomes for us a collection of monstrous images of mass
sadism, blindness, and cultural sterility. In the recent film *The
Atomic Cafe*, government films originally intended to educate the
public about nuclear dangers appear as quite sinister trivializations of
human values. The calm leaders casually discussing the use of nuclear
weapons in conventional war situations show up as insane. The 1950s
images of the bounties of democratic freedom—regimented sub-
urban tracts, motel-like living rooms with a stiff family and a dominating television set, supermarket freezers filled with packaged
food—become in the different frame of *The Atomic Cafe* a parody of
the good life. The images of value and significance are always contingent on the historical moment. They cannot be guaranteed to mean
what is originally intended outside of the historical and political
context in which they are formulated. The suffering and innocent
refugee of 1948 becomes the vicious and elusive pest of 1984.

Goldstein's analysis of the structure of oligarchic totalitarianism
might seem to lie at the pole opposite to the propaganda film. If the
film appeals to Winston Smith in his unenlightened state, Goldstein's
book becomes the bible of his enlightened state, promising him
further enlightenment. If the film appeals to irrational emotion,

Goldstein's book attempts a scientific, sociological explication of the structure and motives of the party. Goldstein's book would, therefore, seem to be in some way free from the kind of misuse the film allows. It is as explicit as it can be.

And yet, despite its explicitness, Goldstein's book, like the film and like Burnham's work, is ambiguous in its rhetorical ends and leaves itself open to different uses. Does such a text intend to warn us away from the coming horror, or does it intend to reconcile us with the inevitable? Like the propaganda film, it is a text which different eras will use to different ends. In the uncomfortable knowledge that the actual issue is not and can never be this simple, let us pretend for now that the book, *Theory and Practice*, is really by Goldstein, that it was written in good faith, and that it was intended to offer some kind of real hope. Even such a document, liberating in the faith that the truth shall make you free, can be used by the Party to obscure the central point, that power is desired for itself and must be sadistic, and to assure its readership of the rationality of power's procedures.

This flexibility of interpretation has, as I am suggesting, a historical component: different eras honor different values. But it is also made possible by a central evasion inherent in the anticipation itself. An anticipation, even while it pretends to allow for choice and free will, actually narrows possibilities. Far from offering a choice of futures, it claims that the future is inevitable. It therefore, while enlightening in a voice of dispassionate description, serves as a device to persuade its readers that the future foreseen will come, whether one wants it or not, and that wisdom consists of accommodating to that inevitable future. Such an anticipation must conceal its actual rhetorical purpose. It must claim to be a neutral description; if it acknowledged any purpose to *persuade*, it would immediately be treated, not as an anticipation, but as a political document. In short, an anticipation is a covert political document which, while seeming to promise control and freedom to its readers, encourages resignation.

This is an obvious paradox at the heart of anticipation, but it is one which is relentlessly denied by anticipators. Thus, Burnham, describing *The Managerial Revolution*, can say,

> What is at issue here is not, we should note, a question of *program*. Neither of these hypotheses—nor any additional alternative hypotheses—raises any problem of what "ought to be," of whether the con-

tinuance of capitalism would be "good" or "bad," whether we "ought" to fight for socialism, or what program "ought" to be adopted by men of good will. The problem is simply one of fact, of what on the basis of the evidence now at our disposal, is most likely to happen. (*PR* 8 [1941]: 184)

It does not take much sophistication to see that there is something disingenuous here, that such dispassionate fatalism, despite its claim to neutrality, is doing its best to undermine the morale of any opposition and to bring about that which it claims to be inevitable.[5]

Such paradox, which characterizes most anticipation, leads to the denial of the possibility of historical change. The roots of this process are embedded in H. G. Wells's lecture of 1902, "The Discovery of the Future," a text which is often invoked by professional forecasters as the beginning of their art. Wells's basic thesis is that just as one can reason backwards in time from the present to the prehistoric state of things, so one should be able to reason forward. It is, he claims, simply a matter of understanding the "operating causes" and following the deductive chains rigorously and without sentiment. Just as the physical sciences can predict the movements of stars, so it should be possible, says Wells, to predict human affairs.

> If I am right in saying that science aims at prophecy, and if the specialist in each science is in fact doing his best now to prophesy within the limits of his field, what is there to stand in the way of our building up this growing body of forecast into an ordered picture of the future that will be just as certain, just as strictly science, and perhaps just as detailed as the picture that has been built up within the last hundred years of the geological past?[6]

The equation of physical science with historical prediction implies a simple determinist idea of a history shaped by rigorous sequences of cause and effect.[7] It is not a view of history that allows one to change the world in any way. But it is just such a view which is more satisfying to a predictor.

The geological image also allows Wells to get around one of the profound difficulties of all forecasting: our own experience of the unpredictability of individual behavior. As he himself remarks, "We are continually surprising ourselves by our own will or want of will" (p. 376); if we cannot predict ourselves how can we expect to predict on a larger scale? Wells ingeniously turns this argument against itself: "I would advance the suggestion that an increase in the number of human beings considered may positively simplify the case instead of complicating it; that as the individuals increase in number they begin to average out" (p. 377). He demonstrates this by analogy to a pile of sand: you can predict the shape of the pile fairly accurately, and even tell which size grains will be where in the pile, even though you have no specific knowledge about any individual grain. In certain respects this is a profound observation; it is just such reasoning which justifies the use of statistics in sociology. But when applied to history and forecasting, this is a problematic analogy, for implicit in the analogy is the assumption that all times reveal themselves as the same. In the name of forecasting history, the method presumes there is no such thing as real history.

The heap of sand raises a second problem because, quite apart from its presumption of the uniformity of all moments, it presumes a perspective which is valuable only to someone outside the pile, that is, outside of history. To someone inside the pile, to the specific and individual grain of sand, the shape of the pile, while of some interest, is less important than the relation of the different grains, how they meet, abut, move against each other. To take a perspective that treats such matters as microscopic and trivial is to assume a position that ignores the important political questions. Wells admits that his model does not allow for "the great man." More significantly, though, it does not allow for *any* conscious action by *anyone*. The grain of sand is entirely passive and all heaps approach the same shape. A meaningful insight needs to see the precise *social* relations and possibilities that allow the heap to exist and of which the shape of the pile is a final but fairly inconsequential expression.

Wells's model, quite apart from the practical issues of whether it will work, has two important consequences which will characterize the rhetoric of much later prediction. First: in claiming that all times, like all heaps of sand, are basically the same, it denies the possibility of different eras with different contours. Second: in the name of history, it denies the importance of the very details of social relations that are the basis of politics itself.

One should mention here a related form of prediction which is really anti-prediction: a stance that explicitly argues the essential unchangingness of the world and, therefore, denies the possibility of any kind of important change. In recent times this is a more common form than we might casually suppose. It is much in evidence in

American SF in the forties and fifties. Hari Seldon's "psychohistory" is perhaps the most popular instance. Asimov's essay, "Social Science Fiction" (1953), clearly argues such a thesis. At one point in his essay Asimov illustrates the unchangingness of history: leaving blanks where specific names might be put, he gives us a one-page description of a revolution, and then he gives us three sets of "right" answers from the English, French, and Russian revolutions. Asimov's point is that a writer predicting the future need only employ the basic paradigm in order to give a fairly accurate picture. Asimov's game, where not simply a statement of the obvious (somebody wins, somebody loses), is trivial. It shows not an understanding of deep mechanisms or structures of history, but an ability to write imprecisely. A sentence such as, "Eventually, a strong government was formed under_____" (p. 280), while it has the air of saying something, is empty. "Eventually" evades the important time issue. The words "strong" and "under" beg all questions about what kind of political arrangement the word "government" entails. And all the important issues of whom this person represented, where politically he came from, and how he consolidated this power, are evaded by the vapid passive, "was formed." Such a sentence tells us nothing of significance about Cromwell, Robespierre, or Lenin as historical figures. In short, such a sentence obscures any actual historical insight and thereby implies that the details of real history do not particularly matter. Meaningful historical thought can begin only after such elementary and trivial similarities have been absorbed.[8]

Asimov invokes broad parallels between past events; Wells invokes the models of scientific prediction. There are, however, other ways of viewing history. Both Asimov and Wells are attempting what Karl Popper would call "naturalistic" modes of prediction, as opposed to "historicist" prediction. It is worth thinking out the ramifications of these two modes of looking at the future, for, while at one level all modes of prediction share a similar rhetorical posture (that is, they try to persuade us by describing the inevitable), at another there are political implications to be drawn from the modes of reasoning.

In *The Poverty of Historicism* Popper argues that philosophers such as Plato and Marx set up a special kind of model for thought about the future, which is essentially different from that we see Wells performing.[9] These "historicists" claim to understand the mechanisms of "history," which, they argue, are unique to history and quite unlike the causal mechanisms of the natural sciences or even the looser statistical patterns used in sociology. The historicists are wary of easy parallels and they argue that every historical moment has to be understood in and of itself, as a distinct stage in historical development. Spengler would talk of the "morphology" of history. Thus, the French and Russian revolutions mark very different historical actions, and any parallels one would want to draw from the two are likely to be misleading and to distract us from the "real" direction of history. Historicism would criticize Wellsian naturalistic prediction which thinks in terms of populations, energy sources, transport systems, and so forth, as being trapped at the level of surface phenomena and, therefore, unable to see in any rigorous or useful way the movement of *history* itself.

One difference between historicist and naturalistic anticipation lies in their different attitudes toward what Darko Suvin, adapting Ernst Bloch, calls the *novum*. Historicist prediction allows for the new (though it certainly does not necessarily entail it!). It tends toward organic rather than mechanistic metaphor and sees all particular historical events as signs of a deep development, whether of growth or decay. The naturalistic models tends to see history as at some basic level static and to treat change as an epiphenomenon.

Goldstein's book is based on a naturalistic premise. The opening thesis of the text poses a configuration which it claims defines all history: "Throughout recorded time, and probably since the end of the Neolithic Age, there have been three kinds of people in the world, The High, the Middle, and the Low" (p. 152). To some extent this is an echo of the beginning of the *Communist Manifesto*. But I would point out an important difference: if Marx and Engels define class struggle as the motive of history, they see class structures as changing. Thus, where Marx and Engels allow for a new form of social organization in the future, Goldstein poses a basic and unchanging unit which will determine rigorously the shape of all societies. If, in positing a structural basis that underlies all societies, Goldstein's analysis shows up as different from historicist futurology, by that same gesture it puts itself close to the ahistoricism of Asimov. The totalitarian Party is, thus, not a new structure at all, but merely the final configuration of a social structure which has always been in place. In this respect, Goldstein's analysis of the oligarchic collective is for us an anticipation which, far from foreseeing any possibility of meaningful change, or even of decline, sees the future as a closed inevitability.

I do not mean to say that Orwell himself meant to argue such a case, but I do mean that such a case is implicit in the naturalistic anticipation, and I imagine that a good part of the power of *Nineteen Eighty-Four* derives as much from these generic imperatives of Goldstein's book as from the more graphic depictions of oppression and mind control.

Goldstein's book, however, is the ultimate sign of a particular turn of Orwell's pessimism. By giving us a sociology of the future, he implies that the choice of the future is closed. In this mode, to talk about the future is to kill the concern for the future that might lead one to try to change the present. Thus, the book, presumed by Winston Smith to serve the purpose of revolutionary education, consolidation, and awareness, for us becomes a warning of the impossibility of meaningful change. Orwell uses the anticipation to deny political possibility. Politically, his position now resembles that of a conservative, like C. S. Lewis, who, in *The Abolition of Man* (1947), was arguing that the scientific-technological renaissance is only a way of granting further power to those already holding too much power and a way of depriving the future of its full range of options.[10]

Goldstein, whatever uses he has been put to, is not an Ingsoc technocrat. His collaboration in the larger projects of the Ministry of Truth may be completely unintentional. But "Goldstein" is, after all, just another of the pen names of Eric Blair. *The Theory and Practice of Oligarchic Collectivism* is, finally, Orwell's *Anticipation*. And for Orwell, unlike Goldstein, such collaboration with the totalitarian end of history is *inevitable*, given the forms by which he thinks.

One Man's Tomorrow Is Another's Today: The Reader's World and Its Impact on *Nineteen Eighty-Four*

Elizabeth Maslen

When politics meets literature, the kind of regime under which a writer is working can have a crucial effect on his or her choice of priorities, especially if the writer's views happen to conflict with those that prevail in places of authority. A writer may or may not have freedom to express these views openly, and this freedom, or lack of it, must inevitably influence any choice of literary form. When a writer lives in a climate where dissenting opinions can be expressed openly, without incurring penalties, then there is a choice between presenting ideas directly to the reader or through such forms of "oblique" writing as science fiction (or, as the Russians call it, *naoútchnaïa fantástika*—scientific fantasy). If the writer lives under a repressive regime, then the choice is likely to be much more limited: if an individual is to survive, or at least survive as a writer, he or she can rarely express dissenting views directly, but must rely on some form of oblique writing, trusting to the reader's willingness and experience to interpret the underlying ideas as intended.

And it is precisely here that the writer runs into problems. Most schools of literary theory today tell us what the fates of Zamyatin's *We* and Orwell's *Nineteen Eighty-Four* all too clearly demonstrate: that when the text leaves the writer's hands, it takes on a life of its own, as it were, and indeed can assume a number of different identities, depending on the circumstances and experience of readers at different times and in different places. To make a broad generalization which I shall be exploring more closely: under a repressive regime, readers who are seriously concerned with politics may become adept at interpreting literature which is ostensibly entertainment of a more or less serious kind, if they sense that a writer has concealed political or social comment. But under regimes where writers have the choice between direct and oblique expression, any political impact that oblique writing has may be dissipated, as readers may well feel that the writer's views cannot be as high a priority as the choice of form, since that choice must have been made on aesthetic grounds rather than for reasons of political discretion.

Here, then, is the dilemma we are faced with when confronting the undoubted popularity of *Nineteen Eighty-Four*. With his last two major works Orwell reached, and has continued to reach, a wider audience than he ever achieved with his earlier works. But whether the reasons for his success are what he wished or intended is a question we debate continually. And what made him turn from his earlier explorations of social realism to oblique writing? Social realism was a respectable mode for political utterance in Orwell's England; he had used it constantly in his journalism, his factually based works, and his earlier novels, apart from the mildest of flirtations with other modes, as in the Joycean chapter in *The Clergyman's Daughter*. Certainly, among those English writers that Orwell is known to have admired, Swift and Kipling used animal fable for social comment, while Wells and Huxley used futuristic fiction for something akin to Orwell's own purposes; but he must have suspected that most of his contemporaries, in England at least, read them for their literary rather than their political and social implications.

So what had these two genres, the animal fable and futuristic fiction, to offer an English writer intent on making political points? First and foremost, they entertain, so luring at least some readers to confront ideas which they might repudiate out-of-hand in more direct modes of writing. Second, by their very nature, fable and futuristic fiction announce that they expect the reader to explore other worlds: they need not be, at their best, overtly dogmatic and so can flatter any reader into feeling the only valid interpreter. Of course, these very qualities of entertainment and obliqueness have their dangers too: precisely because they rely on a reader's perspicacity, they are at the mercy of that reader's prejudices and prejudgments. But weighing advantage against disadvantage, their main attraction for Orwell may well have been that he could cast lures to a wide audience. Whereas "humankind / Cannot bear very much reality," a wide audience is willing to be entertained, and so possibly his political message might reach more people than if he were to spell it out more explicitly.

But was Orwell seduced into dissipating his political message in his later works? Freedom of expression can breed political fantasy as well as political apathy in all but a few; so was Orwell's choice of entertaining forms paradoxically esoteric, if he really meant to get his political points across? Had he seen the power of oblique writing under repressive regimes, and come to believe that the same climate prevailed in England as he saw it, affecting the writer and his readership alike? And, most important, had he failed to see that even under repressive regimes, the full political content of oblique writing is only going to reach the relatively few who are prepared to wrestle, and so break its code, and apply its implications to their own situations—and quite possibly recreate the text in ways the author did not intend?

Certainly there is good reason why Orwell may have come to distrust full-scale social realism as a sure channel of communication between writer and reader. The reception of his nonfictional *Homage to Catalonia* during the late thirties had shown that a realistic mode need not spare a writer from interpretations quite other than his own: few readers rallied to his defence of the POUM; even the Left Book Club deserted him for his support of suspected fascist sympathizers. Yet the POUM, while not Trotskyite, was well-disposed to Trotsky's ideas. It is not very surprising that, over the next decade, Orwell not only acquainted himself with Trotsky's life, work, and fate, incorporating the essence of what he interpreted in the portrayal of Goldstein in *Nineteen Eighty-Four*, but also that he should have lost faith in the capacity of unadulterated social realism to communicate ideas. And it is interesting to compare his move from the mainstream of this literary mode with the changing direction of Doris Lessing's writings since *The Golden Notebook*, published in 1962.

Up to the time of writing *The Golden Notebook*, Doris Lessing had produced realistic novels. Like Orwell, she was socially committed, and, although, unlike him, she joined the Communist Party, she soon came to eschew party politics as such. Like Orwell, she came (in her novels, that is) to use artistic expression primarily as a means for conveying ideas. In *The Golden Notebook* she experimented with "layered" form, the telling of one tale in five different ways, all apparently resolved in a sixth telling. Her chief purpose was, as she protests in her preface added in 1971, to say "implicitly and explicitly, that we must not divide things off, must not compartmentalise." Instead she found, on giving the manuscript "to publisher and friends . . . that I had written a tract about the sex war, and fast discovered that nothing I said then could change that diagnosis".[1]

What is fascinating about *The Golden Notebook*, significant for Lessing's future development, and relevant to Orwell's last work, is the way in which the text throws the responsibility for its interpretation very heavily upon the reader, although this would not appear to have been Lessing's intention while writing it. In a way, it is ironic that her preface reveals the need to explain so fully the writer's intentions when producing *The Golden Notebook*. Because the writer-protagonist in the work shows a constant distrust of her own capacity to express the truth; is horrified when, in a dream, her "idea" of her novel, and that of the film director who sets out to produce it, differ utterly in their interpretation of what she wrote; and repeatedly stresses the treachery of language. The very fact that Lessing's readers are presented with six different versions of the same material allows them to choose, consciously or not, the dominant theme as they see it. The form of the novel invites them to do this, whether Lessing intends it or not, because, by selecting this form, she has virtually written her own intentions out of the text.

She admits as much at the end of the 1971 preface, seeing the conflicting interpretations of her work as raising "questions of what people see when they read a book, and why one person sees one pattern and nothing at all of another pattern, and how odd it is to have, as author, such a clear picture of a book, that is seen so differently by its readers." From the time of writing that preface, she has turned to modes of writing that leave more and more room for readers to interpret and "recreate" her works by, for instance, deliberately not explaining the role of the animal Hugo in *Memoirs of a Survivor*, or the relation between inner and outer space in this and other of her later works. More recently, in her *Canopus in Argos: Archives* series, she has turned entirely to "space" fiction, as she calls it, as a means of expressing her ideas, while at the same time consciously leaving the reader's world to have its own impact on her novels. And she has said: "The old "realistic" novel is being changed . . . because of influences from that genre loosely described as space fiction. . . . Space fiction, with science fiction, makes up the most original branch of literature now."[2]

We can see from this that Lessing's experience with *The Golden Notebook* and Orwell's experience with *Homage to Catalonia* have much in common; and Lessing's description of the lessons she learned from her book's reception may well throw some light on Orwell's own change of approach in his last two major works. Yet, intriguingly, Lessing's preface also serves to highlight Orwell's unwillingness to admit, a decade after the critical reception of *Homage to Catalonia*, that readers do not always recreate a text in the way a writer anticipates, or can anticipate; for some of the problems raised by *Nineteen Eighty-Four* are similar to those raised by *The Golden Notebook*. Orwell's unwillingness to learn about the uncertainty of reader-response to a writer's ideas after his own earlier experience is certainly implied in his essay "Why I Write," published in 1946, when *Animal Farm* had been in print for a year and *Nineteen Eighty-Four* partially planned for two years at the very least.[3] In this essay Orwell writes, after asserting his ten-year commitment to writing against totalitarianism and for democratic socialism. "As I understand it . . . it seems to me nonsense, in a period like our own, to think that one can avoid writing of such subjects. Everyone writes of them in one guise or another. It is simply a question of which side one takes and what approach one follows. And the more one is conscious of one's political bias, the more chance one has of acting politically, without sacrificing one's aesthetic and intellectual integrity."[4]

This passage is surely a classic statement of wishful thinking. *Does* everyone write of these things, or is Orwell's sense of what constitutes political matter so broad by the time he writes this essay as to be beyond the bounds of definition? Is the question of which side one takes and what approach one follows so simple? Is a consciousness of one's political bias always an easy matter, and, if it is, does it give one more chance of *acting* politically without sacrifice of aesthetic and intellectual integrity?

So why did Orwell make such passionate assertions in his 1946 essay? His growing obsession with totalitarianism and his fear that it would swamp the England he knew offer the most popular explanation; but I would like to make a further suggestion: while he clung to his faith in his own "aesthetic and intellectual integrity," his political judgement as to choice of literary vehicles for his message may have been distorted by his awareness of other writers using similar subject matter in a variety of ways and under differing circumstances. All share with Orwell the difficulty of putting across ideas which have an extraordinary capacity for shape-changing and reinterpretation, depending on whether their audience accepts the political environment of the text at the time of its creation; how they see its relevance to their own situations; and how successful the writer's message is in crossing political frontiers of time and space. Some of the most important of these minds were formed in Eastern Europe; and, while *Animal Farm* and *Nineteen Eighty-Four* are set in England, those works rooted in other regimes and other places had a considerable effect on Orwell and his contemporaries, in many ways helping us to understand why he chose the forms he did, and why difficulties arise from these choices.

For instance, in Russia, oblique political writing has had a long history under both Czarist and Soviet censorship. Bertram Wolfe sums up how this kind of writing works: "By innocent-seeming tales of other lands or times, by complicated parables, animal fables, double meanings, overtones, by investing apparently trivial events with the pent-up energies possessing the writer, . . . the reader [is] compelled to dwell on them until their hidden meanings bec[o]me manifest."[5] Of course, Wolfe refers to the politically conscious reader here, although, being politically conscious himself (and knowing the Russian political scene well), he does not feel the need to make the point. The point is worth making, however, in view of its implications for Orwell's choice of forms in his later words. And the point continues to be valid if we think of the scientific fantasies of, for example, the brothers Strugatski or Siniavski. But this is to take a leap beyond Orwell's time: I want to concentrate on what Orwell himself knew or could have known about Russian oblique writing.

So we can turn, say, to Ivan Krylóv, who translated La Fontaine in the early nineteenth century, and was able to fuse the satirical French fables with traditional Russian folk tales to become, almost overnight, a writer of enduring popular apolitical entertainment, and a practitioner of oblique writing, as he satirized Francophile behavior among the educated of his day (his best fables were written during the Napoleonic era); government muddles ("The Quartet," a tale of the monkey, donkey, goat, and Mishka the bear asking the nightingale how to improve their music and getting the answer: "You need skill and better ears; however you sit, you'll never be musicians," is thought to refer to the reorganization of the Council of State in 1810); laziness and greed in everyday life, and so on. He was still favorite reading matter among the Russian troops in the Second World War, and Bernard Pares's 1926 translations were reprinted in Penguin in 1942, a year before Orwell said he began writing *Animal Farm*.[6] This might appear to have marginal relevance to *Nineteen Eighty-Four* and scientific fantasies; but Krylóv's heir in satire was Saltykóv-Shchedrín, who wrote animal fables[7] but also wrote, for instance, "Story of a Town" in 1870, which describes, among other things, the destruction of a town of fools by one of its governors, and the building of a geometrical replacement with houses all on the same pattern, spies in every block, and uniformed citizens following an exact timetable.[8] Leonid Heller asserts: "*Story of a Town*, in its rage against uniformity, is the most violent caricature ever written about Czarist Russia (and perhaps also, by premonition, about the claustrophobia of collectivism), and a prefiguration of the dystopias of the twentieth century."[9] One might question Heller's idea of premonition, since later readers might well recreate the text in this way, regardless of the author's foresight. But what is equally, if not more important for our central concern is that Saltykóv-Shchedrín, with his skillful blend of sophisticated and folk elements, in style as well as content, is a direct Russian precursor of Zamyatin, as is made clear in Zamyatin's "Theta" fables,[10] as well as in his best known work *We*,[11] which shares several of the concerns of "Story of a Town." Orwell's interest in *We* is well known; but what happened to *We*, and why it happened, give other valuable insights into the problems we face with *Nineteen Eighty-Four*, because *We*'s fate demonstrates dramatically the impact of the reader's world on a text.

Zamyatin had to write obliquely: *We* was not written in exile but in Russia during Lenin's lifetime, when the Party was still faced by opposition groups and a fiercely independent peasantry, and when Trotsky's views on permanent revolution were still discussable. Zamyatin did not manage to get *We* published in Russia; it first appeared in translation abroad, and in 1926 was translated into Czech, also appearing in a Russian émigré magazine published in Prague. When it was first written, the Revolution was only three years old; but by the time the Czech and expatriate Russian versions came out six years later, events were catching up with *We*. It was these versions which made Zamyatin's position as a writer untenable. Of course, Stalin and his aides had been educated in the power of oblique writing to convey a political message,[12] but why had Zamyatin been relatively unharmed by earlier translations in the West, only to be pilloried six years after he had written the book? I have traced the Russian antecedents of *We* as it is, I think, important to see the answers arising from the Soviet situation. Furthermore, Orwell only read the book in the thirties, in its mediocre French translation [form], and his comments on it are affected by the English success of *Brave New World*, Huxley's futuristic fable published in 1932 and written under very different circumstances.

For one thing, the leader of the community in *We* is actually present in the tale, visibly seen as the controlling force at all important functions; he is visibly seen as ultimately responsible, just as the Czar, Lenin, and later Stalin were seen as ultimately responsible for their regimes and policies. Second, Zamyatin's Green Wall, which serves as a bulwark against the world of nature and those who lurk there, is an oblique but clear reference to the Revolution's agrarian policy, which turned to something infinitely more repressive under Stalin, and so more dangerous to Zamyatin through the 1926 publications. A third important feature of *We* is that the protagonist does not surrender of his own volition: he is operated on but, in his lobotomized condition, is still able to report that revolution goes on. It is worth noting that in Huxley's *Brave New World* there is no revolution: his characters Marx and Helmholtz opt out, the Savage hangs himself. So while Zamyatin squarely blames the State for the destruction of the individual, while suggesting that the revolution is still in the balance at the end of his book, the departure of Huxley's individualists leaves no reverberations behind. What is more, in Zamyatin's *We*, the girl protagonist has insisted that revolution must, of necessity, be continuous, seeing stasis as unnatural by definition and denying any such thing as an ultimate revolution.[13] It is not very surprising that Zamyatin could not get his work published in Lenin's Russia; in the readers' changing world of the late twenties and early thirties, it is astonishing that he got out of Stalin's Russia alive.

Orwell reviewed the English translation of *We* in 1946, and has even been accused of plagiarizing when writing *Nineteen Eighty-Four*. But while he quotes in his review a passage on revolution as being enough to have publication banned in Russia, his main interest in *We* would seem to lie elsewhere. Although *We* may not suggest to all readers that anti-industrialism or anti-bureaucracy predominate as themes, Orwell would seem to want to relate its core to all industrial societies, seeing it as attacking The Machine in general, not in particular, and he is keen to point out that Zamyatin spent a number of years in England. Orwell was the first to connect *We* and *Brave New World*, but, while he finds Huxley's work better "put together," Zamyatin's "not of the first order," he asserts that *We* "is on the whole more relevant to our own situation," and sees the male protagonist as "a sort of Utopian Billy Brown of London Town."[14] Most importantly, at no point does he mention the reasons for oblique writing under a repressive regime, or the fact that Huxley could choose his literary form for mainly aesthetic reasons. And this surely suggests that Orwell was recreating Zamyatin's text according to his own world as a reader, disregarding (despite his acceptance of why *We* was banned) the implications of repressive and liberal regimes on the crucial matter of choice of form, and the impact of different readers' worlds on Zamyatin's text—including Orwell's own.

Certainly *Nineteen Eighty-Four* owes something to *We*. The central love affair is an obvious link, although it is amusing to see that Orwell makes the female of the species basically apolitical, a reversal of Zamyatin's tack with his female protagonist; the pressing need to exterminate genuine passion, imagination, and any kind of individual choice is shared, and so on. But the main links are not to the Russian heritage which forms at least a vital part of *We*; they connect more obviously to Orwell's recreation of *We* as a Western reader. In many ways, *Nineteen Eighty-Four* is closer to Huxley: neither Huxley nor Orwell hint at any sizeable revolution in progress; the questioning of The Machine is left to individuals. And unlike Zamyatin, Orwell does not stress the world beyond the city.

Nor did Orwell feel the urge to set his work far in the future: he does not appear to have been naturally drawn to this aspect of oblique writing. According to Peter Davison's edition of the facsimile, Orwell appears to have toyed with a number of titles, *1980* and *1982* as late as 1947, while *The Last Man in Europe* (a possibility from early days, conceivably as early as 1944) only gave way to *Nineteen Eighty-Four* at the end of 1948.[15] And *Nineteen Eighty-Four* as a title has had much to answer for, with regard to readers' worlds and their impact on Orwell's text, raising complex and disturbing issues.[16] One reason for this is, surely, that Orwell hovers between realism and fantasy; the result is a work very like the dystopian caricatures of timeless Bosch or period Hogarth. Caricature, used seriously, is a treacherous art: it must be sufficiently like what it represents to be identifiable, while at the same time it must deliberately distort what it wishes to emphasize. The caricature relies on its audience for its interpretation, of course; but by presenting, say, a recognizable human face and then distorting it, vulnerability to an audience's point of view is immeasurably increased. An audience may even see caricature as social realism, on its own terms, which may not correspond to the artist's: the caricature of the artist's ideas, if he is bent on conveying ideas, may well be the paradoxical result.

I am emphasizing my view of *Nineteen Eighty-Four* as political caricature partly as one possible reading of the text, and partly because so many arguments about Orwell's last major work have centered on whether or not it is meant as prophetic fable. But academic debate cannot ignore the fact that, as it stands, the work is called *Nineteen Eighty-Four*, and a prophetic work it has become for a large readership. For some English readers, as Mark Reader has pointed out, the focal point is the English setting in a still recognizable London, so that while Winston Smith may have forgotten much of his past, English readers of a certain age are tempted to fill in his background for him, and so, as it were, become accomplices to his nightmare vision;[17] and this impact of the English readers' world has been used by differing political groups in differing ways. Meanwhile, Isaac Deutscher saw it as a seminal work for McCarthyism;[18] while Fyvel said in 1959 that "when recently published in Warsaw, *Nineteen Eighty-Four* was received by young Polish intellectuals with avid appreciation and an astonishment that an English outsider should have shown such insight into Stalinist society," a view shared by Ghanaian intellectuals of the same era under another man's rule.[19] Last year, some Indonesian intellectuals said in private conversation that Orwell's book exactly reflected current experience in their country; and in *Le Monde* of 15 May this year, the Czech writer Vaclav Havel, who still resides in his own country, speaks of the "struggle against automatism" in his land, defines impersonal power as "a universal principle, not just emanating from Moscow," and finishes by speaking of "la novlangue du monde," asking "has the

New Speak of the real world already replaced natural human language, to the point where two persons cannot even share the simplest experience any more?"[20] Clearly, the tomorrow of Orwell's title is Havel's today, as he experiences it.

So, if Orwell meant to write on his today, offering warnings rather than prophecies about his tomorrow, does my suggestion about caricature in the text help to explain why so many readers find it mirroring their different experiences? I have already pointed to Russian oblique writing as one possible source for the potential split between Orwell's ideas and their execution; another may be the undoubted link between Orwell's book and Koestler's *Darkness at Noon*.[21] Koestler, brought up in Hungary, only left Budapest in 1922 when he was seventeen, after Béla Kun's ill-fated attempt to set up a soviet there. He took part in the Spanish Civil War as a communist, and spent some time in a death cell there. He was deeply shocked by the Great Purge trials which soon followed in Russia, and, out of his disillusionment, wrote *Darkness at Noon*, his great realistic novel based on just such a trial, where the only element of fantasy is kept for the vision of the Promised Land in the protagonist's imagination. *Darkness at Noon* was published in 1940 and was well received critically; but it had little impact until after the war years. There are a number of possible reasons why this should have been so. The most widely accepted view is that most readers quite simply did not want to acknowledge what was happening in Russia; fascism was enough, and so Koestler's revelations either suffered a similar fate to Orwell's in *Homage to Catalonia*, since they disturbed so many readers' world view; or they were read as Kafkaesque, which for many meant fantasy.

Kafka's work had enormous impact on English readers in the thirties. He was brought up, like Koestler, with German as his first language and lived in Prague, contemporary with Zamyatin, and writing throughout the First World War and the first years of the Russian revolution; as in Koestler's case, turbulent politics were right on his doorstep. He died two years before those two publications of *We*, so disastrous to Zamyatin, were brought out in Prague itself. Readings of Kafka's work are legion, but on some things most readers agree: his style, if not his meaning, is lucid; he has a rich sense of the absurd, both comic and horrific; and, as in Orwell's case, it is almost impossible to disentangle autobiographical and fictional elements in his writing. It is a work like *The Trial* which I would maintain affected interpretations of *Darkness at Noon*, and may have encouraged the caricature element found in *Nineteen Eighty-Four*.

What is so striking about *The Trial* is the way in which Kafka treats the ordinary little things of daily life with complete realism; treats his protagonist's rather self-righteous rectitude with humor; and yet gradually builds up an atmosphere of nightmare, where the individual is powerless either to understand or influence the intangible menace of persecution. *The Trial* was first published in England in 1935, a date just prior to the Spanish Civil War, which was to bring in its wake a growing awareness of fascism and Stalinism; so *The Trial* became imbued—for thinking people at least—with significances which may or may not have been intended by Kafka, but which (as in Zamyatin's case) were overtaken by events beyond the writer's immediate concerns. His nightmare vision, according to Samuel Hynes, became a sophisticated parable for writers in the thirties;[22] and it is this which may have led many readers to recreate Koestler's later novel as a nonrealistic fiction, and may have been a further factor in encouraging Orwell to eschew full-scale realism, while trying to avoid the fate of *Homage to Catalonia* and *Darkness at Noon*—or so I suggest.

Finally, I should like to focus on just one point in *Nineteen Eighty-Four* to show how completely, if unintentionally, Orwell surrenders control of his text to his readers' worlds; and that is in the handling of Goldstein's book. Winston Smith never finishes the book; he simply imagines how it will end. Now, for a reader like Deutscher, this element of fantasy in Smith's make-up (already apparent in his "dream" or O'Brien, a Kafkaesque merging of hypothesis and fact which is skillfully never fully explained) was unimportant; Deutscher knew Trotsky, saw Goldstein's book as a summary of *The Revolution Betrayed*, and did not mention Smith's fantasy ending, since it squares (more or less; some readers might think rather less than fully) with Trotsky's own conclusions.[23] But what of readers who do not know Trotsky's work, or fail to recognize Trotsky in Goldstein? To them, Goldstein's book may seem unnecessarily longwinded, holding up the action; or the imagined ending may seem a wish-fulfilment of Smith's daydreams about the proles which may appear, in the context of the entire novel, utterly unjustified, and so on. O'Brien's assertion that Goldstein's book is a fabrication anyway may be taken at face value, or, for those who know Trotsky's fate, as an accurate account of the Stalinist deconstruction and absorption of another's lifework. However one reads Goldstein, it seems fair to say that Orwell was taking a bizarre risk in including this version of historical text if he intended his novel, set in the future, to be a vehicle for his own ideas; and his unwillingness to offer any clue as to the independent or fabricated existence of Goldstein's book both shows his failure to perceive the implications of his choice of form for *Nineteen Eighty-Four*, and demonstrates the surrender of his message both to his day and ours.

Echoes and departures from Zamyatin's necessarily oblique writing, Huxley's chosen futuristic form, Kafka's realism as fable, Koestler's realism as fact—all these and much more vie for our attention through the legend of Orwell's window pane prose and so appear, as it were, on equal terms. And so the novel becomes all things to all people, here and now, as factual prophecy or fabulous invention. But let me end with a quotation: "It is not only childish of a writer to want readers to see what he sees, to understand the shape and aim of a novel as he sees it—his wanting this means that he has not understood a most fundamental point. Which is that the book is alive and potent and fructifying and able to promote thought and discussion *only* when its plan and shape and intention are not understood, because that moment of seeing the shape and plan and intention is also the moment when there isn't anything more to be got out of it."[24] The writer is Doris Lessing, but her words might well serve as an epigraph for Orwell's *Nineteen Eighty-Four*.

Big Brother Antichrist: Orwell, Apocalypse, and Overpopulation

W. M. S. Russell and Claire Russell

In *Nineteen Eighty-Four*, as everyone knows, George Orwell depicted Britain as part of an American national socialist state. He himself explicitly described the novel as a warning and not a prediction. "I do not believe," he wrote in 1949, "that the kind of society I describe *will* arrive, but I believe (allowing, of course, for the fact that the book is a satire) that something resembling it *could* arrive" (his italics).[1] He had earlier complained of people who tried to "spread the idea that totalitarianism is *unavoidable*, and that we must therefore do nothing to oppose it" (his italics).[2]

Orwell himself was well aware, however, that he was prone to apocalyptic feelings and visions, to seeing the future in terms of golden promise and/or fearful menace. His comments on Koestler in 1945 apply equally to himself.[3] Koestler had described himself as a "short-term pessimist," and by implication a long-term optimist. Orwell commented that Koestler had no view of the future, or rather "two which cancel out"; but he himself clearly shared this combination of ultimate hopes and immediate forebodings. In 1946, he was writing with sympathy of the utopian dreams underlying democratic socialism,[4] and during the blitz he viewed the scenes of destruction with an expectation of "immense changes," ultimately for the better.[5] Sometimes hope and fear were exactly balanced. The hero of his novel *Coming Up for Air* foresees a future of totalitarian oppression and dictator worship. "It's all going to happen," he says. "Or isn't it? Some days I know it's impossible, other days I know it's inevitable."[6] But the dark visions generally prevailed. In a poem written when he left Burma, he could conceive of blazing stars raining on the earth in the style of the Book of Revelation.[7] In the early 1930s, he wrote of "the horrors that will be happening within ten years," and sometimes had an urge to "start calling down curses from Heaven like Jeremiah or Ezra or somebody."[8] His friend George Woodcock wrote of him that "often, indeed, it seemed as though one had been listening to the voice of Jeremiah."[9] In 1935, he wrote a little poem about being born in an evil time, and how "a happy vicar I might have been / Two hundred years ago"; but even in this daydream his clerical occupation is "to preach upon eternal doom" as well as to "watch my walnuts grow."[10] At the end of 1945, he made fun of his own apocalyptic leanings in an article of horrific prophecies he called "Old George's Almanac."[11]

In view of all this, in considering *Nineteen Eighty-Four*, it is worth looking at apocalyptic beliefs, with their positive and negative aspects, their visions of wonders and horrors in the future. There are two types, cyclical and once-for-all. The Indians believed in a recurrent cycle of ages: things begin well, get worse and worse, and end in the destruction of the, by now, thoroughly evil universe, and its replacement by a new and good one.[12] In the cult of Vishnu, the god appears in his tenth incarnation as a kind of messiah at the end of the present cycle, but this idea may have come from the West.[13] Some Greek thinkers shared the Indian conception of cycles. The Stoics developed this into a rather depressing notion that each cycle exactly repeats the last one, so that another Socrates will marry another Xanthippe, and so on, next time around. They did concede that a freckle-faced person might conceivably not have freckles in the next cycle, but this is cold comfort.[14]

The second type of apocalypse involves a once-for-all destruction and renovation of civilization and the universe. There are Persian, Moslem and Scandinavian versions, but all these have been influenced by the Judeo-Christian apocalypse, though both Bousset and, more recently, H. R. Ellis Davidson have shown that the Scandinavian vision of Ragnorok probably had independent origins in the paganism of the North.[15] By far the most important for European culture is the Judeo-Christian literature, which has been described as supreme among all manifestations of popular thought in reflecting "the impression produced by historical events on contemporary generations, on their ideas, hopes and fears."[16]

In its most familiar form, the Judeo-Christian apocalypse is a vision of a time of troubles followed by a time of bliss. A succession of disasters, including tyranny, war, famine, and pestilence, kill millions of people. Then follows a millennium, a thousand-year period, of peace and prosperity for the lucky fraction of survivors. Of the Jewish and Christian apocalyptic writings, by far the best known, and to most people the only one known, is the Book of Revelation, for the obvious reason that it forms part of the new Testament. When the Christian Church became established, it began to frown upon apocalyptic writings, with their overtones of revolution and catastrophe in the near future.[17] The Book of Revelation was the only such work to be admitted to the scriptural canon, because it was believed to be the work of St. John the Apostle, who was probably dead long before it was composed.[18] This book has contributed some unforgettable images, such as the four horsemen, representing tyranny, war, famine, and pestilence. However, in 1895 Wilhelm Bousset showed that Revelation is a highly garbled account of a much more coherent vision of the end of the world. By a beautiful piece of detective work, he was able to reconstruct this vision from scattered passages in the Old and New Testaments and the early Christian Fathers, and from a couple of dozen Jewish and Christian apocalyptic works in various languages.[19] The Jewish and Christian ideas interacted in various ways,[20] and each writer tried to weave in the political forces and events of his own time, but, despite this, there emerges a clear picture of the last days. The most striking feature is the rise and reign of a deceiving tyrant, the antimessiah or Antichrist, behind whom lurks the demon Belial or Beliar.[21] The Dead Sea Scrolls, discovered after the Second World War, fit in well with Bousset's picture; they refer to the demon Belial or Beliar, and to a wicked priest or Prophet of Untruth,[22] clearly the Antichrist. In the tradition revealed by Bousset, antichrist reigns for about three-and-a-half years, before being overthrown by the genuine messiah or by the Archangel Michael; but since time is traditionally somewhat distorted in these last days, the reign of Antichrist could either be much shorter or much longer than this.[23] According to one view, the defeat of antichrist is followed at once by the final destruction of the world and the last judgment. According to another view, the one followed by the author of Revelation, the millennium of earthly happiness intervenes.[24] In either view, the tyranny of antichrist is the main feature of the time of troubles, accompanied by war, famine, and pestilence.

Ever since Pompey profaned the Temple, the Jews hated Rome, and they consistently gave their antichrist a Roman origin, at times even calling him Romulus.[25] Some early Christians, though not St. Paul, shared this view. Matters were complicated by a Near Eastern folk belief about the survival or revival of the emperor Nero, who actually died in *A.D.* 68.[26] The author of Revelation, using a degraded form of totemic imagery, split the figure of Antichrist into a false prophet and two Beasts:[27] thereafter, Antichrist was often called the Beast. But as soon as there was any hope of even toleration by the Empire, the Christians began to soft-pedal Antichrist's Roman origin, and when the Empire became Christian, they naturally dropped it altogether. Insofar as they tolerated apocalyptic ideas at all, they now switched decisively to a Jewish origin for Antichrist.[28]

The Jewishness of Antichrist gave a great boost to medieval hate campaigns against Jews, who were regarded as his agents.[29] Antichrist plays, such as the German *Herzog von Burgund*, which ends in a massacre of Jews, must have had an incendiary effect. When this play was produced in Frankfurt in 1469, the town council, greatly to their credit, passed a special ordinance to protect their Jewish population, but other Jewish communities were less fortunate.[30] As Norman Cohn has shown, would-be totalitarian movements throughout the Middle Ages found the millennium a convenient bait, and Antichrist and the Jews convenient hate objects.[31] Since these movements were revolutionary, the Church generally opposed them. But in the fourteenth and especially the sixteenth centuries, the church's rule was shaken by schisms, and the church itself, in a totalitarian vein, sanctioned apocalyptic ideas for propaganda purposes. Hence, as Jean Delumeau has shown, preachers instigated pogroms with growing official support, and there emerged, in his words, "an antijudaeism unified, theorised, generalised, clericalised."[32]

As Christopher Hill has shown, the Protestants, especially in embattled England, reverted to the Jewish version of Antichrist as of Roman origin.[33] The equation of the Pope with Antichrist was virtually official doctrine in the Elizabethan Church.[34] The English Protestants even felt some affinity with the Jews, and the instant voluntary conversion of the whole Jewish people became an important item in the timetable of apocalyptic events. This may have influenced "Cromwell's decision to readmit the Jews to England in 1656."[35]

On the Continent, the writers of the Counter Reformation

counterattacked by reemphasizing the Jewishness of Antichrist,[36] and, of course, in the orthodox realm in Eastern Europe no reformation occurred. So, as Norman Cohn has shown, the link between apocalyptic beliefs and anti-Judaism continued right down to Hitler's promise, fortunately over-sanguine, of a thousand-year Reich.[37] The famous *Protocols of the Elders of Zion*, much used by Hitler, purport to be the program of a worldwide Jewish conspiracy of destruction. They were forged by the Csarist Russian police as part of their policy of instigating pogroms to divert peasant resentment away from the Csarist government, and published in good faith in 1905 by a Russian religious crank, in a book called *Antichrist as an Imminent Political Possibility.*[38]

If we now turn to *Nineteen Eighty-Four*, it is clear that Orwell is at one level satirizing the use of an Antichrist figure, for diverting resentment, in the very explicit hate sessions against the Jewish archenemy Emmanuel Goldstein. But at a more fundamental level, for Orwell himself, there is an excellent candidate for the figure of Antichrist in Big Brother, or rather the oligarchy that uses this shadowy figure-head, for Antichrist has often stood for institutions as well as individuals. This becomes clear when we consider the traditional character of Antichrist and his tyranny. In the sources studied by Bousset, Antichrist demands worship from all, and has his image set up in all the cities; all the people invite each other to praise him.[39] He simulates benevolence, without benefiting anybody.[40] He is, in general, supremely a deceiver, and his subjects and dupes suffer from strong delusions and a distorted mental vision.[41] He uses dens of vice as bait.[42] When deception fails, he uses terror, destroying all who refuse him worship.[43] He claims to control the past totally, asserting that before him there was no one.[44] Under his reign, "cruelty shall flourish, and love be dried . . . brother shall betray brother unto death and father son."[45]

The writers of seventeenth-century England sharpened the picture. They considered it a mark of Antichrist to "engage all to unity and uniformity."[46] They listed the features of his reign as conformity and cruelty, using censorship and persecution for dissent.[47] One of them observed that "a restraint of the press is usually practiced where Antichrist has his throne,"[48] "By the mark of the Beast in the forehead," wrote a commentator on Revelation, "I understand the irrationality of obedience of those that subject themselves blindfold in all things."[49] Milton himself wrote that Antichrist, whom he identified with the Pope, "assumes to himself this infallibility over both the conscience and the Scripture."[50] All this adds up to a striking portrait of Big Brother and his creators, and of the totalitarian world of *Nineteen Eighty-Four*.

We do not suggest that Orwell was familiar with the Jewish and Christian apocalyptic literature. He did not need to be. The Judeo-Christian apocalyptic vision has had a vast and many-sided influence on European culture. Until the eighteenth century it was taken literally by many, if not most, people. In the romantic era, as M. H. Abrams has shown in detail, it was reshaped by German philosophers and German and British poets as a secular message about psychology and world history, and in this form it permeates much of modern literature.[51] This new message took some odd forms, especially among the philosophers. But at least the romantics, disillusioned by the outcome of the French Revolution, realized that violence was not the way to a better future. They saw their millennium in terms of heightened consciousness, a constructive attitude to the natural environment, and a greater emotional awareness of other people; and they perceived that art, especially literature, had an important part to play in bringing these changes about. Following another path, both Roger Bacon and Francis Bacon related the wonders of the millennium to progress in science and technology.[52] Along yet another line, apocalyptic writings evolved into more or less realistic histories of the future, a genre extremely important for the development of science fiction. The transition from apocalyptic fantasy to circumstantial prediction can be credited to the remarkable Portuguese Jesuit, Antonio Vieira, who lived from 1608 to 1697. Statesman, diplomat, teacher, missionary, and explorer of the Amazon, Vieira was a humane and liberal-minded man who campaigned valiantly on behalf of the Portuguese Jewish Christians, the Brazilian Indians, and the black slaves. He had more than one brush with the Inquisition, but secured royal and papal protection. His book, *History of the Future*, predicted a world of the King of Portugal.[53] Though emerging from previous apocalyptic writings in Portugal, this was, in effect, a detailed political forecast. It was followed by many more histories of the future, up to, and beyond, those of H. G. Wells, with their alternation of promise and foreboding.[54] Vieira's idea of world government was a particularly fruitful one, even if he inevitably backed the wrong horse in the Portuguese empire, already being nibbled away by the Dutch.

Besides these literary offshoots, apocalyptic imagery has been used again and again in European history as a weapon of political propaganda. Those labeled as Antichrist by their enemies or victims include Archbishop Laud, Louis XIV, Peter the Great, Lenin, and European colonial governments in Africa.[55] In the proliferation of sects and parties in seventeenth century England, especially under the Commonwealth, this antichristening activity ran riot. Everybody called everybody else Antichrist.[56] Cromwell, who had of course been antichristened himself by the radicals, told one of his critics bitterly: "You fix the name of antichristian upon anything."[57] The word "beast" was so heavily used as Revelation's synonym for Antichrist that a new word was needed for ordinary beasts, and Christopher Hill has suggested this explains the emergence at this time of the word "animal."[58]

Orwell may not have known the apocalyptic literature analyzed by Bousset, but he was an heir to all these apocalyptic influences in many ways. From his boyhood, Wells was one of his favourite authors[59], and, of course, both positive and negative aspects of the apocalyptic tradition are constantly present in the work of Wells. W. M. S. Russell has shown, for instance, how Wells used imagery direct from the Book of Revelation in *The War of the Worlds*.[60] At one time, Orwell thought of writing a biography of Mark Twain,[61] whose work, from the *Connecticut Yankee* onward, is full of apocalyptic nightmares. In any case, Orwell knew his Bible, and must have been familiar with Revelation and the other biblical apocalyptic passages. He was also at home in seventeenth century English political literature.[62] During the Second World War, when he was broadcasting specimens of British culture to Asia, he reminded a colleague that Milton had been a propagandist for the Commonwealth, had himself chosen to include the *Areopagitica* in his broadcasts.[63] He knew the work of Winstanley, a great antichristener of oppressive rulers.[64] "The pamphlets of Gerrard Winstanley," he wrote in 1946, "are in some ways strangely close to modern Left Wing literature."[65] He was quite familiar with the concept of Antichrist. In 1941, he wrote that "the people who say that Hitler is Antichrist . . . are nearer an understanding of the truth" than those who had failed to take the Nazi menace seriously.[66] In his novel *Keep the Aspidistra Flying* he invented a literary magazine called *Antichrist*, based loosely on a real one he wrote for himself called *Adelphi*, which of course means "brothers" in Greek.[67] From all this, it seems not unreasonable to conclude with some degree of certainty that Big Brother has something of Antichrist about him, and that *Nineteen Eighty-Four* takes its origin in the apocalyptic tradition.

The old apocalypses are full of fantasies about monsters and falling stars. Orwell's novel, on the other hand, is perfectly naturalistic, and full of accurate predictions and extrapolations of trends to be observed when he wrote it. Our world in 1984 is measurably more like the world of Orwell's novel that it was in 1948. Claire Russell has expressed this thought in the following poem, written towards the end of 1983:

> *They're coming through the windows,*
> *They're coming through the doors,*
> *They're coming through the ceilings,*
> *They're coming through the floors.*
>
> *There's no more fun on celluloid;*
> *Big Brother Bug's a paranoid.*
> *When "What the Butler Saw" was mild,*
> *The blue-taped video-show's gone wild.*
>
> *Adherents of a phobic creed*
> *Fear that the end is drawing near*
> *With its delays and numbered days.*
> *The ritual must proceed.*
>
> *The ritual goes on and on,*
> *And no-one has a care,*
> *That long ago the time has gone,*
> *When everything bid fair.*

Orwell correctly predicted the growth of pornography and the technology of surveillance. These were perhaps relatively easy predictions, but Orwell showed uncommon perceptiveness in harping, both in the novel and in his nonfiction, on the link between violent pornography and power worship.[68] For the ethological basis for the connection between dominance and pseudosexual displacement activities was only discovered by A. H. Maslow and Claire Russell in the nineteen-fifties;[69] besides these displacement activities, pornography also reflects the experiences of a stressful upbringing.[70] Orwell was quick to emphasize the phenomenon of terrorism. The grimmest moment in the whole of *Nineteen Eighty-Four* is that when Winston and Julia, believing they are joining a movement against the Party, agree, if necessary, to throw acid in a child's face, as O'Brien later reminds him.[71] But the most astonishing feat of prediction in the book is the third chapter of the Goldstein document, which discusses the Cold War.[72] We need only compare this chapter, called "War is Peace," with the actual history of the Cold War, to be awed by Orwell's prophetic powers. Even his account of the precise geography of hot and cold war is extraordinarily near the historical facts since his death: he said he began to think on these lines in 1944 "as a result of the Teheran Conference."[73]

How, then, can we compare Orwell's sober and often accurate predictions with wild fantasies of the apocalyptic writings? The answer is that they too contain a large measure of underlying realism. They can in general be dissected into bizarre events in the natural world, such as stars falling like leaves,[74] and perfectly realistic disasters affecting human societies—tyranny, war, famine, and pestilence. We have shown a few years ago, in studies of totemism, that human beings took a long time to distinguish between events and processes in human societies and those in the natural environment, and have still not fully eliminated this confusion between society and nature.[75] The falling stars result from this confusion; the monsters, from symbolism. When they are stripped away, we are left with the essential sequence of events we summarized earlier, as follows: "A succession of disasters, including tyranny, war, famine and pestilence, kill millions of people. Then follows a millennium, a thousand-year period, of peace and prosperity for the lucky fraction of survivors." This sequence of events has occurred again and again in human history.[76] Every so often, a population began seriously to outgrow its current supply of resources. It then entered a period of population crisis, with well-marked effects, including tyranny, war, famine, and pestilence. Specifically, the combination of famine, chronic malnutrition, and social stress lowered resistance to infection, so that epidemics killed millions. Malthus, who well understood all this, put the process in apocalyptic words. "The vices of mankind," he wrote, "are active and able ministers of depopulation.

They are the precursors in the great army of destruction; and often finish the dreadful work themselves. But should they fail in this war of extermination, sickly seasons, epidemics, pestilence, and plague, advance in terrific array, and sweep off their thousands and ten thousands."[77]

As a result of each such crisis of overpopulation, numbers would be drastically cut down, and this, for a time, improved the situation, because the surviving population was much reduced, relative to its current resource supply. Hence such relief periods were items of economic, political, social and cultural advance, often called renaissances. Unfortunately the relief has never been more than relative, and no such relief period has ever lasted a thousand years. But in all other respects the apocalyptic narratives simply describe the course of population crises and relief periods, even to such details as the price inflation characteristic of the crisis period,[78] referred to in the Book of Revelation in connection with the third horseman, in the ominous phrase "a measure of wheat for a penny," that is for a large sum of money.[79] Apocalyptic ideas were, in fact, most active and intense during periods of population crisis, such as those of the fourteenth century, and the sixteenth and seventeenth centuries, in Europe, with a mild recrudescence in the incipient crisis at the end of the eighteenth century.[80]

Tyranny has been a feature of all population crises. But it has taken particularly frightful forms in the densely populated irrigated regions of the Near East, the Far East, and the New World, at times when large areas along rivers were being unified into what Sprague de Camp has called "watershed empires."[81] From a number of competing states, the winner was always the one nearest the watershed, for instance, the Assyrians, the Inca, and the Ch'in State on the Yellow River. The wars of unification developed savagely militaristic states, of which the winner was usually the worst: it collapsed during the relief period brought about by the drop in population due to war and tyranny, and was replaced by a milder regime, such as the Persian Empire or the Han Dynasty.

For all his great insight, Orwell was wrong in supposing that totalitarianism is something new.[82] Stanislav Andreski has shown that only its "combination with a progressive technology" is new, and that states like those of the Inca and the Ch'in were thoroughly totalitarian.[83] The principles of the Ch'in state were expounded in a book by Kung-Sun Yang, Lord of Shang, a Ch'in minister who was himself executed in 338 B.C.[84] Andreski called this book "altogether a faithful picture of modern totalitarian rule."[85] W. M. S. Russell wrote that it "reads like a satire by Orwell," and summarized it as follows.[86] The author

> defined "virtue" as unquestioning obedience to the state. The worst deviations from virtue, according to him, were care for old people, not working (at farming or war—nothing else counted as work), personal ambition, a taste for beauty, and love. The people were to be adjusted to total obedience by inflicting severe punishment for even the slightest deviation; then the really serious crimes, like art or love, would never occur. When actually executing a criminal, it was important to find out what death he most feared, and then inflict it. Anyone failing to denounce a friend for law-breaking was sawn in half.

In 213 B.C., when the King of Ch'in had become the Emperor Ch'in Shih Huang Ti, he made a determined effort to burn the whole of existing Chinese literature, except certain technical works. This was done, as a later Chinese historian wrote, "for the purpose of keeping the people ignorant, and of bringing it about that none within the Empire should use the past to discredit the present."[87] Clearly the Ch'in rulers shared the view of the *Nineteen Eighty-Four* Party: "who controls the past controls the future: who controls the present controls the past."[88]

Modern industrial civilization has finally attained population densities and urban aggregations comparable to, and even exceeding, those of the great irrigation civilizations. It shows similar symptoms of bureaucratic growth and monoculture in food production. The logic of world resource use calls for a rational world government of the kind dreamed of by Vieira or Wells, but the world is divided among warring states like those of the Yellow River valley in the fifth and third centuries *B.C.* Orwell's nightmare is, therefore, not an empty threat.

The sequence of crisis and relief has recurred many times in human societies, the cycles being staggered in different regions. For instance, we have described seven such cycles in the history of China, and five in the history of Europe during the Christian era alone.[89] From this point of view, the Indians and Stoics were nearer the truth with their concept of recurrent cycles. But now, with modern military

technology, and overpopulation synchronized everywhere to produce a world-wide crisis, we are facing the possibility of once-for-all
catastrophe. And this time, though the stars would not fall like
leaves, there could be effects of apocalyptic proportions on our
natural environment. The solution, of course, is to reduce our swol-
len population densities by humane means instead of cruel ones, to
substitute voluntary birth control for involuntary death control. This
was the point made, in apocalyptic terms, by Robert McNamara to
the World Bank Group in 1968: "I do not believe that anyone would
wish to reintroduce pestilence—or any other of the four horsemen of
the apocalypse—as a 'natural' solution to the population problem."[90]
Orwell's novel may be one of the many warnings that will help to turn
mankind in the direction of voluntary birth control. With populations
reduced in this way, we may at last hope to escape forever apocalyptic nightmares, and to prepare the way for something much better
than apocalyptic dreams.

For the apocalyptic legends, so realistic about the horrors of
overpopulation, were anything but realistic in predicting an instant
millennium. Past periods of relief and renaissance, in which population pressure was somewhat reduced, give us some inkling of what is
really involved in human progress. These periods saw an enhanced
emotional awareness, a development of parental behavior and its
offshoot, social welfare, and a revival of science and art. When
voluntary birth control gives us the necessary relief from population
pressure, the task of building a better world will only begin. We need
to enhance those social parental activities which at present tend to be
undervalued and, in concrete terms, underpaid. Whereas the totalitarian state, as Orwell described, withers science and loses all touch
with reality, we need all the scientific enterprise envisaged by the two
Bacons, to inform us about human needs and natural resources,
always remembering the words of Francis Bacon, that "nature is not
to be commanded, except by being obeyed." As the romantic writers
saw, we need artistic creation to heighten consciousness and mutual
emotional awareness; and, as Orwell himself showed, language and
literature are vital here. We need to promote, in short, all that the
Party in Orwell's novel, and the Ch'in State in reality, sought to
destroy. Instead of the instant eternity of static bliss for a few, that
follows the millennium in apocalyptic writing, we can foresee for

mankind a continuing need and opportunity for creative endeavor. And perhaps this is the crucial message of the best science fiction, shining even through Orwell's last novel as if through a photographic negative, that, in the words of Isaac Asimov,[91] "the end of eternity is the beginning of infinity."

Variations on Newspeak: The Open Question of *Nineteen Eighty-Four*

T. A. Shippey

In a letter to the *Times* on 6 January 1984, Professor Bernard Crick, author of *George Orwell: A Life* and editor of the Clarendon Press annotated *Nineteen Eighty-Four*, attacked the *Times* fiercely for having maintained in a previous editorial that the "principal message" of George Orwell's novel was "about the use and abuse of language for political purposes." This was "body-snatching," he replied (meaning that Orwell, safely dead, was being appropriated to stand for opinions and institutions he would never have tolerated); it led also to "a comfortable, distancing reading of the text." Worst of all, it presented Orwell as a simple writer, ignored the true complexity of *Nineteen Eighty-Four*, and failed to observe the multiplicity of its "main satiric thrusts" (of which Crick identified seven). The final sentence of Crick's letter declared that "when anyone says it [*Nineteen Eighty-Four*] has a single or principal message they are wrong: and such assertions tell one more about the reader than about the book."

There is much in this reaction with which one can sympathize. One might well think that the *Times* had a certain vested interest in ignoring some of the objects of satire in *Nineteen Eighty-Four*, since it is one of them. Winston Smith spends much of his time in the Records Department of the Ministry of Truth falsifying reports in the *Times*, which has clearly become totally identified with the government (rather than just very largely, as in Orwell's own day). It is also nearly always acceptable in the terms of modern critical discourse to speak up for a work of art's complexity, and to accuse rivals of oversimplifying. Finally no one is in favor of comfortable readings, the taste for the challenging or disturbing having become firmly established. Nevertheless, there is something ominous about Crick's last clause. It sounds rather like a threat ("if you persist in offering single or principal interpretations you will show yourself up in ways you are not aware of"). And in a situation where Crick's opinions, via the biography and now the "standard edition" of the text, are likely to become dominant, it seems only right that even his most critically mainstream pronouncements should be scrutinized. Is there nothing to be said, after all, for the view that *Nineteen Eighty-Four does* have a "principal message," and that this is indeed not far from the theme of the assault on language?

One clarification which should be made immediately, of course, is that talking about messages of any kind is liable to be distracting when one is discussing a novel.[1] It would be better, at least initially, to consider structure: and here one has to say that however complex (or otherwise) Orwell may have been as a writer, the *structure* of *Nineteen Eighty-Four* at any rate is fairly simple, even conceivably too simple. It consists of three parts, none of them labelled or titled by Orwell.[2] In part 1, Winston Smith is introduced, and the scene is set of his home, his work, his neighbors, and his frustrations. Part 2 details his love affair with Julia and his recruitment by O'Brien. Part 3 is set almost entirely in the cells of the Ministry of Love, and consists very largely of a long conversation with O'Brien.

This structure is, furthermore, in several respects rather clumsy. In a letter to Anthony Powell on 15 November 1948 Orwell wrote that the book was "a ghastly mess," adding in a further letter to Julian Symons on 4 February 1949 that he had "ballsed it up."[3] Commentators usually take these remarks as the result of modesty, or of a sense (of course entirely plausible) that Orwell's terminal illness had prevented execution from matching intention. Nevertheless, and without any intention of carping, there are some odd things in the structure of *Nineteen Eighty-Four*. Movement between chapters, for instance, is very jerky, as one can see by looking at the chapter openings, so many of them simple-sentence, past progressive or pluperfect: there is often little continuity between one scene and the next.[4] It has surprisingly few characters: in part 1 there are only five major speaking parts besides Winston; namely, Parsons, Mrs. Parsons, Syme, the old prole of chapter 8, and Mr. Charrington, and, arguably, none of these *is* major. In chapter 1, indeed, the only words we hear from anyone at all are "Swine! Swine! Swine!" from Julia (at this stage nameless), "My Saviour!" (from another woman never named), and "B-B! . . . B-B!" (from everyone communally). Common in the novel are fragments of overheard conversation; for example, from the proles in chapter 8, or Julia and the "duckspeaker" in the canteen in chapter 5, while several characters are reduced entirely to the status of "noises off," like Winston's wife Katherine, or, of course, Comrade Ogilvy, who never exists at all. None of these comments, naturally, need disbar *Nineteen Eighty-Four* from being entirely successful in its own way. However, they may well suggest that as a narrative it is *not* complex, however many its satiric thrusts. The overall effect at times is of a series of silent stills, while at the heart of the whole novel there lies Winston's abject failure of a diary, a journal with no dates, a book its author does not know how to write, a text whose principal message is quite unambiguously "DOWN WITH BIG BROTHER," written "over and over again." Winston is not Orwell, nor is his diary *Nineteen Eighty-Four:* but it may be significant that the novel springs from an extraordinarily unselfconscious and craftless literary artifact, and one presented to us with far more respect than contempt.

If we return to the novel's structure, the unspoken question most readers must find themelves asking would then appear to be, not (as Crick would have it) "what messages emerge from this work's complex syntax?" but more simply "what holds these disparate scenes, outcries, or fragments together?" And if the structure of *Nineteen Eighty-Four* is simple, the answer to the latter question ought to be simple as well: the strand running through the majority of the disconnected scenes and overhead conversations is that of Winston trying to recapture the past. Crick indeed suggests that the book's "positive themes" are once again not single, but double, "*memory* and *mutual trust*,"[5] and once again it may seem heartless to argue for the removal of one of them. However, there is oddly little about "mutual trust" in *Nineteen Eighty-Four*, even as an absence, apart, of course, from the central love and betrayal of Winston and Julia. By contrast, the theme of memory is pervasive. Winston is liable to introduce the subject at any moment, however unexpectedly, and there is a sense that throughout the novel Winston (and Orwell too) is trying to convert the reader to an appreciation of the vital importance, not the mere desirability, of objective evidence and recorded history. Thus, Winston rejects all the more obvious toasts which O'Brien proposes on his recruitment to "the Brotherhood"—"To the confusion of the

Thought Police? To the death of Big Brother? To humanity? To the future?"—and insists on making it "to the past." "'The past is more important,' agreed O'Brien gravely." Goldstein's book says flatly, "The mutability of the past is the central tenet of Ingsoc"; and though it may be said that this is all a fiction composed in the cellars of Miniluv (I shall argue below that it is not), this particular statement rings true. One should add that there is obvious symbolic importance in beginning *Nineteen Eighty-Four* with the purchase of a diary: for diaries are to record the past *in*, and, furthermore, the diary that Winston buys attracts him simply because its very texture and beauty seem to him a proof that the past *had happened* (and had been different).

The diary, indeed, like the glass paperweight and the photograph of Jones, Aaronson, and Rutherford, functions as "a little chunk of history that they've forgotten to alter." It is a mute testimony. Other slightly more articulate ones are the nursery rhyme of "oranges and lemons," and the garbled stories of the old prole whom Winston interrogates in the pub: these at least reach the level of words, though they are not words that Winston can understand (the reader is in a different position). Outnumbering and overpowering these memorial kernels, however, are the repeated memories, dreams, and failures of memory of Winston himself. Even statistically, these must take up a considerable proportion of the book, and they extend from the book's sixth paragraph—when Winston is trying to "squeeze out some childhood memory that should tell him whether London had always been quite like this"—to its penultimate page, when Winston suffers the "uncalled" and "false" memory of himself playing Snakes and Ladders with his vanished mother. The climax of *Nineteen Eighty-Four* is, of course, its last sentence, "He loved Big Brother." But one might feel that the true collapse is not that maudlin moment, nor the terrified betrayal of Julia, but this spectacle of Winston, the diarist, the committed quester for memories, for the first time trying not to squeeze one out, but to reject one which has come without his seeking. In any case, in between the book's second page and its second last, there are at least ten sequences in which Winston drifts into a retrospect of one kind or another, remembering an air raid shelter, or the taste of chocolate, or a scene of women buying saucepans, or a dream of his mother and the Golden Country; and this does not count the repeated scenes in which Winston notes others apparently *failing* to remember about the war with Eurasia, or the reduction of the chocolate ration, even though these trigger most prominently reflections on "ancestral memory," Winston's loneliness, and the way the past "has been actually abolished."

Winston's job, furthermore—another entirely unpredictable piece of ironic invention—is to destroy the past by means of his speakwrite and his "memory hole." It does not seem too much to say first, that part 1 of *Nineteen Eighty-Four* consists entirely of a series of variations on the theme of recapturing, or abolishing, the past; and, second, that even after Julia and O'Brien have entered the plot to provide it with some narrative movement, this theme remains dominant or principal, even if not exclusive.

Professor Crick, it must be said, would certainly stigmatize this as mere one-sided delusion. He notes wryly that "the intensity of Orwell's writing gives the illusion of a single hidden truth, and indeed many people have searched for the key and, even worse, claim to have found it."[6] It may be some excuse to say that the impression *Nineteen Eighty-Four* makes on this reader is not that of a hidden truth but of an area of bewilderment, a set of questions to which Winston and Orwell obsessively return, but to which neither knows the answer. It is an obvious pointer that Winston's reading of the Goldstein book breaks off just as he is about to learn the ultimate answer of *why* the Party has decided "to freeze history at a particular moment of time." He gets as far as "this motive really consists . . . ," then discovers Julia is asleep, and puts the book aside for a later moment that never comes, reflecting as he does so that so far he has learned nothing he did not know already. Clearly Orwell also got no further than posing himself the riddle. But this particularly obvious unanswered question is only part of a general bewilderment which sweeps over Winston repeatedly, as to why he is alone, why no one else thinks as he does, and also (this one strongly shared by the reader) how everyone else in the story seems to manage to accept total contradiction effortlessly and without breaking down. "Was he, then, *alone* in the possession of a memory?" Winston asks himself in the canteen. Later on, he watches with utter amazement as the Hate Week speaker changes from Eurasia to Eastasia "actually in mid-sentence, not only without a pause, but without even breaking the syntax"—and the crowd of Parsonses, for all their involvement with hundreds of meters of bunting and posters, follows him with no apparent trace of strain or remembrance. The story insists on telling us that people *can* do this. It gives up on the question of why; and even on the question of how, the answers given—"doublethink," "blackwhite," and "crimestop," among others—remain barely comprehensible. Nevertheless, the psychology of the *other* inhabitants of Airstrip One is the basic puzzle, or the basic challenge, of *Nineteen Eighty-Four*; and the puzzling element in it is that their minds seem able to shut off critical areas (like memory) at will, and with'out apparent loss of efficiency elsewhere. O'Brien, in short, has something missing. But he is not stupid. Is he mad?

Professor Crick, confronting this problem at the one moment when it reaches the level of the bizarre, is quite clear that the answer to the last question is "yes." His critical introduction to *Nineteen Eighty-Four* says so three times: O'Brien "is mad" on page 31; on page 48 his claims "that 'our control over matter is absolute,' that 'the earth is the centre of the universe,' and that he could levitate if he wished, just as the Party could reach the stars . . . are absurd, as Winston and the reader realize"; and on page 64 "O'Brien turns out to be insane, he thinks he can levitate and reach the stars," while for good measure we are reminded in note 94 that "all this, and 'I could float off the floor like a soap-bubble if I wished to,' must indicate that absolute power has driven O'Brien mad." Of course common sense is entirely on Crick's side. Just the same, calling O'Brien mad (however many times) does not settle the issue. He is, after all, telling Winston that beliefs ought to rest on evidence: and Winston has no evidence, except memory, which is entirely subjective. It is true that the *reader* has evidence, any amount of hard and tangible evidence, not only that O'Brien's evidence does not exist, but that O'Brien does not exist either, nor the Party, nor Oceania, nor Airstrip One. But to bring this in is to destroy the whole effect of the novel. *Nineteen Eighty-Four* could not work without at least the entertainment of a belief that people could practice doublethink, that people *do* practice doublethink, that we may be doing it ourselves, that Winston may be wrong, O'Brien right, and common sense an extremely poor shield to trust in.

It may be appropriate at this moment to raise the issue of genre. *Nineteen Eighty-Four* is on the whole regarded as only marginally related to science fiction, a judgement which is on the whole correct (if only for Orwell's rather surprising lack of interest in technology). However, there are moments—including the episode in which O'Brien sets himself above the law of gravity—in which it comes close to the science fiction subgenre of the "enclosed universe." Of this, the paradigm is Wells's short story "The Country of the Blind" (1904), set in an enclosed valley inhabited only by blind people. Later examples, like Robert A. Heinlein's *Orphans of the Sky* (1941) or Brian Aldiss's *Non-Stop* (1958), are set in enormous "generation starships" where inhabitants have forgotten that their world is artificial, or in sightless caverns beneath the earth, like Daniel E. Galouye's *Dark Universe* (1961). Whatever the setting, though, some points and some tensions seem to remain fixed. One is that the reader has to be asked to identify with a central character who is sighted (not blind), or who knows his world is artificial (not natural), or who, at worst, seeks to break out from a situation he finds intolerable, instead of accepting it as part of the natural order of things, like his fellows. Tension comes, however, from the fact that the reader has simultaneously to be made to understand that the majority of supporters of the status quo has in a sense right on its side. Their beliefs may be wrong (because of their limited evidence), but they are not illogical; while, at the same time, the thought is projected that no one's evidence is anything but limited, and that the reader is more likely to resemble the conservative majority than the initiating hero. In Heinlein's *Orphans of the Sky* one character, rather like O'Brien, insists that the stars are only an optical illusion, created by tiny lights behind glass in a small unlit compartment; he rests his belief on logic, common sense, and natural facts. Orwell had probably not read this.[7] He had, however, almost certainly read Wells's "Country of the Blind," in which the sighted Nunez totally fails to shake the belief of the blind sages that they are living in an enormous stone cavern, and that all the evidence Nunez points to is susceptible of some other explanation. He cannot even convince them that he can see (for they all *know* they cannot).

The parallels between *Nineteen Eighty-Four* and the "enclosed universe" are then easy to draw. Winston's universe is, for one thing, quite tightly enclosed: he never gets far from London,[8] and even what he sees in London (he slowly realizes) could be faked, as perhaps are the rocket bombs. He is very largely at the mercy of what he is told. Yet, like the heroes of Heinlein, or Aldiss, or later authors, he does not *believe* what he is told, preferring instead to be driven by "some kind of ancestral memory that things had once been different." Like Wells's Nunez, he has a faculty (memory, as Nunez's is sight) which appears to be completely lacking in his fellows; even Julia, like Nunez's partner Medina-saroté, shows little belief or interest in it. The most important parallel, though, lies in the strategy of dealing with the reader, where Orwell and his science fiction successors and predecessors operate so similarly as to make one think their procedure intrinsic to stories of this type. As has been said, the reader naturally identifies with the sighted person, or the rebel, or the man with a memory, the hero who is making his way toward an awareness of truth. Yet, at the same time, the reader cannot help seeing how partial and limited this character's knowledge really is. When, for instance, Winston reads the Party history book, we know (but he does not) that people did wear top hats before the Revolution: but that this was by no means a uniform, nor the prerogative of the capitalists.[9] The answer to Winston's question, "could you tell how much of it was lies?" is obvious to us—as is the answer to his later difficulties in sorting out the old prole's account of top hats and Boat Race night, and his second "huge and simple question, 'Was life better before the Revolution than it is now?'" But just as we recognize how easy these answers are, outside the enclosed universe, we also recognize how literally impossible it is for someone inside the enclosed universe to reach them at all. All such stories, then, face the problem of how the hero or the rebel is to come to an understanding of his universe which, by the logic of the story, he cannot possibly reach on the available evidence alone. The normal solution in such cases is to provide a "captain's log"—a document of some kind which explains what has happened and is somehow (often with very little plausibility) transferred to the hero's possession.[10]

In the case of *Nineteen Eighty-Four* the analogue to the captain's log is of course the Goldstein book, a device with almost no logical plausibility at all! O'Brien says he wrote it (in which case it ought to be totally false). On the other hand, he says that as a "description" it is true (and it is only the description we read, not the program for revolt). But there seems no reason why a real O'Brien should allow a true history to circulate, or even know enough to create one. The fact is that Orwell uses the Goldstein book to deliver an authorial lecture, or, one might say, to bridge the otherwise uncrossable gap between

Winston's awareness and our own. There has to be an explanation for
Airstrip One, or else *Nineteen Eighty-Four* would slide toward fantasy; but no one in the story could provide it in propria persona
except at the cost of breaching the characters' mental enclosure.

The force of reclassifying *Nineteen Eighty-Four* with enclosed
universes and "The Country of the Blind" is in a way to make excuses
for O'Brien. According to our understanding of the universe, he is
mad; but then so is the Captain who refuses to believe in the stars in
Heinlein's novel, and so are the "blind men of genius" who devise
"new and saner explanations" for the universe (devoid of space and
sight) in Wells's story. But it would be wrong to think that Wells's
blind philosophers were *not* "men of genius." They were, given that
they could not see. And O'Brien is sane, given that he has no memory
and no interests outside the Party. It is true that in Wells's gentler
fable even the blind men who propose to remove Nunez's eyes do so
with the best of intentions, meaning only to make him sane; but then
O'Brien too insists that he means to "cure" Winston. The real
difference is that in the Edwardian story a cured rebel would be
allowed to live.

It seems wrong, then, simply to insist that modern readers' views
are too secure to be shaken, and that O'Brien can be dismissed as
clinically insane. Both Orwell and Winston are too bewildered for
that. The area of their bewilderment is largely psychological. Winston never really manages to answer the questions central to, and
generated by, the whole one-track structure of *Nineteen Eighty-
Four*: how can people be intelligent in some areas (like the technicali-
ties of Newspeak) and utter fools in others? Do they repress unwanted knowledge, or do they manage somehow never to take it in?
Above all, what are the mechanics of oblivion? Winston understands
the mechanics of his job well enough, which is, of course, dedicated
to eliminating documentary evidence. Just the same, a history of
sorts (he feels) ought to be reconstructable from mere personal
memories, like his own and the old prole's, and maybe Julia's or
Charrington's. However, the story insists that he is wrong. The rest
of the population of Airstrip One can do something, mentally, that
he cannot. It is on this ability, even more than on falsifying the *Times*,
that the Party depends. It is against this shared consensus that Winston, all through part I and later, assembles his dreams and his
memories, and his diary.

Orwell, of course, felt that there was a basis for the Airstrip One mentality in real life; otherwise he would hardly have bothered to write *Nineteen Eighty-Four*. His *Collected Essays*, however, suggest that though he recognized the phenomenon he was not very much more able than Winston to imagine how it was actually produced. The scene in Hate Week when the speaker changes in mid-sentence from denouncing Eurasia to denouncing Eastasia has an evident root in Orwell's analysis of the state of mind of a convinced Communist before and after the start of the Second World War. "For years before September 1939" everything he wrote had to be "a denunciation of Hitler"; then for twenty months (between the Nazi-Soviet Non-Aggression Pact and Hitler's invasion of Russia) he had to become pro-German, while "the word 'Nazi,' at least so far as print went, had to drop right out of his vocabulary." But then, "immediately after hearing the eight o'clock news bulletin on the morning of 22nd June 1941, he had to start believing once again that Nazism was the most hideous evil the world had ever seen."[11] The ludicrous, if truthful, precision of timing, and the interesting momentary focus on vocabulary, are clearly seeds for scenes in *Nineteen Eighty-Four*. However, Orwell went on in that essay only to talk about stultifying effects on literature, not about the problems of the mind. In the same way, though one may feel sure that his fear that controlling the press was the same as "actually" abolishing or "actually" destroying the past[12] came from his own experiences in Catalonia, these do not seem to have led him to any clear nonfictional portrait of how the mind of a censor (or a self-censor) works. Probably the nearest he got to it was in his excellent and still-valuable "Notes on Nationalism," of 1945, in which he asserts that nationalism as he defines it is "widespread among the English intelligentsia" as a "habit of mind," that it leads to a general "indifference to objective truth," a fascination with the idea of altering the past, and an ability to know facts "in a sense" or on one level, but nevertheless simultaneously to find them completely "inadmissible."[13] One might say that all this made literally true and supported by an immense organization of enforcement gives us the world of *Nineteen Eighty-Four*. Still, the motivation behind the "nationalist" escapes Orwell as it escapes Goldstein. So does the trick of doublethink, of letting a fact, as it were, penetrate the mind only so far and no further.

Is doublethink not really a matter of language? Orwell hesitates to say as much, and there are some arguments against the theory. In Winston's time, for instance, Newspeak is by no means firmly established, though he sees vagueness and oblivion already all around him. On the other hand, there is also continuing evidence of thought-crime: and the point of Newspeak, as Syme says, is to make thought-crime "literally impossible, because there will be no words in which to express it." Furthermore, it looks as if Newspeak is only a development of mentally stultifying forms of Oldspeak; the man in the canteen, whom Winston overhears with horror in chapter 5, is talking English, though the words he says are "not speech in the true sense: it was a noise uttered in unconsciousness, like the quacking of a duck."

Unconscious speech is admittedly hardly more comprehensible than doublethink, but from such scenes, and from Orwell's other remarks on language, one can construct a theory which is at least implicit in *Nineteen Eighty-Four*, and which goes some way to explaining the novel's central bewilderments. It is in some respects not a very *strong* theory, for Orwell's grounding in the English language at Eton was totally inadequate and left him at the mercy of linguistic prejudice ever after.[14] But it would go something like this. To begin with, Orwell thought that the structure of a language had something to do with the character of its speakers. One can see from his notes on "The English Language" in "The English People" (1942)[15] that he thought English was intrinsically an *anarchic* language (which is very far from the truth); but that this healthy inheritance was vulnerable to all sorts of corruptions. Hence the space given in the "Appendix" on Newspeak to the regularization of noun and verb declensions (a matter of little importance), together with the complete absence of comment on all the things a real "1984" state would feel obliged to eliminate from English (like the powerful time-classifications of the English verb system, about which Orwell knew, consciously, nothing useful whatever).

Going on from there, Orwell thought that it was easy enough for words to exist without things to refer to (see his remarks on "lackey" and "flunkey" in "As I Please" for 17 March 1944),[16] but that in such cases the words came to dominate the mind of their user. The same was true of the absence of words. The abolition of "nazi" from the vocabulary of the conscientious 1940 communist did nothing about nazis, but it did at least inhibit any consistent recognition of the fact that the German state was run by an anticommunist party—not much of a loss, one might think, but a beginning. From such observations sprang the idea of Newspeak as a means of political control. But their ludicrous nature seems also to take us straight to doublethink. Did the 1940 communist not *know* that the Germans with whom Britain was at war were nazis? Of course he did. But refusing to put a true label on them somehow prevented him from having to take the knowledge any further. One would like to say that this state of mind remains incomprehensible, but by this stage most of us must begin to feel twinges of guilt: such exercises in mislabelling are too common to feel distanced from. Newspeak, then, may be our best avenue into doublethink, and into the whole area of bewilderment over psychology in which Winston and Orwell both flounder, but to which they constantly direct us. It may, therefore, not be completely unreasonable to say first, that the connecting thread of *Nineteen Eighty-Four* is abolition of the past, and of memory; but, second, that insofar as this is considered rationally explicable, and not mere fantasy or nightmare, the explanation lies in a deliberate assault on language which we are capable of recognizing as an exaggeration of genuine and observable linguistic habits—not exactly what the *Times* said in its leader of 31 December 1983, but close enough.

No one could deny, furthermore, that this has remained a live issue. Few would follow Orwell's assumption, in the Newspeak "Appendix," that the relation between word and thought was one-to-one. However, the question of what the relation *is* has remained fascinating; as has the problem which Orwell left unsolved, of how to get inside the mind of a "doublethinker." Finally, while not everyone has been able to agree with the assumptions of Newspeak, few would disagree with Orwell's earlier remark in "Politics and the English Language" (1946) that "[the English language] becomes ugly and inaccurate because our thoughts are foolish, but the slovenliness of our language makes it easier for us to have foolish thoughts."[17] Slovenly and foolish variants of English have been framing thoughts ever since Orwell's novel was written; they might not have become subjects for fiction if other writers had not read *Nineteen Eighty-Four* the *Times* way.

The clearest Orwell-inheritor as language-satirist seems to be Ursula Le Guin. It seems undeniable that at least some of her work is a conscious reaction to *Nineteen Eighty-Four* and Newspeak, or an

engagement with it. However, before considering that (in her novel
The Dispossessed, 1974), it may make sense to look at her relatively
elementary satire/parody of 1972, *The Word for World is Forest*.[18]
This is quite clearly a comment, even a homily, on Vietnam; but it is
distinguished first by an attempt to do what Orwell could not (namely
probe the mental processes of an extreme, doublethinking nationalist); and, second, by its demonstration of the ruinous effects of
jargon.

The first of these effects is achieved in the presentation of the
book's main villain, one Captain Davidson, largely through the
device of *style indirect libre*. As the novel opens, with Davidson
waking up, we seem to be reading a description of his mind by the
traditional novelistic omniscient narrator: "Two pieces of yesterday
were in Captain Davidson's mind when he woke, and he lay looking
at them in the darkness for a while." Since it *is* Davidson's mind,
though, a majority of the vocabulary and grammar is his: "It looked
like that bigdome Kees was right . . . " A shock-effect, however, is
created by the merging of the two modes, omniscient narration and
direct quotation, as in Davidson's sudden vision of what the alien
world will become: "a paradise, a real Eden. A better world than
worn-out Earth. And it would be his world. For that's what Davidson
was, way down deep inside him: a world-tamer. He wasn't a boastful
man, but he knew his own size. It just happened to be the way he was
made." Here, there are several indicators of indirect speech: past
tenses, like "would" and "was," use of the third person in "his" and
"He" and "Davidson." All these predispose us to accept the sentences as the work of the omniscient narrator, and, therefore, true.
But the sentence beginning "for that's what Davidson was" is simply
too boastful to be accepted that way. One realizes suddenly that it is
in fact a translation of what Davidson is saying to himself, "That's
what *I am*, way deep down inside *me . . . I'm* not a boastful man." But
when Davidson says he isn't boastful, he is! And when the narrator
appears to say "that's what Davidson was," it's neither truly what he
was nor the voice of the narrator. One finds oneself reevaluating
everything that has gone before, to try to sort out its reliability; and
from then on the reader is continually waiting, even in passages of
apparent narration, for the Davidson personality to signal itself by
vocabulary, grammar, or paranoid opinion.

One main result is that attention is very strongly directed to what is distinctive about Davidson's thoughts, and the language that controls them. Probably his most identifiable trait is a refusal to accept or need explanations. Thus, in fairly quick succession, we have:

> He knew his own size. It just happened to be the way he was made. (P. 37)
> "It's a fact you have to face, it happens to be the way things are." (P. 38, direct speech)
> He was a patriotic man, it just happened to be the way he was made. (P. 43)[19]
> Some men, especially the asiatiforms and hindi types, are actually born traitors. Not all, but some. Certain other men are born survivors. It just happened to be the way they were made. (P. 77)

Along with this there goes a very heavy use of the adverbs "actually," "really," locutions like "the fact is," the adjectives "normal," "practical," and (especially) "realistic," along with the noun "reality." Davidson, one can see, is committed to "the way things are." Or rather, he thinks he is. His tragedy is first that he cannot tell his own opinion from reality, and second (much more seriously and less commonly) that his own continuing denial that there is any need for explanations prevents him from any form of self-analysis. He has an aggressive ideology based on denying that he possesses anything as unnatural as an ideology at all. Appropriately, then, his own internal monologue drifts in and out of the narrator's comments; we see that his mind has been irretrievably poisoned by false meanings and ready phrases.

More interesting as satire, though, if not as fictional experiment is the presentation of Davidson's superior Colonel Dongh. By one of the book's most obvious ironies, he is a Vietnamese; and the English he talks is clearly a parody of that already tediously familiar to Le Guin from official American communiqués. One is obliged to give fairly extensive samples. In example 1, Colonel Dongh is responding to an accusation from the anthropologist Lyubov that an alien assault on one of his outposts has been motivated by human enslavement of the aliens:

> (1) "Captain Lyubov is expressing his personal opinions and theories," said Colonel Dongh, "which I should state I consider possibly to be erroneous, and he and I have discussed this kind of thing previously, although the present context is unsuitable. We do not employ slaves,

sir. Some of the natives serve a useful role in our community. The Voluntary Autochthonous Labor Corps is a part of all but the temporary camps here. We have very limited personnel to accomplish our tasks here and we need workers and use all that we can get, but on any kind of basis that could be called a slavery basis, certainly not." (Pp. 67–68)

In example 2 the Colonel is speaking directly and reprovingly to Lyubov:

(2) The Colonel went on. "It appears to us that you made some serious erroneous judgements concerning the peacefulness and non-aggressiveness of the natives here, and because we counted on this specialist description of them as non-aggressive is why we left ourselves open to this terrible tragedy at Smith Camp, Captain Lyubov. So I think we have to wait until some other specialists in hilfs have had time to study them, because evidently your theories were basically erroneous to some extent." (P. 74)

In example 3 the Colonel has been captured by the aliens and imprisoned, with all his surviving men, apart from outposts under Davidson. He is helpless, but trying to bargain his way out:

(3) The point is, without introducing into this any beside the point or erroneous factors, now we are certainly greatly outnumbered by your forces, but we have the four helicopters at the camps, which there's no use you trying to disable as they are under fully armed guard at all times now, and also all the serious fire-power, so that the cold reality of the situation is we can pretty much call it a draw and speak in positions of mutual equality. This of course is a temporary situation. If necessary we are enabled to maintain a defensive police action to prevent all-out war. Moreover we have behind us the entire fire-power of the Terran Interstellar Fleet, which could blow your entire planet right out of the sky. But these ideas are pretty intangible to you, so let's just put it as plainly and simply as I can, that we're prepared to negotiate with you for the present time, in terms of an equal frame of reference. (P. 106)

One can see that some of the features of this jargon would have been immediately familiar to Orwell: primarily, of course, the euphemisms. Orwell's brutal juxtaposition of the words *pacification* or *rectification* with the facts they represent is well known.[20] Exactly the same phenomenon (except that here it is sincerely meant) appears in Dongh's rejection of "slaves" in favor of "Voluntary

Autochthonous Labor Corps," in example 1, or his use of "defensive police action," in 3, to mean airstrikes with napalm bombs against undefended villages. Orwell also noted the use of "pretentious diction," which Dongh exemplifies by "previously," for "before," "very limited personnel to accomplish our tasks," instead of "very few people to get the job done," and the preference for the "ready-made phrase" like "for the present time" or "in positions of mutual equality," instead of words like "now" or "as equals."

Other features, however, and more interestingly, appear to be new growths. When one considers that Dongh is a military man, accustomed to the use of weapons of terrible destructiveness, it is odd to notice how consistently tentative his speech is. The prime example in the samples given is the end of 2. How anything can be "basically erroneous" but only "*to some extent*" defeats the mind. But one notes also how at the start of 1, an underlying "which I think are maybe wrong" is not only inflated with long words but also extended with the needless "I should state." Why should Dongh state it? Why should he ask others to notice he is stating it? There is a formal, guarded punctilio about his speech which resembles nothing very much in Orwell's list of dislikes.

Added to this there is what one might call a "hatred of foreground." Dongh uses, in 1, the words "context" and "basis," in 3, "factors," "situation," "frame of reference." All imply something behind the event, something contributing to it or even enclosing it, but not the event itself. Some of them, like "frame of reference," are among Dongh's favorite phrases. What does this preference imply? Before deciding, one should note at least three other fairly consistent features. One is a deep uncertainty over grammatical connection: "because . . . is why," in 2 is clearly tautologous, "which there's no use," in 3 is a conflation of two different constructions, and both the "and" in line 3 of 1 and the "although" in line 4 seem on reflection either to be unnecessary or actively misleading. Uncertainty is furthermore particularly acute over grammatical cohesion: "them" in line 7 of 2 is a long way from the antecedent "judgements" to which it refers (or does it refer to "natives?"); "and also all the serious fire-power" in 3 is confusingly split from "the four helicopters" to which it is parallel, and the verb "have" to which it acts as object. Finally, Dongh has a simple habit of repeating words: "any kind of basis that could be called a slavery basis," "The point is . . . beside the point," "the entire fire-power . . . your entire planet." Euphemizing, one can see, may be used deliberately and tactically. But many of Dongh's linguistic habits seem to be just clumsy and pointless.

Yet they foster a variant of doublethink. Just as Le Guin has taken up, in Davidson, the challenge of penetrating the mind of a "nationalist," so in Dongh she illustrates how slovenliness of language makes it easier to have "foolish thoughts," thoughts which may lead to genocide. Dongh's language *is not morally neutral.* In brief, one might say that his basic trouble is an inability to admit a contradiction, or a failure. Like Davidson, in this respect, his adopted posture is one of omnipotence. Nothing ever goes wrong. Some "factors" of it may have been "erroneous"; but the assumption is that these can and will be corrected. Since, however, even Dongh notices that things do go wrong, a certain guardedness of speech at all times has to be built in. Along with this there seems to go a willingness to be distracted from the grammatical line of a sentence (for there are many factors to keep track of and Dongh needs to list them all), and a feeble perception of cause and effect. More could be said (the point made earlier about repetition, for example, still remains inscrutable). However, the final effect is of assumed omnipotence wandering in indecision: a strange correlation (given the Vietnam references) of syntax and strategy.

There is, furthermore, no doubt that Dongh's language was drawn from life. Which particular American spokesman or spokesmen Le Guin noticed one cannot now say, but the interesting point is that Dongh's is not an idiolect, a one-man variant. It seems instead to be a class dialect or trade jargon of the United States government. To many it will be familiar not even from Vietnam, but from the experience of listening to President Nixon's defenders on television. Samples here could be given very nearly literally ad nauseam, but I choose one from the developing Watergate scandal of 1973: after Le Guin's work, one should notice, but absolutely certainly unaffected by it. Its date rubs in the point that Dongh's language parodies not a party, but certainly a whole subclass or governmental faction. The example is from a White House briefing of 22 May 1973.[21] Someone had just read to Leonard Garment, President Nixon's counsel, an earlier statement by President Nixon (one notes en passant its tentative but inflated diction) that he had been "advised" shortly after the

Watergate break-in "that there was a possibility of CIA involvement in some way." Who, the questioner asked, "advised" the president of this? To the question Garment replied:

> There are some transactions that can be stated with certainty. There are others that must be stated with a certain degree of generality. The question of who, out of a possible number of persons, whether it be two, three, or four, who might have drawn particular information to his attention, or the totality of circumstances from which that suspicion or knowledge of supposed fact came, is something that really cannot be stated with certainty at this time.

Most of the linguistic features of Le Guin's parody are here present. There is the choice of pretentious words: "transaction" is especially odd for a scene in which someone can only have told the president something, or written him a letter. It goes of course with the president's "advised." We also note the ready-made phrase "drawn . . . to his attention," as well as (and this brings in the preference for backgrounding) "totality of circumstances." Especially confusing in the whole answer is loss of grammatical cohesion: "who" in line 3 is far separated from the verb phrase to which it acts as subject, "might have drawn"—so far that it makes one wonder whether perhaps it is the "who" in line 4 which is the subject of "might have drawn," in which case one would have to reconsider the sentence's entire structure. The objects of "might have drawn" add further confusion. Finally one notes once again the repetition of "stated . . . stated . . . stated." In this last case, it must be said, one might possibly think that Garment was aiming for a kind of rhetorical balance. But this flattering opinion tends to evaporate as one reads on. A little later the questioner indicated an apparent contradiction in an earlier presidential statement, and asked if the statement was wrong. To this Garment could quite honorably have replied that it *was* wrong, as the president had realized later, or that it had only been paritally right. However, he actually replied: "No. I think the April 30th statement represented the President's knowledge and recollection at that point stated to the finest state of certainty, and that process of investigation and examination has continued since then, and this statement is a more complete statement." Here the repetition "statement . . . stated . . . state" (!) has no possible rhetorical defense. For good measure, "that process" looks as if it ought to oppose "this statement." But it is merely another false trail.[22]

Many observers, watching Garment and his like, must admittedly have felt that this was not doublethink but doubletalk: a word recorded from 1938 and showing a rapid shift of meaning from "deliberately unintelligible speech" to "deliberately ambiguous or imprecise language; used esp. of political language."[23] Garment, in other words, replied as he did simply in order to confuse questioners and drive them away. That motivation was no doubt present. However, it would be even more worrying if, as seems likely, presidential advisers both political and military simply could not turn this form of language off! If, that is to say, their confusion of syntax both reflected and created their thoughts, This would take us indeed from doubletalk to doublethink, and strongly reinforce the Orwellian thesis that a new form of language could inhibit perception and prevent the most obvious facts from ever getting through. It is true that "Garment speech"—prolix, confused, and full of synonyms—is quite unlike Newspeak stylistically. However, the effect is much the same.

To return to Le Guin: it seems likely that *The Word for World is Forest* is only a parallel to *Nineteen Eighty-Four*, not a commentary on it. But this does not seem to be true of her later work, *The Dispossessed* (1974), which includes within it more or less overt reactions to most of the major European utopias and dystopias from Plato on. A major feature of the novel is that half the characters speak a language, Pravic, which has been designed specifically to correct, to make unthinkable, the error of its parent language, Iotic. Unlike Newspeak, Pravic is designed with the best of intentions, and to foster anarchy rather than state control. Nevertheless, *The Dispossessed* does offer a fictional answer to the *Nineteen Eighty-Four* thesis that "thoughtcrime" will become "literally impossible" without the right words to think it in. Le Guin, though, suggests strongly that Orwell was wrong.

A reader's first impression is that the experiment of Pravic has been a success. In an early scene an Iotic speaker uses the word "bastard." His Pravic-speaking listener does not understand it. In Pravic, "marriage" does not exist either as a word or as an institution; there is, therefore, no concept of legitimacy, and no force in an accusation of illegitimacy. Bastardy furthermore has strong connections with rights to inheritance; but in Pravic no one inherits anything, for "money" also exists neither as word nor as thing. The same is true of "buy," "profit," "bet," "private," "propertied class," "class," "status," and much of the English vocabulary of possession. Even "my," though it exists in Pravic, is not used as it is in English. On the whole, one sees rapidly and with approval that in this imagined world large areas of possessiveness, and of self-definition at others' expense, have been eliminated from tongue and brain.

The trouble is that they do not stay eliminated. Profit does not exist in Pravic, but the word "profiteer" is used—to mean, strictly speaking, a speaker of Iotic, a member of a capitalist society, or someone who behaves like one. But just as in English people say "bastard" to insult others, so in Pravic "profiteer" has become a term of simple abuse. "You're one of those little profiteers who goes to school to keep his hands clean," says one character. "I've always wanted to knock the shit out of one of you."[24] There are no such people in the Pravic society; dirty work is rotated; everyone goes to the same kind of school. "Profiteer" has become a simple reversal of "bastard" ("rich person," as it were, as opposed to "propertyless person" in our thinking). "Shit" is also significant. In Pravic this is not a taboo word and carries no sense of obscenity or insult: "shit-stool" for WC is the normal word. This too could be approved of, as natural and logical. However, in another strange reversal the term "excrement" (to us a euphemism) has in Pravic acquired a strong political meaning for anything excessive, commercialized, unnecessary. "Excrement," therefore, is used noneuphemistically, and again almost without meaning, as a swear word. It seems as if semantic spaces, however carefully vacated, have to be filled.[25] With the best will in the world, Pravic is turning back towards Iotic.

There is, furthermore, a strong sense in Le Guin's novel that the thing *can* exist without the word. "Buying" and "selling" do not exist, in theory, in Pravic—one character rubs the point in by getting the first word wrong and pronouncing it "bay." This does not mean, however, that people cannot be bought and sold, even if no money changes hands. In an important scene the book's hero, a physicist, forces the right to have his work published by an implied threat to submit no more. This is a kind of bargain: "They had bargained, he and Sabul, bargained like profiteers. It had not been a battle, but a sale. You give me this and I'll give you that. Refuse me and I'll refuse

you. Sold? Sold!" As the book goes on, its Pravic-speaking characters come to the realization that in spite of all verbal quarantining
their anarchic society has spontaneously regenerated "government"
and "politicians." By symmetry it has also allowed its own carefully
invented vocabulary of social comment, which rests on such notions
as the "functional," the "dysfunctional," and the "organic," to become a deceptive jargon like that of the profiteers. "Who do you
think is lying to us?" demands the hero. The answer is, "Who but
ourselves?"—with its implication that doubletalk (if it ever existed)
has become doublethink, and that some Pravic speakers are as confused as Colonel Dongh or the unfortunate aides of President Nixon.

It is not clear which of several possible conclusions one should
draw from *The Dispossessed*. The simplest is to say that it tries to
refute Orwell, claiming that no Newspeak could forever overpower
the natural qualities of the human mind. Less optimistically, one
might think that both *Nineteen Eighty-Four* and *The Word for World
is Forest*, on the one hand, and *The Dispossessed* on the other, could
be right: in other words, that improving the human mind by verbal
engineering, whether Pravic or Basic English, is hard, but that de-
grading it through Newspeak or Vietnam English is all too easy.
However, the reader of these novels is at least directed to an open
question, and a live issue. Does language control thought? Are the
many appalling forms of English we hear really meant, or translated
out of some clearer language? Or do the forms of jargon which many
of us are taught actually *prevent* us from ever seeing matters straight?
It is troubling that to these questions there are no available answers,
and very few published contributions.[26] In some cases—as for instance that of the highly stylized student revolutionary jargon of
1968—even the documents have vanished, and one is left, like Winston Smith, working from inadequate memories alone.

The war in Vietnam, one may think, would not have surprised
Orwell (except in so far as it gave the lie to his theory of all-powerful
superstates). He would also not have been surprised even by new
forms of perversion of political English. There can be no doubt,
either, that he would have been entirely against "comfortable, distancing" readings of his text, and that to this extent Professor Crick's
reminders that *Nineteen Eighty-Four* is not simply about Russia or
totalitarianism are valuable ones. I do not feel, however, that listing
Orwell's many "satiric thrusts" necessarily makes his novel more

relevant or even represents it well. In particular ("body-snatching" though it may be), I cannot imagine that Orwell would have welcomed too much distraction from his central uncertainty—how could people deceive themselves as so many of his generation's intellectuals had?—and from the central theme of his novel *Nineteen Eighty-Four*, namely the difference between a mind that tries to capture truth and a mentality that tries to abolish it by destroying language, on paper, in dictionaries, and at the roots of thought. Finally, it seems to me significant of cardinal error that the Crick edition of *Nineteen Eighty-Four*, besides repeating often that O'Brien is simply mad, finds itself obliged to maintain the thesis that the final "Appendix" on "The Principles of Newspeak" must be a joke, "delightfully satiric."[27] We are told on page 55 that when the "Appendix" says it is "difficult" to translate writers like Shakespeare, Milton, Swift, Byron, and Dickens into Newspeak, we are meant to assume automatically that the job is impossible, to be protracted even beyond "so late a day as 2050"; on page 74 this becomes "we know that the target for the final adoption of Newspeak will have to be postponed again and again"; while on page 119 (and this *is* "body-snatching") Crick finds it "absolutely clear" that Orwell really thought Newspeak "impossible" and that "language will always escape from official control." Note 37 finally paraphrases the last words of the "Appendix" as "no regime can simplify Shakespeare and it is barbarism to try."

One would like to be so confident, in Shakespeare or in language. There seems, however, to be no great difficulty in simplifying literature, as long as one does not care how banal the result is. As for language escaping official control, this does seem very likely (witness *The Dispossessed*) but a really thorough experiment has never been tried. Quite small-scale ones (witness Colonel Dongh) have been far too successful. Orwell's awareness of language, I would conclude, had no great technical rigor, but was the result of sharp observation, the most painful experience, and genuine anxiety. Whatever else was drawn into *Nineteen Eighty-Four*, doublethink and Newspeak are at the heart of it.

Part 3
Alienation, Prognostication, and Apocalypse

Aliens for the Alienated

Kenneth V. Bailey

Constance Irwin opens her book *Fair Gods and Stone Faces* with a description of the approach in 1519 of Cortes's conquistador ships to the eastern coast of Mexico. "The Indians," she writes "looked out over the 'waters of heaven,' and noticed some peculiar objects out to sea. [They were] floating towers . . . which grew larger, and larger, swept in towards shore and anchored." The men who emerged from them were white faced and black bearded. "To the beardless yellow-brown Indians," she says "the newcomers seemed as alien as creatures from space." Yet there was at that time expectation among the Aztecs of salvation coming from "the waters of heaven" out of which the sun rose each day, a tradition inherited from the conquered Toltecs. A stressful, warring, military race, the Aztecs in the person of Montezuma welcomed the alien gods. This quite quickly led not only to Montezuma's destruction but to that of their entire culture. The reality did not live up to the myth of redemption projected onto it.

This fragment of history incorporates a motif which, in various guises, repeats itself in troublesome times, particularly in times of social and cultural disintegration, discord and schism. Central cores of belief having been eroded, there then appear, and are reflected in popular lore and literature, two distinct, though complementary trends. A. J. Toynbee in *A Study of History* defines them as *archaism* and *futurism*; and both are recognizable as symptoms of the human condition of alienation. When Marx used this concept to indicate the separation of the proleterian producer from the products of his work, his corollary was that the product thus objictified was of no interest or concern to those in this way alienated. In its more extended sense the term now implies a fissure between personality and environment, or group and environment—environment embracing a spectrum spread from the domestic to the cosmic.

The external fissure so defined is paralleled by a fissure within the individual psyche. The healing of this, the reconciliation of opposites, and the consequent achievement of wholeness as between the individual and his or her shifting complex of environments, mirrored in the "interior environment," is in Jung's terminology the process of individuation. In the course of it, the opposite or "opponent," the ambivalently good/bad, guilt or anxiety-bearing "dark brother," a shadow figure rising from the unconscious, may, in the imagination, in fantasy, in literature, take many forms—demon, Mr. Hyde, Frankensteinian monster, Caliban, extraterrestrial, or whatever.

These groupings and sequences of interior experiences are, of course, much more labyrinthine than a sketch in this context can convey. Other symbolic images rising from the unconscious, and relevant to the individuation process, are variously identified as anima, animus, Wise Old Man, Magna Mater, hero archetype, and so on. Moreover, it will be apparent even from this brief outline that alienation is perennially a phenomenon of the human condition, as is the motivation to attain a measure of wholeness. It is, however, in circumstances of social stress that its occurrence is most clearly discernible. The literatures of such periods are its faithful indicators. In the early part of this century, for example, the writings of D. H. Lawrence provide many instances. His poem "New Heaven, New Earth" is a very anatomy of alienation. His longing for organic relationships and his search for a wholeness in sexual fulfillment were often associated with an idealization of past or primitive figures, or races, whom he saw as being more fully alive, more completely human, than the men and women conditioned to the values and mores of his own day. His poem "Cypresses" ends: "There is only one evil, to deny life / As Rome denied Etruria / And mechanical America Montezuma still." Lawrence, in fact, had his own variation on the Quetzalcoatl theme in *The Plumed Serpent*. There he writes of his archetypal hero character, Ramón: "Only he had the strong power for bringing together the two great human impulses to the point of fusion, for being the bird between the vast wings of the dual-created power to which man has access and in which man has his being. The Morning Star between the breath of the dawn and the deeps of the dark."[1]

The phenomenon of dualism in nineteenth and twentieth century literatures can also be considered in its Freudian aspect, and has been extensively so treated by Rosemary Jackson who, developing further the work of Jacques Lacan in her book *Fantasy: The Literature of Subversion*, has shown how such dualism may be the dramatization of a conflict in which the "self" is torn between a primary narcissism and an "ideal ego." The fantasized return to a state of undifferentiation is in correspondence with the idea of achieving a unity, of attaining the "paradisal" or unalienated state.

The creative arts today offer many examples of this kind of dramatization. A recent Italian production of *The Tempest* represented Caliban and Ariel as projective aspects of Prospero, so that his freeing and pardoning of those two elementals (or elements in his nature) gave point to his own prayer in the Epilogue for pardon, release, and a return to his native inheritance. In this century science fiction and fantasy have been powerful media for the working out of such psychological/cultural metaphors. The film *Forbidden Planet* actually develops a not dissimilar interpretation of *The Tempest*. From the literature of science fiction I cite briefly three examples, each of which, and each in a different key, demonstrates a species of wholeness being established through processes of disintegration, metamorphosis and fusion. There is something like a return to the paradisal in the dying-ancient/cosmic-foetus images in Clarke's *2001: A Space Odyssey* (both in the film and in the novel). Philip K. Dick's macabre story "The Father-Thing" presents an oedipally energized state of duality and alienation, resolved (if, indeed, it is resolved) through trauma and disintegrative violence. The Pohl-Williamson *Starchild* novels run, space-operatically, a gamut of variations on reshaping, dividing, merging identities through a sequence of environments ranging from corpse-banks to sun-bursts, which lead eventually, again through disjunction and transference, to the unitive "be one with Almalik" finale of *Rogue Star*.[2]

After that short tour of inner space and some of its projections, let us reconsider, now in the context of history, those Toynbeean concepts of *archaism* and *futurism*, both of which he sees to be reacting against or destructive of the contemporary ethos within which they exist. In archaism there is a return to origins and roots. In the civilization of our own times the dominance of an urban technology founded on empirical sciences and positivist philosophies has been accompanied by minority movements toward archaism, with corresponding literatures. Contemporary "return to origins" movements have existed in parallel with, and have often drawn sustaining imaginative impetus from, a proliferation of Middle Earth fantasies, including regression as far back as to the Pliocene. Indeed, the fancifully folk-costumed members of Group Green, refugees from the Galactic Milieu entering *The Many-Coloured Land* of Julian May's tetralogy, are as good an example of the rebellious and escapist aspects of archaism as one could wish for.

Turning back a century, we find W. S. Gilbert's libretto[3] for *Patience* encapsulating, while satirizing, the opposition of Victorian metropolitanism and archaism when it makes Reginald Bunthorne sing of walking down Piccadilly "with a poppy or a lily in your mediaeval hand," and puts first its chorus of aesthetes and then its chorus of guardsmen into what Gilbert called "stained glass attitudes." William Morris's Merton Abbey workshops had their literary counterpart in fantasies such as *The Well at the World's End* (almost contemporary with *The Time Machine*); and, although there is a large escapist element in his later writings, the strength of Moriss's practical, and even political, contribution to the reaction against a good deal that was basely ugly in that period should not be undervalued. Although he read John Stuart Mill and Marx, it would, as William Gaunt suggests in *The Pre-Raphaelite Dream*, be near the truth to say that he was converted to socialism by the *Morte d'Arthur* and Rouen cathedral.

Writers who, somewhat in the Gothic tradition, worked on the overlapping fringes of proto-science fiction and fantasy in the last decade of the nineteenth century, hark back similarly to the Middle Ages and beyond: as, romantically, in Arthur Machen's *Great God Pan*, or as in, with a sort of cynical appreciation, stories such as "The Bell of Saint Euschemon" and "The Elixir of Life" in Richard Garnett's *Twilight of the Gods*. Both of these books were contemporaries of *The Time Machine*, and, although futurism is more obviously the keynote in Wells's early science fiction novels, there is in many of them the same nostalgia for paradise, however ambivalently felt and expressed. It is there in his depicting of the Sweet Auburn aspects of the village of Cheasing Eyebright in *The Food of the Gods*, and in the recollected premechanized landscape of the Weald in *The Sleeper Awakes*. It is there half a century after *The Time Machine* in *The Happy Turning*; and it is certainly there in *The Time Machine* itself—but that we will come to later.

Wells's scientific romances appear as works of the greatest significance as we continue to examine the relationships between archaism/futurism and our theme of alienation. It will be useful to look a little closely at three of them: *The Island of Doctor Moreau*, *The War of the Worlds*, and *The Time Machine*. They are of their time but continue to have relevance to ours. In each there is a vein hostile to the then established social and industrial conditions. They belong to a decade in which both the anarchist disciples of Kropotkin and the gradualist Fabian socialists led by Sidney Webb came to recognize a truth in Bernard Shaw's assessment of humanity as it had by then matured—that it would be as productive of an army of light as thistles might be expected to be of grapes.

Now, although Wells's stormy liaison with the Fabians did not begin until 1903, he had as a student sat at the feet of both T. H. Huxley and William Morris (as a young member of the Kropotkin-influenced circle that met in Hammersmith). These experiences probably nurtured ideas and images which eventually entered into his essentially Frankensteinian fiction, *The Island of Doctor Moreau*. It is set in the 1880s and its unpleasant exercises in creature-creation take place somewhere in the South Pacific; but the subsequent horror that was "well-nigh unsupportable" to Edward Prendick was that felt in London. He was sickened there "by the blank expressionless faces of people in streets, in omnibuses, in trains—people who seemed to him to be those transformed, conditioned, but essentially unchanged animals of the island. He describes them as "furtive", "prowling", "gibbering," or, alternatively, as weary pale, proletarian creatures who passed him by like "wounded deer." There is here, I believe, a projection of a state of alienation into the making of which enter, first the gospel of his mentor Thomas Huxley, that natural man's conduct is shaped by "pain and pleasure at his elbow, telling him to do this and avoid that"; and, second, by what lay behind the Shavian "grapes and thistles" estimate. Prendick retreats from his urban nightmare to pastoral Downland, takes up astronomy, and finds peace and protection in contemplating those empty spaces and glittering hosts of heaven that so frightened Blaise Pascal. As for Wells, he continued to range space and time, looking into the future to see what kind of a screen that might provide for his projections and attempted resolutions.

Those projections to the future had two main strands. One was of hope, involving new evolutionary sports, nourished by food of the gods, or changed by cometary smoke, or even involving, with varying degrees of ambivalence, aliens such as Martians or Selenites. At the end of *The War of the Worlds* his narrator says of the Martian brains: "To them and not to us perhaps is the future ordained." In the other strand he mixed a despair engendered by a realization of the entropic fate of all things with a pessimistic intuition that the utopia of his turn-of-the-century *Anticipations* could easily become the dystopia of his own *When the Sleeper Wakes*. That book observed trends in the exercise of power and persuasion which Orwell half a century later explored further in *Animal Farm* and *Nineteen Eighty-Four*.

Along with the hopes Wells placed in the emergence of a dedicated new *Samurai* caste went a savagely apocalyptic strain, appearing early and persisting through to *Mind at the End of its Tether*. As Norman and Jeanne Mackenzie so neatly put it (in their book *The Time Traveller*): "Fusing the Book of Revelation with *The Origin of Species*, he developed that idea into a secular version of the Second Coming in which a new and superior breed of men would 'take the world in hand' and create a 'sane order'." Certainly the destructiveness of the alien invasion in *The War of the Worlds* is distinctly apocalyptic in incident and tone. In that book Wells introduces images and ideas often through the witness of minor and later discarded characters, but these images and ideas greatly color the book. The judgement motif issues from the weak and terrified Curate: "What sins have we done? The morning service over, I was walking through the roads to clear my brain for the afternoon, and then—fire, earthquake, death! As if it were Sodom and Gomorrah!" He sees the aliens as operating "the wine press of God." The new order motif is voiced by the Artilleryman. His diatribe is reminiscent of that pronouncing doom on the flute players, the merchants, the wearers of fine linen, in the Book of Revelation: "There won't be any more blessed concerts for a million years or so; there won't be any Royal Academy of Arts, and no nice little feeds at restaurants." He describes the fate of the dancing drunken orgy in Regent Street at the hands of the Martians. For the future he envisages the formation of a band of "able-bodied, clean-minded men. . . . Life is real again, and the useless and cumbersome and mischievous have to die." Although Wells soon discredits this protofascist philistine, the same voice echoes in his work at times. As late as 1941, in a letter to Bernard Shaw (quoted by the MacKenzies) concerning retaliatory bombing, he said that he didn't care if all the art treasures of the world were ground to powder; he even seems to see this as necessary if he was ever to realize his expressed wish to see humanity decultivated, to make a fresh start.

In *The Time Machine*, the earliest of the three books, the Traveller "saw in the growing pile of civilisation only a foolish heaping that must inevitably fall back and destroy its makers in the end." This is symbolized in the Palace of Green Porcelain with its decaying books, rusting machinery and fit-to-be-desecrated idols—a description symptomatic of the iconoclasm which is, as Toynbee points out, a syndrome of futurism. In his chapter "The Saviour with the Time Machine," Toynbee, referring to the Wells novel, writes of seeking salvation from irreparable social damage "in a return to an idealised past or a plunge into an idealised future." In this early Wellsian future, however, there are no *Samurai*: only a dominant but degenerate and cannibalistic "Have-not" proletariat, and the hedonistic "beautiful people," with the trappings of an Edenesque past, but actually the effete descendants of the nineteenth century "haves," pursuing "pleasure, comfort and beauty." Their earthly paradise with its splendid buildings, sun drenched landscape, serene skies, and blue undulating hills has obviously an appeal for Traveller/Wells. For all his disillusion he still describes it as "that Golden Age." Childlike, the Eloi welcome him as having "come from the sun in a thunderstorm." After the final epoch of cold and the last apocalyptic eclipse the Traveller narrates that in journeying back "the sun got golden again, the sky blue. I breathed with greater freedom." These symbols of cosmic renewal may here be subconscious in Wells, but they chime with those of the "solution" to alienation of D. H. Lawrence's *Apocalypse* (published in 1933—the year of *The Shape of Things to Come*): "re-establish the living organic connections with the cosmos, the sun, the earth, with mankind and family. Start with the sun, and the rest will slowly happen."[4]

Our own point in time is a century on from late Morris and early

Wells; a half century from late Wells and Lawrence; a third of a
century from Orwell's *Nineteen Eighty-Four*. We have moved further
into an era when, in Lewis Mumford's terminology, the dehumanized ego of posthistoric man will fill the future stage, unless, that is,
patterns of social organization are achieved which, in Mumford's
words, "put the highest concerns of man at the centre of all of his
activities, [uniting] the scattered fragments of the human personality,
turning artificially dismembered men—bureaucrats, specialists . . .
'experts', depersonalised agents into complete human beings."

When he writes of artificially dismembered man, fragmented
and incomplete, Mumford employs a Frankensteinian trope. An
artificial nonintegrative reassemblage may result in a man partially
incorporated into a machine to function in a limited and depersonalized way. In their purely functional aspects, such may be the astronaut, the assembly line worker, the cog in an administrative hierar-
chy. Science fiction has frequently dramatized and represented
symbolically such roles. One recalls D-503 in Zamyatin's *We*, the
rocket captain, Hollis, in Bradbury's *Illustrated Man*, and, one of the
most sophisticatedly conceived examples, Pohl's character Roger
Torraway in *Man Plus*.

Torraway is monster, demigod, cyborg, hacked about, cas-
trated, tinkered together, implanted, and fitted for adaptation to an
unearthly planetary habitat. With his optic circuits operational, "he
looked at himself in the mirror he had demanded they install: insect
eyes, bat wing, dully gleaming flesh. He amused himself by letting his
visual interpretations flow from bat to giant fly to demon." He has
also in his incompletely conditioned state some of the characteristics
of a werewolf. When he, a metamorphosed human, escapes and is
tracked down in something resembling a mad wolf hunt, there is a
fearful, though unfulfilled, expectancy that he will have torn his
unfaithful wife's body to pieces—violence typical of lycanthropy. He
is described as looking like the devil from the Disney/Moussorgsky
"Night on a Bare Mountain." Dr. William Russell and Claire Russell
have pointed out in their paper "The Social Biology of Werewolves"
that in medieval England the maneating, rabies spreading, and
allegedly shape changing wolf could be a symbol of the devil. Thus we
have in Roger Torraway a semi automated monster, with an unhu-
man range of senses, a more than human strength, and an almost
fatal isolation from normal human contacts, conduct, and environ-

ment, a figure capable of engendering innumerable atavistic reso-
nances, and the very prototype of those creatures onto whom the
alienated may project their alienation.

Putting these two themes together—first the Frankensteinian
creation, and then the projection for which it is the created recepta-
cle, we find a pattern which is basic to three further milestone books,
each separated from the other by about three-quarters of a century;
and I propose to look at them in a little detail. They are Mary
Shelley's *Frankenstein* (1818); again, but in differing perspective,
H. G. Wells's *War of the Worlds* (1898); and Ian Watson's *Embedding* (1973).

In *Frankenstein*, the monster is a creature of conjoined remnants
of what once had natural life, what Rosemary Jackson has termed
"the *disjecta membra* of a dead society raised up again as the living
dead." The mental counterpart of this social metaphor is the image of
the creator's, Count Frankenstein's, dark alter ego, reflecting the
wish to be wholly restored, but, unable to achieve an integrated
existence, venting frustrated and destructive energies on its environment, physical and human. In Brian Aldiss's virtuoso variation on
the theme (*Frankenstein Unbound*) the confrontation is perfectly
captured in the passage in which his time-transported protagonist,
Bodenland, says to the Monster, "We are of different universes. I am
a natural creation, you are a—a horror, unalive. I was born, you were
made." To which the reply is, "Our universe is the same universe,
where pain and retribution rule." The Monster's last words are,
"Though you seek to bury me, yet you will continuously resurrect
me. Once I am unbound, I am unbounded!" In other words, the
Monster says that as a personification of the alienated element in the
human condition it has a kind of immortality, cannot be banished.

The War of the Worlds has a not dissimilar concept at its core. It
appeared during a critical and transitional phase of the first, or
mechanical, industrial revolution. In it, humans are threatened by
aliens embodying the technological power and ruthlessness of a
future race—a race representing man's intelligence dehumanized.
The Martians, with their different range of sense registerings, are
"mere brains wearing different [machine] bodies to suit their needs."
Wells's ambivalence toward these aliens is (as previously noted)
similar to that which he displays towards the Selenites in *The First
Men in the Moon*, and towards the young giants in *The Food of the*

Gods. On the one hand, the Martians are pitiless, blood drinking ogres; on the other, as his narrator comments, "We men, with our bicycles and road skates, our Lilienthal soaring machines, our guns and sticks and so forth, are just in the beginning of the evolution that the Martians have worked out." Eventually, of course, the planet strikes back. Bacillary infection decimates the aliens until only their artificial carapaces remain: "They glittered now, harmless tripod towers of shining metal, in the brightness of the rising sun." Life returns to normal, but in the book's strangely disturbing conclusion the dehumanizing alienation pattern (as in *Doctor Moreau*) is again superimposed on normality. The narrator describes all the renewed bustle of traffic and human activity, and he speaks of his own happily restored domestic life, but then he says that it can all suddenly become vague and unreal. It seems to him that the busy multitudes in Fleet Street and the Strand "are but the ghosts of the past, haunting the streets, that I have seen silent and wretched, going to and fro in a dead city, the mockery of life in a galvanised body."

The "mockery of life" motif and that of the evolved monster are also in Ian Watson's *Embedding*. In this complex novel human subjects are being "shaped" and exploited by what are essentially Frankensteinian protagonists. The Amazonian Indians endeavor to produce their magic child, drug conditioned, from the womb of the woman in the taboo hut; when released, it is a monster. Christopher Sole, the experimental neurologist/semanticist, aims to create a new type of human being in his psycho-lab. His prime subject is a Pakistani orphan, and his work's objective is to embed an artificial language as a key to more sophisticated and more universal modes of logic and perception. To do this he uses computerized linguistic reshufflings, drugs, and illusions: an overstressed and overloaded brain sends the child destructively mad in an episode which is a close Frankensteinian analogue.

These two motifs are interwoven with that of the alien Sp'thra's offer to trade technological knowhow for human brains. They are creating an artificial mind, dependent on living brains collected throughout the galaxy, in furtherance of a communications project designed to alleviate their own alienated condition. After the destruction of their starship, its Chamber of Brains is entered. Rows of crystal lifesupport boxes, towering to the domed roof, contain creeper-like tendrils of wire leading to naked brains set in plastic jelly, attached to segments of straight or curly spine and to sense organs on muscular cords or bony supports. Anatomically, we are back with Mary Shelley; but the monster is not now a symbolic alter ego, but a collectivity. Moreover, what motivates the creation of all of these monsters is less a desire for greater knowledge or power than a need for more liberating modes of communication.

The concept of a whole historical, technological, or epistemological assemblage being welded into one accessible encyclopedic bank is common to early and to contemporary science fiction. All past things exist in Wells's Palace of Green Porcelain. In the case of his Selenites, "all knowledge is stored in extended brains . . . the lunar Somerset House and the lunar British Museum Library are collections of living brains." More recently we find sophisticated variations in Barrington Bayley's "Bees of Knowledge" (in *The Knights of the Limits*), in Michael Moorcock's *Rituals of Infinity*,[5] and in such widely differing constructs as the psychic sea in Lem's *Solaris* and Silverberg's labyrinth-deep "House of Records" (*Majipoor Chronicles*). In these two latter examples it is respectively the planetary ocean, and (in such episodes as "The Soul-Painter and the Shape-Shifter" and "Thesme and the Ghayrog") archetypal alien beings which are the projection-media. They function to mirror the processes of communication, both between the self and the macrocosmic world which it confronts, and between the conscious and the unconscious. At the same time, they are agents in dramas of psychic disruption and/or reintegration.

Such dramas may be exemplified further from two recent works: a novel and a short story. First, from Arthur C. Clarke's *2010: Odyssey Two*: in this sequel, as in its predecessor, there is metaphysical speculation as to what kind of communication between denizens of the universe, computers and bodiless minds included, may be achieved at molecular, electronic, or other levels. A prime instance is that of the HAL 9000/Bowman/Chandra relationship. The two humans are Frankensteins of sorts, having respectively operational and creative roles, with Hal in the role of monster. In this role Hal is mirror and human surrogate, reflecting both sentient mind and human automatism. This is depicted in the dismantling of Hal, when the autointellection panel is broken down, and Hal's poignant protests ("You are destroying my mind. . . . Don't you understand? . . . I will become childish. . . . I will become nothing.") give way to initial memory-implant babble and eventually to the pathetic "Daisy, Daisy" song and mechanically intoned training responses. After Hal is reconstituted, to avoid further dangerous schizophrenia, Chandra insists that Hal be given truthful information on the Jupiter escape schedule. When Max protests, "He's only a machine," Chandra replies, "So are we all, Mr. Brailovsky . . . whether we are based on carbon or silicon makes no fundamental difference." In the final synthesis Bowman and Hal become, in effect, components of a fused identity. As Clarke puts it: "Their thoughts melded together with the speed of light," dispensing with the medium of words tapped on a keyboard or spoken into a microphone.

In our second example, Robert Silverberg's story "Basileus," the protagonist, Cunningham, is put under stress through his work on the structuring of defense strategy and simulations. He has, in the course of this, cracked the technique of feeding potentially destructive messages to superpowers' central computers. As a hobbyist he has studied angelology and can summon onto the screen over a thousand angels. Some, like Cunningham, have unstable personalities, but he knows them to be only magnetic impulses under his control. One, an original creation, is Basileus, imperial in stature, but of shadowy, uncertain function. A conference with other angels leads to the setting up of Basileus as apocalyptic arbiter, a Judge of Worlds. As Cunningham's personal, social, and sexual life disintegrates, the curia of angels tells him to look into the screen when he calls up Basileus: the face will be his own. "Come now, Basileus, we are one," are his words as he feeds in judgement and world's end to both east and west. This is the perfect projection of an alienation in the mode of what Lewis Mumford calls the "negative syndrome."

The outcome of "Basileus" is downbeat. It may, on the other hand, be upbeat, as in the narrator's projective experience in Olaf Stapledon's *Star Maker* when he identifies with what he calls "the cosmical mind" and perceives a symphonic beauty in the "ultimate cosmos." This he describes as a "creature"that "embraced within its own organic texture the essences of all its predecessors." Its relation to each earlier cosmos was that of our own cosmos to a human being, and the life of each contributory cosmos related to its life much as a brain cell relates to the life of a human mind.[6]

The crosstides flowing between the life of the imagination (be that a life resulting in "dangerous visions" or poetic insight) and life

as lived day by day in the frequently alienating contemporary milieu
energize much current science fiction and fantasy. We are like planet
dwellers receiving disturbing images from Helliconia, or, more
actively, like the Aldiss character in *The Interpreter* who says: "I have
one eye cocked on the universe and one to my inner self. Yet at the
same time I am aware of this thug sliding towards me from a side
street." The surface self is endlessly preoccupied with the contingencies of existence, and the question implied is how can inner self and
that self which confront's the outer universe communicate effectively
and function integrally.

I have here been concerned chiefly with elements in various
modes of science fiction and fantasy which, by creating a projection
of the human condition onto an alien image—animal, android, extraterrestrial, planet, or star, assists the processes of self-realization,
of self-orientation, and individuation in a universe of which the self is
at once component part and microcosm. Aliens, in these contexts,
are fictions, and much of the "scenery" of science fiction is devised to
provide for them plausible realistic and/or symbolic habitats.

Carl Sagan has suggested that science fiction may perform a
service in readying contemporary minds for the possible future shock
of contact with an actual alien mind. Probabilities of this happening
do not seem immediately to be great; but were it to happen I believe
that science fiction, far from declining, would be stimulated by new
horizons opening up—just as when Martian canals and lunar subter-
rains lost any but mythic or symbolic status (they still retain these);
the fresh perspectives provided by black holes, worm holes, dolphin
language, computer language, and all the ramifications of exploratory anthropological and psychological research have marked out
avenues of development for speculative fiction. My guess is that
serious science fiction will continue to involve itself closely with
issues of communication, exploring the implications of intercultural,
interspecies, interintelligence exchanges and, within these parameters, will often use its dramatizations and extrapolations to create
models of the ways in which the self confronts its internal and
external environments as these change with time. In such functioning
it offers not a faith but a variety of therapies, playing, according to
writer, vision, and bias, admonitory, cautionary, stabilizing, revolutionary, cathartic, or simply greatly exhilarating and mindflexing
roles. Angels created may become collaborators. Demons created

may be analyzed, empathized with, and exorcised. Its readers will
not be allowed to elude the significance of Nietzsche's dictum (in
Beyond Good and Evil):[7] "He who fights with monsters should look
to it that he does not become a monster. And when you gaze long
enough into the abyss the abyss also gazes into you." Abyss-gazing is,
perhaps, as good a definition of science fiction as any.

News vs. Fiction: Reflections on Prognostication

Gary Kern

Missives of Doom

> Oft expectation fails, and most oft there
> Where most it promises, and oft it hits
> Where hope is coldest and despair most fits.
> —Shakespeare, *All's Well That Ends Well*

Recently Dr. Paul Ehrlich of Stanford University, author of *The Population Bomb, Extinction*, and other important studies, sent me his projection for the year 2030—less than fifty years from today. As Ehrlich sees it, "80 million more people are coming here for breakfast, lunch and dinner," and he recommended that I take a part in the work of Zero Population Growth. A few days later, Captain Jacques Cousteau wrote me to express his alarm at the pollution of the ocean, which might cause the melting of the ice caps, drastic changes in global temperature and the exodus of coastal populations inland, where they will encounter famine, chaos, and disease. Cousteau set no date for the worldwide catastrophe, since, as he put it, one cannot "describe being tossed about in an on-coming cyclone," but he advised that I take a part in the work of the Cousteau Society. In the following days, I received letters from presidents of organizations advocating a sane population policy, immigration reform, sex information, planned parenthood, voluntary sterilization, and negative population growth, each of whom voiced dire concern for the future in terms of millions of physically, mentally, and spiritually stunted human beings. Separately, each letter confirmed my pessimistic thoughts about the future, yet taken together gave rise to a perverse optimism. Clearly, if all of them were true, some were false, since only one future will occur. For example, if people flee inland from putrid waves of poisonous surf, as Cousteau foresees, illegal immigration to California will surely abate, reproduction of the natives conceivably will drop and fewer people will be coming to this spot for supper than Ehrlich predicts. I need only consider the forecast of a major earthquake in California before the end of the century to cancel all other predictions for the state, as well as the organizations which make them.

But if the San Andreas Fault holds firm, and the Pacific waves of filth do not sterilize the surfers, what disastrous future should I pick? And on what basis? Ehrlich, after all, did not really write to me. His letter was photoprocessed by ZPG and mailed to me three times; but since I have never contacted ZPG, it addressed not me, but my name.[1] Sad to say, Cousteau and all the others but the last were equally unacquainted and impersonal. They must have acquired my name from Negative Population Growth, to which I once sent ten dollars, on the calculated probability that I would make a donation. The fact that I did not was no doubt subsumed in a predictable percentage of negative responses, so in a sense I fulfilled a function of the future and validated their prognostication. But if they could predict the noninvolvement of a certain number of names, could they fail to foretell the success or failure of their mission, and, with it, the falsehood or the futility of their initial prediction?

Prognostication, I thought, is a paradox. It presumes to predict the future, but not the reaction to the prediction. World destruction is inevitable, unless we apply all our efforts to stop it. World utopia is inevitable, but we must help it through the birth pangs. We can change the movement of history, but we must all move in the opposite direction. We can't change the movement of history, but we can delay it by failing to understand it. There are forces dependent on human will, but we must will other forces. There are forces independent of human will, but we must align ourselves with them. We are surviving today, but on the basis of unconscious principles; so we must make conscious tomorrow the principles for our survival. We anticipate, we predict, we prognosticate our future as a sort of surplus activity accumulating from past and present. If we really knew what we were going to do, we would not have to consult megatrends; if we really knew the megatrends, we would not have to plan what we're going to do.

Metaprognostics

> Wilt thou reach stars,
> because they shine on thee?
> —Shakespeare, *Two Gentlemen of Verona*

Prognostication must be inevitable, but not all alike. I was intrigued by the double premise of my impersonal missives of doom, and I thought it might be worthwhile to list all the ways I could of looking into the future, particularly since I've been writing a novel set a modest five years ahead. Some methods of prognostication (Greek *pro + gignoskein* = "to know in advance") struck me as older than others, so I attempted a sort of genealogy, without a pretense of demonstrable truth. The ways that I found were ten—actually a few more, which I forced into the preferred number.

1. *Instinct (Forecasting*–1). Intelligence in the universe is unconscious, and prior to man, protoverbal. Without a known plan, it builds up hierarchies of processes with interconnecting systems, some of which are incorporated in the living creatures produced.[2] The intelligence in plants, animals, and natural processes. The repetition in tides, seasons, and generations. The earliest intelligence of man instinctually assumed that things would repeat—cycles, revolutions, millennia. Modern intelligence changes the names—trends, projections, prospects. What else but instinctual anticipation, raised to the level of eschatology, can explain the importance the world has attached to the dates, 1984, 2000, 2001?[3]

2. *Prophecy.* Dependence on cycles, anticipation of a millennium, invokes good or bad fortune, divine will. Prophecy expresses this will as a revelation, usually in the form of a promise or warning. The prophet hears the words of the gods which others can hear but faintly, or not at all. When even he cannot hear them, the gods must be coaxed by divination, sacrifice, or augury.[4] Should this fail, the grand plan must be read by the tossing of bones or dice.[5] Today, prophecy is replaced by "precognition" (the Latin equivalent of *pro-gnosis*), and the grand plan by a daily horoscope amusement. With the atomization of society and the increase of doubt, everyone becomes mantic, a questionable prophet of his own future doom.

3. *Mythmaking.* Mysteries remain, and men transmit their explanations over generations to serve as guides to the individual stages of life. The events of life are meaningful, predictable, but beyond a

single person's ken. Myths relate us to the collective experience. They are laughed away as mere fairytales and are recognized as soulpiercing truths by one and the same mortal.

 4. *Predetermination.* Having perceived order in the universe, man conceives it as self-enclosed, self-sufficient, and self-perpetuating. Once an atom is set in motion, it has a track to follow, as does a man. God becomes the first mover. The universe takes the form of a machine, described by Euclid and Newton, which God might interrupt with a miracle, but not constitutionally alter. Enter the scientific method: cause and effect, the programmable utopia (Chernyshevsky), the implacable law (Malthus). The reductivism of Darwin, Marx, and Freud. When reality spoils the scheme, then the theory of relativity, the uncertainty principle, and the laws of probability take its place. One way or another, in large matters and small, we must know in advance what will happen.

 5. *Historical determinism.* History invested with a moral purpose. Class conflict instituted as the basic process, the masses blessed, the exploiters damned. Philosophy is pragmatized, religion secularized, wrong thinkers vilified, right thinkers deified. Predictions are promoted with propaganda, five-year plans, and thought control; mistakes are eliminated by doublethink, newspeak, and the memory hole. Activists treat the dogma as a game plan, while revisionists reduce its predictive value to a position of wait and see.[6]

 6. *Extrapolation.* What works in one place must work in another. From prehistory to history, from continent to continent, from planet to planet. The earth evolved in a solar system—there are other solar systems. Intelligent life requires stereoscopic vision, complex limbs for work and locomotion, a body for provisioning energy and a brain for efficient control, so we can expect to see these features in spacemen from other worlds. We peer to the end of the universe and behold the reflection of our own face.

 7. *Data analysis (Forecasting–2).* From small to large, from large to small. Statistics, birth and mortality rates, demographics, public-opinion polls—all assume that percentages of human processes can be predetermined with negligible plus or minus degrees of error. One problem is contamination of data: if people find out the prediction, they may change their behavior and disprove the projection. Or the prophecy may be self-fulfilling: they may cause the

result. In any event, unpredicted reactions to the forecast can be reabsorbed as "feedback" leading to more refined analysis.[7]

8. *Determination.* The impatient doer predicts the future by making it happen. Yet, however forceful, he is not omniscient and not the master of all events. As Tolstoi pointed out in *War and Peace*, the leader cannot issue commands to account for every contingency: he has real power, but no knowledge where it will lead. Thus, Napoleon, Hitler, and American policy in Vietnam, where as one soldier put it, "We never lost a single battle, yet we lost the war."[8] In daily life this method is used by the person "looking out for number one," expecting "to profit from the coming bad times," planning "to survive and prosper in the next war or revolution."[9] There is a pacifist, communal version: We can end world hunger, we can abolish war, we can make friends with the Russian people, "if only we really try."[10] All these doers refuse to accept the frightening possibility that no one is in control—of himself, his people, the world. As Stephen Vizinczey puts it: events converge on a time and a place; each time has a place and each place has a time; increase either and you decrease control: time + place = chance. He advises his readers to aim for an immediate goal in the next few minutes.[11]

9. *Scenario making.* Aware of the folly of outright prediction, thinkers in think tanks design alternative versions of the future as contingency plans, so that a recognized situation may be met with a maximum of preconceived thought. Paragon of the method is Herman Kahn, *Thinking about the Unthinkable* (1962). From Pentagon scenarios of Mutually Assured Destruction (MAD) the method has spread to the wider society in the form of alternative press statements, courtroom tactics, football game plans. The problem is that without a real test, a real situation, the method may multiply into infinite scenarios in the attempt to account for all contingencies. When the test comes, all the prepackaged scenarios but one collapse, and this one fits, but unevenly. In science fiction, visions of the future proliferate into mutually exclusive scenarios, each shredded in turn by the slow forward grind of reality.

10. *Straightforward projection.* Common sense tells us we'll have more of the same—more good, more bad, and if problems pop up we'll fix them. This is the working model for most of us in our daily affairs, the government in its foreign policy, and the news media in its

world coverage. The rub is that developments in human society do not proceed from A to B to C. As James Burke graphically demonstrated in his book and television series *Connections* (1978), an innovation in one area sets up conditions which trigger innovations in other areas. Technological growth is zig-zag, exponential, and obliterative of the past. In literature, the Russian formalist Viktor Shklovsky hinted at the same thing when he stated: "Not from father to son, but from uncle to nephew." Those who rely on commonsense projections open themselves up to a lifetime of surprises.[12]

In addition to these ten types of prognostication, I should mention the more general *rapture of the future* which sets tasks and goals for the future without a specific method of determining what that future will be. Its basic tenet is a superprediction: Unless there is more preparation for the future (i.e., more prediction), there will be individual and societal disorientation, confusion and chaos threatening the very existence of mankind.[13] To forestall this outcome, the futurologist makes the necessary proposals. For the individual: new studies, new lifestyles, checklists of progress with emotional plusses and minusses. For society: new forms of education, councils of the future, futuristic training villages. We must teach our youth to map *probable futures*, institute committees to select *preferable futures*, and change politics to facilitate *possible futures*. This rapturous vision has the same value for the individual as a Ben Franklin list of good and bad deeds, a Leo Tolstoi diary of activities planned for every hour of the day, an enthusiastic scribble of New Year's resolutions. As for society, it founders on the axiomatic "we." "We" must anticipate, "we" must plan, "we" must decide. "If only we all . . ."[14] Such futurological we-mongering has lost contact with reality. The nation is not a homogenous community of "we," but a plurality of contending interests and antipathies. The tribal feeling of "we" erupts only in war and revolution, electrical blackouts, and sports stadiums—and even then with contention. The social commentator infected with a rapture of the future lacks any method, any philosophy, and within the year proves himself as out of date as a headhunter snapped by a Polaroid.

The uncomfortable fact is that omniscience cannot be had in past, present, or future. A part cannot understand the whole of which it is a part: a self cannot define itself without becoming a second self, a mind cannot discover the mind of which it is the expression, an eye cannot see the eye without making itself a reflection, nor concentrate on a point without blurring the periphery. Therefore, an individual cannot comprehend the mass, a contemporary cannot surmount the age, a mortal cannot circumvent the immortal. All knowledge is preliminary, and our conception of the future premature. In such a state of affairs, each new fact impresses us with its thingness, its graininess, its reality. This reality may confirm our predictions, and a high score of confirmations—our method, but we cannot honestly believe that before a specific event we know what will happen. Thus, whether it confirms or crushes our expectation, each event brings a surprise—a little one in the first case and a big one in the second. And the broader our outlook, the more concentrated our focus, the more surprises we experience as the future bombards us with unforeseeable, unstoppable happenings instantly converted into the immediate present.

Fantastic Reality

Truly, if you pursue some fact of real life, even one not particularly striking at first glance, and if only you have the strength and the vision, you will find in it a depth which is lacking in Shakespeare.
—Dostoevsky, "Two Suicides,"
Diary of a Writer, Oct. 1876

It seems that certainty increases as we draw back to the present, the arena of all our real actions. This present is conceived as broad and continuous, a sort of breathing bubble in the fluid of time. It retains the immediate past and seems already to contain the most immediate future—that future constantly impinging, slipping across the border, and becoming established fact. That is, the future as news. Each morning the news refreshes itself, and at points throughout the day; we attend to it and react to it, feeling it within our grasp. Perhaps here, on the brink of the future, yet still, as it were, within the present, we can manage our lives, our society, our world. Not so much by prognostication, as by the speed of our reaction to events, and by our awareness of the time. Each person acts in his own way: one makes a capital investment, another requests a donation, a third dispenses birth control pills, a fourth contains a riot, and I write fiction.

As previously mentioned, the letters of concern for the future came as I was writing a novel. At the same time, as chance would have it, I had come in my daily reading of Dostoevsky to his *Diary of a Writer* (*Dnvenik pisatelya*) for the year 1876. The conjunction of the two seemed fortuitous, the letters posing the problem of dealing with the time, the *Diary* providing a historical example. With this work, Dostoevsky, an avid reader of newspapers, created an entirely new literary form in order to keep abreast, and even ahead of events, month by month sharing with his subscribers all the things that concerned him, all things seen, heard, and read, all the major issues of his time and place. His concerns sound remarkably modern: deterioration of the family, dependent status of women, child abuse, cruelty to animals, destruction of forests, threats of war, social apathy, legalistic immorality, suicide, reality and fantasy. Writing furiously to meet deadlines, Dostoevsky nevertheless did not merely report the news or provide a running commentary, but, rather, philosophized through the news, shifting the focus from incident to society, from Russia to Europe, from present to past to future. At one time, a personal reaction; another time, a social analysis; a third time, a fictional work. Always, in whatever form, he sought the chief idea in an event, its essence, its reality. "I have my own special view of reality," he wrote to a friend, "and that which the majority call exceptional and almost fantastical, for me sometimes constitutes the very essence of reality."[15]

With his monthly journal Dostoevsky attempted: (1) to advance literary, social, and philosophical arguments; (2) to keep abreast of events by the speed of his reaction; (3) to cope with the mass of events by penetrating to their essence; (4) to discover the exceptional and fantastic twist that sometimes reveals a hidden reality; and (5) to make an impact on the time—the present, immediate future, and long-range future. In this latter intention he realized that he could not predict any specific events. He was too well aware of the quirky, uncontrollable nature of everyday reality:

> Never will a novelist present such improbabilities as those which reality presents to us every day by the thousands, in the form of the most ordinary things. No fantasy could think it up in any other way. And what superiority over a novel! Just try it, *compose* an episode in a novel . . . and next Sunday a critic, in a feuilleton, will prove to you clearly and triumphantly that you are raving and that in reality this never

happens and moreover never could happen, for such and such reason. In the end, you will be ashamed and agree with him. But then you get [the newspaper] *Golos* [*The Voice*], and suddenly you read in it a whole episode. . . . At first you read with surprise, horrible surprise, so that even while you are reading you do not believe anything; but you come to the end, put away the newspaper and all at once, without knowing why, say to yourself: "Yes, this is the way it should have happened." And another will even add: "I had a presentiment of this."[16]

Although he could not predict the specifics, Dostoevsky still believed he could catch the general sweep of the time. In answer to the perennial demand to portray reality "as it is," he objected: "There is no such reality at all, and there never has been on earth, because the essence of things is inaccessible to man, he apprehends nature as it is reflected in his idea, proceeding through his feelings; consequently, you must give greater vent to the idea and not fear the ideal."[17]

With such a flexible, yet controlled response to his time, Dostoevsky could write journalistic articles keen in their topicality, yet lasting in their relevance to a civilized society. Such is the account of the Advocate Spasovich, who by the act of humiliating a little girl on the stand successfully defended her father against the charge of beating her brutally (Feb. 1876, chap. 2). Dostoevsky could also incorporate the news of his day into imaginative fiction, such as the story "The Meek One" (*Krotkaya*), where he combined newspaper reports of various suicides into one most pathetic suicide, and imagined word-for-word the inner monologue of the man who had caused it (Nov. 1876). And he could turn his sociological analysis into a religious ideal, prophesying that the people of the soil, embodying the moral virtues of selflessness, receptivity, and love, would lead Russia into an era of brotherhood and freedom, awakening the whole of mankind into a realization of Christ's way. This ideal, like the kingdom of heaven on earth, or the free communist society, was not necessarily disproved by events, but postponed by its believers beyond the life of the prophet to an ever receding future.

Dostoevsky serves as a paragon of the writer concerned with his time, and his methods would answer most questions for me were it not for a peculiar twist of our own. In his time, Dostoevsky could pick out the most significant story and reveal its hidden essence. On the basis of a single political murder, he could develop a huge prophetic

novel, *The Devils* (*Besy*, 1872). And, although suicides in Russia
appeared on the increase, he had time to comment on nearly every
one. This situation, I believe, does not apply to our time and place,
where a suicide attracts no individual attention and anonymously fills
out bulging statistics. Twenty years ago, our nation was appalled by
the report that apartment dwellers in New York City had watched
while a woman was knifed to death on the street and had not moved
an inch to help her. The Kitty Genovese case seemed a crystallization
of social apathy, entered the textbooks of sociology, and inspired
made-for-TV movies. Today, crowds cheer the murderer, neighbors
join the rapist, passersby laugh at the corpse, and business goes on as
usual. (I can cite reports for each of these items.) For a writer today,
it is impossible to pick the worst, most characteristic alleged incident.
Impossible to invent outrages against the human spirit which could
match the charges filed daily against freedom-loving Americans released on their own recognizance. Such is my opinion, but then I am
not Dostoevsky, and theoretically someone as sensitive as he could
grasp the all-time worst, most characteristic event encapsulating the
ruin of our society.

Or could he? Aside from the worsening of our times, which
some blithe spirits might contest, there is a quickening of the pace,
which few today would deny. What is the writer to do, especially one
without his own daily column, his own monthly journal? Slavishly
follow the grisly course of events, only to fall behind in energy and
inventiveness, all the while suspecting that his work will be shunted
aside by the life story of one of the criminals, as told to another failed
novelist? Here, the example of Dostoevsky, with his one-man philo-
sophical-literary journal, seems an impossible dream.

The Acceleration of Events

> I find it difficult to imagine works by Lev Tolstoi based on good
> sanitation. I find it difficult to imagine readers really excited by such a
> good, sanitary Tolstoi.
>
> —Evgeny Zamyatin, "The Goal"

There was a reason why I set my novel five years ahead. My
thinking was this: it would take a year to write, another year to find a
publisher; in the third year the book would come out in hardcover,
and in the fourth year in paperback. Finally, in the fifth year, a movie

producer would buy it, and professors would assign it to their classes. At that fond date I did not want it to be behind the times. Therefore, my task was set: to ignore the dross of my day, the blather of airhead celebrities, the media hype of problems beside the point, and to concentrate on the constituitive factors, the signals of future developments, the essence. In short, to keep a bit ahead of the news. As I have indicated, this task proved beyond my abilities. Recognizing, for example, that we live in a society of random violence where each person plays roulette with thugs, I hit on the idea of including real, but slightly altered news items in the novel, so that my hero would hear on the radio and read in the papers only this kind of report. I opened the local section of the *Press-Enterprise* and saw on a single page three separate accounts of unidentified bodies discovered along the highways. Again, in the novel, I wrote a scene with a dozen emotionally disturbed children learning to ride a horse, intending by this to emphasize the increase of abused children in our society. This intention was validated, but dwarfed by the case of the McMartin Preschool of Manhattan Beach, where teachers were charged with molesting, raping, terrorizing, and photographing for pornographic purposes more than a hundred children for a decade. Again, I sent my dogcatcher hero to China, where I planned for him to answer questions about dog pounds, the overpopulation of pets in the USA, and so on. A week later I read in the *Los Angeles Times* of a campaign against dogs in Beijing, where gangs of conscientious citizens were chasing strays and bludgeoning them to death with clubs. If I could not equal any specifics, how could I compose the configuration—the world five years hence with all of its social and electronic dysfunctions?

The problem is not quite the same which Dostoevsky tried to solve. There is not only the eternal onrush of the future, but a quickening of the pace. By this I mean two things: an acceleration of events and an acceleration of news. For the first, I cite all those charts of the timetable of evolution, where man is seen to appear in the last tiny colored strip; all those imaginary clocks where the age of the earth is reduced to twenty-four hours, human history to the last half-second, and the industrial revolution, automobile, jet airplane, nuclear weaponry, and miniaturization to progressively smaller fractions of that last half-second. And to living memory, which can look back over the better part of the century and see a new technological environment for each generation, almost for each decade. In his book, *Future Shock*, Alvin Toffler sums up the situation with his concept of the eight-hundredth lifetime:

> If the last 50,000 years of man's existence were divided into lifetimes of approximately sixty-two years each, there have been about 800 such lifetimes. Of these 800, fully 650 were spent in caves.
>   . . . Only during the last six lifetimes did masses of men ever see a printed word. Only during the last four has it been possible to measure time with any precision. Only in the last two has anyone used an electric motor. And the overwhelming majority of all the material goods we use in daily life today have been developed within the present, the 800th, lifetime.[18]

No doubt future shock was felt by an ancient province conquered in turn by the Persians, the Greeks, and the Romans; yet, on a worldwide scale, the statistics confirm our sensation of accelerating change. As Toffler shows, speed itself has speeded up, from 8 mph in 6,000 B.C., to 13 mph in 1825, to 100 mph at the end of the century, to 400 mph in 1938, to 18,000 in the orbiting space capsules of 1970.[19] Similar horrific statistics are given for the increasing production of print, the multiplication of scientific discoveries, and the consequent increasing ignorance of each individual in respect to the total output. Our breathing bubble of the present is shooting through the fluid of time, and though we may seek security in memories of the good old days or in wish-fulfillment fantasies, we cannot escape the sensation of perilous, revolutionary speed, exceeding not only our anticipation, but also our imagination. Fiction pales before fact. In the popular media a maximum effort is made to convert news into docudramas, novels of fact, and topical hit songs as quickly as possible—can it be not only to make money, but to tame the news, to make it conventional? Interesting items in the newspaper, in fact, are no longer available to the inspired Dostoevskian novelist: the rights to them are purchased, sealed, and handed to a hired hack. But even five days after Jonestown, when the instant book on the involuntary mass suicide was stocked at eye level on the supermarket stands, the news looked stale, a dreary printout of the features already supplied by the newspapers, magazines, radio, and television, and the accustomed public turned to fresh horrors. As for writing a fictional work which would expose religious cultism in America, it would hardly serve any purpose. A careful psychological probing, of course, would take many months and could hardly command wide appeal.

Once again I find a parallel in the literary experience of Russia, where a few decades after Dostoevsky the waves of revolution accelerated events and made new demands upon writers. After the October Revolution, the notion that news was more exciting than art was advanced everywhere, both by uneducated new writers and opportunistic old hands. Every artist had to deal with it, and in the theater of Vsevolod Meyerhold a play might be interrupted by a motorcycle shooting down the aisle, up a ramp, and onto the stage, where the Red Army messenger would announce the news from the front. Pageants of the Revolution and Civil War were enacted in the streets, and proletarian writers insisted that novels must move into the factories, express the pathos of construction, the "new reality." (Curiously, restagings of the classics enjoyed a vogue, much like the BBC productions which today serve our country's cultural needs.) Of all the extreme literary manifestoes of the twenties, the argument for fact over fiction attained its zenith in the statement of Sergei Tret-yakov, spokesman for the New Left Front of the Arts (Novyi LEF), who won everlasting glory for himself by declaring the daily news-paper superior to Tolstoi. He wrote:

> The sufferers among us are whining: Where is the monumental art of the Revolution? Where are the "broad canvasses" of the red epos? Where are our red Homers and red Tolstois? . . .
>
> We have no reason to wait for Tolstois, for we have our own epos. Our epos is the newspaper . . .
>
> The entire anonymous newspaper staff, from the workers' corre-spondent to the lead reporter—this is the collective Tolstoi of our day . . .
>
> How can there be any talk of some *War and Peace* when every morning, as we grab the newspaper, we in effect turn a new page of that astonishing novel which goes by the name of our modern life. The *dramatis personnae* of this novel are its writers and readers—we ourselves.[20]

Tretyakov wielded little influence. In fact, he was attacked by Party critics and eventually liquidated in Stalin's purges. Yet at the end of the twenties he enunciated an attitude that had been growing since the Revolution: the primacy of fact over fiction, pragmatic task over imagination. The Party, while destroying some of its exponents, accepted factualism as an essential ingredient of literature, which, when guided and shaped by the proper ideology, would produce inspiring works of socialist realism. During the first five-year plan (1928–32), brigades of writers were sent to construction sites to describe the building of socialism; fictionalists were set quotas the same as daily reporters. Most of this scribbling has entered the history lists of Soviet Russian literature and is inflicted only on Soviet high school students and foreign specialists, but from among the hundreds of titles one exception shines bright as a work filled with energy, excitement and the quickened pace of its time. It is the novel *Time, Forward! (Vremya, Vperyod!)*, completed in 1932 by Valentin Katayev. Here a competition for pouring cement at the construction site of a chemical combine sets the stage for a lively picture of workers rushing over wooden planks with barrows of gravel, sand, and cement, casting short radial shadows crisscrossing each other, counting their mixtures against the clock and the previous record.

At the same time that Katayev was writing his hallelujah to industrialization, a lesser-known writer by the name of Andrei Platonov was working out his own approach to the reconstruction of society. In his novel *The Foundation Pit (Kotlovan*, 1930), he describes the building of a future utopia—a housing block for the proletariat, where the pit grows ever deeper and the workers live in a shack. Here the communist ideal does not motivate men identically and produce a sterling team effort, but rather moves through the mind of each individual believer. The narrative is slow, belabored, working out the thoughts of the hunched-over diggers.

These two approaches to the "new reality" make a striking contrast. Katayev is swift, easy, one-dimensional. His characters may be of various sorts, but existentially they are all the same. The reality posited beneath his text is firm, discernible, and exploitable. The world is challenging, but conquerable by energy, will, and right understanding, while reflection, doubt, and daydreaming will only waste time. Platonov, on the other hand, is strange, difficult, rough-edged. Each character has his own attitude and destiny, his own eccentric understanding of the world, and no one understanding is taken as right. Reality is consequently fragmented into as many truths as there are individual minds, yet uniformly serious and necessitous. Platonov creates a world of infinite original constructions of reality, countless private agreements with nature and life, driven by a never fully revealed universal mechanics, where the chief physical experience is want, and the chief mental activity is delirium. A "cruel and beautiful world," as he titled one of his stories.

By the standards of his day, Katayev best caught the tempo of revolution and matched the onrush of events. Platonov was out of step, quirky, disturbing. Katayev was accepted for publication and celebrated. Platonov was rejected and pilloried. *Time, Forward!* enjoyed critical acclaim, entered literary history and anthologies. *Kotlovan* passed decades in oblivion and was published only recently outside of Russia. Comparing the novels today, more than fifty years after their writing, one cannot fail to distinguish the vital difference. Katayev is an interesting historical document. Platonov is literature.

So then, it would be easy to conclude that in times of rapid change the work which comes closest to journalism, reportage, news, stands the best chance of success in its day and may qualify for a historical document in the future, while the work which explores less familiar areas of reality and creates its own fictional form may fail in its day, but aspire to immortal posterity. At this stage the question becomes one of a presumed "test of time," which must overcome popular taste and sneak past the gatekeepers of the media. And there the matter may stand, as regards the acceleration of events. But this was only half of the problem.

The Acceleration of News

The window on the world can be covered with a newspaper.
—Stanislaw Lem, *Unkempt Thoughts*

Are there more murders today, or more reported murders? More suicides, or more recorded suicides? More homosexuals, or more declared homosexuals? For the social statistician, the true figures perhaps can be found. But for the ordinary citizen, more reports equal more events. The instantaneous registry of every news-worthy event in the world, its storage, retrieval, and reproduction by an international communications network, has not produced univer-sal understanding and harmony as visionaries of the past presaged (Edward Bellamy, Velimir Khlebnikov). On the contrary, it has made each citizen of the planet into an impotent atom, powerless to stop explosions of human misery, or even to slow down the furious round of sensational thrills. How can the writer, especially the fictionalist, stand against this stinging swarm of tragedies, this minute-by-minute attack of athletic diversions, the onslaught of happy endings with little kids and their doggies from the other side of the globe? One method of defense is to recognize that the news is a phantom.

Many things occur in the world, and no one can know every one. The news is a grill predesigned to sift the flow of events. On the basis of certain assumptions about public interest and need, the grill admits discrete incidents and lets pass the overall flow.[21] Editors arrange the incidents admitted as newsworthy in an order familiar to us all: international news (disruptions, protests, terrorist attacks, and wars); national news (governmental press releases, criminal cases, obituaries, activities of beautiful people); economic news (stocks and statistics); sports news (all sorts of games, stats, and interviews); and finally the human-interest story (sweepstakes winners, eccentrics, pandas, and little bunnies). These categories are constantly re-shuffled to produce the top story, the continuation, the closing story, and an attempt is even made to keep track of the overall flow in the form of an abbreviated "in-depth" report. Nevertheless, most developments in most countries escape notice until they match the grill; then the news provides maps of Vietnam, Iran, and El Salvador to bring the public up to date. Likewise, the ongoing work of major scientists, inventors, and artists attracts no attention, but the results may receive mention at an awards ceremony or in an obit. Thus, the news calms us by giving a familiar shape to the ever-impinging future, yet at the same time alarms us by singling out shocks and surprises, keeping us ignorant of the formative forces.

Not too many years ago, Marshall McLuhan, known as the "media guru," predicted the global village and its social effects, but already his predictions seem tame. By its instantaneous omni-presence, the media environment creates the illusion of an eternal continuum of news, existing here and there in sight and sound and print, and shared by all as a daily vicarious experience. In this uniform, predictable, self-enclosed world, distinctions between art and life, fact and fiction, past and present are obliterated, or at least made inoperative. The writer who maintains these distinctions finds himself at a disadvantage, in tune with the heritage of human thought and creation, but cut off in silence and obscurity from the social structure of his day.

Once it was possible to isolate ordinary life from art—that is, the moments of life spent while not experiencing a work of art. It was assumed that the time spent on a work of art was in some way worth more than an equal time of ordinary life: the artist took more time to produce his work than for the recipient to receive it, or, by his genius, packed more intelligence into it than another person could gather on his own in the same amount of time, and so there was a profit. If not, the game was not worth the candle. But today, the average American spends morning to night in the midst of artistic products, whether of the supermarket or museum variety, whether in public or private. As Toffler puts it, modern man spends almost all of his waking hours taking in "coded messages," many of them "artfully fashioned by communications experts."[22] He may read the newspaper or a magazine as much as an hour a day; he hears countless songs in cars, elevators, telephones on hold, dentist chairs, psychiatric waiting rooms; and he watches television seven hours and five minutes every day of the year.[23] Consequently, raw experience—that is, uncoded, unfashioned, unaccompanied activity—is reduced to the sleeping hours, and daily life comes closer to a walking dream. As a rule, the recipient of art compares not his own experience and thoughts to the artistic work at hand (e.g., "Dallas"), but rather another work of the same variety (e.g., "Dynasty"). Since art itself is cheapened in its mass replications, comparison is, therefore, made between a range of unworthy objects. On the other hand, the artist himself can narrow the distance between art and life by speeding up his production, and by means of computer, word processor, and minicam produce in nearly the same amount of time it takes to consume it. Or he can transmit raw experience immediately as an artistic product (e.g., "An American Family," PBS 1973), with the result that the raw experience, aware of the camera, becomes an act. It would seem that time is saved, but only for the artist. For the recipient, the weaker the distinction between art and life, the more time is lost.

When art and life are fused, distinctions of form cease to matter. A book can become a movie; a movie, a book. A commercial can become a hit song; a hit song, a commercial. A gospel can become a musical. Within the convertible forms, the genres become convertible. A tragedy can become a comedy; a comedy, a tragedy. A news story can become a fictionalized drama; a fictionalized drama, a news story. The roles in the convertible genres of the convertible forms themselves become convertible. An actor can become a director; a director, an actor. A movie star can become a writer; a writer, a movie star. Actor, director, writer, producer, politican, president— all are convertible in every direction, save that a sports star can become everything else, but an out-of-shape celebrity can convert only to a friend of sports stars, a participant in beer commercials with sports stars, and so on, but not to an actual athletic competitor. The touchstone of convertibility, the magic key to success, which converts the actress Jane Fonda into a politician, the politician William F. Buckley into a novelist, the scientist Carl Sagan into a television producer, the comedian Rodney Dangerfield into an actor, a beer salesman, and a singer in the video of his own record, is celebrity-hood—known in the trade as "recognition value."[24] The lure is held out to every aspiring writer: get recognized, and you can do anything; develop and display your talents (even those you don't have yet) through the fullest range of human potentials. All you need to do to gain celebrityhood is pass through one or another of the media portals, providentially guarded by the keepers of the stencils. At the gate of fictional literature, whatever the genre pathway (sci-fi, detective story, horror, romance) an editor-clone holds the stencil which you are expected to match: a thin, dried husk of the nineteenth century realistic novel, fed as the mass communion wafer just before the movie in the necropolis of the entertained zombies.

It will have been noticed that entertainment, no-news, has slipped into the discussion. News cannot be isolated from the media at large, which transmit entertainment. Aldous Huxley, in *Brave New World Revisited* (1958), faulted previous prognosticators, himself included, with the observation: "They did not foresee what in fact has happened, above all in our Western capitalist countries—the development of a vast mass communications industry, concerned in the main neither with the true nor the false, but with the unreal, the more or less totally irrelevant. In a word, they failed to take into account man's almost infinite appetite for distractions."[25]

More recent critics have remarked on the tendency of news itself to become entertainment—for example, Paddy Chayevsky's scathing film, *Network* (1976), itself turned into an innocuous television entertainment, intersticed with commercials and consumed by the uncritical viewers. With its increasing homogeneity, the media environment blurs not only the distinction between life and art, but also between news and fiction. An outstanding case in point was the ABC-TV broadcast of the film *The Day After* (27 November 1983). As part of the preshow publicity, the network arranged for a public showing of the film in West Germany, where the question of nuclear armament was particularly intense, then reported the reactions of the West German moviegoers—*as news*. By the time of the USA television showing, the film had made the cover of *Newsweek*—*as news*. Immediately after the showing, ABC held a formal discussion with experts on nuclear warfare, and their responses were reshown by all the networks *on the news*. The mediocre quality of the film, its artistic phoniness, were occasionally noted, but regarded as beside the point. In the next week, ABC followed its coup with a series of war game scenarios, using former and present members of government in the fictional roles of president and his staff of advisers. Both *The Day After* and *The War Game* then entered the archives, thence no doubt to return as reruns, where fact and fiction are one.[26]

Reruns, repeats, reproductions of every recorded fact and feature in any time and place create the wraparound of a universal present tense. This morning's news can be seen tonight; yesterday's news, next week; and next week's news, if not yesterday, then at least prepackaged and instantly replayable. In this universal present, people are ageless, or rather all ages. Bob Hope has quipped that he can turn the television dial and watch his hairline recede; should he turn the dial the other way, he could watch it fill back out. Here fads and fashions need never go out of fashion; no instant celebrity need ever pass from the scene. Deceased stars perform with living ones to live audiences of some former year, or with laughtracks of presently embalmed cadavers, and only the recipients of the residuals know who's up and about, and who's resting in Forest Lawn. If you own a video cassette recorder, you may preserve the favorite film of your youth and keep both it and yourself forever young. Where once great exploits were recorded by memory and shaped by imagination into legend, today they are put on instant replay and trivialized by four different angles. The assassination of JFK can be witnessed again and again, on a progam devoted to the subject, or in the middle of a variety show, or as part of a fictionalized movie. At the press of a button, the flick of a dial, the consumer enters an eternal present tense wonderland, where life and art, reality and fiction, tragedy and comedy, actor and human being, living and dead, memory and instant replay are convertible, equally important, and equally unimportant.

"Control over communications services," writes Daniel Bell, "is a source of power, and access to communication is a condition of freedom."[27] The same must be said about entertainment services— that is, the industry which produces and transmits plays, films, novels, and songs. In the post-information revolution, the two services have merged into a communications-entertainment complex, so that the movie rights to the novel based on the killing, for example, are settled before the body is cold. (In the case of Gary Gilmore, before the body is dead.) This brings the discussion of this paper down to the eternal question of freedom. The would-be novelist today, like the literary greats of the past, must not only contend with the unknown future, the speed of events and a world of illusion, he must choose: to compromise or not to compromise. To match the stencils, prostitute his art, and hope to become a celebrity. Or to hold out, experiment, win honor, poverty, and oblivion, but to hope against hope for posterity. Or possibly to entertain another hope: that the communications-entertainment complex will eat itself up, convert into unheard Muzak, make itself obsolete. Or, just as a shock in one's private life—such as an accident, a crime, or a punch in the nose—can wake a person up to the meaninglessness of most of our public expression, so a shock to the nation might blast away the puffery and set the condition for a vital art.[28]

In the meantime, the instruments of the mass media are diffusing into society, so that the individual consumer can assemble his own electronic den and record and reproduce whatever he wants from the multibillion-dollar networks. In this way he can create an alternative environment, more congenial to his soul and mind. Collecting his own images and sounds, he can divorce himself from the song in the air, the broadcast in progress. He can recognize that the morning soap, the primetime special, the latenight talkshow are not live events, but prerecorded reproductions which he counters with his own. With computer and software, he can print out his own writings, his own newspaper, become a desktop publisher. A new time-sense is created, in which the self-conscious individual becomes his own reporter, his own entertainer and critic. Where this will lead I cannot predict—to ever greater social fragmentation, to isolated pockets of culture, to solipsism? However, in our present media environment, I see only three choices: to become an indiscriminate slave to the stimuli of the mass media, to become a discriminate thief of the media in order to create your own environment, or to turn it all off and become a recluse.

Envoy

> All yet seems well, and if it end so meet,
> The bitter past, more welcome is the sweet.
> —Shakespeare, *All's Well That Ends Well*

My intention was to discuss problems which I believe face honest writers and, additionally, anyone concerned with the prospects of the future. But I can only make choices for myself. They are: To counter the impending cataclysms with a modest contribution to the cause of my choice. To counter the mass media with my own alternative environment, my own time. To account all prognostication as fiction, and the news as a fictional grid. To write my own fiction in the attempt to grasp reality. To accept that with the acceleration of events I will often be surprised, and with the acceleration of news I will often fall behind. To expect that my novel will be rejected, but if accepted make little change in the world. Yet to remain inspired by the insight of Dostoevsky, the originality of Platonov, the irreconcilable spirit of Karl Kraus. To have faith in my imagination, because in the very worst of times it refuses to be extinguished.

Boring Dates:
Reflections on the Apocalypse Game

Frank McConnell

To satisfy what I am sure must be keen anticipation at my title, let me give you the complete list of boring dates, in chronological order. They are 1984, 1999, 2001, 2010, 2419, and—the first shall be last, I recall hearing somewhere—802,701.

Of course you recognize most of them. But, without being condescending, let me remind you that 2419 is the date of Philip Francis Nowlan's original Buck Rogers story, *Armageddon 2419* A.D., 802,701 is the date of the central action of *The Time Machine*, and 1999 is the title of a song by the outrageous rock and roller, Prince, which contains the following, rather brilliantly apocalyptic lyrics:

> *I was dreamin' when I wrote this*
> *So sue me if I go too fast,*
> *But life is just a party*
> *And a party wasn't meant to last.*
> *Two thousand zero zero,*
> *Party's over 'cause we're out of time,*
> *So tonight we're gonna party*
> *Like it's nineteen ninety-nine.*

Petronius couldn't have said it better, nor the man who called himself John of Patmos and wrote the Book of Revelation. Prince, Petronius, and pseudo-John share not only an initial but a sense of the terminal, the sense—as Frank Kermode calls it in his splendid book—of an ending, the imagination of the end. It is an imagination Orwell shares, and those are the terms under which I choose to celebrate him.

Mind you, it is the numbers which are boring, and not by any

232

means the texts those numbers inhabit. And, in its way, that is an indication of one of the problems of apocalyptic writing, and one of the more virulent bacteria infesting science-fiction criticism, that is, the belief that science-fiction is in any way *predictive*.

Many of my distinguished colleagues and friends, I know, disagree fraternally but severely with my opinion—especially that kind and wise man, Frederik Pohl. But, each year at the Eaton Conference, I introduce that divisive theme into the proceedings: a harmlessly academic and diffident version of Poe's Red Death.

William Blake, the first great theorist of SF, put it this way: a prophet does not tell you what is *going* to happen, he tells you that, if you go on the way you're going, this is what you're going to *look* like. And Eric S. Rabkin, a spiritual heir of Blake, has argued that SF matters precisely because it raises in an especially acute fashion the general phenomenological and historical problems of storytelling altogether. I would go farther than Rabkin and suggest that at least the utopian/dystopian variety of SF raises serious questions about the nature of writing itself.

Let me put it this way: my boring dates are boring because they *are* inscribed, and because the act of inscription is, per se, a fixative that can tend to diminish the radiance or the luster of the very image it preserves.

Now that sounds almost perverse and paradoxical enough to have been translated from the French. But anyone who has ever written will recognize that the proposition is not so complicated. To write it down is to *fix* it; and to fix it is to confront, inevitably, the fissure between expectation and execution, idea and act. Jean Genet, that maestro of unpleasantness, compares his writing, in *Our Lady of the Flowers*, to fecal matter that, once produced, grows progressively cold and alien to the producer.

To be sure, many readers of Genet will want to observe that, in his case, this is a remarkable act of self-assessment. But it is *generally* true. Genet writes from prison, and for him to write is simultaneously to be freed from confinement and to realize a new, other kind of confinement: the confinement of having *uttered*.

Genet in prison, Frederick Douglass in slavery, Winston Smith in the bowels of the Party, Jack Abbot in the belly of the beast: for all of them, to write is to realize what it is to be free, and what it is to be enslaved. Remember that *Nineteen Eighty-Four* is primarily, the record of a record, a book about the production of Winston Smith's journal and its effect upon his consciousness. "He was a lonely ghost uttering a truth that nobody would ever hear. But so long as he uttered it, in some obscure way the continuity was not broken." That is what Winston thinks to himself at the very inception of his journal. "It was not by making yourself heard but by staying sane that you carried on the human heritage." And on the very next page he comes to the central insight of the prison journalist: "Now that he had recognized himself as a dead man it became important to stay alive as long as possible."

There speak, I submit, both the crucial political and prophetic voice of the novel, and also the peculiarly despairing voice of the professional writer who understands both the importance and the folly of his elected vocation. As Peter Stansky and William Abrahams reassert in their splendid biography of Orwell, his initial commitment was not to politics, but to that distinctively modern disease, the idea of being a writer: the political prophecy followed upon the artistic quest, as it did in the case of that other great esthete-turned-polymath, H. G. Wells. Indeed, *Homage to Catalonia*, where Orwell discovers in the same moment his passionate political libertarianism and his full vigor as a writer, may almost be taken as the mirror image of Winston Smith's journal. For the author of *Homage*, writing shows him the way out of his self-constructed cage; for the author *in Nineteen Eighty-Four*, writing shows him the bars of his cell.

Or rather, not the bars, but the screens. Notice again the brilliance of the scene in which Winston begins to write. He has to hide the blank notebook from the omnipresent telescreen: which is to say he has to conceal his seditious act of inscription from the very technology that, in our age, most threatens the privacy, the loneliness, and the sublime arrogance of the act of writing. And under that indictment I include, of course, not just television but its older brother, film. The second film version of *Nineteen Eighty-Four*, vastly wiser than the first version, concentrates on this aspect of the novel, on screens within screens and the omnipresence of the visual, as opposed to the written, image. And on that level, it cannot help but remind us of a film like George Lucas's *THX 1138* (another arbitrary number!) where the entire structure of society is video-monitored; which is to say simply that we are reminded of how much

Orwell's vision *is* a vision not only of our world but of our nightmares about that world.

Twenty-four hours before I wrote this, I had a long conversation and a rather Daliesque dinner with a hyperintelligent and distinguished SF writer who has also written extensively for and about television. He made the compelling point, over the lamb tandoori, that trying to write *good* television is an immoral act, since watching television is itself an immoral act, and good television would only seduce us into more time in front of the tube, more time not writing or reading or thinking for ourselves.

To be sure, the argument can be described as paradoxical. The cure for America's malaise of the spirit is not less but more "Laverne and Shirley": homeopathic medicine, indeed (as in "emetic"). But it is not necessarily wrong. Here is a distinguished imaginative writer—he despises the term SF—Harlan Ellison, in the preface to his collection, *Strange Wine*:

"The *act* of watching television for protracted periods (and there's no way to insure the narcotic effects won't take you over) is deleterious to the human animal. The medium itself insists you sit there quietly and cease thinking."

Having expended a number of words, and a larger amount of energy, upon arguing that film and literature are equivalently noble and serious acts of the primal, mythmaking imagination, I find this a distressing utterance. But part of my distress is that I cannot entirely dismiss it. Remember that Orwell's overriding passion was to be a *writer*, a writer of any sort, but a man whose life was lived with and within words. Indeed, it is difficult to think of Orwell, with his love of the language and his compulsive sense of the work to be done, without thinking of that other magisterial British consumptive, Keats. Both men were obsessed with, dedicated to, the business of inscription. And both men felt it to be an existential gamble.

What Ellison is saying is really a paraphrase of the myth of *Nineteen Eighty-Four*, and a fine paraphrase at that: I find it significant and moving that one of his best stories, "Repent, Harlequin! Said the Ticktockman," virtually concludes with a reference to Orwell's book. To produce a sound and image track is not to write, but, precisely, to *produce*—to manufacture an object of consumption that bears no more relationship to your inner life than your next pack of cigarettes or your next White Tower hamburger. Maybe, come to think of it, less.

Now I do not really believe this. But I think it is important *not* to believe it, and to understand why we don't have to believe it. Notice that one of the first things Winston remembers in his journal is the propaganda film showing Oceanian helicopters strafing Eurasian soldiers and citizens alike. The audience—except for Winston, who is already an embryonic humanist—is delighted at the carnage. This may have appeared, in 1948, to be a perverse view of film, or a pessimistically unreal view of human nature. But of course we have watched audiences watch *Straw Dogs, Dirty Harry*, and any number of even more shocking films (*I Spit on Your Grave* and *Bring Me the Head of Alfredo Garcia* come to mind as two of the more elegantly self-descriptive titles in human history). And so we know that Orwell may never have been more of a prophet than in this area.

But that is a secondary point. The main point is that Orwell perceives a tension between the written and the filmed tale—a tension that can be either therapeutic or deleterious. The 1954 film of *Nineteen Eighty-Four* has not been rereleased, thanks mainly to the venality of theatrical distributors. This is a pity, because it is a very fine film. But, in fact, in that film of this book about books and film, the important scene of Winston viewing the helicopters is not shown. It is a thematic mistake of the first order. Think, for example, of what a Truffaut or a Stanley Kubrick could have done with it.

Because, of course, both Truffaut and Kubrick *did* do something with it. *2001*, which may well be the most nonverbal sound film ever made, features printed legends—as in a silent film, reminding us once again that we are hearing what we see—at each major junction of the film. It is a film about language: THE DAWN OF MAN is the first legend we see on the screen, and that writing is not solely writing, but also writing *about* writing. After the development of sound, it is impossible to make a truly silent film (Charlie Chaplin in *Modern Times* and Mel Brooks in *Silent Movie* both tried, with failed if wonderful results): but Kubrick comes as close as any director can to that precarious eminence. For *2001* is, ultimately, a film about language and the ways in which language not only reflects, but constitutes human consciousness. We did not need, nor did we want, *2010* to explain to us that Hal goes bonkers in *2001* because he has become truly linguistic (i.e., truly human; i.e., has been taught to lie). We *knew* that, if we had watched the film successfully at all. Arthur C. Clarke, like Hal, has failed to learn one important lesson: when to shut up.

Truffaut's *Fahrenheit 451* plays even more subtly with the tension between writing and filming than does *2001*—and a great deal more subtly than Ray Bradbury's original novel. To begin with, there is one place in a film where the written word is absolutely necessary: the main title sequence, of course. But in *Fahrenheit 451*, this dyslexic dystopia, the credits are only spoken, while the camera shows us a forest—an electromagnetic *selva oscura*—of television antennae. It is a clever trick, but it is also (as is usual with Truffaut's clever tricks) more than that. It is a reminder that the spoken word, even when spoken through the medium of the sound track, is perishable, and that the written word, even when only seen on the screen, somehow *stays*. Jacques Derrida argues seriously that, at least in the metaphysical acceptance of priority, writing is *before* speech. Bradbury's novel argues the same thing, rather faintly, and Truffaut's film establishes it with, for me, unrelenting authority. *Fahrenheit 451* is in its way the ideal reverse-image of the novel *Nineteen Eighty-Four*: for just as in the novel, the written word is continually threatened by the video image, so in the film, the video image continually impinges upon the authority of the written word.

Montag the fireman—his job is to set fire to books—becomes seduced by literature and finally becomes a subversive, which is to say, in this world, a literate man. He is an anti–Winston Smith in that for him freedom is the discovery of reading rather than writing, and in that the television screens in his world are primarily things that you watch rather than things that watch you. Nevertheless, the same fundamental equations apply in both stories.

Except that they apply more bitterly, and perhaps more realistically, in Orwell's tale than in Bradbury/Truffaut's. For *Fahrenheit 451*, after all, depends upon the same thesis that sustains almost every second-rate humanities and literature course taught in American or British universities: the brave but pathetic faith, that is, that in a soulless society literature will save you because it is, God help us all, *good* for you. Depressed? Read Jane Austen. In despair? Check out Dickens. Suicidal? Try Shakespeare.

Orwell will not allow us that easy option. Not because he knows more about life than Bradbury does, but precisely because he knows more about literature, more about being a writer. If we are the words we live by, then the possibility of cheapening those words is also the possibility of cheapening ourselves. George Steiner, in a brilliant discussion of *Mein Kampf* in his book *Language and Silence*, observes that the cheapening of the national psyche under the Third Reich is anticipated by the cheapening of that marvelous instrument, the German language, in Hitler's autobiography. Of course it is "Politics and the English Language," and of course it is the grammatology of the Vietnam War and every other officially sanctioned debacle of a sickening century. But it is also an indication of the degree to which Orwell perceived, and preserved for us, the right semantics of our time.

Nineteen Eighty-Four is not a book, it is a mythogem; a metaphor that we can not really escape even if we wanted to, a boring date that will remain forever one of the *words* by which we define ourselves. Orwell succeeded better at his act of inscription than he perhaps intended, but succeed he did. "Philosophers have heretofore only tried to understand the world," wrote the young Marx in the most famous of his theses on Feuerbach. "The point, however, is to change it." It is Orwell's permanent glory that he wrote us a book and forged us a myth that inverts the Marxian formula and convinces us again that, in some range of identity, understanding still matters.

Notes

Biographical Notes

Index

Notes

Storm Warnings and Dead Zones: Imagination and the Future

1. Ray Bradbury, *The October Country* (New York: Ballantine Books, 1974), pp. 175–91.

2. Robert Scholes, *Structuralism in Literature* (New Haven: Yale University Press, 1974), p. 193.

3. Faustus's pact grants him power over nature for exactly twenty-four years. His search to conquer earth and heaven soon leads him to realize, however, that he has not world enough and time. To this anxiety Mephistopheles replies, ironically, that these heavens are not half so fair as man because they were made for man. For man, now damned to have a future, the old static, homocentric world, the vision that drove Faustus to rebel in the first place, is now evoked as a refuge, an ironic haven from the terrors of a human future which, despite promises, has the necessary limits of our condition.

4. Edward W. Said, "Abecedarium Culturae," in *Modern French Criticism: From Proust and Valery to Structuralism*, ed. John K. Simon (Chicago: University of Chicago Press, 1972), p. 350. "In achieving a position of mastery over man, language has reduced him to a grammatical function." Said's analysis of Foucault and Lévi-Strauss is based on this adversarial relationship between man and system.

5. Scholes, p. 200. "The role of a properly structuralist imagination will of necessity be futuristic." He says elsewhere: "In the structuralist vision of man, a new awareness of the nature of language and the processes of thought has led to a new awareness of human universality" (p. 190).

6. Said, p. 531. "In other words, man now lives in a circle without a center, or in a maze without a way out."

7. Scholes, p. 199. He goes on, significantly, to discuss the fall in terms of Faustian power: "The fall of man is neither a myth from prehistory nor an

event at the beginning of human time. It is a process that has been occurring for centuries, and it is not so much a fall into knowledge as into power—the power to work great changes in ouselves and our immediate environment, the power to destroy our planet in various ways."

8. Norbert Wiener, *The Human Use of Human Beings* (New York: Anchor/Doubleday, 1954), has this to say of "feedback": "I repeat, feedback is a method of controlling a system by reinserting into it the results of its past performance" (p. 61).

9. Isaac Asimov, "Social Science Fiction," in *Science Fiction: The Future*, edited by Dick Allen (New York: Harcourt, Brace, Jovanovich, 1971), p. 288. "It would be nice, however, if science fiction could be said to point actively in a worthwhile direction. It would seem that it cannot. It presents a thousand possible futures and there is no way of telling which of these will resemble the real future or even whether any of them will resemble the real future."

10. Asimov, p. 285. "[SF] can, first and most important, accustom the reader to the notion of change. The force of change is all about us, it is the essence of our society. Science Fiction is the literature of social change, and it treats social change as the norm."

11. In the George Pal film (1960), the Morlocks are depicted as hoary white creatures, old beast-men.

12. George Orwell, *Nineteen Eighty-Four* (New York: Signet Books, 1961), pp. 217–18.

13. Dario Zanelli, "From the Planet Rome," in Federico Fellini, *Fellini's Satyricon* (New York: Ballantine Books, 1970), p. 8. "It's a film about Martians, a science-fiction film. It should be as fascinating to its spectators as the first Japanese films were to us: films which left you with a continuous feeling of uncertainty."

14. Bernardino Zapponi, "The Strange Journey," in *Fellini's Satyricon*, p. 35.

15. "Documentary of a Dream: A Dialogue between Alberto Moravia and Federico Fellini," in *Fellini's Satyricon*, p. 25. a curious current runs from Fellini's remark about the "leprosy of time" and the fact that Wells's sphinx, as the riddle of time, has a leprous white face.

16. Asimov, p. 285.

17. *The Illuminated Blake*, annot. David V. Erdman (Garden City, N.Y.: Anchor Press/Doubleday, 1974), p. 389.

18. Jean Gattégno, *La Science-fiction* (Paris: Presses universitaires de France, 1971), pp. 40–41. "La 'fonctionnalisation' de chaque Sélénite, imitée de la fourmilière, ajoute à l'inhumanité de cette univers, où la haine est souveraine."

19. Gary Zukav, *The Dancing Wu Li Masters: An Overview of the New Physics* (New York: William Morrow & Company, 1979), pp. 42–43.

20. Northrop Frye, *Fearful Symmetry: A Study of William Blake* (Boston: Beacon Press, 1947), p. 209. "Urizen is a skygod, for the remoteness and mystery of heaven is the first principle of his religion. He is old, but his age implies senility rather than wisdom. He is cruel, for he stands for the barring of nature against the desires and hopes of man."

21. Michel Butor, "Science Fiction: The Crisis of Its Growth," trans. Richard Howard, *Partisan Review* 34 (Fall 1967): 595–602.

22. *The Dune Encyclopedia*, comp. Dr. Willis E. McNelly (New York: Berkley Books, 1984), pp. 193–94.

Origins of Futuristic Fiction: Felix Bodin's *Novel of the Future*

1. See for example I. F. Clarke, *The Pattern of Expectation: 1644–2001* (New York: Basic Books, 1979); and Darko Suvin, *Metamorphoses of Science Fiction: On the Poetics and History of a Literary Genre* (New Haven & London: Yale University Press, 1979), pp. 115–44.

2. See for example Chris Morgan, *The Shapes of Futures Past: The Story of Prediction* (Exeter, England: Webb & Bower, 1980).

3. Alexandre Cioranescu, *"Epigone,* le premier roman de l'avenir," *Revue des sciences humaines* 39, n. 155 (Juillet–Septembre 1974): 441–48.

4. For bibliographic guides see I. F. Clarke, *Tale of the Future from the Beginning to the Present Day*, 3rd ed. (London: The Library Association, 1978); and Pierre Versins, *Encyclopédie de l'utopie, des voyages extraordinaires, et de la science fiction* (Lausanne: Editions L'Age d'Homme, 1972): articles on "Anticipation" and "Guttin, Jacques."

5. Raymond Trousson, *Voyages aux pays de nulle part: histoire littéraire de la pensée utopique*, 2nd ed. (Bruxelles: Editions de l'université de Bruxelles, 1979), pp. 174–81; Frank E. Manuel & Fritzie P. Manuel, *Utopian Thought in the Western World* (Cambridge, Mass.: Harvard University Press, 1979), pp. 458–60. See also Trousson's excellent introduction to Louis-Sébastien Mercier, *L'An deux mille quatre cent quarante: rêve s'il en fut jamais*, ed. Raymond Trousson (Bordeaux: Editions Ducros, 1971).

6. Robert Galbreath, "Ambiguous Apocalypse: Transcendental Versions of the End," in Eric S. Rabkin, Martin H. Greenberg & Joseph D. Olander, eds. *The End of the World* (Carbondale and Edwardsville: Southern Illinois University Press, 1983), p. 56. Grainvile's role in the secularization of apocalypse is briefly discussed in W. Warren Wagar, *Terminal Visions: The Literature of Last Things* (Bloomington: Indiana University Press, 1982), p. 16. For the classic discussion of apocalypse as a fundamental trope of modern science fiction, see David Ketterer, *New Worlds for Old: The Apocalyptic Imagination, Science Fiction, and American Literature* (Bloomington & London: Indiana University Press, 1974).

7. Robert Scholes, *Structural Fabulation: An Essay on Fiction of the Future* (Notre Dame and London: University of Notre Dame Press, 1975), pp. 17–18.

8. "On rêvait les fins du monde et le dernier homme." Felix Bodin, *Le Roman de l'avenir* (Paris, 1834), p. 16. Subsequent citations to this book will be given in parenthesis in my text. Translations are my own. I have used the British Library's copy of *Le Roman de l'avenir*. So far as I know the only discussion in English of Bodin's book is in Clarke, *The Pattern of Expectation*, pp. 69–72. For Clarke, who does not take up the aesthetic issues raised by Bodin, "the main value of his book lies in the evidence it provides for believing that the intellectual revolution implied in the idea of progress had been completed by the 1830s" (p. 72). See also the entry "Bodin (Felix)" in Versins' *Encyclopédie*.

9. "En effet, je n'ai connaissance d'aucune action romanesque transportée au milieu d'un etat social ou politique future" (p. 397).

10. "Sans donner ni relief ni movement aux choses ou aux personnes . . . sans aborder enfin la création vivante d'un monde à venir quelconque."

11. "Si jamais quelqu'un réussit à faire le roman, l'épopée de l'avenir, il aura puisé à une vaste source de merveilleux et d'un merveilleux tout vraisemblable, s'il se peut dire, qui énorgueillira la raison au lieu di la choquer ou de la rvbaler comme l'ont fait toutes les machines à merveilleux épique, qu'il a été convenu de mettre en jeu jusqu'à présent. En offrant la perfectibilité sous la forme pittoresque, narrative et dramatique, il aura trouvé un moyen de saisir, de remuer les imaginations, et de hâter les progrès de l'humanité, bien autrement puissant que les meilleurs exposés de systèmes, fussent-ils présentés avec la plus haute éloquence."

12. "Chacun s'arrange un avenir à sa fantaisie; chaque système, chaque secte a le sien" (p. 26).

13. "La peuvent se trouver des révélations de somnambules, des courses dans les airs, des voyages au fond de l'océan, comme on voit dans la poésie du passé des sibylles, des hippogriffes et des grottes de nymphes; mais le merveilleux de l'avenir, comme je l'ai dit précédement, ne resemble point à l'autre, en ce qu'il est tout croyable, tout naturel, tout possible, et dès-lors il peut frapper l'imagination plus vivement, et la saisir en s'y peignant comme la réalité. On aura trouvé ainsi un monde nouveau un milieu tout fantastique, et pourtant pas invraisemblable . . . "

14. "Pour le moment, la question est de savoir si, après les grotesques et audacieuses fantaisies de Rabelais, les amusantes et satiriques inventions de Cyrano et de Swift, et les pétillans romans philosophiques de Voltaire, il était possible de trouver quelque chose de nouveau et toutefois d'analogue; quelque chose qui ne fût ni d'une fantaisie trop dévergondée, ni d'une intention purement critique, ni de cet esprit philosophique qui nuit a l'intérêt

et à l'illusion en substituant toujours des idées aux personnages, et en subordonnant l'action et les caractères à la thèse qu'il soutient; et pourtant une chose à la fois fantastique, romanesque, philosophique et un peu critique; un livre où une imagination brillante, riche, et vagabonde, pût se déployer à son aise; enfin, un livre amusant sans être futile. Je crois que ce livre était possible; mais je suis encore parfaitement convaincu qu'il n'est pas fait."

15. Trousson, p. xxx.

16. The only theory I know which implies that resort to future time must involve a switch in genre is Mikhail M. Bakhtin's discussion of "Forms of Time and the Chronotope in the Novel," in his *Dialogic Imagination* (Austin and London: University of Texas Press, 1981), pp. 84–258. For Bakhtin the chronotope—i.e., the relationship of fictive time and space—is above all "a formally constitutive category of literature" which "has an intrinsic *generic* significance" because "it is precisely the chronotope that defines genre and generic distinctions, for in literature the primary category in the chronotope is time" (pp. 84–85). It follows from this insight, which merits wider application, that a significant alteration of genre will always be among the results of displacing novelistic action from the past, present, or "once upon a time" to the future. Bakhtin, however, does not pursue this issue or even mention futuristic fiction.

17. For a superb account of how that overwhelming majority of today's science fiction which *is* set in the future exploits the formal consequences of its proleptic structure, see Thomas A. Hanzo, "The Past of Science Fiction," in George E. Slusser, George R. Guffey, and Mark Rose, eds., *Bridges to Science Fiction* (Carbondale and Edwardsville: Southern Illinois University Press, 1980), pp. 131–46.

18. Paul Alkon, "Samuel Madden's *Memoirs of the Twentieth Century*," *Science-Fiction Studies* 12 (July 1985): 184–201.

19. [Jane Webb], *The Mummy! A Tale of the Twenty-Second Century. By Mrs. Loudon* (London: Frederick Warne & Co., 1872) pp. v–viii. My discussion is based upon the Eaton Collection copy of this edition. *The Mummy!* was first published anonymously in 1827. Among its admirers, unfortunately, was the landscape gardening expert John Claudius Loudon, who eventually discovered, fell in love with, and married its author: a disastrous marriage for the history of futuristic fiction because it deflected Jane Webb's considerable talents from writing any more tales of the future to publication instead of botanical books with such dreary titles as *The Ladies' Companion to the Flower Garden*, *The Ladies' Flower Garden of Ornamental Annuals*, and *The Ladies' Flower Garden of Bulbous Plants*.

20. For support of my research on early futuristic fiction I am grateful to the John Simon Guggenheim Memorial Foundation.

Anticipating the Past: The Time Riddle in Science Fiction

1. On biblical prophecy, see Maurice Blanchot, *Le Livre à venir* (Paris: Gallimard, 1970), pp. 117–28; and Jacques Derrida, *D'un Ton Apocalyptique adopté naguère en Philosophie* (Paris: Galilee, 1983), pp. 86–92; on prophecy as a genre, M. H. Huet, "La Voix prophétique," *Littérature* 31 (Oct. 1978): 90–98.

2. For a recent interpretation of Nostradamus, see J. C. Pichon, *Nostradamus en clair* (Paris: Laffon, 1970).

3. Those are the dates of George Orwell's *Nineteen Eighty-Four*, Arthur C. Clarke's *2001: A Space Odyssey*, Ursula K. Le Guin's *Lathe of Heaven*, Ray Bradbury's *Martian Chronicles*, Robert Heinlein's *Moon Is a Harsh Mistress*.

4. "Pendant le cours de l'annee 186–, le monde entier fut singulièrement ému par une tentative scientifique sans précédents dans les annales de la science." *Autour de la Lune* (Paris: Hetzel, 1870), p. 1.

5. "L'année 1866 fut marquée par un événement bizarre, un phénomène inexpliqué et inexplicable que personne n'a sans doute oublié."

6. Both titles have been published in a posthumous volume of collected stories, *Hier et demain*, (Paris: Hetzel, 1910).

7. *Le Chateau des Carpathes* (Paris: Hetzel, 1892) p. 1.

8. Une multitude de Systèmes différents qui se fondent pour ainsi dire les uns dans les autres pour ne former qu'un seul ordre de choses." Diderot, *Oeuvres Completes* (Paris: Assezat-Tourneux), tomme 1, p. 369.

9. See in particular, Condillac, *Essai sur l'origine des connaissances humaines* (Paris: Galilee, 1973), pp. 125–31.

10. Darwin, *Origin of Species* (Collier Books: New York, 1962), p. 484. Emphasis mine. See also pp. 479 and 483

11. Ernst Haeckel, *The Evolution of Man*, trans. Joseph McCabe, (London: Watts, 1910), vol. 1, p. 6. See also *Climbing Man's Family Tree: A Collection of Major Writings on Human Phylogeny, 1699 to 1971*, ed. Theodore D. McCown and Kenneth A. R. Kennedy (Englewood Cliffs: Prentice Hall, 1972). My thanks to Vincent Sarich, Professor of Anthropology at the University of California, Berkeley, for his helpful suggestions.

12. Ibid., p. 5.

13. See Freud's discussion of Darwin's twentieth chapter of *The Descent of Man* in "The Infantile Recurrence of Totemism," *Totem and Taboo*, in *The Basic Writings of Sigmund Freud* (New York: Random House, 1938), pp. 884–930.

14. *The Descent of Man* (New York: D. Appleton, 1897), p. 65.

15. See Rosny ainé, *La Guerre du Feu*, published in 1909, a speculative history of the origins of society. See also René Barjavel's *Le Voyageur*

imprudent, published in 1958, in which another time traveller choses to explore the past; his *Ravage*, published in 1943, where one of Nostradamus's prophesies is realized; Philip K. Dick's *Now Wait for Last Year*, 1966; Pierre Boulle's *La Planète des singes*, 1963, and *Une Nuit interminable*, 1952; and A. E. Van Vogt's *Seesaw*, 1941.

16. Eric S. Rabkin, *The Fantastic in Literature* (Princeton, N.J.: Princeton University Press, 1976), p. 4.

The Thing of Shapes to Come: Science Fiction as Anatomy of the Future

1. Samuel R. Delany, in an essay entitled "About 5,750 Words," in his criticism collection *The Jewel-Hinged Jaw* (New York: Berkley, 1977), makes some similar points on the use of tenses in science fiction. He deals primarily with Saussurean "levels of subjunctivity"; my approach is different: I am considering the need for an authoritative stance which makes such levels of subjunctivity useful to speaker or writer.

2. Almost any high school or collegiate basic physics text can provide these models, but more interesting variants can be seen in Rudy Rucker, *Infinity and the Mind: The Science and Philosophy of the Infinite* (Boston: Birkhauser, 1982), pp. 10–15.

3. All page numbers for Walter M. Miller, Jr.'s *Canticle* are from the Bantam paperback edition, seventh printing.

4. All page numbers for Damon Knight's *Dio* are from the Groff Conklin anthology, *Five Unearthly Visions* (New York: Fawcett Publications, 1965) where I first ran across *Dio*. The novella originally appeared in *Infinity Science Fiction*, September 1957.

5. All page numbers for *2010: Odyssey Two* are from the first U.S. edition (New York: Del Rey Books, 1984).

Knowing the Unknown: Heinlein, Lem, and the Future

1. Stanislaw Lem, *Solaris* (New York: Berkley, 1970); Robert A. Heinlein, *Time Enough for Love* (New York: G. Putnam's Sons, 1973). These editions are used for citation.

2. Leonard Krieger, "Autonomy of Intellectual History," *Journal of the History of Ideas* 34 (Oct. 1973): 499–516.

3. Daniel J. Boorstin, *The Americans: The Colonial Experience* (New York: Random House, 1958), pp. 149–63, 185–88.

4. See also Darko Suvin, "Afterword," *Solaris*, p. 223.

Reactionary Utopias

1. "In a World of Her Own," *Mother Jones*, January 1984, 23–27 and 51–53.

2. Samuel R. Delany, "To Read *The Dispossessed*," in *The Jewel-Hinged Jaw* (New York: Berkley, 1977).

3. Joanna Russ, "Recent Feminist Fictions," in *Future Females*, ed. Marleen S. Barr (Bowling Green, Oh.: Bowling Green Popular Press, 1981).

4. I thank Charles Platt, George Slusser, Sheila Finch and Kathleen Spencer for discussions of the manuscript.

Media, Messages, and Myths: Three Fictionists for the Near Future

1. George Orwell, *Collected Essays, Letters and Journalism* (Harmondsworth: Penguin, 1971), vol. 2, p. 377.

2. Bertolt Brecht, "Radio—eine vorsintflutliche Erfindung?" in *Gesammelte Werke* (Frankfurt & Main: Suhrkamp, 1967), vol. 18, pp. 120–21. My translation.

3. Brecht, "Der Rundfunk als Kommunikationsapparat," in *Gesammelte Werke*, pp. 127–34.

4. Hans Magnus Enzensberger, "Baukasten zu einer Theorie der Medien," *Kursbuch* 15 (1969): 160–61. I have translated "Bewusstseinsindustrie" (literally, "industry of consciousness") by "mind industry," as the author does himself in his other text cited below (note 34).

5. Ibid. 161–62

6. The telescreen behaves like a radio, while in our world television has in many respects replaced radio, even in its social function. This is, incidentally, the reason why, in Philip K. Dick's *Ubik*, the TV set "reverts" to a radio in the time regression sequences (chap. 10). Here there is a correct understanding of the social function of radio and TV (in spite of Platonic considerations); in *Nineteen Eighty-Four* it seems to be the lack of scientific understanding that prevents the full extrapolation of the two broadcasting systems as such.

7. *The Best of Philip K. Dick*, ed. John Brunner (New York: Ballantine, 1977), p. 417. See Carl Freedman, "Towards a Theory of Paranoia: The Science Fiction of P. K. Dick," *Science Fiction Studies* 32 (March 1984) 15–24. Freedman's article interestingly relates Freud's views on paranoia and paranoid thinking with Marx's theory of commodity fetishism and applies his conclusions to science fiction in general, and Dick's opus in particular, especially *Ubik*.

8. Raymond Williams, *Television: Technology and Cultural Form* (London: Fontana, 1974), especially pp. 139–40; but see also his *Communi-*

cations, 3rd ed. Harmondsworth: Penguin, 1976), pp. 129–37, on "the four main kinds of communication system."

9. This is very clear in some of Ballard's work, when the ludicrousness of scientific explanation contrasts with the credibility of landscape and characters. I am thinking of "The Cage of Sand" (1961), "Deep End" (1961), and *The Drought* (1964).

10. Let me comment aside, and very personally, that I disagree with Raymond Williams in the new chapter of his *Orwell*, "*Nineteen Eighty-Four* in 1984," first published in *Marxism Today*, January 1984, 12; "Three layers of the novel . . . the third, a superstructure, including many of the most memorable elements, in which, by a method ranging from fantasy to satire and parody, the cruelty and repression of the society are made to appear at once ludicrous and savagely absurd." For me these words would apply beautifully to Pohl and Kornbluth's *The Space Merchants* (1952); here I do not find the sense of humor of which, incidentally, Orwell was capable in *Animal Farm* (1945).

11. I use "near future" in a broad sense, as something particularly opposed to far future fiction and which maintains many features of our familiar world. *Solar Lottery*, taking place in 2203, is no less "near future" in this sense than *Flow My Tears, the Policeman Said* in 1988 or *Dr. Bloodmoney* in 1981. Even presents like *Crash* and *VALIS* (1981) share this "near futurity" which is the alternative place, the place not far from our experience (as near future is the time not far from it as well; cf., note 32 below).

12. This merger-confusion between medium and message is more heuristic on my part than a McLuhanism on behalf of Dick's part.

13. Peter Fitting, "*Ubik*: The Deconstruction of Bourgeois SF," *Science Fiction Studies* 5 (March 1975): 49–50.

14. Or the mad capitalist, as Darko Suvin puts it, speaking of Palmer Eldritch, "P. K. Dick's Opus: Artifice as Refuge and World View," *Science Fiction Studies* 5 (March 1975): 14.

15. The "war is on" excuse is recurrent in dystopias of this kind; e.g., Dick's *The Penultimate Truth* (1964) or Bradbury's *Fahrenheit 451* (1952). Cf., Ellison's "'Repent Harlequin!' Said the Ticktockman" (1965): "It was, after all, patriotic. The schedules had to be met. After all, there was a war on! But, wasn't there always?"

16. Drugs are paradigmatic of the entropy of consumerism: they are addictive (i.e., causing dependence), hallucinatory (alienating) and eventually destructive. They are, then, the terminal commodity of consumerism. In this sense, they symbolize all other commodities of the system, of which they are co-referential.

17. Gérard Klein, "Discontent in American Science Fiction," *Science Fiction Studies* 11 (November 1977): 8.

18. In this last work the sense of fealty is baffled when the hero, Bob

Arctor, enters the recovery clinic; he sees himself sent/sold by his liege to the enemy. The fiefs try to outmaneuver each other just like Oceania, Eurasia, and Eastasia; and the fact that Bob had allowed the Narc Brigade to spy (by means of a device not wholly unlike the telescreen) on him and his real friends reveals a curious variation of the hidden camera—as hidden as the poppies in the cornfields where addicts are restored to sanity through occupational therapy.

19. In *We Can Build You* (1972) the Frauenzimmer androids (*the* Lincoln, *the* Stanton) are human because they are labors of love, products of artistry and craftsmanship (Pris and the engineer are genial "outcasts") in contrast to the John Wilkes Booth android fabricated by Sam K. Barrows.

20. While the Presidents, the "Der Alte" figures, are regularly and constitutionally replaced, the First Lady is eternal, as Big Brother is, because there is no ban on dates, as in Airstrip One; it is said that "she's been in office for seventy three years; . . . On TV she looks around twenty" (chap. 9). Cf. *Nineteen Eighty-Four*, part 2, chap. 9: "Nobody has ever seen big Brother. He is a face in the hoardings, a voice on the telescreen. We may be reasonably sure that he will never die." Note he is a *voice* on the telescreen!

21. Robert Plank, "Die Welt in der Glaskugel," in Franz Rottensteiner ed. *Quarber Merkur, Aufsätze zur Science Fiction und phantastischen Literatur*, (Frankfurt/Main: Suhrkamp, 1979), pp. 93–110. Lost childhoods are here the worlds destroyed by the war efforts of Oceanic, Eurasian and Eastasian bureaucrats, as is the creative and thriving Abe Lincoln America destroyed by the industrial big sharks. This drabness and misery accounts also for the multiplication of ersatz products, from Victory Gin to the stainless steel teeth of Palmer Eldritch.

22. Literally, to the end of the (socially acceptable, or inhabitable) world, as in *A Scanner Darkly* with the poppies, or in *Electric Sheep* with the toad; to the end of the solar system, as in "Sales Pitch" (1954); to the end of one's life, as in *Ubik*.

23. The vitiated message may lead us, along another line of thought, to the media as yet another veil interposed between the cognizing subject and the truth, always penultimate. Hence, the search for the Man in the High Castle—and the final concern with the gnosis.

24. Quoted in Robert Louit's interview with Ballard, published in *Foundation* 9 (1977): 50.

25. At the other end of the spectrum, in "The Voices of Time" (1960), we find a telecommunicative situation, but its content is reduced ro the minimum, this being the ultimate bit of information, the countdown to the death of the universe.

26. The name of the satellite, Echo, is used elsewhere in a transposed manner, e.g., through magic. In *The Crystal World* (1966) "Echo" becomes synonymous of crystalline structure (crystals being "echoes" of elementary

structures, a "parallel spatial matrix" [chap. 7]). The Echo satellite is itself an echo of Venus: "The satellite? Yes, an impressive sight. Venus has now two lamps" (chap. 5). What is true of land and skyscape is also valid for people and their relationships (Sanders-Louise consciously echoes Sanders-Suzanne, etc.).

27. Interview with Robert Louit, *Foundation* 9: 53.

28. "From Shanghai to Shepperton," *Foundation* 24 (February 1982): 18.

29. Interview with Robert Louit, *Foundation* 9: 53.

30. "Es wäre ein Irrtum, über die Zukunft zu schreiben": interview with Reiner Zondergeld and Joerg Krichbaum, in *Quarber Merkur*, Rottensteiner, ed., p. 15.

31. Enzensberger, "The Mind Industry," *Partisan Review* 36 (Winter 1969): 103.

32. "Do you mean the military and political reasons?" "No, I don't." . . . "I mean the *real* reasons," . . . "Do you seriously believe that, Lieutenant? 'The spirit of exploration'! My God! what a fantastic idea!" ("A Question of Re-entry"). Spatial trips are unnecessary as temporal trips: hence the stories occur in the present or near future (see also his interview in *Quarber Merkur*).

33. Ivan Illich, *Deschooling Society* (Harmondsworth: Penguin, 1973), p. 109.

34. This is the longest lineage of Ballardian characters, starting with Strangman in *The Drowned World* (1962) and having as latest avatar "President" Manson in *Hello America*.

35. See the interview in *Quarber Merkur*, especially pp. 153–54 (the same theme is discussed in the Louit interview, but with less development).

36. "Introduction to the French Edition of *Crash!*" *Foundation* 9: 48.

37. Ballard has acknowledged the influence of and his fascination with the media and technology as help for the enlargement of "inner space" (e.g., in an interview with *Penthouse*, April 1979). That he is becoming optimistic about (earthbound) technology has not prevented him from writing only disaster novels, even though in a renewed form (*The Unlimited Dream Company* [1979] is perhaps a freak, a much elongated novella lacking the sustained violence of *Crash*.) On the other hand, all his dystopias are to be found in the stories—"Build Up" (1957), "Chronopolis" (1960), and "Billennium" (1961).

Images of *Nineteen Eighty-Four*: Fiction and Prediction

1. George Orwell, *Nineteen Eighty-Four* (London: Secker & Warburg, 1949), p. 43. all references are to this edition unless otherwise specified.

2. Orwell, p. 33.

3. Orwell, p. 128.

4. Neil Kinnock, "Shadow of the Thought Police," *Times*, 31 Dec. 1983, p. 8.

5. See Paul Lashmar, "Information as Power," in *Nineteen Eighty-Four in 1984: Autonomy, Control and Communication*, ed. Paul Chilton and Crispin Aubrey (London: Comedia, 1983), p. 79.

6. Orwell, p. 39.

7. Orwell, *Nineteen Eighty-Four* (Harmondsworth: Penguin, 1954; reprint, 1981), back cover.

8. David Bowie, "1984," *Diamond Dogs*, RCA, APL1 0576, 1974.

9. "1984speak," *Times*, 31 Dec. 1983, p. 9.

10. Orwell, p. 34.

11. Orwell, p. 46.

12. See Jeremy Seabrook and Trevor Blackwell, "Mrs. Thatcher's Religious Pilgrimage," *Granta*, no. 6 (1983): 39–52.

13. Anthony Burgess, *1985* (Boston: Little, Brown, 1978).

14. Orwell, p. 30.

15. Burgess, p. 29.

16. György Dalos, *1985*, trans. Stuart Hood and Estella Schmid (London: Pluto, 1983).

17. Thomas M. Disch, "The Man Who Had No Idea," *The Magazine of Fantasy and Science Fiction*, Oct. 1978, 5–33.

18. Ursula K. Le Guin, "The New Atlantis," in *The New Atlantis and Other Novellas of Science Fiction*, ed. Robert Silverberg (New York: Hawthorn, 1975), pp. 61–86

Orwell and the Uses of the Future

1. Orwell, *Essays*, vol. 4 (London: Secker and Warburg, 1968), pp. 329–30. Though he distinguishes between "naturalist novel" and "book of anticipations," we can clearly read the description as allowing and including both. One can argue that such a distinction makes no difference, that even the naturalistic novel is prophecy. See, for instance, Matthew Hodgart, "From *Animal Farm* to *Nineteen Eighty-Four*," in *The World of George Orwell*, ed. Miriam Gross (London: Weidenfield and Nicholson, 1971), p. 139.

2. See Charles Elkins, "Science Fiction versus Futurology: Dramatic Versus Rational Models," *Science-Fiction Studies* 6 (March 1979): 20–31.

3. William Steinhoff, *George Orwell and the Origins of 1984* (Ann Arbor: University of Michigan Press, 1975), pp. 43–54, 201.

4. Burnham's "realism" was not universally convincing. Dwight McDonald wrote a couple of devastating reviews of Burnham's work which argue the emptiness of his basic concepts.

5. John Naisbitt is working the same paradox when he concludes *Megatrends*, his prediction of the information-saturated future, with these words: "In a time of the parenthesis (i.e. in our own time between two eras) we have extraordinary leverage and influence—individually, professionally, and institutionally—if we can only get a clear sense, a clear conception, a clear vision of the road ahead." *Megatrends* (New York: Warner Books, 1983), p. 252. If the vision of the road ahead is so clear, then one must wonder what is the use of the "leverage and influence" that we are offered.

6. H. G. Wells, "The Discovery of the Future," in *The Atlantic Edition of the Works of H. G. Wells* (New York: Scribner's, 1924), vol. 4, p. 375.

7. We might note that within a few years, in his *Modern Utopia* and in his socialist pamphlets, Wells will be directly contradicting this determinist view. See my *Logic of Fantasy* (New York: Columbia University Press, 1982), pp. 119–25.

8. The Asimov sentence appears in "Social Science Fiction," in *Science Fiction: The Future*, ed. Dick Allen (New York: Harcourt Brace Jovanovich, 1971) p. 280. The deadening impact of Asimov's parallels might be alleviated by looking at some real history writing, Crane Brinton's comparative study of revolutions, for instance, or more recently, Barrington Moore's examinations of the difference between the Russian and German "revolutions."

9. 1957, rpt. New York: Harper Torchbook, 1964.

10. 1947, rpt. New York: Macmillan, 1965.

One Man's Tomorrow Is Another's Today: The Reader's World and Its Impact on *Nineteen Eighty-Four*

1. Doris Lessing, from the preface added in 1971 to *The Golden Notebook* (London: Michael Joseph, 1962; New York; Simon and Schuster, 1962). All quotations from this preface are taken from the paperback edition (Chicago: Granada, Panther Books, 1974), pp. 7–22.

2. Doris Lessing, *Re: Colonized Planet 5, Shikasta* (London: Cape, 1979; New York: Knopf, 1979), p. ix.

3. George Orwell, *Animal Farm* (London: Secker and Warburg, 1945). For the development of *Nineteen Eighty-Four* in conception, outline, and drafts, see Bernard Crick, *George Orwell: A Life* (London: Secker and Warburg, 1980), pp. 407–09. Also Peter Davison, ed., *George Orwell, Nineteen Eighty-Four: The Facsimile* (London: Secker and Warburg, 1984), pp. ix–xiii.

4. George Orwell, "Why I Write," in *The Collected Essays, Journalism and Letters of George Orwell*, vol. 1, ed. Sonia Orwell and Ian Argus (Harmondsworth: Penguin, 1970), p. 28.

5. Bertram D. Wolfe, *Three Who Made a Revolution: A Biographical*

History (London: Thames and Hudson, 1956), p. 36. Originally printed in USA, 1948.

6. *Russian Fables of Ivan Krylóv*, trans. Bernard Pares (Harmondsworth: Penguin, 1942). I am deeply indebted to Peter Caracciolo of the Department of English, Royal Holloway and Bedford Colleges (University of London) for pointing out the date of the Penguin edition, which is of interest for *Animal Farm* as well as for my current argument.

7. M. E. Saltykóv-Shchedrín, *Izbrannyje Skazki* (Moscow: State Literary Publishing House, 1950).

8. *Oeuvres de Nicolas Leskov et de M. E. Saltykov-Chtchédrine*, trans. and ed. Sylvie Luneau et al. (Bibliotheque de la Pleiade, NRF, 1967), pp. 1013–221.

9. *La Science-Fiction Soviétique*, ed. Leonid Heller (*Le livre d'or de la science-fiction*, gen. ed. Jacques Goimard, Presses Pocket, 1983), p. 19. My translation.

10. E. Zamiatine, "Les contes de Théta," in *La Science-Fiction Soviétique*, pp. 43–52. I do not, of course, discount Zamyatin's debt to H. G. Wells, but wish to point out his native heritage.

11. Yevgeny Zamyatin, *We* (Harmondsworth: Penguin Modern Classics, 1983). It is worth noting that Orwell first read *We* in an inadequate French translation.

12. Wolfe, p. 221. Also Lionel Kochan and Richard Abraham, *The Making of Modern Russia* (Harmondsworth: Penguin, 1983), pp. 378–79.

13. Zamyatin, p. 170.

14. Orwell, *Essays*, vol. 4, pp. 95–99.

15. Davison, *Facsimile*, pp. ix–x and xvi for discussion of title; also p. 23 for corrections of date in Smith's diary.

16. Davison, p. xvi, note 8 for reference to anonymous article re: Jewish calendar equivalent to 1984. Proven or not, this link is indeed prophetic about much reader response!

17. Mark Reader, *Political Criticism of George Orwell* (Ph.D. diss., University of Michigan, 1966), pp. 114 and 125. A copy is in the Orwell Archive, University College, London.

18. Isaac Deutscher, "1984—The Mysticism of Cruelty," in *George Orwell: A Collection of Critical Essays*, ed. Raymond Williams (Englewood Cliffs, N.J.: Prentice Hall, Spectrum, 1974), pp. 119–32.

19. T. R. Fyvel, "George Orwell and Eric Blair—Glimpses of a Dual Life," *Encounter* 13 (July 1959): 60–65.

20. My translation from the French.

21. For recent comment on this, see John Wain, "From Diagnosis to Nightmare," *Encounter* 61 (Sept.-Oct. 1983): 45–49. I have, of course, no wish to dispute other links, as with H. G. Wells's *Modern Utopia*, Jack London's *Iron Heel*, Katharine Burdekin's *Swastika Night*, and so on.

22. Samuel Hynes, *The Auden Generation: Literature and Politics in England in the 1930s* (London: Faber and Faber, 1976), p. 316.

23. Deutscher, pp. 119–32.

24. Lessing's preface to *The Golden Notebook*, p. 22.

Big Brother Antichrist: Orwell, Apocalypse, and Overpopulation

1. Cited by W. Steinhoff, *The Road to 1984* (London: Weidenfeld and Nicolson, 1975), p. 199.

2. Cited by B. Crick, *George Orwell: A Life* (Harmondsworth: Penguin, 1982), p. 445.

3. Ibid., p. 468.

4. Ibid., p. 507.

5. Ibid., p. 392.

6. Ibid., p. 371.

7. Ibid., pp. 170–71.

8. Ibid., pp. 239, 248.

9. Steinhoff, p. 194.

10. Crick, p. 193.

11. Ibid., p. 505. for other indications of Orwell's apocalyptic leanings, see Crick, pp. 207–71, 386–8, 391.

12. W. D. O'Flaherty, ed. and trans., *Hindu Myths* (Harmondsworth: Penguin, 1975), pp. 43, 236; V. Ions, *Indian Mythology* (London: Hamlyn, 1967), pp. 24–25, 72.

13. O'Flaherty, p. 236.

14. D. E. Hahm, *The Origins of Stoic Cosmology* (Columbus: Ohio State University Press, 1977), chap. 6, especially p. 195, n. 1.

15. Persian: W. Bousset, *The Antichrist Legend: A Chapter in Christian and Jewish Folklore*, trans. A. H. Keane (London: Hutchinson, 1896), pp. 115–16; Moslem: ibid., pp. 116–17; Scandinavian: ibid., pp. 112–14; H. R. Ellis Davidson, *God's and Myths of Northern Europe* (Harmondsworth: Penguin, 1964), pp, 202–10.

16. Gutschmid, cited by Bousset, p. ix.

17. N. Cohn, *The Pursuit of the Millennium* (London: Mercury Books, Heinemann, 1962), pp. 13–14.

18. G. Quispel, *The Secret Book of Revelation*, trans. P. Staples (London: Collins, 1979), pp. 8–9; cf. R. Grant, *A Historical Introduction to the New Testament* (London: Collins, 1971), pp. 235–37.

19. Bousset, passim; cf. also Cohn, pp. 1–21; F. E. Manuel and F. P. Manuel, *Utopian Thought in the Western World* (Oxford: Blackwell, 1979), pp. 44–48.

20. Bousset, pp. 111–12.

21. Ibid., re. Antichrist, passim; re. Beliar, pp. 82, 96–97, 136–37, 153–56.

22. E. Wilson, *The Dead Sea Scrolls 1947–1969* (London: W. H. Allen, 1969), pp. 71, 65..

23. Bousset, pp. 218–19.

24. Ibid., pp. 245–46; Manuel and Manuel, pp. 38–41.

25. Bousset, pp. 105, 107, 185–86.

26. Ibid., index, s.v. "Nero" and "Nero redevivus."

27. Ibid., pp. 182–88.

28. Ibid., pp. 186–88, 123–31.

29. G. K. Anderson, *The Legend of the Wandering Jew* (Providence R.I.: Brown University Press, 1965), pp. 38–41; J. Delumeau, *La Peur en Occident* (Paris: Fayard, 1978), pp. 356–97.

30. Anderson, p. 39; Delumeau, pp. 364–66.

31. Cohn, pp. 60–65, 138–39.

32. Delumeau, pp. 356–97, quotation p. 397 (our trans.).

33. C. Hill, *Antichrist in Seventeenth-Century England* (London: Oxford University Press, 1971), pp. 4–40.

34. Ibid., pp. 31–33, 177.

35. Ibid., pp. 114–15, 175–76, quotation p. 115.

36. Bousset, pp. 131–32; Hill, p. 38.

37. Cohn, pp. 309–11.

38. Ibid.; Hill, pp. 175, 179.

39. Bousset, pp. 22, 255, 161, 179, 192.

40. Ibid., pp. 171, 178.

41. Ibid., pp. 22, 177.

42. Ibid., p. 65.

43. Ibid., pp. 64, 211.

44. Ibid., p. 161.

45. Ibid., p. 254.

46. Hill, p. 91

47. Ibid., pp. 128, 94.

48. Ibid., p. 131.

49. Ibid., p. 94.

50. Ibid.

51. M. H. Abrams, *Natural Supernaturalism: Tradition and Revolution in Romantic Literature* (London: W. W. Norton, 1973), passim.

52. For reference to Roger Bacon: W. M. S. Russell, *Man, Nature and History*, (London: Aldus, 1967), p. 177; and Francis Bacon: Abrams, pp. 59–60.

53. R. Cantel, *Prophétisme at Messianisme dans L'Oeuvre d'Antonio Vieira* (Paris: Ediciones Hispano-Americanas, 1960), passim.

54. I. F. Clarke, *The Pattern of Expectation 1644–2001* (London: Cape, 1979), passim.

55. Hill, pp. 70, 184, 155, and 182.

56. Ibid., pp. 41–145.

57. Ibid., pp. 121–22, 132.

58. Ibid., p. 40.

59. Steinhoff, pp. 5–10; Crick, pp. 81, 87, 93, 128–29.

60. W. M. S. Russell, "Folktales and H. G. Wells," *The Wellsian* 5 (1982): 2–18.

61. Crick, p. 247.

62. G. Orwell, "Inside the Whale," *Collected Essays* (London: Heinemann, 1961), p. 153.

63. Crick, pp. 417, 420.

64. Hill, pp. 116–18.

65. Cited by Crick, p. 507.

66. Orwell, "Wells, Hitler and the World State," *Collected Essays*, p. 162.

67. Crick, p. 251.

68. Orwell, "Boys' Weeklies," in *Collected Essays*, pp. 108–09; and pp. 244–45, in "Raffles and Miss Blandish."

69. C. Russell, "The Concept of Pseudosex," *Guy's Hospital Gazette* 84 (1970): 241–45.

70. C. Russell and W. M. S. Russell, *Human Behaviour: A New Approach* (London: Deutsch, 1961), chap. 6.

71. G. Orwell, *Nineteen Eighty-Four* (Harmondsworth: Penguin, 1954), pp. 153, 233.

72. Ibid., pp. 163–73.

73. Crick, p. 550.

74. Bousset, p. 241.

75. C. Russell and W. M. S. Russell, "The Social Biology of Totemism" and "Space, Time and Totemism," *Biology and Human Affairs* 41 (1976): 53–79, and 42 (1977): 57–80.

76. See C. Russell and W. M. S. Russell, *Violence, Monkeys and Man* (London: Macmillan, 1968); and "Scarcities and Societal Objectives," in *Growth without Ecodisasters?* ed. N. Polunin (London: Macmillan, 1979), pp. 409–28; and W. M. S. Russell, "The Palaeodemographic View," in *Disease in Ancient Man*, ed. G. D. Hart (Toronto: Clarke Irwin, 1983), pp. 217–53.

77. Cited by W. M. S. Russell, "The Palaeodemographic View," pp. 235–6.

78. W. M. S. Russell, "Population and Inflation," *Ecologist* 1, no. 8 (1971): 4–8.

79. Revelation 6:6.

80. Hill, pp. 155, 164; Delumeau, pp. 278–87.

81. Russell and Russell (n. 76, 1968), p. 212, cf. Russell (n. 52), pp. 90–139; L. Sprague de Camp, *The Ancient Engineers* (London: Tandem, 1977), p. 23.

82. Crick, pp. 367, 371.

83. S. Andrzejewski, *Military Organization and Society* (London: Routledge and Kegan Paul, 1954), pp. 108–15; S. Andreski, *Elements of Comparative Sociology* (London: Weidenfeld and Nicolson, 1964), pp. 311–22, quotation p. 322.

84. J. Needham, *Science and Civilisation in China*, vol. 2 (Cambridge: University Press, 1956), p, 205.

85. Andrzejewski, p. 113.

86. Russell (n. 52), p. 124. The words "by Orwell," present in draft, were actually cut in the course of the compression necessary to reduce this history of mankind to 63,000 words of print. For more detail about Lord Shang's book, see Needham, pp. 206–13.

87. Cited by L. Cottrell, *The Tiger of Ch'in* (London: Pan Books, 1964), p. 130.

88. Orwell, *Nineteen Eighty-Four*, p. 213.

89. Russell and Russell (n. 76, 1979), pp. 412–15.

90. "Address to the Board of Governors," *Advances in Fertility Control* 4 (1969): 1–3.

91. I. Asimov, *The End of Eternity* (New York: New American Library, Signet, 1958), p. 192.

Variations on Newspeak: The Open Question of *Nineteen Eighty-Four*

1. This is indeed recognized by Crick; see George Orwell, *Nineteen Eighty-Four*, with critical introduction and annotations by Bernard Crick (Oxford: Clarendon Press, 1984), p. 8. This edition is used for all future references to *Nineteen Eighty-Four*.

2. Crick supplies part and chapter headings on the contents page of his edition, but does not introduce them to the text.

3. See *The Collected Essays, Journalism and Letters of George Orwell*, ed. Sonia Orwell and Ian Angus (London: Penguin, 1970), vol. 4, pp. 513 and 536 respectively.

4. For instance 1, chap. 3, "Winston was dreaming of his mother," 1, chap. 6, "Winston was writing in his diary," 2, chap. 5, "Syme had vanished," 2, chap. 6, "It had happened at last," 2, chap 8, "They had done it, they had done it at last!" 3, chap. 1, "He did not know where he was."

5. *Nineteen Eighty-Four*, p. 11.

6. *Nineteen Eighty-Four*, p. 19.

7. It appeared as two connected novellas, "Universe" and "Common Sense," in *Astounding Science Fiction* (1941), but not in book form till after Orwell's death. Orwell had come across "Yank mags," but there is no sign that he had ever read that one.

8. It is strange and implausible that he is able to go on the outing with Julia in 2, chap. 2. Such visions of "the outside" are, however, common (essential?) in "enclosed universe" stories, They provide reinforcement for the hero's otherwise unlikely urge to escape. Hugh Hoyland sees the stars in Heinlein's novel; Roy Complain, the sun in Aldiss's.

9. In the Heinlein novel one character reads a physics textbook, and then delivers an allegorical commentary on it. The reader realizes the textbook is true, the commentary a product of the enclosed universe. In Orwell's Party history textbook, the truth and error are more thoroughly mixed; but once again the reader is in no doubt as to which is which.

10. Both Heinlein and Aldiss use this device, as (with slight updating) does Harry Harrison in *Captive Universe* (1969).

11. *Collected Essays*, vol. 4, p. 89.

12. The adverb is used insistently by Winston, though one's natural reaction is to think it a mistake, see *Nineteen Eighty-Four*, p. 187, p. 290.

13. *Collected Essays*, vol. 3, pp. 412, 420–21, 428.

14. He confessed that "English" was hardly a subject at all in his schooldays, see *Collected Essays*, vol. 3, p. 210. Some analysis of Orwell's linguistic mistakes is made by Roy Harris, "The Misunderstanding of Newspeak," *TLS*, 6 January 1984.

15. *Collected Essays*, vol. 3, pp. 40–46.

16. *Collected Essays*, vol. 3, p. 135.

17. *Collected Essays*, vol. 4, p. 157.

18. Published first in the anthology *Again, Dangerous Visions*, ed. Harlan Ellison (New York: Doubleday, 1972), and cited from the authorized Signet reprint.

19. One might note that Orwell spoke up for "patriotism," as opposed to "nationalism," in "Notes on Nationalism," *Collected Essays*, vol. 3, p. 411; but Le Guin feels the word has been poisoned.

20. *Collected Essays*, vol. 4, p. 166.

21. Cited from *Watergate: Chronology of a Crisis*, ed. Mercer Cross and Elder Witt, *Congressional Quarterly:* Washington, D.C., 1975, p. 88.

22. Garment's official White House biography says that before becoming Nixon's counsel, he worked "on a variety of various projects"! See *Watergate*, p. 43.

23. See *A Supplement to the Oxford English Dictionary*, vol. 1, A–G (Oxford: Clarendon Press, 1972).

24. Citations are from the first British edition, Ursula LeGuin, *The Dispossessed* (London: Gollancz, 1974).

25. Anthony Burgess notes that this could be expected to happen even in Newspeak, in his *1985* (London: Hutchinson, 1978), p. 51. "Pejorative semantic change is a feature of all linguistic history": in other words, people would use "Big Brother!" where we might say "Jesus Christ!"

26. An exception is the book *Language and Control*, by R. G. Fowler et. al. (London and Boston: Routledge & Kegan Paul, 1979). The first essay in this collection is "Orwellian Linguistics," by Bob Hodge and Roger Fowler. This too has its own bias, however. Like Crick (see below), it insists that "Appendix" on Newspeak must be taken ironically; I feel this view is untenable even from Hodge and Fowler's own citations.

27. *Nineteen Eighty-Four*, p. 55.

Aliens for the Alienated

1. Lawrence's projection of a natural "wholeness" onto animals (which, after all, are aliens of sorts) is similarly an indication of his own alienation. In the poem "Snake" he depises his own petty aggression against the snake, seen as "Like a king in exile, uncrowned in the underworld . . ."; and "Lizard" ends: "If men were as much men as lizards are lizards / they'd be worth looking at."

2. In *The Reefs of Space* Dondevero's escape from the body bank is achieved by his being disassembled and then put together again without the conditioning collar, while a substitute patchwork man made up of "junk" parts is assembled inside the collar. In this variation on the artificial monster-reintegrated man themes, the controlling collar is symbolic of alienating servitude and compulsion.

3. Gilbert's librettos register well how the satirical eye regarded the then prevailing literary modes—*Patience* lampooning the aesthetic medieval cult; *Ruddigore*, the Gothic romance; *Iolanthe*, or *The Peer and the Peri*, Victorian fantasy in the George Macdonald vein. But there are depths beneath their comic surfaces. *Iolanthe*, for example, is centred in the archism of Arcady, which is the land of Faery and home of the bi-natured shepherd Strephon and his immortal mother, whose "golden age" dispensation those earthy beings, members of the nineteenth century House of Lords and Regiment of Guards, are brought both by "magic" and by nuptial stratagems to comply with.

4. In Wells's *The First Men in the Moon* there is a significant passage in chapter 13 ("In the Sunlight") where Cavor and Bedford ascending from the moon's interior see the sunlight circle above them grow, and then in over-whelming light feel that "the fear and stress of our flight through the dim

passages and fissures below had fallen from us" and that "we seemed to have come into our own province again." This is followed shortly by Bedford's "mystic" experiences of alienation, unity, and individuation during his sun-drawn, earth-shine illuminated journey back to his home planet (chapter 20: "Mr. Bedford in Infinite Space").

5. There is in Moorcock's *Rituals of Infinity* a collection of created subspatial alternate worlds which run the gamut of possible geologies, ecologies, cultural scenarios, etc. They share the doom of decline and decay; but when the thirteen planets by a kind of "star maker" experimental act are phased into ordinary space-time, to function symbiotically, the tone becomes "paradisal." The golden sunlit bridges which eventually come into being to link them, Faustaff says, "mean understanding; communication."

6. It should be remarked, however, that a dualism persists throughout *Star Maker*: a dualism felt within the narrator and perceived in, or projected onto, the Star Maker. The narrator says that he experiences both praise and anguish when he senses the nature of the ultimate. He also says (of the "ultimate"): "And though there was love there was also hate comprised within the spirit's temper."

7. Bertrand Russell wrote of Nietzche's philosophy that it bordered on the half-mad King Lear's vision: "I will do such things— / What they are yet I know not—but they shall be / the terror of the earth." This is an alienation of ambivalent negative/positive potency. Nietzche's writings contain many insights which find echoes in contemporary science fiction. One of his Maxims with some relevance for the present essay reads: "Around the hero everything becomes a tragedy, around the demigod a satyr-play; and around God everything becomes what? Perhaps a world?"

News versus Fiction: Reflections on Prognostication

1. Undated form letter, beginning: "You'd better start making some major plans—because 80 million more people are coming here for breakfast, lunch and dinner." Zero Population Growth, 1346 Conn. Ave., Wash., D.C. 20036.

2. Cf. Michael Polanyi, *The Tacit Dimension* (New York: Doubleday, 1966).

3. Note the unfortunate case of Andrei Amalrik. In 1969, returned from Siberian exile, the young Russian dissident wrote the essay, *Will the Soviet Union Survive until 1984?* (New York: Harper & Row, 1970). His prognosis was war with China, secession of the Warsaw-Pact countries and collapse of the Soviet empire. When 1984 dawned, Amalrik himself was not present, having fallen victim to a traffic accident in November 1980, while the Soviet Union was headed by Yuri Andropov, Chief of the KGB when

Amalrik had penned his wish-fulfillment. Andropov himself passed away in 1984, but the Soviet Union survived.

4. Cf. Julian Jaynes, *The Origin of Consciousness in the Breakdown of the Bicameral Mind* (Boston: Houghton Mifflin, 1976), esp. book 2, chap. 4.

5. The Valentinian Gnostics, who regarded God the Creator as a subordinate deity, believed each member of the group could have direct access to the higher power through the Holy Spirit. Accordingly, they drew lots to decide who would act as priest, as bishop, and as prophet at each of their meetings. Elaine Pagels, *The Gnostic Gospels* (New York: Vintage, 1981).

6. "Soc-ism is an imaginary social order which would come into being if individuals were to behave to one another within society in complete accordance with the social laws. It can in fact never be attained because of the falsity of the premises on which it is based. Like every extra-historical absurdity, soc-ism has its own erroneous theory and incorrect practice, but it is almost impossible to establish either in theory or practice what the theory and practice of soc-ism actually are, and to distinguish between them." Alexander Zinoiviev, *The Yawning Heights*, trans. Gordon Clough (London: The Bodley Head, 1974), p. 9.

7. Jonas Salk, discounting predictions of overpopulation: "I am convinced that a number of factors—pollution, overcrowding, pressure on natural resources—will constitute a feedback mechanism that will reduce the population to a level that is optimal for survival. I think that this mechanism is genetically implanted." "A Conversation with Jonas Salk," *Psychology Today*, March 1983, 54.

8. Orwell's vision of an eternal party, able to alter the past and control the future to the extent that $2 \times 2 = 5$, is in some ways a debate with Tolstoy. Also with Dostoevsky's underground man, who tries to escape the tyranny of $2 \times 2 = 4$. See *Nineteen Eighty-Four*, part 3, chap. 3.

9. For further titles, such as *How to Steal a Job*, *How to Launder Money*, *How to Start Your Own Country*, write to Loompanics Unlimited, P.O. Box 1197, Port Townsend, WA 98368.

10. "Beyond War: A New Way of Thinking," Creative Initiative, 222 High St., Palo Alto, CA 94301.

11. Stephen Vizinczey, *The Rules of Chaos, or Why Tomorrow Doesn't Work* (New York: McCall, 1969), p. 36. Yet one must agree with Milton Himmelfarb: "The one man Lenin was responsible for the Bolshevik Revolution . . . Hitler willed the Holocaust." In "No Hitler, No Holocaust," *Commentary*, March 1984.

12. For the most reasonable approach to personal planning, cf. Bertrand de Jouvenel, *The Art of Conjecture*, trans. Nikita Lary (New York: Basic Books, 1967).

13. Alvin Toffler, *Future Shock* (New York: Bantam, 1974), p. 11, 35. Also Jonas Salk, "A Conversation," pp. 50–56.

14. See Toffler's use of "we must," p. 437.

15. F. Dostoevsky, to N. Strakhov, 26 Feb. 1869, *Sobranie sochinenii v 30-kh tomakh*, vol. 17 (Moscow: Nauka, 1976), p. 373.

16. Ibid., "Diary of a Writer for 1876" (March), vol. 22 (1981), pp. 91–92.

17. Ibid., "Diary of a Writer for 1873," vol. 21 (1981), p. 75.

18. Toffler, p. 19.

19. Ibid., p. 26. There is a book devoted solely to the accelerated clock, or the new science of chronography: Nigel Calder, *Timescale: An Atlas of the Fourth Dimension* (New York: Viking, 1983).

20. Sergei Tret 'yakov, "Novyi Lev Tolstoi," *Novyi Lef: Zhurnal levogo fronta iskusstv* (Moscow: Gosizdat), No. 1, 1927, pp. 34–38. The writer Mikhail Zoshchenko claimed that the times demanded not a red Tolstoy, but minor forms such as the humoresque. See "About Myself, My Critics and My Work" (1927), *Russian Literature Triquarterly* 14 (Ann Arbor: Ardis, 1977), p. 403. Note also Toffler: "it may now be too difficult for any individual writer, no matter how gifted, to describe a convincingly complex future," p. 466.

21. Donald Graham, publisher of *The Washington Post*, recently defined the news in terms of various types of "story"—e.g., the hard-to-get story, the well-detailed story, the investigative story, the daily-beat story. As to the criterion of "story," he referred to "public interest." In answer to my question (from the audience) if the press ever tried to determine what the public needed to know, he strenuously insisted on the contrary, yet allowed that he carried "important stories" of "minimal readership." From this and other indications, I surmise that newspapermen do not perceive their own cliches. (The Annual Press-Enterprise Lecture, March 20, 1984, University of California, Riverside.)

22. Toffler, p. 164.

23. A. C. Nielsen survey for 1983, reported by the Associated Press, 26 Jan. 1984.

24. One sickening example will suffice: "It took the influence of a Jackie Kennedy Onassis to convince Michael Jackson to do the unheard of: bare his soul in a book. Jackie O., hardly a trendie, nevertheless has been tuned in to Michael's music thanks to kids Caroline and John Kennedy, fans since his Jackson 5 days. Mrs O. actually renewed an earlier acquaintance with the singer last fall by paying him a visit in California. She returned shortly after with a book deal from Doubleday, her employer. The deal (worth well over $1 million) will have Michael and Jackie working exclusively together. He'll provide the life story, poems, drawings and dance secrets;

she'll provide the polish as editor. When not hard at work, they can slip away to her favorite Manhattan lunch haunts or browse in movie memorabilia shops, which they've already done as part of their campaign to 'get to know one another better.' Expect the fruits of this literary collaboration next spring." Mikki Dorsey and Dawn Baskerville, *US*, 7 May 1984, 35.

25. Aldous Huxley, *Brave New World Revisited* (New York: Harper & Row, 1965), p. 28–29.

26. What a pity that Peter Weir's film *The Last Wave* (1977) could not stimulate such nationwide attention; although it is no more fictional than *The Day After*, it is much more profound and disturbing, and artistically honest. However, it too lives in reruns and may prove the more enduring vision.

27. Daniel Bell, *The Winding Passage: Essays and Sociological Journeys 1960–1980* (Cambridge, Mass.: ABT Books, 1980), p. 43.

28. After the present talk, a voice from the audience advised me: "You should read some of the late and middle Wells, where again and again he has cataclysms that bring the world to sanity."

Biographical Notes

PAUL ALKON is Leo S. Bing Professor of English at the University of Southern California. He has just completed a book on fiction of the future.

KENNETH V. BAILEY has been Senior Lecturer in History at Daneshill College and Chief Education Officer to the BBC. He is presently a freelance writer.

GREGORY BENFORD is Professor of Physics at the University of California, Irvine, and a Nebula Award–winning writer. His most recent novel is *Artifact*.

COLIN GREENLAND is a novelist, literary journalist, and critic. His reviews appear regularly in the *Times Literary Supplement* and *Foundation*.

HOWARD V. HENDRIX is a graduate student in English literature at the University of California, Riverside. He was a 1985 winner of the Writers of the Future Award.

MARIE-HÉLÈNE HUET is Professor of French at Amherst College. She has written books on Jules Verne and the staging of Marat's death.

JOHN HUNTINGTON is Professor of English at the University of Illinois at Chicago. He is the author of *The Logic of Fantasy: H. G. Wells and Science Fiction*.

GARY KERN has published on Soviet literature and Solzhenitsyn and is the translator of Khlebnikov and Lev Kopelev. He has recently co-edited a book on the Strugatskys with George Slusser.

BRADFORD LYAU is a graduate student in intellectual history at the University of Chicago, with a dissertation on French science fiction. He was on the editorial staff of the Encyclopedia Brittanica.

ELIZABETH MASLEN is Lecturer of English at Westfield College, University of London. She has written on South African dissident writing, Slavonic literature, and the visual arts.

FRANK MCCONNELL is Professor of English at the University of California, Santa Barbara. He is the author of *Storytelling and Mythmaking* and writes mystery fiction.

José Manuel Mota teaches American literature at the University of Coimbra in Portugal. He has written extensively on science fiction.

Frederik Pohl is a well-known science fiction writer. He has won both the Hugo and Nebula awards.

Eric S. Rabkin is Professor of English at the University of Michigan. He is the author of *The Fantastic in Literature*.

Claire and W. M. S. Russell are authors of some 120 publications on animal and human behavior. Claire Russell is a practicing psychoanalyst and poet; her husband William is Reader in Sociology at the University of Reading and past president of the Folklore Society.

T. A. Shippey is Professor of English and Medieval Literature at the University of Leeds. He is the author of *The Road to Middle Earth*.

George E. Slusser is Curator of the Eaton Collection and Adjunct Professor of Comparative Literature at the University of California, Riverside. He is winner of the Science Fiction Research Association's Pilgrim Award for 1986.

Index